P I N P O I N T

by

Sheila Mary Taylor

ISBN   1461049148

EAN   978-1461049142

'Pinpoint' was first published by Night Publishing, a trading name of Valley Strategies Ltd., a UK-registered private limited-liability company, registration number 5796186. Night Publishing can be contacted at: http://www.nightpublishing.com.

All characters are fictional, and any resemblance to anyone living or dead is accidental. Although some of the places and establishments in and around Manchester, East Cheshire and Derbyshire UK, which form the physical background to this story, are real, or were once real, there are also some born purely of the author's imagination.

ACKNOWLEDGEMENTS

It never ceases to amaze me how generous people are in sharing unstintingly their expert knowledge with writers.

I could not have written this novel without the help of many friends and strangers, in particular the exceptionally generous and specialised help of one top class lawyer and one top class policeman. There were other lawyers and policemen who also gave willingly of their help, and add to those an orthopaedic surgeon, a physician, a paramedic, a marriage registrar and an instructor in self-protection for women, and many others who answered my never-ending questions, including those wonderful friends in my two writers' groups who read the manuscript and gave constructive criticism. They know who they are, and to them all I offer my heart-felt thanks and appreciation. Any mistakes are mine, not theirs.

I also owe a huge thank you to Tim Roux of Night Publishing for believing in the novel and bringing it to life.

And to the artist Muriel Clutten for the cover image, and Monica Eringin for her graphic expertise.

A mist, a cloud, the form and substance of my hope.
It darkens and grows steadfast to my gazing.

Dora Taylor

For my husband, Colin, and my three sons, Colin, Peter and Andrew

Strangeways Prison, Manchester, England (*September 1994*)

I've represented many murderers and am often surprised at how normal they appear. But this one is different. As he walks into the interview room he stops dead. His mouth drops open. His eyes bulge. His elbows clamp to his sides as though a knife has plunged into his back. And he looks straight at me unlike most who bow their heads till I say something to make them feel at ease, and who look past me when they tell me their stories. Not this one.

'Please sit down,' I say. His name is Smith. Sam Smith. This is what it says on his file cover. It's what he called himself when he was interviewed by the police.

'I know it seems stupid,' I say, 'but can I ask you to confirm your name. Your full name.'

I don't know. I just don't see him as a Sam Smith. Stupid name anyway. Nobody calls their kid that. Maybe I'll know from the way he tells me. The name, when he says it himself, will either sound like it belongs or like he's pretending.

'Sam Smith,' he says, and something in the timbre of his voice gels with the curve of his lips and the way his slightly protruding eyes follow mine . . .

And now he's nodding his head. Or am I imagining it? And there's an almost imperceptible smile on his face. That smile. And those eyes. I grip the desk. I can't breathe. My skin turns cold, clammy. My fingers tingle. A fragment of long forgotten memory skitters through my head then vanishes . . .

There's only one person I've ever known with eyes like those. And my darling twin brother died twenty-six years ago. Before my real life began.

Scary coincidence.

But let's get on with it and start the job – it's going to be a long haul, and he's got a lot to do to beat the charge. Murder. Horrible, cold-blooded, psychopathic, sexually motivated sadism.

And I think I know him.

FRIDAY

Eight Months Later

The door to the jury room swung open. The seven men and five women filed in and took their seats. Julia Grant glanced at the dock. Perched behind the thick protective glass Sam Smith looked immaculate in a fresh white shirt, the blond beard newly trimmed, nothing moving except those marble-blue eyes.

She noticed that Detective Chief Superintendent Paul Moxon was already back with the small group of officers who had gathered, sitting opposite the jury benches and eyeballing the jurors throughout the trial. Old trick, hard to get the judges to move them away, to persuade them that they are engaging in deliberate psychological warfare for the jury's votes. Paul smiled at her — a slow half smile and a slightly raised eyebrow, as if to say that for only one of them would today's verdict spell success.

She smiled back. Defence versus Prosecution. Part of the day's work. Only this time the stakes were higher than usual.

She looked towards the dock and saw that Sam Smith was also watching her. Their eyes met, but there was not a blink of recognition, his face so alien it was hard to imagine how the thoughts haunting her in the eight months she had been preparing his defence had ever entered her mind. Eight months studying his face across the narrow interview table for some tell-tale sign. But right now there was nothing in that face she could relate to. Nothing that even hinted at a link. Nothing that drew her to him. Good-looking men seldom delivered what their looks promised, she thought. Some unsuspecting female might be attracted until she looked into his eyes. Fish eyes. Cold and hard. Shut off from the rest of the world except for rare fleeting expressions of sadness when they seemed to drift into the past — and drag Julia with them.

The Clerk of the Court rose to his feet. 'Court stand,' he blurted in his usual offhand way.

The door opened. Mr Justice Dale strode to his red leather chair, scarlet and ermine robes flowing, wig well down his forehead. He nodded to the crowded court and sat down.

Julia pressed her shoulders against the back of the solicitors' bench. Another five minutes and it would all be over. And what then?

He might be free, but would she ever be?

The Clerk of the Court cleared his throat. 'Will the foreman of the jury please stand.' He looked directly at the foreman. 'To the charge of murder, have you reached a verdict upon which all of you are agreed?'

'Yes.'

Something made her glance at Smith again as if he'd called her name out loud. Instead of looking at the foreman, who was the person about to pronounce on the rest of his life, his gaze was fixed on her, waiting for her to turn and look at him, knowing that she would. Oh, that stare. That look. He thinks he has some power over me, she thought. Some right of claim. Men always expect to have power over women. One way or another. Even Sam Smith.

Or whoever he really was.

'Do you find the defendant guilty, or not guilty?' the Clerk of the Court asked in his precise, clipped voice.

Even a hardened criminal like Smith must surely feel some trepidation now. But there was not even a flicker to show he registered one iota of emotion.

Julia sat back in her seat, determined not to look at Smith again.

The hushed court waited.

The pause between the Clerk's question and delivery of the reply was like a gap in the fabric of time, allowing her mind to wander through the whole of her experience of dealing with this man. From prison to this court, through all the painful sessions of trying to get to know him. And of giving up her inner self to him. The hours she had spent in the interview room at Strangeways Prison fast-forwarded through her mind as bit by bit she'd wrenched from him the facts, piecing it all together so that she could convince QC Geoff Atherton, who would try to convince the jury that Sam Smith had not raped, tortured, knifed, mutilated and strangled to death seventeen year old Joanne Perkins.

'Guilty,' the foreman said.

'You bastard!' someone in the gallery yelled. There was no one rooting for Smith.

She looked straight ahead. Remembering what Ben Lloyd had told her this morning, she cringed with embarrassment. 'You're one of the best criminal solicitors in Manchester, but I just can't see how the firm is going to win on this,' he'd said. 'If he's acquitted you're the bent brief who got him off to the disgust of the general public. If he's convicted you'll be the laughing stock for having taken on the case in the first place. How are you going to uphold your reputation?'

A fat lot of good her reputation was doing her now.

She forced herself not to turn around again. Smith could signal as much as he liked with those slightly protruding eyes and Michelangelo lips, but her part in this was finished. It was all over bar the sentencing. And that was a foregone conclusion. No adjournment for reports here, no expectation of leniency.

She wondered, with a gut wrenching emptiness, why she still cared what happened to the man. She had listened to the evidence, weighed up the judge's closing speech. She knew in her heart it was a true verdict, beyond appeal. Her client was guilty. He had shown no mercy and was not about to get any now from Dale. Not a chance. So the pain in her heart was another part of the mystery of being this man's lawyer. Why couldn't she let it go – consign him to the dustbin of her no-hoper cases?

Ignoring the rumble from the public gallery, Mr Justice Dale invited Atherton to address him on sentence. Julia and Geoff had rehearsed how this phase of the case should be dealt with if the verdict went against Smith. They had persuaded Smith without a fight that it would be best to just get on with it: recite the facts of his painful history – the abuse, neglect, alienation and detachment from real childhood. All they had received from their client on the subject was a cold, unemotional,

'Yeah, whatever.' And so Geoff reeled off, with little ceremony, his prepared comments. 'My client will, I know, not accept the jury's verdict, My Lord, but he knows the matter is now in your hands.' Barely allowing anyone in the courtroom to have time to shift in their seats or mutter a comment to their neighbour, Dale addressed himself to the dock.

'Sam Smith, you have been found guilty of one of the most heinous crimes known to mankind. There is only one penalty the law can impose on you and that is a sentence of life imprisonment. I find the wickedness of your crime, your contempt for your victim, and your complete lack of remorse so repugnant that I will recommend to the Home Secretary that the sentence be served by you for at least thirty years.'

Julia's tongue stuck to the roof of her mouth. It was as if the words had been directed at her instead of to her client. She almost found herself turning to Smith to say sorry, but caught herself just in time. She was so confused she didn't know whether to laugh or cry. And she didn't dare look at Paul Moxon.

'I cannot order that you spend the rest of your life in jail,' the judge continued. 'But if this were possible I would further recommend that no parole be granted until you have drawn your final breath. This is the only way society can be adequately protected, and you can be properly punished. Take him down.'

Julia leaned back. Thank God, she thought, dismissing the notion that was invading her thoughts.

A weight of silence bore down on her as though she was under water. *No*, she told herself, taking a deep breath. Apart from the colour of our hair . . . but her thoughts still refused to line up into any semblance of logic.

She glanced at Geoff Atherton, sitting immediately in front of her. At that moment he turned and looked at her. His face showed none of the irritation he must be feeling. As one of Manchester's most revered Queen's Counsel, he wasn't used to losing a case, especially one for which he had received instructions from Julia. He smiled a half smile. He shrugged a win-some-lose-some shrug. She half-smiled back. Then with a theatrical flick of her eyelids she looked up at the ceiling, flexed the tension from her shoulders and began gathering up the files in front of her. She had to keep making this look like a perfectly ordinary case. Behind her a voice pierced the silence of the courtroom like a shot from a gun.

'Julia!'

She spun round towards the dock. Two dock officers were holding Smith between them. Like a coil of spring-steel he burst free from their grip. Two more officers appeared and manacled his hands behind his back. As they hauled him to the top of the stairs leading to the cells, he twisted round to face her.

'You'll pay for this, Julia fucking Grant.' His voice soared above the hubbub in the court. 'And for everything else, you fucking bitch. Just you bloody wait.'

- 2 -

The hubbub in court rose rapidly to a crescendo as files were gathered up into boxes and counsel who had been at each other's throats for the past fortnight exchanged jokes. Police officers engaged in self-congratulatory, macho banter, and news reporters circled for whatever sensational comment could be swept from the air. Julia, blocking her ears, fled down the stairs and pushed through the smoky glass doors of the Crown Court.

Dodging the gaggle of voice recorders and long-lens cameras, she dismissed the dozens of reporters and TV cameramen with a polite 'No comment' and walked in a daze into the wide-open space of Crown Square. She glanced over her shoulder. Geoff Atherton was obliging the cameramen with a statement that would be televised around the country within the next few hours.

With Smith's threat still ringing in her ears she stopped to take a revitalising breath of fresh air. The fragrance from the newly cut lawns mingled with an enticing whiff of coffee wafting from the *Bar San Georgio*. A coffee would save her life. She walked quickly past a Piccadilly Gold news car, then stopped and turned back to face the court, her thoughts drawn against her will to Smith.

Yet another television crew was besieging Geoff. Was he telling them about Smith's threat? Usually she knew exactly how her clients would react to their verdicts, yet nothing had armed her for Smith's outburst from the dock. Nor for his final poisoned look.

He's down there now, she thought, locked in the cells below the court. I should be light-headed with relief. I'll never see him again. After an outburst like that, she had a good mind to write a terse letter, expressing her disappointment at the result, but making it clear that she would not tolerate, under even the most extenuating circumstances, being threatened and abused as he had just done. Smith had just given Julia her get-out. If he needed further advice, he should nominate alternative solicitors and she would pass the file to them.

But would it be as easy as that? Would she ever be able to forget the voice, those eyes, that hauntingly familiar look?

She was torn between believing and not believing. Between wanting and not wanting. Between loving and not loving. Such a situation had no precedent, she was sure. Nothing in her legal training had prepared her for this. She felt as though her sense of logic had been turned upside down, threatening to make her act contrary to the legal principles she normally upheld, actions contrary to the advice she gave to her clients. She hated herself for this apparent weakness, but seemed powerless to overcome it. When she thought of her long lost dead brother, and Smith, in the same mental breath, she found the paradox offensive, but she had no idea why she could not keep her sacred, almost mythically precious thoughts of her brother separate from those of this callous, manipulative and deeply depraved man.

The gaping hole in her memory had started twenty-six years ago on the very last day she saw him. All she remembered after that was being told that her twin brother was dead. And then being adopted by David and Jessie, when a new life with no past began.

The question had been gnawing away at her soul since almost the very first moment of meeting Smith: Is he, could he be, that loved and longed-for brother whose name she could not even remember? The idea was as ridiculous as it was impossible to dismiss from her mind.

That day at Strangeways, when he had walked into the interview room for the first time, he had sensed something too, of that she'd been certain. But even now she was confused about why she had almost had a panic attack. For twenty-six years she had dreamed the dream of a child, that her brother would be restored to her. Now she sometimes doubted he had ever existed. She longed for what was surely only an impression in her unconscious, a nebulous sensation of loss rather than of any specific being.

And never a person such as this.

Coincidence? she asked herself. It couldn't be anything but.

Maybe, Julia. Maybe, she mused, looking round in case anyone could see her mouthing these words to herself and begin to question her sanity. Maybe something that happens by chance in a surprising or remarkable way is how most people would categorize coincidence, wouldn't they? Yes, but too often in my career I see happenings which appear to occur by chance but are never just coincidence. They're always part of a chain of events which can be manipulated to go one way or another. Sometimes you're not even aware of this manipulation. You reach a crossroads. You can't decide which way to go. But somehow your subconscious is busy computing that chain of links. It comes up with an answer. You start marching down one of the roads. Afterwards you have no idea why you chose this particular road but surprisingly, just by sheer chance, it is the right one.

Come on, Julia. It's simple. If you were to trace backwards through that chain you'd eventually reach a solid brick wall through which you could no longer see the event that "just by chance" triggered the one that followed. Maybe then, but only then, you could say that it was just a coincidence.

Forget it, she told herself. Your imagination has been blazing unchecked. Smile. It's over. It doesn't matter who he is. He is who he says he is. And if he isn't it's none of your business. He's just a killer who's got his just deserts. The faint likeness you thought you saw was clearly the twisted result of your obsessive yearning for your lost twin brother, the only person in those desperate days before your adoption who was kind to you.

17

She stopped walking, and stood rooted to the ground as though this would sharpen her memory. But he tried to protect me, she thought, though not knowing why. And the thought would not go away. The only person who had loved her . . .

No, Julia, she said emphatically to herself. Not your bloody brother. Just a nasty piece of work you had the misfortune to represent, who nearly manipulated the life blood from you and tapped into your sense of longing after you foolishly showed him too many – far too many – of your personal cards. The hand you shouldn't show to your clients. More fool you, Julia. This man called Smith is behind bars now. Removed for all intents and purposes from this world. Amen.

There you are. Nothing could have been easier. The door is locked. The key thrown away. Now, get on with your life.

Smiling to herself, she carried on towards Bridge Street. She wouldn't need the coffee now. Simon had always said how a simple smile could banish negative thoughts. Even though he had been dead for almost six years she had never forgotten her husband's golden advice, though lately she had noticed it hadn't always worked. More often it was this weird ability of hers to debate the problem with herself, as though she were talking to an alter ego.

Geoff Atherton was suddenly beside her. Falling into step with her he took her arm, always the perfect gentleman. 'Well, what was that tirade all about?'

'Well, let's face it,' Julia said. 'You've got to blame someone when the bottom suddenly falls out of your universe. A pretty natural reaction if you've just been condemned to spend the rest of your life in prison.' She looked up at him and smiled. 'As threats go, I've had worse.'

'Typical Julia,' he said, shaking his head. 'Stoic. Stubborn. And so magnanimous.' He stopped and turned to her, shielding her from the wind. 'But why you? Why not me? Or the police. It's not usual for them to threaten their solicitors.'

'You know, I think you're right. Though I have suffered my fair share of being expected to shoulder responsibility for the sins of my clients. The thing is, I think he trusted me. More than they usually do. He has no one else to blame,' she said, more to herself than to Geoff. She tossed her hair over her shoulder and smiled. It was important to carry on looking normal. 'He doesn't mean it, you know. He was just letting off steam.'

Geoff raised his eyebrows. 'You really believe that?'

'Who cares? He'll be inside for at least thirty years. And I won't be sending him Christmas cards in the interim.'

'I'm not convinced by your casual flippancy, Julia, and I wouldn't blame you if you felt bloody offended, even if it wouldn't do you any good.' She didn't answer. 'You're pale,' he said. 'You look as though you could do with a drink.'

She forced another smile. The idea was tempting. Counsel's chambers were next door to the Lloyd Grant offices and it wasn't unusual to meet at the end of the day for a chat and a drink at the *San Georgio*. Or at the Mark Addy where they'd watch the River Irwell oozing past the big plate glass windows of the old river-bus station. She glanced at her watch. 'Bit early for a drink, isn't it?'

'It's Friday, Julia. The Smith trial's over. Okay, just a coffee?'

She was about to say yes when she saw Paul, a crowd of reporters pressing around him. Geoff followed her gaze.

'Friend of yours?'

In his tone she noted the censure. In his eyes she saw the doubt. 'Yes,' she said.

The legal world was small. People talked. And when they didn't know the full story they embellished. Geoff will have heard rumours, but she wasn't prepared to discuss her ambiguous relationship with DS Paul Moxon.

She looked across at the tall, well-set figure. He was on call this weekend, he had told her, so wouldn't be dropping in to see her and her daughter Nicky as he usually did on Friday evenings. Their strange, tantalising relationship had been evolving at a geologically slow pace for some time, and she had no idea where it might lead, if anywhere. And even less idea what other people might think about it. Not that she even advertised its existence.

Moxon had his back to her, engrossed, together with Prosecuting Counsel, in animated conversation with members of the press. They were laughing and patting each other on the back.

'Well, at least they're pleased with the verdict,' Geoff said.

This made Julia acutely conscious of the professional chasm between Paul and herself. Today the yardsticks by which they measured success in the courtroom seemed more divergent than ever. Sam Smith was one of Paul's particular bêtes noires. Right now he would be jubilant. He would feel like rubbing her nose in it, not to spite her but because of what he was, a copper first, and the rest of him a distant second. No, she didn't want to see him so soon after the Smith verdict. She turned back to Geoff.

He gestured towards the *San Georgio*, eyebrows raised.

It would mean a post-mortem on the Smith case and Julia wasn't sure she could handle that. 'Thanks, Geoff. I'd really love to. But there're a million things to do at the office and I must get home to Nicky early. It's her nanny's night off.'

As she walked away a frightening image flashed across her vision. It had begun while she was watching Smith in the dock. She had tried holding on to it but just as it was doing now, it slithered away and refused to return. Something she had done. Something she had fled from into her amnesia. Something too horrific to contemplate.

- 3 -

Relieved to find no clients waiting to see her, Julia peeped into her personal assistant's office. There'd be a plethora of phone messages and she was hardly through the door when Linda started.

'Joey Gallagher's pissed off 'cause you haven't returned his calls. Call him back before five or he's going to sack you. Mrs Carruthers says why isn't Jimmy out on bail yet? Wants you to ring back and explain. Hindley Remand Centre cancelled Monday's slot to see Dave Harkin 'cause he's been moved to Hull Prison. The Listing Office said the judge insists the Jeffreys case is not taken out of the list.'

'What d'you mean not taken out? The prosecution's got no objection.'

'Well, that's what they said. Oh, and the fruitcake's been on again.

20

Wants to know if you've got his damages yet off the police and if you have he'll call in later to pick up the cheque.'

Julia shook her head. 'I wish I could help him. The poor old bugger may be delusional but it's about time he did his deluding somewhere else. If he comes in here again tell him to go away and bloody well call the police if he doesn't.'

Linda smiled and carried on with the messages. 'The Listing Office again. Want to know if it's okay to take the Jameson case out of the list.'

'Thanks, Linda. You're a star. Luckily they'll all wait until Monday.' She scooped up the bundle of messages and files Linda would have sorted into order of urgency, and fled down the passage to her own office at the front of the building. She regretted her display of impatience but had been unable to stop herself. She needed to be on her own.

With a lingering glance at the photo of Nicky, long blonde hair neatly combed, one tooth missing, and at the beautiful portrait of Simon – eyes looking straight at hers, the last before the plane crash, she sank into the chair behind her desk. She made a few phone calls, then began ploughing through outstanding mail, working like a robot, giving instructions into her dictaphone for Linda to deal with later. At this frenzied rate she would be home well in time for Wendy to keep her hair appointment, and for her to take Nicky and Duke for their favourite walk in The Carrs.

She was gathering the files she needed to work on at the weekend when Ben appeared in the doorway.

'I heard the verdict,' he said. 'Want to talk?

Not now, she thought. She didn't need this. But on the other hand, if she didn't, he would hound her. She looked pointedly at her watch. 'Okay. But I can only spare five minutes.' She gave him a swift smile. Keep looking normal, she reminded herself.

- 4 -

Julia watched Ben pour the coffee.

He handed her a mug. 'News travels fast, especially when it's bad.

21

What's all this about him threatening you? Before you ask, it was on Piccadilly Radio a few minutes ago.'

She told him in as few words as possible about Smith's outburst from the dock.

'I'm surprised they didn't handcuff him sooner,' he said.

She closed her eyes, then quickly opened them again. Now take it easy, she told herself. Be careful not to defend him too much. 'In fairness, there was no perceived need. He was as gentle as a lamb. Throughout remand his behaviour's been impeccable.' From Ben's expression, even that was overdoing it. 'Anyway, handcuffs are out of fashion in the dock these days,' she added quickly. 'Needless physical restraint might have conveyed to the jury that he was a risk. And therefore criminally guilty. I never had a moment's trouble with him.'

'Not a bit like Fred Kodjo, eh, Julia? I don't know how you handle him.'

She was not fooled by the honey tones. He was trying to humour her. Why, she wondered. 'Fred's no more difficult than any other client,' she said.

'He's maximum security for God's sake. They don't even move him without sixteen prison officers, police cars, armed police officers, motorbike outriders.'

'When I visit Fred, he behaves perfectly.'

Ben nodded. 'Yeah. You could probably tame a lion if it came to the push.' He gave her one of those incongruous smiles she had lately become wary of. 'Do you think Smith will appeal?' he asked.

What's up with Ben today, she wondered, not oblivious to the sudden change of tack. 'Told me this morning there'd be no need.' She shrugged. 'Anyway, after his performance in the dock, he's just got himself another lawyer.' She looked out the window, then back again at Ben. 'Strange what he said, though. I asked him why, but . . .'

A puzzled look spread across Ben's face. Julia followed his gaze and realised with a start that she had been stirring her coffee throughout their conversation even though she never took sugar. Avoiding his eyes, she put the spoon on the tray and carried on calmly. 'It was really odd how certain he appeared to be that we'd already won his case for him.'

'I think he's far cleverer than your average criminal,' Ben said. He paused, but Julia wasn't taking the bait. 'You've probably got to know him better than any other law abiding citizen.'

'Yes,' she answered. And her thoughts drifted away, wondering if Smith had felt the same possibility as she had. And if so he would be wondering who she was too, so why had he never said anything.

'Strange, isn't it,' she said, 'how you build up a kind of . . . friendship with your client. Well, you know what I mean,' she hastened to add. 'I've never quite understood how it happens.'

Careful, Julia, she told herself. Ben knows you too well. But you wouldn't like him to know you might be the twin sister of a cold blooded murderer, now would you?

'Not really, Julia. Most of us get on well with our clients. Some better than others, but if we didn't try to get on with them we'd end up with none.'

'Yes. But sometimes you can do both. You can dislike them. Despise them. Abhor their behaviour. Hate them for what they've done. Or for what you think they've done. At the same time you can actually feel . . . sorry for them, and begin to think you understand exactly why they've done what they've done. But as far as Smith is concerned, he's just a billing exercise now.' She was not about to reveal to Ben what was going on beneath the surface.

What was there to tell him, anyway? Nothing was definite. And if even the slightest hint of a connection with Smith leaked out, the media would have a field day with the headlines: SOLICITOR JULIA GRANT TWIN SISTER OF BRUTAL MURDERER SHE DEFENDED. What would that do to her career, and more importantly to Nicky?

'I think you're right,' Ben said. 'Forget it, Julia. It's over now. When you know they're guilty and you've given them an adequate defence — in his case more than adequate — you just walk away. You've done your duty. And that's it.'

It's okay for you, she thought. In any other case Ben would be right, but she doubted that getting Smith out of her system was going to be that easy. 'I couldn't agree more,' she managed to say, trying to maintain an air of confidence. 'but, you know, I thought we might just have had a chance.'

She was not oblivious to the incongruity of it all. She liked to win. Her reputation depended on a fair percentage of success but in this instance, professionally, it was a relief to have lost. She had never defended anyone in whose guilt she so firmly believed. But because of who he might be, and because of her deep empathy with the appalling events that had moulded and twisted him, she had craved for him to be innocent.

Ben narrowed his eyes. 'In the end it's all about winning, isn't it?'

'No, it's not. It's about getting the fairest deal for your client — Jesus, Ben, you know that.' Julia bit her lip until she was sure it must be bleeding. 'But when you do win,' she said, giving him her most relaxed smile, 'it sure gives you a boost.'

'Yes, but let's be honest, with this one you never had a chance.'

'I don't really know where you're going with all this, Ben. We did have a chance. Some of the evidence was all over the place. There were cops hell-bent on nailing him who lied through their teeth and were like naughty kids who'd been caught with their hands in the sweetie jar when they were cross-examined. There were major cock-ups with continuity on the forensics. Oh, and I nearly forgot, my client told me he hadn't done it. So what was I to do, walk all over him and get him to plead? I don't think so, Ben. And anyway, you know as well as I do, every case of murder's a gamble. So much depends on the prejudices of the jury.' She bit her lip again. She was protesting too much.

Ben frowned and shook his head in a way that Julia recognised. It was an almost theatrical look that often presaged one of her partner's insightful perceptions.

She flicked a wisp of hair from her eyes.

'What's up, Ben?' she asked with studied nonchalance.

'You're normally so predictable, Julia, but — I don't know how to put this — you've behaved strangely over the Smith case right from the beginning. Take day one. Your face was like chalk when you came back from that first visit . . .' He clasped his hands together until his fingers turned white. 'If . . . if there's anything I can do — I mean, you look . . . well — I'd like to help.'

'I'm fine,' she said, relieved that help was the only thing on his mind.

'Good. I'm glad,' he said.

'And I have to go. Dog and daughter beckon. Friday and the weekend are upon me."

Ben quickly finished his coffee. He took a deep breath and rubbed his chin, drawing his eyes together in another worried frown. Julia pushed her chair back and was about to stand, ready to go, when he spoke.

'You know something? You'd have made a damned good barrister.'

She smiled. Now who was behaving strangely? He was so transparent. Why all this flattery? 'No. I'd have hated dealing with all the stuffy formality — the bowing and scraping. I've always gone for the one-to-one contact. Finding out what makes clients tick. Delving deep into their psyche to find out what really happened. Why they became criminals. Some of them may be the scum of the earth,' she said, twisting Simon's ring round and round her finger, 'but every one of them is still entitled to the very best, the most thorough defence it is humanly possible to — '

'Sure. And if anyone can make a silk purse out of a sow's ear, it's you.'

Julia acknowledged his sugary praise with yet another smile. But why now? She could do without all this. She was fond of Ben. He had guided her professionally and for this she was grateful. But she often found him gazing at her in a way that made her wary of him, even after all these years working as his partner. Not for the first time she thought that perhaps, as Simon's best friend, he felt entitled to set himself up as Simon's successor. In defence she restricted social contact with him to the occasional lunch or a quick drink after work. He was only ever invited to the house when there would be other guests there. No way was she ever going to risk sending him mixed messages.

'I don't like losing,' she said, trying to keep the conversation as general as possible, 'any more than you do. When we win I can tell myself I've done a hell of a good job. When we lose I still know I've done a hell of a good job. But then I wonder whether I couldn't have done just that little bit better.'

'Yes. But there'll be other trials to win.'

She looked at her watch. 'Listen, Ben, I've really got to get moving. I have to get home. I'll see you Monday.'

He stood up. She could see his mind had switched direction. He took several steps towards her, then stopped.

'Julia.'

She dug for her car keys in the side pocket of her handbag and leapt for the door before he could suggest they go out for a drink. 'Yes?'

'Do you want . . . protection?'

He looked quite pathetic in his attempt to keep her talking, yet she couldn't help laughing with relief.

'Protection? Thank you, but that's the last thing I need. Smith will be inside for at least thirty years.'

- 5 -

At dead on four-fifty Sam Smith watched the big white sixteen-ton prison van reverse through the electronically operated gates into the secure area at cell level behind the Crown Court on Gartside Street.

There were three other prisoners going to Strangeways this afternoon. All Cat-A's, Sam noted with interest. He hated being close to anyone else at the best of times, especially cons. It was just his bad luck to be handcuffed to the one he detested the most. A nonce. Indecently assaulted and knifed to death a seven-year old boy behind the Community Centre in Moss Side — the scum. Third child offence. A child for Chrissake. An innocent little child . . .

Still, it wouldn't be for long. He would just have to bear it. Soon they'd be in the sweatbox, each locked in a cell on their own for the journey to Strangeways.

And that wouldn't be for long either. Not if Frank and Stringer and Joe Sagoe were on the ball. Sometimes it was good to be one of the boys. They owed him one. When the heat was on to name names over the Carstairs robbery they'd all have done a stretch if he hadn't kept his mouth zipped up. Anyway, they knew there'd be a juicy prize for them this time.

If everything went according to plan.

At four fifty-five the prison officer escorted them into the cellular van. The screw, stocky with shaved head and gorilla hands, unhandcuffed them for fuck's sake, then locked each one into their individual cells. Bless him for being so considerate. Passenger comfort and all that.

Sam got the first cell at the front. Sitting on the cold bare seat, he peered through the mesh window into the passage dividing the two rows of cells. Great stuff. He could see the entrance. Only one screw today, though, instead of the usual two. Birthday and Christmas rolled into one.

He gazed around the small steel cell. Not much bigger than the head on the yacht he and Joe Sagoe had done their one and only drug-run on from Tangiers to Gibraltar, when you had to come out before you could get your pants back on. Still, it was better than sitting next to the nonce.

At precisely ten past five he felt the engine begin to vibrate. The concertina gates clanged open and his shoulder pressed against the cold steel as they turned left down Gartside Street. He grinned to himself. No armed escort – he wasn't good enough for that – he wasn't a terrorist or a prison rioter, so he didn't qualify. What a trusting bloody shower they were.

Fucking hell, he wished he could see out. But this was the old type sweatbox, painted white to look like the new ones that had small, double-glazed windows on the outside. This thing was just a big reinforced steel box, like a giant Securicor van. Good thing he had insisted on the locomotive unit from an articulated lorry. Power, weight, nifty acceleration were essential, he'd told the boys. Christ, you needed something really solid to take on the weight of this fucking tank.

Apart from the limited view of the passageway all he could see were the four steel walls crowding in on him. Better than looking at the nonce though. Or having to touch him or smell him or see the evil look in his eyes.

He knew the route well. By now Frank would have the getaway car parked at the junction of Gartside and Quay Street. He would have

27

spotted them coming through the gates and he'd be on his latest nicked mobile phone to Joe Sagoe now. And that fat old bugger Sagoe'd better have the loco unit in the proper position, just like he had worked it all out for them. Just like he'd instructed them to do.

A right turning now, into Quay Street. They'd be looking straight at his favourite sign in Manchester. The one opposite Granada TV Studios that said BECOME RICH OVERNIGHT, if it was still there. *Exactly* what he intended to do, don't worry. Fifty grand for the escape pay-off and the rest for him. And that was just for starters if that shower had done the homework he had ordered them to do on Julia fucking Grant.

Julia Grant. No time to think of her now. Later . . .

They must be under the green railway bridge now. Into Trinity Way. In a minute they'd turn into their final approach towards Strangeways.

Come on, Sagoe. Come on.

He pressed his knuckles into the sides of the cell. His pulse raced as he waited for the bang.

Christ, Joe. Where the fuck are you?

He held his breath.

Nothing.

Maybe Joe's had another heart attack. Fat fucker.

Maybe the prison driver had spotted the loco unit. Maybe he was wondering what it was doing in the middle of Manchester without a trailer attached.

Christ. Maybe the bugger suspected something.

And then he heard it.

The sudden roar of the loco unit.

The deafening crash, hurling him against the wall of the cell.

Good old Joe. A dream coming true.

Screeching brakes, shouts and screams, the smell of oil, adrenaline pumping through his veins and behind him the nonce yelling and bawling his head off.

Peering through the grid. The screw staggering to his feet, blood pouring from his head.

Joe Sagoe's raucous voice. 'Out!'

A dragging sound. Scuffling. Shouting. More screeching of brakes.

For Chrissake, Joe. Hurry.

Joe's voice again. 'Open up now or I'll blow your head off.'

Stringer's. 'Now. Or I'll shoot.'

The blessed noise of the chain. The brass key in the lock. The crash of metal. The door opening. The smell of Mace . . .

And then his spine slamming against the back seat of the Scorpio, squashed between Joe Sagoe and Stringer with Frank at the wheel, all four of them rocking with laughter.

A few moments later they roared past the prison, its brick façade glowing orange red in the late afternoon sun.

'Here,' Joe said, handing Sam a big plastic carrier bag, 'change of clothes, extra shirts, razor and blades, gloves, money, water. Dark glasses, screw-driver, paper clip. Jemmy. Map. Cloned number plates And all the extra dope you wanted 'bout the Grant family. Address. Phone number. Husband's family tree. Figures on estate agency chain before they flogged it – gonna blow you away when you see how filthy rich the pigs were. Everythin' you asked for. The lot, includin' the passport which cost a fuckin' packet. And by the way, there's an empty house opposite the mansion in Wilmslow. Bad state of repair. Might be handy. But watch it. Could be handy for the Dibble too. Oh yes, and there's a park behind her house, called The Carrs. Lots of handy trees. And you'll need this.' Joe passed him a nine-millimetre Beretta. 'Silencer too,' he added with a grin. 'And, of course, a knife. Wouldn't be Smart Sam without your precious flick-knife, now would it.'

'Nice one.' Sam took the plastic bag and put the knife and the gun into his pocket. The bulge felt good, though he had no intention of using the firearm. Not now anyway. No sense in drawing attention to himself. It was just a precaution. In case things went wrong later.

He gave Joe his most winning smile. Joe was a real mate. Frank and Stringer had proved useful too and still had plenty of work to do to earn their pay-off.

His excitement mounted as the reality began to sink in. He was free. Not only of Strangeways, but free of having to behave like a ridiculously docile reformed character for the last eight months.

Yes, Julia. No, Julia. If you say so, Julia . . .

If he hadn't, he'd have got nowhere.

Leaning over Joe's bloated stomach he buzzed open the car window and took a long, slow, deep breath, savouring the delicious feeling that enveloped him like a shroud of silk in a whore's bedroom.

Free too of the uncertainty, because now, no matter what, he was committed to only one way forward.

- 6 -

Julia hurried past the law courts towards the multi-storey car park in Gartside Street. The media crowd had dispersed. Paul was nowhere in sight. He must have gone back to Chester House or to the Mark Addy for a quick celebratory drink with his mates. Well, it didn't matter. It was still too soon to see him.

In spite of the stiff breeze it was reasonably warm for May. With luck she would still be home in time to take Nicky and Duke for a walk in The Carrs. And for a change she would read her daughter a bedtime story instead of Wendy.

She slid a crisp new note into the pay machine, still thinking about Smith. She would never admit to anyone how much his look, even more than his threatening words as he was taken down, had unnerved her. After all they'd been through together in the preparation of his defence, it didn't make sense.

She hurried towards her red Mercedes SLK. Not your average transport for a legal aid lawyer – even a good one – but it was possible because of the inheritance from Simon's estate. She was conservative in her tastes generally, but she had her weaknesses.

With tyres shrieking she manoeuvred to the exit, Paul's final words on the phone just before she had left for work this morning echoing in her ears:

'Tell Nicky I'm really sorry I can't see her this evening,' he had said.

Nicky loved those Friday visits when Wendy left early for her hairdo. Julia loved them too. Especially when he stayed for supper and after Nicky went to bed they'd have a drink together and a chat. 'She'll be disappointed,' she had answered lamely, a feeling of emptiness flooding through her. And he had said, 'I hope you'll go home early for a change. Sometimes I think that kid doesn't even know she has a mother.' All day his words had haunted her. Haunted her and hurt her because she knew they were true.

She zoomed down the ramp, Paul still on her mind. It was an odd friendship, the policeman and the six-year old girl. But Paul and Nicky had hit it off from the first day they met. That had been a Friday too, just before his promotion to Detective Chief Superintendent and not long after Sam Smith had been arrested for the murder of Joanne Perkins. Julia had taken on the case. Met Smith. Almost had one of her panic attacks. She had been served with the original bundle of statements for the Prosecution. But not prepared to sit around for six weeks waiting for the depositions before she could start preparing her client's defence, she had demanded a courtesy bundle of prosecution papers. Paul had unexpectedly called on her at home with two boxes of statements, exhibits and interview transcripts.

He stood on the doorstep. 'Courtesy bundle as requested,' he said, giving her a lop-sided grin and another one for Nicky, who'd sidled up to Julia when she heard the deep male voice. And even more unexpectedly he had said, 'Any chance of a coffee?' *Cheeky bastard*, she had thought, suppressing a smile.

Julia buzzed her window down and fed her ticket into the box at the bottom of the ramp. It vanished with a slurp and the barrier lifted. As she turned right into Gartside Street she glanced at the gates at the back of the Crown Court. Soon a steel van will emerge carrying Sam Smith safely back to Strangeways Prison, or perhaps it's already gone. Out of my life forever, she mused.

Forever? Is that possible? Bloody well ought to be after that outburst.

She turned left into Quay Street and got the lights on green crossing over Deansgate onto John Dalton Street. She drove past the old Free Trade Hall, the now elderly and neglected *grande dame* of classical music in Manchester. She saw it every day, and every day without fail it reminded her of years ago listening to Jessie playing Mozart's 21st piano concerto with the Hallé, the highlight of her adoptive mother's career before arthritis tragically cut it short.

Her thoughts flew back to Paul's remark this morning. 'I'd be with her twenty-four hours a day if I could,' she had told him, the sudden pain of guilt eating into her. She wished she'd had a more satisfactory answer to his unusually outspoken complaint.

She thought about their relationship, if that's what it was. Like his friendship with Nicky, theirs was also an unusual one — policeman and defence lawyer — and one that Ben was quick to frown upon. Yet in spite of operating on different sides of the law they'd become friends.

The first time they'd seen each other was four years ago at Bootle Street police station, tucked behind that maze of buildings over there on her left. Her client had been charged and the police were keen that bail should be withheld. There had been fireworks. The second time was at an identification parade. Fireworks again. The third was at the scene of a crime. Her client had been charged with bludgeoning his wife to death in the garage of their home. She had wanted to check the layout of the house, the views along the street at the back and front. All sorts of things she could get her own forensic expert to check on later, but she had needed to get a feel for the scene. Even though the blood had been pressure-hosed off the floor, nobody had paid any heed to the sprayed-on pattern of blood on the whitewashed walls. Julia had felt a sympathetic blind panic at the sight of the blood and had almost passed out. All she could think of was the terror of the victim, the excruciating pain as her cranium was shattered, blow by blow, the certain knowledge, even as the hammer came down, that she was dying . . . Paul had half carried her to the car, stayed with her until she had recovered. They hadn't said another word to each other but something indefinable had been established.

For the next couple of years they'd rubbed along together, yet all the time he'd be trying to get something out of her, trying to get her to say: Now listen, we're all in this together, we all want to see the truth come out, don't we? Except that Paul's truth and Julia's truth were often diametrically opposed.

Then one day coming out of the Crown Court he had said, 'I'll buy you a coffee at the San Giorgio. Bloody awful one that, isn't it? Terrible.'

And she had said, the tears inside, 'Yes. It is terrible, Paul. Really terrible.' It was a case of mutual sounding-out in those days. Cat and mouse. Behind every encounter, despite their growing friendship, they had opposing agendas. Julia was forever trying to ferret out some information about a case, something not disclosed on the face of the papers, and Paul would egg her on to disclose what her clients were saying. On opposite sides they worked on high profile cases, and the edges between social and professional contact became blurred.

It suited Julia that Paul seemed content to let their friendship remain uncomplicated, yet imperceptibly it was changing. Neither he nor Julia had put this into words, and certainly not into actions, though more and more often she was experiencing a sensual undertone.

A lucky run of green lights took her past the Town Hall and into Princess Street. Settling into the middle lane she reached over and flicked off the radio; the news would be full of the Smith verdict. Instead she slotted in Mozart's Clarinet Concerto, felt for her mobile phone and squeezed the off-button. She filled her lungs then slowly breathed out, letting the day's tension float away on the soaring swell of the notes. On Monday she would bill the Smith file, put it in the billed cabinet. When it was paid someone else would move it on to archiving. Six years later it would be shredded. She never wanted to see it again, not because she had lost, but because she couldn't bear to be reminded of this thing. This thing — this ghastly thing — these unbelievable snippets of memories that through Smith had been seeping back into her mind, that even now, she dared not formulate in words.

Yes. Switch off now, Julia. Think instead of mountain streams and your beloved Pennine hills. Switch off Smith. Put him out of your mind.

But that was easier said than done.

The question of what might have turned him into a murderer clawed at her brain, dragging her back to the brightly-lit cubicle at Strangeways where once or twice a week for eight months, closeted almost eyeball to eyeball, he had become a part of her life.

She put her foot down and slipped into the inside lane. Oh God, she thought, if only I could stop the dark, fearful past from trickling into my consciousness.

The phone was ringing as Paul Moxon walked into his office. This was not going to be a good night. Slinging his jacket over the back of his chair, he sat down and swivelled round to gaze through the plate glass window with its panoramic view of the domain over which he controlled the detection of crime.

Damn that phone. He picked it up. 'Oh hi, Kevin. Yeah, just walked in this minute.'

'Suppose you've heard the news, boss. Smith.'

'Yeah. Had a call coming down Chester Road on the way back from town. Damned near hit the guy in front of me. Give me a couple of minutes, Kev, then come up. There're things we must tie up tonight. He'll be at it again if we don't nab him soon.'

'Have you spoken to Julia Grant?' Kevin asked.

'Been trying ever since I got the news. Not at home. Not in her office. Mobile's switched off.' Paul thought the question was a little close to home, but it was well intended.

He put down the phone then immediately picked it up again and dialled Ken Riding's office at Cheshire Constabulary headquarters in Chester.

'Hello, Ken. Paul Moxon. How are you?'

'Fine, Paul. Been a long time. What can I do for you?'

'Got a problem, Ken. Urgent. We've had a case going on against this guy Sam Smith. He's just gone down for life. And now he's escaped this afternoon on the way to Strangeways.'

'I heard. Crafty bugger. Where do I come into this?'

'His brief was Julia Grant. She probably crops up in Chester Crown Court cases from time to time. The thing is, she lives in your patch. Smith may try to make contact. Maybe worse. He came out with a load of pretty threatening stuff against her as he was taken down from the dock. I don't want to tread on any toes, Ken, but I'd like one of my own men down there to help keep obs and liaise with your men over at

34

Wilmslow. Could do anything, this one.'

'Not a problem, Paul. I'll put Bob Bennett, the senior DS at Wilmslow, onto it straightaway – ask him to contact you direct. You can make the arrangements through him.'

'Great. Thanks, Ken.'

'Don't mention it. You'll get our fullest cooperation. How are things, by the way?'

'Fine. And you, Ken? Isn't it about time you retired?'

'What about you, Paul, you're getting a bit of an old codger yourself? Forty-four if my sums are right.'

'Don't tell me,' Paul said, laughing as he put down the phone. Since Police College at Hendon they'd remained good friends, though they seldom met now. He knew he could count on Ken.

He punched memory recall, followed by the number one button. The automated voice told him the phone was switched off but if he left his message after the tone his call would be returned.

'Damn.' She'll have that bloody Mozart blaring out. What's the bloody point in mobile phones if you keep them switched off? He pressed re-dial and got the same message. He banged it down and immediately it began ringing with an incoming call. He picked it up, hoping it was Julia.

'DS Bob Bennett, Sir, Wilmslow CID. Superintendent Riding asked me to give you a call regarding the Smith escape. We've already heard about it on the bush telegraph. What do you need from Cheshire?'

Paul filled him in. Short, sharp and to the point police-speak.

'Does Smith have access to firearms, Sir?'

'It's not in his MO, but on this occasion I can't rule it out. According to eyewitnesses, his accomplices were armed and masked.'

'Right, Sir. I'll ask the ACC to authorise a firearms support unit stand-by. Or, if you think it's necessary, I could call in an armed response vehicle first. As a stopgap?'

'Anything's possible with Sam Smith,' Paul said. 'Could have been an idle threat. You know what they're like when they first hear their sentence, but I don't want to take any chances.' *Not where Julia Grant is concerned*, Paul mouthed to himself.

'Right,' said Bennett. 'I'll start with surveillance for the time being and get things in motion for armed response. And where will the brief be now, Sir?'

Paul looked at his watch. 'My best guess is she'll be on the way home, may even be there by now. But she could be anywhere.'

'Married?'

'Widow.'

'Family?'

'A daughter, aged six.'

'Any ideas how Smith might arrive if he comes down this way?' Bennett asked.

'Our patrols are keeping their eyes peeled for anything suspicious. I suggest you do the same on the main approaches to Wilmslow, and round Grant's house.' He gave Bennett the address. 'We need to get this guy locked up again. Soon as possible.'

'We'll be happy to beat GMP to it, Sir.'

As Paul finished the call with the usual pleasantries he heard the familiar heavy knock of his right hand man, Kevin Moorsley, who walked in without waiting for Paul's response. He redialled Julia's mobile phone again, gesturing Moorsley to take a seat. Julia's phone was still switched off. Incredible, he thought. 'That was the senior Detective Sergeant at Wilmslow,' he told Moorsley. 'I've just been briefing him in case Smith makes a beeline for Julia Grant.'

Paul turned towards the window. His shoulders slumped despondently. He stared out in the direction of the prominent red-brick tower at Strangeways, wishing he could feel more confident about when Smith would once again be safely tucked away behind its imposing Victorian walls.

Kevin joined him at the window. He followed Paul's gaze. 'Quite a landmark, isn't it, boss.'

Paul undid the top button of his shirt and loosened his tie. Back in the 1830s it would have been the largest, finest building for miles around. A symbol of power, dominating the people's lives. 'Yeah,' he said with a distinct touch of acrimony in his voice, 'where Sam bloody Smith will be very soon if I have anything to do with it.'

He gestured again towards the leather chair on the other side of his desk. 'What's happening?'

'Not a lot, I'm afraid to say,' said Moorsley. 'Bootle Street had a team on the scene within minutes. Another one rounding up witnesses. I've asked for a further briefing for nine o'clock and we're setting up an incident room at Stockport. But in terms of results or even hard leads, not a bloody sausage.'

Paul nodded. 'Look, Kev, I know it's getting late but tonight we must pull out all the stops.'

'Tell me what you want,' Moorsley prompted.

'You've got his known associates list?'

Moorsley nodded.

Paul cracked his knuckles one by one as though each clashing of the bones marked the bullet points of the action he had in mind. 'I want you to set up coordinated raids on all of them. We're only talking about maybe three, possibly four, addresses. Firearms teams on all of the jobs with uniformed backup, okay? We'll obviously be looking for Smith himself but we'll also want to scare the living bejesus out of them all, or their women, and see if any of them coughs anything. Oh, and dogs. Get something with Eau de Smith on it, you know, sheets from his cell, something you can give to the dogs when they go in at each address. If he's at any of them they'll give us a steer.'

'I like it, boss.' Kevin smiled as though the re-capture had already been accomplished. 'And if he isn't at any of the locations we'll have given them all such a fright they won't want to know his case.'

Paul strode to the map of Greater Manchester that monopolised one entire wall of his office. 'He'll be lying low. He's a Manchester man. He won't go far. Moss Side. Cheetham Hill. Salford . . . we'll cover all his favourite haunts.'

Kevin looked at his watch. 'We're already covering his likely pubs and clubs, and tapping our local snouts. Something like this should have gone round the houses like wild fire.' He stood up to leave. He wasn't one to waste time. 'From what I've heard, the escape was carried out like a military operation. Takes a lot of planning, that. There've got to be people out there . . .'

Paul rubbed the day-long stubble along the line of his jaw. Being out-manoeuvred by Sam Smith was not something he was prepared to tolerate. 'There was I thinking how good it was that justice had been done. I still had this big cheesy grin all over my face when I get the news he's scarpered.' He shook his head, still wondering whether it was all a bad dream.

He walked back to his desk, sat down and picked up a cold, half full Maxpax cup, not sure if it was his or had been left by someone else. He looked at the contents, hesitated a second and then drained it. 'It's pissing me off, Kev. We all worked so hard on this case, you, me, the lads and lasses on the team. Jesus, for once even the wallies in the CPS played a blinder. We should have got him for the Jennifer Dunn job though. Maybe we'll have another pop when we get him locked up again. Let's make sure we do, Kev.'

'We'll get him. Don't worry. And you'd better get your jacket back on. Press and Publicity have arranged a TV interview for you down at the scene. Six-thirty sharp.'

'I'll be there. But number one is to stake out Mrs Grant's house. I want one of our own plain-clothes men there now, to team up with Bob Bennett's lads from Wilmslow. They know every nook and cranny. But I want them invisible, Kev. We need the element of surprise.'

'Got it, boss.'

Paul stood up and saw him to the door. 'Make sure an All Ports Bulletin goes out too, just in case. Train stations, airports, seaports. Message switch system. Fax. E-mail. Interpol, the lot.'

Kevin grinned. Adversity rarely dampened his humour. 'Done that already, Chief.'

- 8 -

The traffic lights at Mauldeth Road turned red. Julia jammed on her brakes and realised she had spent the past fifteen minutes on automatic pilot. While she waited, her thoughts leapt back to Sam Smith.

She could see him now, superimposed on the ribbon of traffic jamming Kingsway for miles ahead of her. She could even smell the Jeyes Fluid smell of Strangeways . . .

He is only two feet away on the other side of the interview table, the big blue eyes bulging with emotion. 'God, how I hate her,' he says. His mouth twists. His words ring out above the inhuman noises of the prison, the raucous screams, the cries for help, the blasphemy and the threats, all blessedly muffled by the thick floor to ceiling windows of the cubicle. He stares at me, like he does every time we meet, as though I owe him something, but doesn't know quite what it is.

'How can you hate your own mother?' I ask him.

'Would you walk away from your kid, Julia?'

'Of course not.'

'Leave your kid in a bundle on a doorstep? You got any kids, Julia?'

'One.' I look down at the floor, anything rather than face his sudden hurtful look.

'Lucky you.' He sucks in his breath. 'Boy or girl?'

'Girl. She's my whole life. I'd do anything for her.'

'A little *girl*.'

Oh no, he's not a paedophile too, is he? He smiles and I see a wistful look in his eyes that dispels this thought. 'What's her name?' he says.

'Nicky.'

'Nicky? Nice name.' He pauses. Frowns. 'How old?'

'Just turned six.'

An instant of pain crosses his eyes.

'And where's your mother now?' I ask.

'Never seen my mother. The bitch.'

'She may have had no option,' I tell him. 'No money. Nowhere to live. Maybe she was doing what she thought was best for you.' Are these the same reasons that forced my own mother to leave me to the mercy of strangers? Strangers I'm still striving to remember . . .

Smith's eyes close as if he's struggling to conjure up a fresh vision of his mother but still doesn't like what he sees. 'She's just like all of them. Crap.' he says at last.

'But every mother loves her child. She must have cared about you. Maybe she still does.'

39

'No. No one cares about me so I don't care about them. And what I do is for my own good and nobody else's.'

I try a new tactic. 'I'm sure *my* mother cared about me. But . . . but she also abandoned me.'

His eyes open wider. 'She did? Where?'

'Don't know. Ditch. Railway station. Doorstep?'

I'm walking through a graveyard of images . . .

the separate rooms, the high ceilings. Creeping to my brother's room, strong arms dragging me away, the sudden cold without his warmth, crying, crying, all night long, crying . . .

Smith's lips part in another rare smile.

'Did she really abandon you?' he asks.

'Yes. Me and my twin brother.' My breath catches in my throat. Unintentionally the words have spilled out, every self-made rule never to utter those words to strangers broken. But it's too late to take them back.

Twin brother, I repeat inside my head. I love the sound of the words. I must try to make them go away but they're intent on tormenting me to the full now that they are released. Twin brother. Twin brother.

Smith stares at me. It's a look of unexpected empathy, and I think, as I so often do, how normal he appears. Not like a murderer at all.

'Where is your mother now?' I say, hoping I can stop him asking any more questions.

'I don't even know who she is.' He frowns. 'And your . . . twin brother?'

'Don't know. I think he's dead.'

'You think. Don't you know for Chrissake?' He leans across the table as though he wants to shake me.

'Yes. I know he's dead. They told me, just before I was adopted. But I hate to think of him as dead. It's so long ago. I can't even remember his name or what he looks like – only that I loved him.'

She suddenly has a fleeting, out of body experience. She is looking down on herself having this conversation with a suspected psychopathic murderer. *What the hell are you doing, Julia? Why are you telling this man all this stuff? He's a bloody client, not your father confessor!* But she can't stop. The tap has started to drip and there's no way she can turn it off. She is driven to confide in him.

Smith lowers his voice. 'Why the hell didn't you ask?' It's as though he really cares.

'I was too afraid. I pretended he was still alive. Hoping they'd only told me he was dead to keep me quiet.'

'Why would they do that?'

'He was very naughty. That I do remember. Always throwing his flick-knife at cushions. But this didn't stop me loving him. He was all I had. He looked after me. Kept me warm. Took the blame if I did something bad.'

For a long time we stare at one another. Saying nothing.

'Were you ever fostered, Julia?' His voice only just breaks the silence pressing in on me. He puffs on his cigarette as though he doesn't care what the answer is. The smoke curls into the static air.

'I think so but I can't really remember. I only remember clearly the things that happened after I was adopted. As though I'd just been born.'

'Adopted,' he says. He sucks in his breath. 'Lucky devil, weren't you?' Then he frowns. 'When?'

'That same year. Just after my brother.'

Died?

I can't say it. I hate that word. *They're all dead. My brother. My husband. My mother. Father. There's no one left . . .*

Smith's top lip begins to quiver. 'No wonder you made it good,' he says. A tone of envy creeps into his voice. He bends his head to one side. 'How old were you?' he asks very slowly.

'Ten. Yes, I was ten. There's so much that's blanked out. I was so lonely. I used to dream he'd come back.'

'Still dream?' he asks, leaning towards me until his eyes are staring straight into mine.

It's all wrong I tell myself. You don't talk to your clients like this. But I can't stop. 'Sometimes,' I say. 'And once long ago I thought he really had returned. It was soon after I was adopted. New people moved in next door. There was a boy about my age. We played together. I was so happy. I must have thought he was my brother. One day, for no apparent reason, they stopped him coming round. I wasn't allowed out. Some people came to the door. Questioned me, accused me of molesting him. And all I'd done was put my arms around him.' I realise this is the first time I've ever told anyone this story.

Smith looks away.

'I never forgot that,' I say. 'Being accused of something I hadn't done.'

'Did they believe you?'

'No.' And this time I stare into Smith's penetrating eyes. 'And you? Were you adopted?'

'I should be so lucky. Foster homes. One after another. Few months here, few months there. Kicked out, then on to the next. Except for one. Ada. Three years with Ada. She was the last. Bit of a psychologist, Ada. Taught me all sorts of stuff. Mind over matter. That kind of thing. A schizo, Ada.'

He pulls a crumpled photograph from his back pocket. 'This is her.' His eyes glaze over. 'Ada.'

The face is stark but beautiful. And for some reason I cannot fathom, strangely familiar.

And all at once I know. My breathing quickens. Apart from the scene-of-the-crime photographs of Joanne Perkins' body, mutilated and covered in blood, and those of her lying on a slab at the mortuary, I had seen only one snapshot of the seventeen-year-old when she was still alive.

I look at the photograph again.

The resemblance to Joanne Perkins is uncanny.

'All my foster fathers beat me,' he says. 'Left scars. But Ada was much worse than them. See these?' He points to two jagged scars on his cheek, half-hidden by the beard, then to the multiple scars on his hands, wrists and forehead. 'Other places too,' he says.

'Ada did that?'

He nods. 'But that wasn't all.'

'What else did she do?' I hold my breath. I have been sacrificing my secrets, my hidden fearful past. For this. To find out about his own horrific history. To give him an excuse for what he is accused of doing.

'We lived in a caravan. When they first fostered me we lived in a proper house. It was fine until her husband left. I loved her then. But after that she hated me. She said she loved me but she never did. She blamed me for everything — her divorce, for getting pissed. Even for copping off with men who turned out to be pieces of shit. You name it, I got the blame. First off she just poured melted candle wax on me. I soon got used to that. When that didn't make me scream any more she started with cigs. I used to piss and shit myself when she did it. And she always found a new, hidden place so it wouldn't show. The pain was unbelievable. She twisted my fingers. Broke three of 'em. Look.'

He holds out his hands. The joints are thickened, the bones distorted. He pulls up his sleeves. There are scars all the way up his arms.

'I still remember the pain. It was hell,' he says. 'When it got really bad I'd try to make myself go kind of numb so I'd feel nothing. I used to wet my bed every night – couldn't help it – even though I knew I was going to do it. So much fear I was rigid. She wouldn't give me nothing to drink all day. Made me sit in the wet stinking bedding till it dried. Forced me to watch her having sex with strange men. Lots of strange men. They were always drunk or stoned. Afterwards they'd turn on me. Do disgusting things. One of them even kicked me when they'd finished. Said I was a pervert. Me? They were the ones going at it, not me.'

'Do you still hate her?'

He looks down.

'Do you still hate her?' I ask again, knowing the key lies somewhere here.

'More than anything in the world. But I . . .'

'What?' I push him. I've used myself to get him to this point. Then he stops. He gazes at me with the characteristic twist of the head to one side. 'Do you have sexual fantasies, Julia?'

I keep my expression unchanged. 'Most people do, don't they?' I wonder what is coming next. 'Do you?' I have to ask.

He nods. 'Ada's always there. Like for real.'

I'm no psychologist but things are becoming clearer. He's been through enough to become really twisted, though I doubt he would agree. 'What about your own mother?' I say. 'Have you never tried to find her?'

His bitter laugh cuts the still, dank air of the consultation room. 'You kidding? I told you. She didn't want me . . .' His voice fades away, and he frowns again. 'And you, Julia? Have you looked for your mam?'

'No.' He's turned it around again just when I think I have him on the spot. With that voice and those eyes he could easily drag my deepest fears and secrets from me.

A screw puts his head round the door. 'Five minutes, please.' I am saved.

'I'll see you next week,' I say. I shut the file and see the date of birth on the cover. It shouts at me — 15th December. I am forever noticing it and being taken aback as if for the first time. I pick up the file and violently stuff it in my briefcase.

I push the copied courtesy bundle of papers across the desk towards him. 'We didn't need to go through these today, but read them carefully and be prepared to answer difficult questions next time I see you. I want you to talk me through what happened the night Joanne died. Step by step. Exactly as you remember it.'

He takes the file. His eyes fix on mine. I steady my hand.

'If it helps, write some notes. You've got to help me to help you.'

cold, wet, hungry, locked in his arms, watching his eyes . . .

Get a grip, Julia.

* * *

With a jolt Julia heard the car behind hooting. The persistent vision of Smith vanished, sucked into oblivion like a TV being switched off. Quickly she closed the gap between the Merc and the car in front.

Fool. Did I really discover more about him and the motives for his crime by baring my soul to him, she asked herself. Sure, he gained confidence and trust in me. But did that help me?

On the Wilmslow bypass the traffic speeded up. It slowed down at the roundabout on the old A41 and at that moment she remembered what he had said during their last meeting at Strangeways before the trial began, when he was at his lowest ebb.

'I need you, Julia. You're the only woman, the only person, I can trust. Help me, Julia. Please.'

- 9 -

The traffic through Wilmslow was dead slow and Julia was thankful when she finally reached Hillside House, her safe haven on the banks of the swiftly flowing Bollin River. As she drove through the wrought iron gates Nicky burst out of the front door, with Wendy close behind her.

'Mummy, Mummy, Kitty's got six kittens and they're all like little baby tigers. 'Cept one and he's black.'

'He'll be lucky then, won't he, darling.'

'She's had them all in the utility room,' Wendy said, 'and they look fine. She's got water and food. Nicky's dying to show you. Ironing's finished, I've managed to do all the hoovering, and we've done our reading, haven't we, pet? Despite all the excitement.'

'You're an angel as usual, Wendy. Go on, enjoy the King William tonight and have a good weekend and don't do anything I wouldn't,' said Julia, as Nicky attempted to drag her away. Wendy blew a kiss and hurried to her old shiny yellow Mini. Nicky stood waving until the Mini disappeared through the gates. She turned and clasped her hands around Duke.

'And, Mummy,' she said, stroking Duke's slobbering muzzle, 'when Duke went to look at the kittens, Kitty hissed at him and scratched his nose.'

Julia's eyes misted over, marvelling at what a pair they made, this bright as a button little girl and the big, soft attentive hound. Duke squirmed with delight, tail lashing like a whip as Nicky patted his head.

45

'Have you given them names yet?' she asked as she swung the garage door open.

Nicky screwed up her face against the sunlight shafting through the clumps of tall leafy beech trees that lined the garden. 'Wendy says I can't till I know if they're boys or girls. But, Mummy, how d'you know if they're boys or girls? Wendy won't tell me.'

Julia remembered today's olive branch still in the glove box. She handed Nicky the brown paper packet. 'Wendy's very busy, darling. When she's got time I'm sure she'll tell you which kittens are which.'

'Ooh! Look, Duke. Our favourite.' Nicky rattled the miniature boxes of Smarties just out of reach of Duke's drooling lips, then stood clear of the car as Julia drove it into the garage.

'Mummy,' she said, running to join her. 'I wish Wendy could stay here always.'

'Don't be silly, she's got her own home to go to.' She felt a lump in her throat. She couldn't help it. Her daughter probably loved her nanny more than her mother. Did life have to be that complicated, she wondered.

'Mummy, is Paul coming tonight?' Nicky opened her eyes wide, smiling in expectation.

That look. That fleeting expression. Julia's heart missed a beat. Simon used to look at me exactly like that, hoping I'd respond. Never coercing me, but making me feel it would be a gift to him if I did. Until finally I had realised it would be a gift for me. She smiled to herself. It would make Simon laugh. If he was here.

'No, darling,' she said, banishing the bizarre vision. 'Paul's busy this weekend.'

'Is this your weekend off, Mummy?'

'I hope so. I'm not on duty, and I'll try not to get called out.'

'Oh, goody. Then can we take Duke for a walk? We haven't been to the park for ages.'

'Of course,' she said, Paul's words of this morning echoing in her ears.

Nicky's eyes widened again. 'You mean . . . right now?'

Julia glowed inwardly at her daughter's ecstasy, holding back tears

46

that were a strange mixture of relief, happiness, fear, regret, all scrambled together in one big surge of emotion. 'I'll get Duke's lead,' she said, wiping the corner of her eye.

'Yippee!' Nicky careered across the cobbled driveway, Wendy, Paul and the kittens forgotten, Duke following with great bounding leaps of joy. At the foot of the stone steps leading to the front door she waited for Julia, jumping up and down and holding out her hands. 'Come on, Mummy. Let's put on our track suits and our trainers.'

As Julia closed the heavy wooden door, the phone in the entrance hall rang. 'Oh no,' she said, looking at Nicky as she threw herself down on one of the carved mahogany chairs on either side of the telephone table. 'Not a call-out.'

She crossed two fingers of her right hand and winked reassuringly at Nicky. Not convinced, her daughter backed away and slid her arm around Duke. Still staring at Julia, she tightened her grip around the dog's neck and pressed her cheek against his snout.

Duke licked Nicky's face and glanced at Julia with droopy eyes as if he knew he had broken the rules.

Julia picked up the phone. Duke was probably the most important thing in Nicky's life, she thought. At least he was always there when she needed him. And Kitty and Wendy were close behind. And Paul. Funny, he was on the list too. She wondered how that had happened.

She held the receiver to her left ear. I wish with all my heart that I could somehow rustle up a normal life for my child. Where she would feel secure and loved by both a mother and a father. Where she wouldn't have to fall back on the love of a dog for her solace. Or throw herself so embarrassingly at every male friend I have . . .

'Julia Grant speaking. Oh hi, Ben, I'm sorry but unless it's really urgent do you think you could get hold of Mark. Or Caroline. I know that she's – '

'Julia, take it easy, will you?'

Why was Ben's voice so calm? It was the voice he used in the office when he had some pretty nasty assignment for her.

'Okay, Ben. What is it?' She envisaged at the very least an urgent visit to a police station to see a client. Criminals had no respect for

47

office hours. She reached out and touched Nicky's cheek as though to presage as kindly as possible the inevitable disappointment. And poor Wendy. How would she react to her Friday night with Alan being ruined?

'I've defrosted a barbecue pack,' Ben said. 'Will you and Nicky share it with me?'

It wasn't what she had expected, but anything was better than that. His usual ploy was lunch. Now and then a tête-à-tête dinner, which she always avoided. But a cosy family meal had seldom interested him.

Oh, well. Just this once. Any other Friday night she'd have had to say no, but with Paul on duty this weekend, someone to talk to tonight after Nicky went to bed seemed a comforting idea.

Again she winked at Nicky.

'Thanks, Ben. We'd love to see you.'

'I'll be there in one hour,' Ben said.

'Make it one and a half. We're just taking Duke for a walk in The Carrs.' She smiled as Nicky flung both arms around Duke's neck. 'I'll light the fire when we get back.'

'Terrific. But take care. I suppose you've heard the news.'

'What?'

'Sam Smith. He's escaped.'

- 10 -

Sam Smith stroked his smoothly shaven chin. Bloody dogs everywhere, dragging their fucking owners along the banks of the river. But that was okay. If he changed benches now and then there was enough space in this park to keep him inconspicuous until nightfall. Until he was ready to make his move.

The car had been a cinch. Some thickhead in Longsight, not a block away from where they'd dumped the Scorpio, left his pale blue shed unlocked and beggars can't be choosers. But the excitement of it all had made him hungry. He should have stopped at a chippy for a pie. He was thirsty too. And other primary urges made it difficult to sit still. But there was time for all that. Right now there were more important things on the agenda and he could wait. The months of planning were about to pay off.

He sat on a bench watching the clear brown water flow under the bridge. Water under the bridge. That had been his life until now. But it was all about to change.

Something made him look up. In the distance a dog barking. A child laughing, running. A woman. A flash of golden hair.

Jeez.

He had positioned himself right behind her house, but he hadn't reckoned on seeing her here, out on the riverbank. Change of plan, maybe. He watched them approach. What would his life have been like if he'd had her fucking luck?

Now that he was free he was certain it had been something more than chance that when he was arrested, of all the solicitors in Manchester, his mates had recommended Julia Grant. For murder, they'd said, there's no one else. Yeah – fate, not chance.

Grinning to himself he started walking, aiming for a bench further down the river.

- 11 -

'This is my favouritest place in the whole world,' Nicky enthused.

'Mine too, darling,' Julia said, breathing in the fresh country air. Only a mile or so north lay the teeming county of Greater Manchester with its three or four million people and almost, it seemed, as many cars. And here they were, walking along an unspoilt swathe of emerald grassland that edged the River Bollin as it curled and gurgled through the Cheshire countryside.

'Let's go this way first, Mummy. Behind these trees. Let's pretend we're going to see the wizard, like I do with Wendy. Come on. We're off to see the wizard,' she sang, 'the wonderful wizard of Oz.'

Duke streaked ahead, pulling Nicky behind him as he bounded along the narrow lane hidden in the trees directly behind Hillside House.

'Silk Road's my second favourite place on earth,' Julia said, catching up with Nicky. 'I love these huge old beech trees hanging over on each side. It's like being inside a cathedral. And when it rains and then the sun shines on the rain drops in the branches, it looks as though it's lit up with giant crystal chandeliers.'

'Mummy, not Silk Road. It's the *Yellow Brick* road. Why do you always call it Silk Road?'

Julia grasped Nicky's hand. 'Because this is where they used to make silk, of course. There used to be a silk factory just over there, opposite the weir . . . '

She pointed to the river. A man was walking on his own, just beyond the bridge. For a moment she did not move. Another image, dim and distant, smudged the scene before her. She closed her eyes.

Running . . . hiding, stones tearing bare feet, long grass scratching arms and face . . . blood . . .

'Mummy? What's wrong? You look funny. Oh, come on. Duke doesn't want to stop!'

Nicky raced down the slope towards the bridge, rattling the wooden boards and urging Julia to hurry. On the other side Duke dragged her along the path that followed the river.

After a few minutes Julia couldn't take any more. 'It's all right for you, Nicky, but I must sit down.' She flopped onto a vacant wooden bench overlooking the rippling water. 'Whew! I'm so unfit. I think I should join your ballet class on Saturdays.'

'Don't be so silly, you can't do ballet.' Nicky's silvery laughter filled the air as she snuggled close to Julia.

'What do you mean?' Julia protested in mock outrage. 'I'm sure I could.' She pursed her lips, trying to keep a straight face. But it was no good. 'Well, okay,' she said, bursting into laughter too, 'maybe not ballet, but *something* to keep me fit. Aerobics? Judo? Karate? Or . . . self-protection classes.'

Nicky stopped laughing and looked up at her, frowning.

'Mummy?'

'Yes, darling?'

'Who else is coming tonight?'

'Only Ben. And as a special treat you can stay up for a little while.'

'Why isn't Paul coming too?'

Still out of breath, Julia shook her head. 'He said he was sorry, sweetheart, but he's working late. Besides, you can't expect Paul to come and see you every Friday night.'

'Why not?'

'Because —'

'But he's my favourite man. He makes me laugh and makes up silly games.' She cocked her head to one side. 'Mummy?'

'Hmm?'

'Where's my daddy?'

'He — he went away a long time ago, darling.'

'Is he coming back?'

'No.'

'Is he dead?'

The muscles in Julia's neck tightened. What does my daughter know of death?

Nicky twirled her hair around her finger. 'Wendy's daddy isn't ever coming back and he's dead. Wendy told me.'

Grabbing Duke's lead, Julia smiled at a young couple trying to restrain a panting Alsatian. She reached for Nicky's hand, realising that if you learn that someone is dead without ever having seen that person, you have no basis for grief.

'Your daddy died in a plane crash,' she said as gently as she could. 'When you were a tiny baby. His father and mother too. They were your grandpa and granny.'

'Wendy has a grandpa and a granny. And a grandad. And a nan too.'

Julia thought quickly. 'Well, you also have a grandad and a nan. David and Jessie are your grandad and your nan.'

'Then why do we call them David and Jessie?'

Julia hesitated. It would be too much for Nicky to learn all at once that her father died in a plane crash along with her granny and grandpa, and that her other set of grandparents aren't really her grandparents at all, but her mother's adoptive parents.

'Wendy has cousins too,' Nicky said, 'and an uncle. I wish I had an uncle. What are cousins and uncles?'

'Cousins are the children of your parents' brothers and sisters,' she quickly explained. 'But your daddy had no sisters or brothers. And I . . . and I have no sisters. And no brothers. So you have no cousins. No aunts. And no uncles.'

An innocent conversation with her daughter opens the wounds again, thought Julia. They are always there, ready to split and bleed. Every day something triggers the pain of not being able to solve the riddle of her broken, hidden past; not knowing who she was.

'I did have a brother once,' she said.

Nicky's eyes lit up. 'You're playing games with me, Mummy, else he'd be my uncle and you said I haven't got any. And he'd have come to see me, so there. How can you have one and then not have him, silly?' she asked, gripping Julia's arm.

'He's – ' She stopped. There'd already been too much talk of death. 'He went away a long time ago,' she said, almost to herself. 'Far, far away.'

'Is he coming back?'

'Maybe,' she said, then changed her mind. She couldn't even explain things to herself, let alone to Nicky. 'No. I don't think he's coming back.'

'Mummy, I wish Paul was coming tonight.'

Thank God for short attention spans, Julia thought. 'Paul has important things to do. And so have we, young lady. Come on. Time to go home.'

'Oh Mummy! Look at that poor bird in the river. It's trying to get out.'

Julia took one look at the struggling wagtail, ripped off her trainers and slithered down the bank into the swiftly flowing river. Putting both hands under the bird she lifted it out of the water. One flutter and off it flew, while Julia clambered up the bank.

'Mummy, you look so funny. All wet and muddy!'

As they ran laughing towards the bridge, something made Julia look back over her shoulder.

Escaped?

Well, I'm not really all that surprised, she thought. The clever ones always try. But a popular park like The Carrs is the last place he would be. Besides, these days I'm never sure what are illusions and what are strands of long forgotten reality snaking their way back into my consciousness.

- 12 -

The King William was more crowded than usual, even for a Friday night in trendy Wilmslow. Alan took a long slurp of his beer, and licked the foam off his lips as his eyes surfed over Wendy's body.

'Your skin has an extra glow on it tonight, Wendy. And your eyes are sparkling like you're really in the mood.'

Wendy blushed. Dirty bastard, I love him, she thought. He can talk to me like that all night.

'I'm glad you're not too tall. It gives me a feeling of power. And I love all that firm flesh I can grab hold of.' He took a deep breath and looked up at the ceiling. 'I reckon it's because of those twice-weekly Judo sessions you live and die for.'

'I suppose so,' she said, pulling herself up and stretching her neck so that her face was almost level with his.

'You know what? You look smashing tonight. What you done to your hair?'

'I felt like a change.' Wendy's insides trembled. Even after six years he still excited her. She loved the hugeness of him, his strength, his soft fleshy lips and those deep-set eyes that seemed to look right into the heart of you. God, he was sexy and she often wondered why he bothered with a plain, straight-haired girl like her. She smiled, feeling a surge of unexpected feminine allure.

'Glad you like it.' Most of the time Alan never seemed to notice the effort she went to. But she still made the effort — she wasn't about to give up. One day, maybe tonight even, he would say yes.

'Does you good to have a change now and then,' she added, tossing her uncustomary curls so that they swirled around her head and made her feel like the girl on the telly. *Because I'm worth it.*

He screwed up his eyes. 'What d'you mean? A change?'

She tensed her muscles, as though she was about to defend her title in the face of her arch Judo rival. Here goes. 'Well, like all sorts of things. You know. Like I'm fed up with sharing with Janey. Like I'll be twenty-seven Tuesday after next. I want a home of my own, Alan.'

She sneaked a sideways glance at him. He was staring at the froth on top of his glass of beer. He knows what's coming, she thought. 'You must be fed up too,' she went on, not able to stop herself even though she knew it would annoy him. 'Like staying with your sister. Never having any privacy.'

'It suits me, Wendy. I've told you. I'm *not* moving in with you, even if I could find something we could afford. It just wouldn't work. You're out all day and six nights out of seven, when you're not at Judo. Who'd take my phone messages and cook my grub?'

'Answer machine. Mobile phone. Microwave. No problem.' She tried hard to keep the panic out of her voice.

Alan smiled disarmingly and shook his head. 'Come on, Sexpot, let's not argue. We'll have a game of darts, then we can go back to my place. Dawn and Barry won't be home till late and the kids are away on a weekend camp.'

'Alan. Let's talk. We never talk. I want a proper home. Something we can share, instead of having to meet like this at the pub and snatch the odd half-hour at Dawn's.'

'You crazy? You know what a house costs? The extra work to keep it decent? I see some grotty places every day in my job. People out at work. No time for housework. You don't know how lucky you are. Just one room and a bit to keep clean.'

Wendy's spirits sank. This was going the same way it always did. 'I keep the whole of Mrs Grant's house clean too,' she said. 'And I love it.'

'So what more you want? And why the hell don't you move in with Mrs Grant? There's enough room for an army in that mansion. You don't have to live in that poky little studio-flat with Janey.'

'Mrs Grant doesn't want me there all the time. She wants to look after Nicky herself whenever she can. Otherwise she'd never be a mum.'

Mum. What a lovely word. Frightening too. She glanced at her still flat stomach. She was almost certain. She'd missed two periods but hadn't plucked up the courage to go to Boots and buy one of those pregnancy test kit things. Once before she'd missed and it had turned out to be nothing. When it was definite it would make things very different. Not knowing, she could still stay calm. She hoped she wouldn't panic. She hated it when her Judo opponents panicked. It always showed their weakness and then she felt she held an unfair advantage.

'She must be filthy rich,' Alan said, 'living in that house.'

'No, I don't think she is, really. Never buys luxuries and things, except that groovy red car. She inherited the house when she lost her husband and her in-laws.'

'Well, she could sell it. She could give up work, then she wouldn't need you.'

'That's a daft thing to say. She's a career woman. I asked her once why she did it. You know, like defending all those criminals. She said that sometimes the criminals are the victims. She said that long ago she'd been accused of something she never did and nobody believed her but she didn't tell me what it was. Couldn't have been that bad. Not her. No, she wouldn't last a week without working. Anyway, I love my job too, but I wouldn't want to be there all the time. I wouldn't have time for Judo. And I'd never see you. Mind you, I hardly ever do as it is.' Playfully she pushed her shoulder against his. 'Except Friday nights,' she added, looking up at him and half closing her eyes.

Sometimes Wendy felt as though she was already on the shelf. She thought of the six years she had loved him. Of the numerous occasions she'd forgiven him when he had taken other women out. Of her ultimatum last time it happened. 'Only me, or I call it all off,' she had told him, though she knew she never would. In bed they were fantastic together. She didn't want any other man. She would rather do without second best if she couldn't keep her Alan.

'You know I'm called out all hours. Plumbers can't be choosy,' Alan said.

Wendy ignored his excuses. 'Aah, you poor boy. Julia Grant gets called out more than you, and she reckons she gets paid less money for having to go out in the middle of the night than you plumbers do. Besides, I want to start my own family. It was fine when Nicky was a baby but she goes to school now.'

'You and your babies. Can't think why you're so crazy about them. Dawn was just the same. Kept having one after the other.' His voice softened. 'They were real cute when they were little. Not like now, the little thugs, though I still love 'em. Well, don't you go getting any ideas. Like coming off the pill or any of that nonsense.'

'Not a chance,' she said, fluttering her eyelashes. Sometimes lies were necessary and there was no point in spoiling the night. She knew when she was beaten — a lost battle, but not the war, no way. She'd get him.

'Let's go and have that game of darts,' she said. 'Just a quick one.' As he stood up she patted the swell of his neat little butt beneath his belt. 'Then we can go to Dawn's.'

- 13 -

Julia heard the door bell. Duke was barking his head off and she was slightly irritated that Ben should have arrived so early. Still out of breath from hurrying into her clothes after her shower, she stared at the tall, serious looking man standing on the threshold.

'Mrs Julia Grant?'

'Yes?' she said, glancing at the plain black car parked at the front door, trying to place the softly spoken owner. She felt certain she had met him before, but couldn't think where.

He smiled. 'DS Bennett, Wilmslow Police. Er, I'm sure we've met. May I come in?'

Julia had a vague memory of seeing him before, but he'd been in uniform then. Must have had a promotion. What the hell did he want, coming round uninvited like this? Not as if she had any jobs on with him or anything. 'Come in', she said, stepping aside from the door. 'What can I do for you, only I've got a guest coming round shortly.' She glanced at her watch.

'This won't take long,' he said. 'I promise.'

At that moment Nicky appeared at the door, holding on to Duke's collar.

'Make sure Duke has some water, darling. I won't be long.'

She ushered Bennett into the drawing room and offered him a chair, avoiding the one that had once been Simon's favourite.

'I'll come straight to the point, Mrs Grant. We're working closely with Greater Manchester on this case. Within the next few minutes you and your family will have all the police protection you need, twenty-four hours a day. I think, however, that for the first few days we'll . . . '

'Just hang on, Sergeant. Protection, what for? Wait. Please. You mean Smith, I presume, I heard the news. But someone's jumping the gun here. I didn't ask for protection and I can assure you I don't need it. There really isn't anything to worry about.' But even as she spoke a voice inside told her that where Smith was concerned, perhaps it was best to assume nothing.

Bennett looked at her as though he agreed that it was highly unlikely Smith would come to her house, but was carrying out orders and who was he to argue. 'At the end of the day, Mrs Grant, it's up to you, but from what I heard this guy was screaming blue murder — sorry, screaming threats at you from the dock — and next thing he's been sprung in a seriously professional job on his way to prison. Now, if you'll allow me to explain, just as a precaution you understand, we can arrange for you and your daughter to move into a hotel for a short while — we're bound to lock him up again soon.'

'Sergeant, I'm not moving out of my house.'

He nodded. 'No, I thought you'd prefer to remain here and that's why I've arranged for a plain-clothes to be in the house with you. There'll be two men in the garden as well — possibly three for a garden this size. In addition, if you'll let me know what time your child goes to school, there'll be an escort, and of course one for yourself.'

Julia clasped her hands together and tightened her fingers. He's doing it for my own good, she thought, and because he cares. But also because he can — he's got the power. The sort of power that so often tramples good people, as well as bad, underfoot.

She smiled sweetly at the sergeant. 'You're very kind and I

appreciate your concern but, you see, Wendy — that's my daughter's nanny — is with Nicky constantly. She's a little half-pint but she's also a Judo expert. Black belt, in fact. And of course in my job I couldn't possibly have someone trailing around with me. I'm sure you'll understand. Besides, the house is perfectly secure. Telephones in almost every room. A large dog with a very loud voice.'

She stopped. It wouldn't do to protest too much, but she didn't seem to be able to stop herself. So often where Sam Smith was concerned she would find herself on the defensive, without having thought it out, as though that inner voice was dictating and she was merely mouthing the words. 'I don't want my daughter confused by an unnecessary police presence,' she went on. 'I think there's far too much hysteria these days with the media blowing things out of proportion making parents paranoid about their children's safety so they never have any freedom and don't learn to think for themselves.'

'I can assure you, Mrs Grant, we're very serious about this and, as I said, the officers will be very discreet.'

'I'm sure you're right,' she said, making certain her eyes gave not the slightest flicker of fear, 'but I'm afraid I can't allow them in my house, or even in the garden. The dog would never stop barking.'

Bennett smiled and nodded; the experienced cop exercising just the right amount of decorum he thought was needed. Julia was impressed.

'Mrs Grant, you have a very good reputation, even most coppers admire you as far as I can make out. And I can understand why you don't really want to have to take our advice and have us poking your noses into your life.' Julia suppressed a smile. 'We can limit ourselves to a presence outside, on the road,' he continued, as though that had been his plan all along. 'In an unmarked car, of course. As discreet as possible but within sight of the gate at all times. I'm not going to push you any further on this, but I would like you to reconsider. He could be in the area already. But at least you can't complain if we keep a low profile on the road, can you? If you give us a list of the cars, their registration numbers and descriptions of the people who habitually visit, it will cause less disturbance for you and for them. Here's my card — that's my straight through number, my mobile and my email.'

Julia stood up and took the card. 'Thank you. I'll email you a list in a few minutes. There are not many that visit. And I hope you won't think I don't appreciate your concern, it's just that — '

'Enough said, Mrs Grant,' Bennett interrupted, 'but if you change your mind, or the situation worsens in any way, we can review the arrangements.'

'Of course,' she said.

She led him to the door. Before closing it she could not stop herself from pausing and glancing towards the gate, trying to look through the dense hedges.

- 14 -

Paul Moxon was about ready to call it a day. He had been immersed for hours in talking to officers and press. Talking big to reporters, expressing his worst and darkest fears to his team, instilling them with a determination to prosecute the recapture of Smith with extreme prejudice if necessary.

But before leaving he had to try to get hold of Julia once more — he hadn't had a moment to do so for several hours. He rang her number and she picked up almost immediately.

'Julia. At last.'

'Hi. I knew it would be you, but I'm really sorry, Paul, I can't talk now. I've just put Nicky to bed and I don't want to waken her. Also I . . . ' Her voice was a tense whisper. 'Well, I have a visitor. Can we talk tomorrow?'

Paul ground his teeth. A visitor? Who? But he was damned if he was going to ask. 'Just very quickly, then. I've spoken to Chester to have a couple of men on obs at your house. I suppose you've heard.'

'Yes, I know,' she said. 'And thank you, Paul, it's just like you to think of me like that, but, well, this guy Bennett came round and wanted me and Nicky to become refugees virtually. Then he wanted me to turn the place into a B and B cum campsite for his men. In the end we compromised. He's put some people outside on the road. Plain-clothes, in an unmarked car.'

59

'Julia — '

'Really, Paul, it's fine. Duke would have gone berserk and I didn't want Nicky being frightened by a load of Plod knocking about the place.'

'Frightened? That's ridiculous. She's not frightened of *me*.'

'You are Plod,' she said, and he thought he heard a faint chuckle, 'but you're different.'

Paul sensed the change in her voice. If only he could see the expression on her face, he might be able to guess what kind of different she meant. 'Julia I know you probably don't think Smith would carry out his threat, and I know you — are you still there?'

'Yes. But I was just wondering if any other threatened solicitor would receive the same zealous treatment.'

'I'm only doing my job.' Here we go again, he thought, professional hats getting in the way of a closer relationship.

'Yes, but Smith would be a complete idiot if he showed his face within a mile of Hillside House,' she whispered. 'And you know he's not an idiot. Besides, he was only letting off steam.'

'Maybe.' Paul knew his tone did not mask his contempt for Smith. 'But don't worry,' he added, softening his voice. 'As long as they're out on the road now, guarding you, you'll be okay. You won't hear them, or even see them, I'm sure. But knowing they're there will at least give you the peace of mind to have a good night's rest.'

'Yes. All right.'

'And Julia . . . '

'Yes?'

'If you're at all worried I'll ask BT to put a trace on your lines.'

'That's thoughtful of you. But why should I be worried?'

He curbed his irritation. He wished that now and then she would admit to human frailty. But with Julia he always got better results with the soft approach. 'Okay. But it's no big deal, you know. All you do is press digit one on your phone. This activates a printer in BT's Malicious Call Centre. They'll alert us and then — '

'I know. I know all that, Paul. But I don't want the hassle.'

'No hassle. It's all set up remotely.' He paused. 'Actually . . . it just might help us to get him.' He bit his lip. He hoped the unintended sarcasm didn't show. 'Let me know if you change your mind. I'll ring you tomorrow. Give Nicky a hug.'

He put down the phone and spun round to face the window. Why couldn't she be realistic? The man had threatened her, dammit. Now he was on the loose and she was behaving as though nothing had happened. Or was it all an act? A show of bravado for his sake? Why? What was she trying to prove? It's so unlike her normal logical approach. Most women thus threatened would want as much protection as possible. Why didn't she?

Had Smith cast some kind of spell on her, he wondered.

He looked at the sodium glow of the city; Smith was somewhere out there. He had a steadily mounting fear that Smith was going to gravitate towards Julia, whether to harm her or try to get help he wasn't sure. He had so often, in his irrepressible, nosey copper way, tried to get Julia to open up and spill some beans about Smith but she never gave anything away. Nothing tangible anyway. But she did leave him with a sense that the man was having a profound effect on her. It was her long silences, her seriousness. Being on Smith's case had changed her, and it wasn't just because it was high profile, complex or serious — she could handle all that.

He did know from the profile the police had already drawn up on Smith that he was highly intelligent, manipulative, a charmer when he wanted to be but also utterly ruthless. Had he got under Julia's skin? Was he capable of influencing her in a way that went far beyond the bounds of the solicitor client relationship? Perhaps he already had.

He sat down on the edge of his desk. Was there something, anything else he could do before leaving, or something he hadn't thought through, that he could then act on? Dithering was not his style, but that's what he now found himself doing.

- 15 -

Julia tossed a fresh log onto the dying fire and stood for a moment breathing in the evocative smell of wood smoke. It reminded her of

Simon and those few happy years they had together. The summer nights sitting round this fire, planning the future . . .

Ben was watching her again, in that irritating way he had of letting his gaze wander away from her face and slowly down her body.

She bent down and patted Duke, then went back to her chair. Rather than look at Ben she watched the clouds swirl in ever changing patterns across the darkening sky. She hoped it wouldn't rain. She didn't want to be forced into buying one of those modern gas barbecues that lacked the romanticism she still associated with the wood fire.

'Don't you find all this too big just for you and Nicky?' Ben asked. A strange question, she thought, and no doubt it will be something Ben has not just said for something to say.

She followed his gaze. He was looking around at the lush array of shrubs and rustling beech trees surrounding the house, as though he had never seen them before. To her they were special. Familiar shapes and patterns she and Simon had loved together. Simon was still here, in the wood smoke, in the rustling of the trees and the smell of the grass when it was newly mown . . .

'A smaller house on a modern estate would be better for Nicky,' she conceded, 'but Simon would have wanted me to stay. He would have wanted Nicky to be brought up where he'd lived all his life. I love it, really. The space. The peace and quiet. The security. And it keeps Simon alive for me.'

Ben looked down at his almost empty glass, then up again. 'After five years I'm not sure that's very wise.'

Julia said nothing. She could guess where this was going.

'Aren't you sometimes lonely too?' he said.

'I'm too busy to feel lonely.'

He let it go, much to her relief. The wine had made her relax, in spite of the news of Smith's escape and the knowledge that several pairs of police eyes were now fixed on her house. Poor Ben, he seldom missed a chance to make a pass. But he was also kind in a platonic way, and Nicky was fond of him, as though he were an uncle.

She pushed her empty glass towards him. 'You know, that was the best steak I've ever tasted.' She meant it and hoped Ben would not feel she was being insincere.

'Cooking is one of my hobbies, and barbecues just about qualify as cooking,' he said. He poured some more red wine into Julia's glass and some soda water into his.

Julia spotted a slight tremor in his hand and had a fleeting pang of pity for him. She had the feeling he was doing his damnedest to impress her, as though one false move might be his undoing. 'I don't know how you do it,' she said. 'I always char the outside and leave the middle bits red raw, or frazzle it completely. I never really got round to cooking.'

'So, I noticed,' Ben said. 'Shame, in my view. For me it's one of life's joys.'

She gave him a sheepish look. 'First it was Jessie who spoilt me, like no real mother ever would. Then Simon's mother, Natalie the perfect. She never allowed anyone in her kitchen. Now it's Wendy. I simply never learned to cook. And most days I'm just too tired to bother.'

They laughed together quietly, not wanting to waken Nicky whose bedroom window was just above the barbecue patio. Half an hour ago Julia had gone upstairs, leaving Ben to clear away the dishes while she put Nicky to bed with a chapter from *The Wind in the Willows*. And then there'd been Paul's strangely disturbing call, which was still preying on her mind.

'Coffee?' she suggested, when they'd finished their drinks.

Ben nodded. 'But aren't you going to eat your chocolates?' He pointed to the large black and gold box lying unopened on the table.

Julia hugged her arms. All evening she had kept her eyes averted from the chocolates.

Eat these, my dear. Hide them and don't say a word to anyone . . .

The smell of chocolates was enough to make her ill but it had been impossible to refuse his gift. 'I'll save them for tomorrow,' she said, looking up at the sky where the clouds were rushing away from the moon.

Julia prepared the tray while Ben took the glasses to the kitchen.

Back again on the patio he poked at the fire, then poured the coffee. He handed Julia a mug. 'I couldn't mention this in front of Nicky, but what did you really think of Smith's escape? You didn't seem angry or frightened, or even surprised when I told you.'

She moved her chair closer to the fire. All evening she had managed to conceal her concern in a smokescreen of idle chat but it was still uppermost in her mind. With her best legal deadpan face she looked straight into Ben's eyes.

'I suppose it doesn't surprise me. The more serious the criminal the more likely he is to plan his escape.'

'A clever bastard.'

'In some ways, yes. Like being charming and accommodating throughout his period of custody. Not much bad language either. Not like most of them, effing and blinding every second word. But then again, returning to the scene wasn't very clever, was it? There was nothing to tie him to Joanne Perkins except her resemblance to his foster mother Ada, and no one knew about that until by chance I saw a photograph of Ada long after his arrest. Joanne was a random victim he just happened to see in that pub. If he'd stayed away they'd still be looking for him.'

In the sudden silence she saw another scene:

blood, a broken lamp . . .

She closed her eyes tightly. A broken lamp? The details trickle through to me. Fragments. Fleeting glimpses. Leaking into my consciousness. But as usual they ebb away before I can grasp them, before a clear picture can emerge.

She stirred her coffee. Keep your mind on Smith as a psychopath, she told herself. Don't think of him as a person to feel for, or who feels for you. God help me if . . . no, there's that gut-wrenching thought again.

'And don't forget poor Jennifer Dunn.' She heard the agitation in her voice but couldn't stop it. 'Jennifer looked like the foster mother too.

64

She might have been the first victim if something hadn't stopped him at the crucial moment.'

'What, you think he's a serial killer now, do you? He's not a serial killer, for God's sake. Serial killers are loners. Smith's no loner. He'd never have pulled off that escape on his own. What makes you think he's a serial killer?'

'You've been watching too many movies,' she said. 'Serial killers come in all shapes and sizes – loners, party types, shy ones, extroverts. We still don't know much about serial killers. Perhaps Smith's problem isn't really about sex, but revenge. And he'll keep going until he's settled the account. I think he *is* a loner, as a matter of fact. Except when he needs to manipulate people.'

'Julia . . .'

'Yes?'

'Why are you stirring your coffee like that? What's eating you? You never used to have these nervous habits.'

She leapt up and marched over to the fire. Duke followed and pushed his nose against her leg. She stroked his velvet head, and then when she'd finished composing her face she swung round and faced Ben.

'You asked me what I thought about Smith escaping. Well, it bloody annoys me. And it scares me to think what he'll do next. But don't worry about me. Of course I'm angry he's escaped, but as far as I'm concerned the case is closed. And I just don't happen to think there is any serious likelihood that Smith is going to cause me any problems. You know damn well I don't fall into his category of victim.'

'What's wrong with you?' Ben said. 'He threatened you. Jesus, you're in danger and it's no use pretending you're not.'

Julia shook her head. He moved closer. 'You told me you didn't want police protection, but don't worry. I could move in here for a while.' He smiled. 'To Hillside House. My suitcase — I mean — my things are in the car.'

65

16

Paul gulped the remainder of his coffee.

Just then there was a faint knock on his door, as though the intruder was afraid of disturbing him. 'Come,' he said. He would never get home at this rate, especially with half of Friday's paper work still in his in-basket, but his voice did not reflect any of his irritation.

Sergeant Avril Scott peeped around the door. 'Sorry to interrupt, Sir.'

He hadn't seen her often lately, but since moving to the firearms unit she was turning up everywhere. He had bumped into her just after the briefing on tonight's plan of action and had asked her to pop in when she had a spare moment as he'd just received the report on her promotional appraisal.

'Come and sit down,' he said and pulled out a chair for her, remembering the days when he'd been a young aide to the CID and she had been a keen young policewoman. Even then she had shown promise. And if he hadn't been transferred from the division things might have turned out differently between them.

She sat down on the edge of the seat. Paul thought how calm she appeared. Most people would be exhibiting some kind of apprehension as they waited for their assessment, but Avril as always displayed her restraint.

'How've you been?' he asked, taking her file from the basket.

'Just great, Sir.'

He was pleased that she was making progress. He had known her husband, Bob, an outstanding officer in the firearms team. He'd been shot dead when entering a house in Salford, and Avril's determination to emulate her husband's achievements had been intensified by his killing.

A few years after Bob's death he had taken her out a few times, but then he'd met Julia and things had fizzled out between him and Avril. Nevertheless, she was one of the people he most admired in the police force, with a great spirit of dedication and total commitment to her job.

He looked at her now. She was in superb physical condition. When she was out on a job she never drew attention to herself by looking out of place. She could look like a million dollars in one of Manchester's top hotels, but if the assignment was in Cheetham Hill or Moss Side, the transformation was astonishing. And then she always wore black.

Paul dropped his gaze and leafed through the file.

'The appraisal went well, Avril. You've been pretty successful on all these interviews.' He'd been tempted to tell her the good news about her forthcoming promotion, but now decided against it. It would be better done through the proper channels and at the proper time. 'All in all a very good assessment indeed,' he said instead.

'Thank you, Sir.'

Still smiling, she stood up to leave.

'No, please sit down, will you. I've just had a thought.'

He picked up his pen, wrote down a number and the name of a street, tore off the piece of paper and pushed it towards her.

She frowned. 'Joe Sagoe's house. Moss Side. It's where I've been assigned for the dawn raid.'

He nodded. 'I've a hunch Smith might try to hole up there tonight.'

'Yes, Sir,' she said. 'But hardly likely in the circumstances. Joe Sagoe's a possible suspect in the Smith escape. Smith wouldn't dare go near the place. He'd know it was being staked out.'

'Smith thinks he's invincible,' he said. 'He takes great delight in goading us. We must be prepared for the unexpected.'

'Is that all, Sir?'

He nodded. With her voice so gentle, her eyes so kind, it was difficult to believe she had consistently displayed the outstanding physical and mental qualities to have merited her forthcoming new rank of inspector in the firearms unit. He had great faith in her.

'You'd better go home now and get a couple of hours rest before the raid,' he said.

He walked with her to the door.

'Avril, let me know as soon as he's arrested, will you?'

She hesitated. 'But what if you're not on duty?'

'When something urgent comes up I'm always on duty. Call me immediately, please.'

17

Julia gaped at Ben. She felt her cheeks hollow as her mouth dropped open. Quickly she turned away. So that was it. The unexpected barbecue was Ben's way of setting up an easy forum for his latest ploy: protection. Initially he had underplayed the news of Smith's escape, but Ben Lloyd never missed a trick. He was always looking for surreptitious ways of courting her and this was his boldest so far. Identify her as the damsel in distress, he as knight in shining armour and her heart would at last be won. Bless him – a plan so simple in its concept and so unlikely to succeed. She wondered when the penny would drop with Ben. They may have the chemistry to work together but it was never going to lead to love and romance.

'What if I were to tell you there are already police patrols going back and forth outside, watching everything that moves in and out of here.'

'Are there?' Ben asked. He appeared to be startled by Julia's remark – half question, half announcement.

'That would be for me to know and you to guess,' she said. Knowledge is power. 'The truth is, Ben, I feel perfectly safe.'

Julia saw the crestfallen look on his face as though he thought his chance was slipping away.

'You mustn't think I'm trying to use this as – ' he began.

'Oh, come on, Ben, but I do. You're a very sweet man, my friend and my business partner, and I know your feelings for me too. I know they are very genuine, but really – '

'Julia!' He looked at her as though she was mad. 'How many times must I remind you your life is in danger?'

'Oh, don't exaggerate. He thought I'd let him down. They all think that when they go down for life.' She flopped into her chair, hoping he would accept her refusal as final, but read it also as indicative of how far he was from ever winning her affections.

Her words were met with a stony silence. It was for Ben to clear, not her, Julia thought. At last he spoke. 'Don't underestimate him. He managed to organise a brilliant escape and after what was said he's obviously marked your card.'

Julia closed her eyes and took a deep breath. 'Ben, please. We've had a lovely evening. Your cooking was wonderful and you've been helping me, at least until now, to get over it all. So can we just, you know, let it drop? All he's going to do now is get the hell out of town, out of the country if he knows what's good for him. So, no more, okay?'

He stared at her for a few moments, then clasped his hands together. 'Shall I tell you why you're so uptight at the moment?' he said.

She looked at him sharply. 'Thanks for changing the subject, but me, uptight?'

'Definitely,' he said. 'I've been thinking about it and it's all to do with the fact that you've never resolved your true identity. I remember Simon telling me about it, not long before he died. He said one of the things he loved about you, but which also infuriated him, was that sometimes you were like a lost little girl. He said he thought you fell short of your true capacity to give yourself in love because of it.'

Julia could almost feel the hairs on the back of her neck stand up. Well really! She had heard Simon say the same thing — Ben wasn't making this up — but why now? She felt as though he was reading her mind. There's no point in fighting it, she thought. Time to confess and deny. 'And I'm sure Simon also told you I still miss my twin brother. And that I've never been able to summon up the courage to ask my adoptive parents what they know about why he died, and who my real parents were.'

Ben stood up, moved over to her and sat down on the arm of her chair. 'Why don't you, though? Get it all out in the open. Who knows, they might still be out there. You could have a whole family, brothers, sisters, cousins.' He put his hand gently over hers. She pulled her hand away. Ben wasn't letting go so easily — this was just another tack.

'There's just no way I'd ever have wanted to upset David and Jessie. I never called them Mum and Dad, those were not words in my vocabulary. But they did love me, you know. In their own guarded way.'

'I'm sure they still do.' He was edging towards her. 'But it's a mistake to always put other people's needs before your own. What about you, Julia? What do you want?'

Right now she wanted to forget what all her life she had longed to

69

remember. She also admitted to herself she wanted a father for her child, but one she wasn't afraid to love, if that was ever possible. I want . . . oh, if only she really knew what she wanted. So far in her life she had coped with the void, the emotional deficit, and felt she had not been as crippled as some might have been. Like Smith. And now Smith had changed everything.

A breeze fanned the fire, sending a flurry of sparks into the cool night air, rustling the trees and the shrubs and sending her thoughts flying back to Simon.

Ben kept his eyes on her face, waiting for her reply. She could feel a clammy sheen breaking through her pores and wiped her hand across her cheeks. She saw his rapt expression and edged to the other side of her chair. She decided to ignore his question. 'It would break their hearts if I tried to find my real family. David and Jessie have been wonderful to me. Even though they never made a fuss of me. Never hugged or kissed me.'

'You're rather like that yourself. Aren't you, Julia?'

Back off, Ben. Stop pushing. 'Am I?' she responded coldly. She raked her fingers through her hair, thinking it had been a long time since she'd been to see David and Jessie in their retirement home in Southport. 'Poor David and Jessie. I wouldn't know where to start. I would cringe just to ask them what my real name was.'

'I would be too inquisitive not to,' Ben said.

She twiddled Simon's ring. She saw Ben watching her and stopped. 'I *am* inquisitive. But something tells me I should leave things as they are.'

'You must miss your brother,' he said.

Little do you know, Ben. Oh how little. She pressed her palms into the sides of her head and clamped her eyelids closed against a sudden intrusion, so contrary to her thoughts that it almost took her breath away . . .

> *Hairy tobacco-stained fingers . . . pinning me to the bed. The treacly voice . . . then flashes . . . more flashes . . . and his voice —Run Julia run . . . I'll look after you now . . .*

'It's hard to think he'd be thirty-six now,' she managed to say, bewildered as always by the bizarre mixture of memories that zigzagged through her brain like a tangle of crossed wires. All triggered by Smith's sudden appearance in her life, all linking the present to her hazy past in a crazy chain of half-remembered thoughts.

'I'm so sorry, Julia, I've upset you and I had no business . . .' Ben rested his hand back on hers. 'I shouldn't have brought it up. I was just curious. Forgive me.'

Slowly she withdrew her hand again. 'Come off it,' she said, as light-heartedly as she could. 'I'm glad you did. I never get a chance to talk about it.' How long can I keep this up, she asked herself. 'More coffee?' she said, getting up and taking her own mug to refill it from the percolator. He shook his head.

As she poured the coffee she became aware of Ben standing directly behind her. He was so close she could feel his body heat radiating against her. His warm breath brushed against her neck and for a fraction of a second she couldn't move. Then she slammed the percolator down firmly on the coffee tray. She stepped sideways to her left, turned to avoid the kiss and blurted out, 'Ben, Jesus, please, what the hell are you doing.'

Ben almost fell over. He launched himself towards her now, hands reaching for her hips, only to be defeated as she darted sideways again.

He steadied himself, looking like a small boy caught with a pocketful of cream cakes. 'Oh God, Julia, I'm so sorry. I'm really not good at this, am I? My feelings for you are completely honourable and I've made myself look like a fool. You must have realised . . . I mean, after Simon died I've seen your pain, and then I've been through my own. We could be so good for each other, and there's me behaving like a lecherous bastard. I think, I think I ought to go.'

Ben looked lost and pitiful, his eyes downcast as he turned and headed to the kitchen to retrieve his barbecue apron and jacket. 'I don't want to make you feel guilty or anything, if there's no hope for me. But . . .'

Julia followed him to the kitchen door and laid her hand gently on his right shoulder. He stopped dead but did not turn towards her.

'Ben, please don't beat yourself up about it, I understand, really. But I hope you realise that we just aren't going to work as anything but business colleagues — good, close friends too — but nothing else.'

He still didn't turn, but shook his head slowly. 'Good friends, but second best to Paul bloody Moxon.'

Julia snatched her hand away, sympathy turning to anger. 'Just exactly what the hell is that supposed to mean?' she demanded.

'I've seen the signs,' he said, his voice strangely flat. 'I know you. Taking one copper with another, you wouldn't trust them as a breed, and you're even convinced they live by a code in which cops can do no wrong and everyone else is dog shit unless proven otherwise. But not Paul bloody Moxon. Drinks at the Addy, presents for Nicky, and I wonder what bloody else.'

Julia turned and stormed into the kitchen. 'Night-night, Ben. Time for home.' She burst through the door and into the spacious hallway, snatched Ben's keys from the Regency table and rattled them vigorously. 'What you don't know about you shouldn't cross examine. You told me that. And you know nothing.'

Ben followed her into the hallway and grabbed the keys from her outstretched hand.

'On Monday,' she said, her upper lip trembling, 'we will be business partners running a busy criminal firm and we will treat each other as though none of this happened.' She opened the front door for Ben. He paused and turned to her and his mouth twitched as if he was struggling to form a sentence worth saying. Then he stepped out into the night.

She slammed the door and leaned her back against it, as if to prevent any attempt by Ben to change her mind. Her skin prickled as she imagined him grabbing her from behind, overpowering her with soft sickly kisses and words that made her cringe, knowing it was ridiculous and that Ben would never harm her, but feeling it already . . .

his weight, his hairy hands, his rough skin rasping, his tobacco breath . . . it's our secret, Julia . . . don't tell anyone . . . the chocolate's are just for you . . .

She closed her eyes tightly until she heard Ben's BMW roar down the driveway.

At last she opened her eyes, shivering and hugging her arms as the loneliness crept over her.

'Paul. Oh, Paul,' she said, not knowing from whence the words had come.

SATURDAY

18

Sam Smith squinted at the luminous dial of his watch.

'Jeez,' he mouthed silently. 'Five past bloody twelve. Saturday! My first full day of freedom.'

He looked up the steep slope towards the house. He had a clear view of the vast back garden, more like a fucking park than a garden. Crouched behind the fence, limbs stiff, every sense alert, he had waited hours for the right moment to make his move. Earlier he had heard the occasional chatter, seen the outside lights and the faint flicker of flames, smelled the wood smoke. Later a door had slammed and a car had sped down the long curved driveway.

It was the smell of wood smoke and the towering beech trees that reminded him of the caravan, evoking a vivid memory of Ada. He felt as though a bright, intrusive image of her had imprinted itself on his retinas, obscuring his night vision. He blinked repeatedly to erase her mocking face.

Good thing he had cased the joint before darkness fell. The unmarked police car may as well have been in full livery, blue light flashing. Unmistakable, parked on the road like a sore thumb. No way could he have left his heap anywhere on that street, but hopefully it would still be sitting in the King William car park. If not he could ditch it for something faster and not such a sickly colour. Nobody had even glanced at him as he'd walked from the pub, past the church where the road bends towards the river, then into the park where he instantly became just another person taking in the fresh air. He had guessed he might have to wait until after midnight, and what better place than in the shadows of the park.

The dog could be a problem, but nothing he couldn't handle. If he hadn't seen it running with Julia Grant and her daughter along the lane behind the houses, his final plan for getting into the house would have been quite different. Not even Joe Sagoe had suggested it. Or warned him about the dog.

He peered through the gap. His eyes had grown accustomed to the dark and everything stood out clearly. He had seen at least two — maybe three or four — silhouetted figures steal backwards and forwards past the front gate. He'd be stupid not to realise they'd be here. He could kick himself now for his flare-up in the court. The words had just come out, but what the hell. What's done is done. And it might even help to make her scared enough to comply with his demands.

Slowly he scanned the full width of the garden.

Now. Time to move.

Just as he clambered up the high spiked fence the moon appeared above the clouds. Damn. The filth had better not see him perched up here like a bloody performing monkey. With a quick look around he jumped, landing in a pile of leaves behind a beech tree. He felt a stab of pain. Fuck. Trouser leg torn. He licked his finger and pressed it against the gash on his shin. At this rate the clothes Joe had brought him would soon be in rags. Have to be more careful.

He lay still, waiting to see if he had attracted any unwanted attention. After a minute he stood up, flattening himself against a tree trunk as a sudden breeze brought another blast of wood-smoke to his nostrils. Inching his way across the large garden from one tall beech tree to another, he tried hard not to breathe in any more of the smoke drifting across the lawn, but he was too late. Without warning his head reeled. His body swayed. A flock of flashing dots floated across the sky towards him. And over the whine of the wind came Ada's piercing voice.

'You get your fucking arse back up here or I'll tan the hide off of you,' she yells.

And then she is dragging him by one arm back to the caravan, stabbing her lighted cigarette into every part of his flesh she can reach.

Stifling his cries of pain he scrambles to his feet and flings his arms around her leg. She yanks him up. Burying his face in her scrawny body, he clings to her, fighting the panic, smelling the cheap brandy, hiding his burnt and tear-streaked face in her long greasy blonde hair. Slowly he takes the cord out of his pocket. He coils it round her neck, pulling tighter and tighter until her frail body slumps to the ground. He looks down at her, smiles, then slides the knife from his pocket . . .

He blinked as the last of the downstairs lights went off. A moment later a light went on upstairs. His limbs ached. It could be a long wait. But it would be worth it.

He tensed at the faint sound of distant conversation and the steady clip of metal heeled boots coming from the ornate gates at the end of the long driveway. Amateur pillocks, he thought, and smiled to himself. No matter how well they staked out this goddam place they could not be everywhere at the same time. And it wouldn't be long before they got bored, tired and cold. They would go back to their car for a sly snooze before they went for another stroll and a fag.

From his jacket pocket he took out the cutting from the Manchester Evening News Joe had given him. He could just make out the outline of his bearded face. He smiled. VERDICT TODAY the front-page headline said. He folded it and put it carefully in his pocket. 'I'll show these bastards,' he hissed under his breath.

You think you're so clever, Julia fucking Grant. But I'll show you I can do anything I want. Get anything I want. Just like you. You think you're secure, but you're not. And tonight is just the start.

He patted the cold hard bulge under his jacket. Felt the knife in his pocket. Fished for his gloves. Good old Joe.

There was no sign of the dog.

The moon went behind the clouds.

He didn't mind the waiting.

The light upstairs went off.

- 19 -

Julia hated it when something disturbed the dream.

Never before had it seemed so real. 'Julia. This way,' he called, over and over again. If only she could keep the dream alive, just long enough to see his face, but Duke's insistent barking penetrated too deeply.

She kept her eyes tightly closed. She was determined to hang on for one more fleeting second.

I see the jagged rocks, the steep path winding up the mountain, his bare back, the pale skin glistening with patches of blood. Then the mountain spinning, the mist clearing, my hands clawing, slipping, my own voice yelling Wait. Wait! and his faint answer, I'll look after you, Julia. You can't stay here. Hurry . . . Come with me . . .

I could try again in tomorrow night's dream, she thought. Keep on trying forever, until I find him. Until I see his face. Will it be anything like mine, she wondered. Sometimes, if I stare at myself in the mirror, I can squeeze a kind of double image on the side of my face so that for one ephemeral, tantalising moment he is next to me.

She sat up with a start as reality took hold. Duke only barked like that for two reasons: if he heard an unfamiliar sound, or he badly needed to go out.

Through half opened eyes she switched on her bedside lamp and peered at her watch.

'Five past two. Oh, Duke . . .'

She shuffled into the passage. She hoped Duke's barking hadn't wakened Nicky. She was tempted to peep into her room but if she didn't let Duke out soon the kitchen floor would be a disaster.

Halfway down the thickly carpeted stairs she felt a draught on her neck and up her legs. She hugged herself. She should have put on her dressing gown and slippers, but never mind, she could let Duke out and would be back in bed in no time.

The draught again. It puzzled her. She glanced over her shoulder but couldn't work out where it was coming from. It was also strange that Duke would want to go out now, having had the run of the garden until just after Ben had left. Perhaps the wind had rattled something in the kitchen courtyard. Or against her wishes one of the police on patrol had come into the garden.

She squared her shoulders and hurried across the hall. The moment she opened the kitchen door Duke stopped barking. She snapped on the light and there he was with his nose glued to the outside door.

'Oh, you poor darling. You must be desperate.'

He shoved his wet brown nose against her hand and wagged his tail, banging it against the door as she turned the key.

'Shh. You'll wake Nicky. Now you be a good boy and come back quickly.'

He flew past Julia and disappeared into the darkness of the night. Perhaps he heard something after all, she thought. An owl. A cat. The wind in the trees. Or the police officers out on the road, waiting in vain for Sam Smith to appear.

She wandered over to the polished oak table in the centre of the kitchen. In the wide curtainless window her reflection moved towards her. Wendy had left this week's Woman's Weekly on the table. As she flipped through it, she became aware again of her movements in the window.

She looked up. There was the Aga behind her. There were the rows of oak fittings where Natalie's gleaming white china was still displayed. The whole kitchen was mirrored in the window, completely blotting out her view of the garden.

Yet if anyone were out there they would see *me* quite clearly, she thought. And suddenly she felt insecure.

She walked towards the window. Her image walked to meet her. She glanced behind her, then spun her head back to the mirror image.

Idiot. Everything is perfectly normal. What on earth did you expect?

She wished Duke would hurry up. Maybe he did hear something. Maybe it was . . .

Sam Smith?

No. Impossible. There's no way he'd get past the police. And he wouldn't be such a fool to try. And even if he did, would he really want to harm her? Those threatening words were merely words of anger and frustration . . . Help me, Julia, you're the only person I can trust, he had once told her . . .

She opened the door and peered into the darkness. Get a hold on yourself, Julia. See? There's no one out there. No sign of Duke either, though.

And apart from the rustle of the wind in the trees and the faint gurgle of the river, there wasn't a sound to be heard.

'Duke,' she called lightly. 'Du-uke.' If she called any louder she might wake Nicky.

She looked up at the dark clouds that had been building up all evening, just in time to see the moon cruise from behind them, silvering the garden as it maintained a steady course across a choppy sky. She shivered as the breeze ruffled her hair and lifted the hem of her nightgown.

'Du-uke . . .'

To get a better view she stepped down onto the paving stones. The moon flicked in and out of the clouds, casting on the walls giant shadows that were there one moment and gone the next. She hugged her arms to fend off the chilly night breeze, feeling self conscious, as though there were a hundred pairs of prying eyes out there. This is crazy, she thought. I could be standing out here all night waiting for Duke.

She looked down at her flimsy attire. She whipped her head around. There was no one there, of course. But what if there had been? There wasn't even a garden broom she could use to defend herself.

Once more the moon rushed behind the clouds, plunging the garden into darkness. A gust of wind. A sudden bang. The door.

She leapt up the step and yanked it open and threw herself inside, her flimsy night-gown billowing behind her.

She stood at the table, breathing deeply as she flipped over the pages of the Woman's Weekly. 'Where the hell are you, Duke?'

On page twelve she saw a recipe for a cherry cake. Four easy steps. Paul loved cherry cake. If she got up early enough she could make it tomorrow.

Idiot. You can't cook.

She flung the magazine down, went close up to the window and peered out.

'That's it, boy. You can damn well stay out. I'm going back to bed.'

Apart from one slight mistake, Sam Smith was pleased with his night's work, but it wouldn't do to hang around a second longer than necessary. Crouching behind the garage, he waited until he was certain that all was quiet before making his getaway.

After one final look, he crept back down to the bottom of the garden, stopped at the fence, waited again, listened, scrambled over and landed softly in the tree-lined lane. Chuckling quietly to himself he sauntered to his car at the King William.

The streets of Wilmslow were mercifully quiet. So was the road past Styal Prison and the airport. And even the roads to Joe Sagoe's house in Moss Side were all but deserted, so quiet that any patrol car would take notice of just about anything moving and he was glad of his new cloned number plates.

Wherever he could he used minor roads and eventually reached the rows of grim, two-up-two-down houses off Claremont Road. He stopped three streets away from Joe's road, where the houses were derelict, windows and doors gaped darkly, plastic bags flapped and abandoned beds, broken chairs and every other kind of litter lay strewn on the narrow pavements.

He glanced at his watch. Ten past three. Shit. Right now he should be celebrating, not farting around Moss Side. But he knew what his priorities were. He'd already taken care of number one. Now it was time to see Joe for the vital things he'd realised he still needed.

He sat for a moment longer and looked all around him. He must be crazy going there at all. In spite of the nylon stocking over Joe's head, eyewitnesses would have described his friend's enormous size. The filth might have put two and two together. Might at this very moment be watching the house.

Normally he wouldn't risk it. He didn't want to show his face to an increasing number of people; it would only be a matter of time before some smartarse phoned Crimestoppers. But Sagoe had things he needed — more clothes, money, extra ammo in case things got really hot. All essential for his plans.

He closed the car door softly. Turned up the collar of his jacket and put his hands in his pockets. His fingers curled around the cold metal of the gun.

With his eyes skinned he began walking towards Joe's house. Jeez, the whole of Moss Side must be able to hear him. He tried walking softly, putting his toes down before his heels. Just as he reached the bollards at the end of Joe's road, a bicycle shot past into the overgrown back alley to his left, almost knocking him over. His fingers tightened on the gun.

'Hey, watch it, you scum,' he rasped, then almost bit off his tongue because the last thing he wanted was to draw attention to himself. But the drug-crazed lad on the bike didn't even look back. He shook his head. You never knew what you'd find around the next corner in this shit hole. A man must be ready for anything.

His foot hit an empty beer tin, sending it clattering down the road. Christ. What the fuck was he doing here when all the filth in Manchester would be out looking for him tonight? He should get out now, while the going was good —

Money. Fags. Clothes. Slugs . . .

He scanned the row of terraced houses. Joe's peacock-blue door and window frames were more than enough to distinguish his house from all the others, even without the skull and crossbones painted in black. And there it was. Holy mother of Jesus. Plain as daylight, even from this distance. A dim light shone through the curtains. But this didn't mean Joe was home.

He looked over his shoulder. He was a sitting duck if the house was under surveillance. Julia Grant's place was, so this might be too. He stopped. Not a soul in sight, but he'd soon attract attention if he tried to get in at the front door and found it was locked.

He wondered again whether he should be risking it at all. But the coast looked clear. If the cops were down here he was sure he would know. There would be dogs barking, curtains twitching. Surely there'd be at least one idiot prepared to risk arrest by shouting a warning as he approached.

But there was nothing.

Flattening himself against a wall some fifty yards from the house, on the opposite side of the road, he waited. He wasn't going to blunder in. Must be quite sure no one was about. No suspicious vehicles. No movement of any kind. No Dibble. He wasn't called Smart Sam for nothing.

And then, from nowhere, the thought of Joe's West African stew simmering on the Primus filled his mouth with saliva. Until now the surge of adrenaline had kept hunger at bay. He hadn't eaten for more than twenty-four hours and suddenly he couldn't wait another minute.

He tiptoed towards the house.

A light shone in his eyes.

'Don't move. Police. Get on the ground.'

Holy shit. A blonde in black jeans. A bloody cop. Bound to be another one, maybe three or four but hard to see with the torch full in his face.

He thought of all the things he had to gain and what fucking little he had to lose. Dots floated across his vision like snowflakes in a car's headlights, coming at him from every angle.

His eyes glazed over.

Ada!

He whipped out the gun and aimed it straight at the middle of the bitch's chest.

- 21 -

Wendy placed the mug of coffee on Julia's bedside table and the newly delivered *Times* next to her pillow. 'Julia,' she said, softly enough not to startle her.

Something was not right. She never slept this late. 'Julia, shall I get Nicky ready for ballet?' Still no response.

'Julia . . . '

Still getting no answer she stepped back to open the thick blue curtains that covered the bay window overlooking the river and the park. 'You could have a few more minutes in bed,' she said, louder this time, thankful that she'd decided to come over as soon as she heard the dreadful news on the telly.

This time Julia opened her eyes, blinking at the sunlight flooding the room. 'Wendy? What on earth are you doing here? It's Saturday and I'm not working today.'

'Thank goodness you're okay,' Wendy said, closing her eyes in relief.

'Of course I am. I didn't sleep too well but I'm fine. What's up? Why are you so worried?'

'You're safe, that's all,' Wendy blurted out. 'I can't believe you represented that man, Julia, he's gone and killed a policewoman now – haven't you heard?'

Julia's eyes opened wide as she shook her head. The colour seemed to drain from her face and Wendy was suddenly sorry she'd burst in on her like this.

'It was all on the telly this morning,' she said in a rush. 'And there was me thinking he'd come for you too. I saw the photo of him, and Mr Moxon was saying how dangerous he was. The telly said he threatened his lawyer as he was taken out of court. That *was* you, wasn't it? So that's why I had to come.'

'Wendy, I'm fine, really. Nothing to worry about,' Julia said, but she looked far from fine. 'Oh, and before I forget, you'll find a box of Black Magic in the kitchen. I'd like you to have it.'

Wendy was taken aback by Julia's quick, unruffled change of subject. 'Thanks,' she said. She was used to getting Julia's cast-off chocolates. She had never known her eat a single one. 'You have a nice quiet read of the paper,' she said. 'I'll have Nicky ready for nine-thirty. Amazingly the little monkey is still asleep. She'll be cross she's missing another exciting episode of Teenage Mutant Ninja Turtles, so I'd better go and wake her.' She smiled, but Julia did not respond, as though her thoughts were miles away. 'I also saw Mr Moxon on telly last night, you know. He was standing next to that smashed up prison van, looking ever so handsome, asking for witnesses and telling people to watch out for that terrible murderer.'

Wendy bit her lip. She looked at Julia's tense face and shook her head. 'What you need is a good holiday. You haven't had one for two years.'

Julia sipped her coffee. Wendy thought she wasn't going to answer her, but finally she said, 'I know. But I don't mind, as long as I have the odd weekend off.'

'You could always go to the villa. It's been empty now for – '

'No.'

Wendy put her hand to her mouth. How could she have been so thoughtless? If anything ever happened to Alan she would never get over it either. Still, she couldn't understand how an intelligent woman like Julia Grant could go on blaming the family villa in France for the plane crash that killed her husband and his parents as they took off for their holiday six years ago.

'Don't forget the paper,' she reminded Julia, hurrying to the door and wishing she could do more to help this lovely, lonely woman who did so much for her.

* * *

Julia felt a cold shiver run down her spine as she skimmed over the account of yesterday's escape with its pictures of the prison van and the articulated lorry, and the close-up of her ex client – one she had seen many times before. It had been taken at Bootle Street police station on the day he'd been arrested. Shot from below the chin, it dehumanised and criminalised him by virtue of its very genre. But of the killing of a policewoman there was no mention that she could see.

She looked up, startled to see that Wendy was still in the room, hovering in the doorway.

'Julia, could I ask you something?' Wendy said.

'Of course. What's the problem?' She put the paper down and sipped her coffee, glad of the diversion. She hoped it wasn't trouble with Alan. Wendy would be devastated if he ever broke it off.

'It's, well . . . I don't know how to put this. But how can you be on the side of someone like that?' Wendy pointed to the full colour face in *The Times*.

Julia winced as she glanced at the photograph.

'I mean, like you know your client's guilty, like how can you defend

84

them?'

Julia had been asked this question many times. And more than once had also asked herself. 'The fact is, Wendy, that you don't know your client is guilty until he actually tells you he is. Until then, you treat him as though he is not guilty. And sometimes you are right.'

Wendy's eyes narrowed, as if Julia had said the world was flat.

'That's the way the criminal system treats all criminal defendants, at least in theory. They are not guilty until the Crown proves their case.'

Wendy looked down at the carpet, her eyes shifting from left to right.

'And the Crown must prove their case beyond reasonable doubt. And whether you think your client is guilty or not is completely immaterial to the way you deal with the case.'

Wendy looked up at Julia, clearly not convinced.

'And from the criminal lawyer's point of view — not his personal point of view — that doesn't create any moral problem whatsoever.'

'No?' Wendy looked more confused than ever.

'Not as long as certain rules are observed. Look at it this way. I'm bound by my client's confidentiality. But I can still present a defence that highlights the weaknesses in the prosecution's case. I can call evidence to controvert that. And leave it to the jury to draw their own conclusions.'

'I had no idea it was so complicated.'

Julia smiled. 'I suppose that still doesn't answer your question, though, does it?'

'It's all a bit beyond me.' She turned to go, then stopped. 'But I get the gist of it. It's a job. It has strict rules. And you have to follow those rules. No matter what you really feel deep inside you.' She shrugged. 'I don't know how you do it.'

Sometimes, Julia thought, neither do I.

Wendy opened the door, then stopped and turned as though suddenly remembering something of importance. 'I don't want to seem to be criticising you, Julia, but I couldn't help noticing . . .'

She turned again, shaking her head as she began walking away.

Julia sat up straight, almost spilling her coffee. 'Noticing what?'

'Nothing,' Wendy said.

But the hunched shoulders and lowered head spoke volumes. You can't silence the language of the body, Julia thought. 'What is it? Tell me, please.'

'I'm sorry. It was nothing.'

Julia wasn't convinced. Wendy kept the house like a palace. It wouldn't surprise her, she thought, if the disastrous end to her evening with Ben had made her inadvertently leave dirty coffee mugs in the sink.

Just then the phone on her bedside table rang. As she looked up she saw Wendy discreetly slip away. She was tempted to let it ring. She valued the short time she had on her own on Saturday mornings while Nicky watched the telly, to try to make sense of her life. Tears, anger, resentment and panic, all packed into a weekly episode of personal trauma, hidden from the rest of the world.

She picked up the receiver.

'This time he's really done it, Julia. He's shot Sergeant Avril Scott at point blank range. An old friend of mine. Outside Joe Sagoe's house. She's dead.' Paul's voice was shaking with emotion. He didn't wait for Julia to answer. 'Now will you listen to me?'

'I'm so sorry, Paul. Absolutely dreadful. A terrible tragedy.' A wave of nausea swept up Julia's throat. 'Did you get him?' she whispered.

'No. Of course we didn't. Another inexcusable slip-up. Look, Julia, he could be anywhere. You have to have personal police protection. As from right now. This very minute.'

'Paul, I don't know what to say. But I really don't think Smith would harm me. I wish I could tell you why. Let's say it's because I know him so well. Besides, in my job it just isn't feasible to have someone breathing down my neck twenty-four hours a day. You must know that. Anyway, we've got Wendy.'

'And you expect that young woman to be able to defend you? Why, Julia, when we have a whole police force trained to do just that?'

'Wendy's a black-belt. And with twenty-four-hour surveillance on the road outside our house, we'll be just fine.'

She heard Paul's deep sigh. I wish I could tell him, she thought. I wish I could tell him who I think he might be, even though I don't want it to be him and don't even really want to know. I wish I could tell him that if he is . . . if he is . . . he would never harm me. He would always protect me . . .

She blinked her eyes. Oh my God. Where did that come from? Paul's insistence on Julia having personal protection was perfectly natural under normal circumstances. She knew she should accept. She had every reason to trust Paul, and scant reason to trust Smith. If it were any other murderer who had threatened her, she would undoubtedly accept, but Smith wasn't just any murderer. She knew her thinking must seem irrational. She knew her behaviour looked inconsistent. She knew her choices and attitudes did not appear sufficiently justified to anyone who did not have her insight. And she knew how it must irritate Paul.

But until she knew for sure who Smith was, she was trapped inside her irrationality. Irrationality that was dictating to her that if she agreed to twenty-four hour personal police protection, and just say Smith did decide to contact her to seek her help, this would make it easier for them to recapture him. And insanely she did not want them to do that.

She also wished she could tell Paul that every day flashes of memory were returning to build a picture she was still struggling to formulate into thoughts, let alone into words she could accept. Memories from her early childhood with her brother who was the only one who'd loved her; memories intertwined with other sinister memories that were invading her mind and making her cringe with humiliation and shame.

'Okay, Julia,' Paul said at last.

She could hear the exasperation in his voice, but no matter how much more he might try to persuade her, there was no way she could agree.

'But one more move from Smith and I'll have to insist.'

She didn't answer this. She knew how hard it must have been for him to back down.

'Meanwhile,' he said, once more assuming the tone of authority, 'Bennett mentioned that empty house opposite yours. I'm moving the obs team in there today whether you like it or not. They'll have a perfect view of the house and the garden.'

'That's a good idea, Paul.'

'Well, that's something! For once you're agreeing with me. And I suppose you've enrolled for that course in self-protection.'

She said nothing. Paul was always going on about self-protection. Then, as an afterthought: 'Will I see you later?' she asked.

'Christ, Julia, I don't know. All hell has broken loose here at Chester House. Nobody kills a police officer and gets away with it. I can't see myself getting away today.'

'I'm so sorry. Really I am. If there's anything I can do — '

'Just look after yourself.'

'I will.'

She put down the phone and buried her face in the pillow. Oh, God. What would Sam Smith do next?

Hearing Wendy's knock she quickly straightened her hair, relaxed the muscles of her face and took a deep breath. 'Come in, Wendy. I'm sorry, but what were you saying?'

Wendy hesitated. 'Nothing really. I just wondered. I know it's trivial but did you leave the outside kitchen door open when you went to bed last night?'

'The outside door?' Julia rubbed her forehead. And then she remembered Duke. 'You mean — unlocked?'

Last night she'd been a bit groggy when she got up to let Duke out. The dream always did that to her and she could easily have done something absentmindedly.

'No. Not just unlocked. Wide open.'

Julia swung her legs over the edge of the bed. 'Wendy, I let Duke out in the middle of the night. I was too tired to wait for him. It was warm enough for him to stay outside. But I did not leave it open.'

Burglaries were on the increase even in this up-market part of Cheshire, but no one could have got in from the road, she assured herself. Could someone have slipped in from The Carrs? No, the fence was too high. Come on, Julia. If burglars really want to get in, you know they can.

Her head reeled. Smith?

No. Don't be idiotic, she told herself. He was in Moss Side, killing a police officer outside Joe Sagoe's house.

But Duke had heard something. Possibly the PCs themselves, wandering in the garden against their orders, although they were hardly likely to have left her kitchen door wide open.

The thought of a stranger prowling about the house in the dead of night made Julia feel quite sick. 'Is anything missing?' she asked.

'Not that I can see, but I haven't checked yet. I've been giving Nicky her breakfast. I let her help herself and her dish is overflowing with CocoPops. Her eyes glued to the telly.' Wendy frowned and bit the end of her finger. 'Now that I think of it, I didn't see that little photo of Nicky on top of the fridge. The one the superintendent took and you had framed.' She laughed. 'It's probably fallen down behind the fridge . . .' Her voice trailed on but Julia wasn't listening.

'Of course,' she said. She looked up at the ceiling. 'Silly me. No one could possibly have come in. If they had, Duke would have carried on barking.' She was awake most of the night. She would have heard him. Crazily she must have left the door open herself, so she deserved Wendy's admonitions.

Wendy's mouth drooped down at the corners and she looked even more unhappy than before.

Julia stared back at her. 'Wendy? What is it now?'

'Duke.'

'What?'

'He's not here. I've called but — '

With one leap Julia was off the bed, a knot of guilt forming in her stomach for having left him out overnight. Funny, she thought, he barked like hell to get out and then not so much as a yowl to get back in. 'He could have opened the door himself. Like he did last year. With his paw. And then gone out again,' she said, whipping off her nightgown and pulling on an old pair of jeans and a T-shirt.

'If it was unlocked,' Wendy said, looking anxiously at Julia. 'And you know what the old devil's like if there's a bitch in season,' she added with a weak smile.

Julia's mind raced. Wendy knows more than anyone else does what

89

it would do to me, let alone to Nicky, if that dog were lost. Duke has never failed to return for breakfast. Try piecing together your movements after letting him out, she told herself. Ben upset you with his preposterous advances but that was no excuse for behaving irresponsibly .

'But I'm sure I closed the door,' she said, grabbing a pair of trainers. 'I'm always so careful. But I suppose I must have left it unlocked. Anyway Duke would raise the roof if someone opened that door.'

'If he was there,' Wendy said. 'But what if he did go off to see his girl friend?'

Julia smiled, remembering how she had explained a previous disappearance of Duke, after which he had been found in a neighbour's garden making indecent overtures to their diminutive but entrancingly oestrous Poodle bitch. 'I'm sure he'll be back for his breakfast soon, unless . . .' She hated her vivid imagination. Hated it for portraying so graphically the gory sight that filled her mind. A dead dog at the site of a break-in was not an uncommon occurrence these days. Quietly butchered with the nearest heavy object. But she had heard nothing. Besides, the police had been out on the road.

'Wait for me,' she said, doing up her muddy white trainers. 'We must find Duke. Quickly. Before Nicky realises he's missing.'

- 22 -

Julia had been taking Nicky to the Sonya Lake School of Ballet in Cheadle every Saturday since before her fourth birthday. Her daughter's dream was to dance Odette/Odile in Swan Lake at the Palace Theatre in Manchester and nothing was going to stop her. As they walked up the cement pathway to the double glass doors, Nicky tugged at Julia's hand.

'I wish you could watch me today, Mummy. You never watch me.'

'But you know Sonya doesn't like people watching. Besides, I have too much to do this morning.'

She hated herself for having to say that. She could hardly bear to look at the sad blue eyes. 'Nicky, darling, tomorrow I'll play the Swan Lake music for you. I'll watch you practice. Then as a treat you can have

90

one of your favourite ice creams from Sainsbury's.' If it were the last thing she did Julia would make sure she kept these promises. 'Deal?' she said.

Nicky's eyes lit up. 'Okay, Mummy. Deal.'

Julia sighed with a sense of relief she knew she had no right to feel. Once more her daughter had demonstrated the good nature she had inherited from Simon, together with the wide-eyed smile that seemed to light up her face from nowhere.

'But, Mummy,' she said, turning to Julia with a puzzled frown that made her look far older and wiser than her six years, 'you said it was your weekend off.'

'I know, sweetheart. Well, you know what Mummy's job is like.'

'I know. I suppose you have to go to court.'

'No, darling, not today, but there are urgent things I must do.'

She had not told Nicky about the suspected break-in. All she had said was that Duke had gone walkies by himself and hadn't come home yet.

She looked at the sad little face trying so hard to smile. She knew how important it was for children to show off their skills to someone. Someone to give them that necessary reassurance to make them want to go on achieving. Oh, what she wouldn't give for more time with Nicky. She was so like Simon. Not only because of the good nature and the ready smile, but in a host of ways that every day brought him close to her, even though she had long since stopped crying for him. How weird that human beings can inherit character traits even though the person passing on the genes is not even around, has never been around, to exemplify the finer points of those inherited qualities.

Environment versus inheritance. The argument intrigued her. In her professional experience it seemed painfully clear that environment played the bigger part in a person's make-up. But inheritance also fascinated her. Was she like her mother, or her father?

Or like her twin brother.

Over the years she had tried to build up a picture of her brother, working backwards from her own set of physical and mental characteristics. The results were tantalisingly elusive, in spite of the

91

imagined face she sometimes conjured up next to hers.

Nicky broke into her thoughts. 'Will Duke be back when I get home, Mummy?'

She nodded, just as a smiling Sonya Lake appeared at the door.

'Will we see you later, Mrs Grant? I'd like a word.'

'I'll be here at eleven-thirty, unless I'm called out.'

She glanced at Sonya's svelte, leotarded figure. If that's what ballet does for you, maybe I should join an adult class after all, she thought. But they probably don't accept thirty-six year olds, so maybe I'll just settle for the self-defence course Paul is always urging me to take. Last night, if I'd come face to face with an intruder, I wouldn't have had a clue what to do.

She said goodbye and walked away without looking back. A few moments later she felt soft little hands wrap tightly round her waist.

'I love you, Mummy.'

'I love you too, darling. Now run back quickly or you'll be late.'

One day I'll make it up to her, she told herself as she unlocked the car.

She drew the belt across her chest and snapped it in position, grateful when the driver of an old blue Volvo kindly stopped to let her into the solid stream of Cheadle High Street's Saturday morning traffic.

Her mind switched to the tasks before her. Number one priority — find Duke. Then get that old-fashioned lock replaced with a fitting he couldn't open. After a frantic search in the immediate neighbourhood, there'd still been no sign of the dog, and she had left Wendy looking even further afield. 'Shall I ring the police?' were Wendy's last words before Julia had left for Cheadle.

'Not unless we find something missing,' Julia had told her. She was reluctant to call PCs away from more important assignments if it turned out that she *had* left the door unlocked. It wouldn't be the first time Duke had pawed successfully at a door handle when a bitch was on heat. 'I'd hate them to waste time on fingerprints that turn out to be ours. Or Ben's and Paul's,' she had said. 'Anyway, the *Wilmslow Express* said last week that two-thirds of all crimes in this area remain undetected. I'll report it myself later, but only when I'm certain there really was a break-in.'

Turning left onto the A34 she reminded herself that she had a client on the loose, and when he was re-arrested she would have to go to whatever police station they took him to, whether she liked it or not.

Smith. She mumbled his name under her breath. Paul will make sure he's back in Strangeways in under forty-eight hours, and that will be that. End of story. Out of my hands and not a thing I can do about it. So forget it, Julia. Go back to living your life.

Not easy, she thought. She might not even be the person she believed she was, so how could anything in her life be the same again? Had Smith really meant what he said from the dock? And when he was re-arrested, would he still be the avenger he had become after his verdict was pronounced? Or the docile repentant seeking a way out from the violence he had resorted to?

There was no way of knowing.

Coming off the bypass she wondered if she should tell Paul about last night. He would insist on contacting the Wilmslow police. They would send over a couple of PCs and it might turn out to be nothing more than her own stupidity. No, all in all it would be better to wait.

Passing the Blue Bell garage she remembered Nicky's promised treat. Right now shopping was the last thing she needed, but the ice cream was a must.

Turning left after the Water Lane traffic lights she glanced at Hooper's elegant shop windows. It was months since she'd been into a shop to buy anything for herself. Both she and Nicky could do with some new summer clothes, and this year's colours in the windows seemed brighter and more attractive than ever. Coral pink, turquoise, lavender . . . What a refreshing change they'd be from the drab black she wore wear every day to court. If only there was time.

She found a parking space outside the library. She could never look at that library without thinking of Simon. It was where they had first met, one Saturday morning when the scent of spring was in the air. He had looked at her and she had thought she'd never seen such kind eyes. After that he was there every Saturday morning, and they'd discovered they were both students at Manchester University, Julia a late starter and Simon in his final post-grad year. And finally, on the day when it had rained and he'd given her a lift home to David and Jessie's little semi in Lacey Green, she'd been sure he had engineered his position in the queue. From then on they still met every Saturday even if they didn't need to change a book. He always had a lot to talk to her about. He told her about his voluntary work for the homeless, work she felt was akin to what she strove to do for those wrongly accused. Then one day he kissed her and everything began to change. She would run up the stairs to the panelled exhibition room with its neatly stacked square tables and red plastic chairs. He would be waiting for her near the window. He would smile and take her in his arms. She would try to pull away. He would hold her, gently. She would be confused, wanting the closeness and the warmth, yet afraid, wanting to love him but not knowing how; desperate to be loved by him, but still afraid. It wasn't sex she wanted — far from it — but she had this underlying need to belong to somebody. He would wipe away her tears and reassure her. Over the weeks and months she learned to trust him. The fear would still be there but she would reciprocate, wanting to show how much she cared, but unable to express her feelings. And she would lie awake at night wondering what was wrong with her, longing to know how to respond without pretending. The lifts home progressed to drinks at the King William. Then lunch at Hillside House to meet his parents, Natalie and Charles. And finally to the hills. The hills she grew to love, for it was there in a valley, hidden in the trees, that in spite of pain and fear, the long process of discovering the joy of giving had begun. Giving, that would finally lead to the greatest gift of all, a child, that she could love, unreservedly. And who would love her.

Sainsbury's was packed, the queues at the tills infuriatingly slow, and she was glad to get out with the ice cream and a few other essentials for the weekend that Wendy might have forgotten to buy. The Water Lane lights were red again, and she wished the pale blue Volvo behind her would keep his distance.

A few minutes later it was still behind her. Glancing in her rear-view mirror she could see the driver's sun glasses but could not make out through the grimy windscreen whether it was anyone she knew. It was the same kind of car that had let her into Cheadle High Street. She drew in her breath sharply. Surely it couldn't have been behind me all this time –

She turned left. The Volvo turned left too. She slowed down, giving it a chance to overtake. It stayed behind her. I'll begin to worry if it follows me to Hillside House, she thought. I hope the men on obs are wide awake. The world is full of cranks and sometimes we lawyers have to be careful.

The gate was open, which was strange. As she turned in she noted that the Volvo drove past and that the driver was quite clearly not interested in her since he didn't even glance her way. Pull yourself together, Julia, she told herself. That break-in, if that's what it was, seems to have unnerved you more than you realised.

She closed the gate, then drove slowly round the cobbled driveway. The house was partly hidden by the huge cedar tree, but even as she approached she had a feeling that something dreadful had happened.

- 23 -

Julia had never touched a dead dog before. It was strange how like a stuffed animal he felt, like those in a museum you're not supposed to touch and give you a strange feeling when you do. But not only was this fur hard and cold, it was covered with blood from a bullet wound in the head, dark congealed blood that filled Julia's nostrils with its sickly iron odour.

Droplets of sweat broke out on her skin. The beech trees swayed towards her. Feeling Wendy's strong arms steadying her from behind, she remembered the advice the doctor had given her if she felt a panic attack coming on. She took a long, slow, deep breath. Blood or no blood, this was no time to be passing out.

'What happened?' she asked, forcing back the images that were persisting:

> footsteps in the night . . . the brass lamp by the bed . . . the blood . . .

Tears streamed down Wendy's cheeks. 'I found him behind the garage. I carried him here in case he was still . . . I mean . . . I thought that just maybe . . . '

'So there was an intruder. And he must have used a silencer. I wonder what he's stolen.'

She steeled herself to look at Duke, lying so still on the lawn. She gazed into his wide-open brown eyes that once had brimmed over with devotion and were now cold and glassy with surprise. Her hands were drawn again to the matted golden fur, stiff and spiky like an uncut lawn on a frosty morning.

'Wendy,' she whispered. 'This is our beloved Duke. Simon's dog. My dog. Nicky's dog. Our man of the house. What will we tell Nicky? She adores Duke.'

Wendy wiped her eyes and blew her nose. 'Old Margaret next door. Poodle's just had pups. Sure she'll give you one. Bit of a mixture, I think. But soft and white and cuddly.'

Julia stood up and held Wendy's shaking shoulders. 'Thanks,' she whispered. But inside she was trembling with the thought of never having Duke lying on her feet again. Of Nicky never patting his head again. Never holding him tight. And strangely it made her think of her brother, of never touching him again and never feeling his arms around her again. Never seeing his face again. The more I search my memory, she thought, the more it seems to recede, almost within my reach, like when I'm on the mountain and the mist surrounds him and he vanishes, dark, nameless . . .

She looked at Duke and back again at Wendy.

'It's all right, Julia,' Wendy said, taking a deep breath and standing erect again like the little warrior she was. 'I'll bury him at the bottom of the garden. Before Nicky gets home.'

'We should really wait for the police to examine the bullet,' Julia said, making an effort to hold herself together.

Just then the portable phone rang in Wendy's pocket. 'Hello. Yes? Hold on, please. I'll see if she's here. Who shall I say is calling?' She shook her head, then pressed the mute button. 'It's for you. Shall I say you're in?'

Right now Julia didn't want to talk to anyone if she could help it. 'Who is it?'

'He didn't say.'

'He?'

'Shall I ask again?' Wendy knew the voices of Julia's few friends and many of her legal colleagues. She looked annoyed that this one's identity eluded her.

'No. It's all right,' Julia said. 'My job comes first. I might have to attend a remand court or see a client in cells. It could be anything.'

Or perhaps, she thought, perhaps they have already apprehended Smith. 'I'll take it in my study. Ask him to hold on, please.'

She hurried away, rubbing her eyes with the sleeve of her jacket. From the big gold-rimmed mirror in the hall a wild blotchy-faced woman with red swollen eyes and hair awry flashed a look at her as she ran up to her study in the attic. She wondered who was calling. Any one of my clients might be in trouble, she thought. Smith might have given himself up at a police station if he's sunk into one of his manic-depressive moods. I would have to drop everything and go. The weekends were notorious for that, but she had a feeling that this call had nothing to do with her job. It wouldn't be Ben, unless there was an emergency. After last night she doubted he would ever approach her again. Paul? No, that was wishful thinking. He was far too preoccupied with recapturing Smith, especially after the sergeant's tragic murder.

She flopped down at her desk. Her hand hovered over her new state-of-the-art cream telephone-cum-answering machine-cum-everything else, that Paul had persuaded her she should have. Gazing out at the lawn that swept down towards the river, she held back her tears. She lifted the receiver.

'Julia Grant speaking.'

Silence.

'Hello?'

And then she heard it. Not exactly heavy breathing but loud enough to tell that someone was there. Almost certainly what the police would describe as "a malicious call."

She cursed her stupidity. Last time she had spoken to the Crime Prevention Officer at Wilmslow Police Station, they'd briefly discussed the advantage of single women simply saying 'Hello' rather than giving their name to a potential malicious caller. But old habits die hard.

The voice was barely audible. 'You sound different on the phone, Julia.'

Smith?

'Your accent sounds not quite so posh. More like mine. Why is that, Julia?'

Never answer any questions, no matter how innocent they may seem, unless the caller is known to you. That's what the CPO had said. But she couldn't help herself.

'What do you mean?' she demanded. 'Who is this?'

It can't be Smith. I'd have recognised his voice.

'You mean you don't know?' The voice was muffled. An old trick often resorted to by the likes of her clientèle. She pressed the two-way record button.

'Listen carefully, Julia.'

'Who are you?'

'Never mind that now. Just listen.'

She searched for a telltale word, a familiar vowel, but was unable to connect the flat, smothered tones with any of her clients. 'I'm going to put this phone down unless you tell me who you are,' she said.

'You're wasting precious time, Julia.'

'Stop calling me Julia.' Most of her long-standing clients called her Julia. In fact everyone she knew, apart from judges, called her Julia. Smith? And if it was, why would he disguise his voice? 'Who are you?' she demanded.

'You'll know soon enough,' the voice answered, the tonelessness adding a degree of menace to the implied intimidation.

'In that case, why the secrecy?'

'No secret, Julia.'

She gripped the receiver. Either he is crazy or he is deliberately trying to frighten me. 'What do you want?'

'That's better. That's much better. What do I want? Well now, that's quite simple. And no bloody trouble for you.'

'Oh? Really?'

'Two hundred and fifty grand wouldn't even cause a ripple in your fucking bank account, would it now, Julia?'

'You're crazy.'

She slammed down the receiver, breathed in, then quickly let the air out through her nostrils, as though to close the episode for good. She'd had her fair share of ex-convicts phoning her at the office, playing on what they assumed was her feminine weakness when they thought she owed them for not winning their cases. Most criminal lawyers had the same problem.

She had often argued with Paul that in her experience long prison sentences were not always more effective than short ones, that prison works for dangerous prisoners, but not as well for less serious offenders. That often when they came out they were more of a threat than when they went in. Certainly when many of them came out they were unemployable, and two of her clients had told her recently that there was nothing in life for them now but to go on being criminals. But a quarter of a million pounds! Anyway, she had successfully got rid of this one, so that was that.

She glanced at her watch. Ten-thirty. Probably too late now on a Saturday morning to find any locksmiths in, but she ought to give it a try. Duke would never open that door again, poor darling, but someone else might. Silly to take any chances. *Change the locks if you're in doubt*, the Crime Prevention leaflet said.

Fighting back a renewed stream of tears she opened the left-hand bottom desk drawer and hauled out the yellow pages, found a Wilmslow locksmith and scribbled the number on her pad. She dialled and was lucky. The man said he'd call later and quickly she emailed his details to DS Bennett at the Wilmslow police so that he would have no trouble getting in.

She decided she had better phone Paul now and tell him about Duke's violent death. He was fond of Duke too. She would have to tell him some time, and then he would wonder why she hadn't told him sooner. Especially as Duke had been killed with a firearm.

She pulled the phone list towards her and found the number of his flat in Didsbury. Moxon. Paul. 0161 – 445 . . .

Then she remembered he was on duty this weekend and he'd be in his office. She was about to look up his direct number when through the window she saw Wendy walk across the lawn. Over her shoulder she carried a heavily laden sack. Julia gazed unbelievingly at the shape in the sack. Duke. My beloved Duke is in that sack.

'This burglar has murdered our dog!' she shouted, knowing no-one could hear her but wishing she could tell the whole world. 'I will tell the police,' she said, still talking to herself. 'And to hell with the hassle, and then I'll call Paul.'

Just then the phone rang.

She picked up the receiver.

'Julia?'

It was the same muffled voice. The same crank wanting the two hundred and fifty thousand pounds.

Keep your cool, she told herself. 'I'm afraid I don't have time to talk to you now, whoever you are,' she said, making sure her voice was as polite, calm, and as controlled as possible. 'If you feel you have a claim to make, you can do this in writing to the courts. Your case is closed and I am no longer in a position to act for you.'

'Julia, Julia. That's a load of crap.'

There was a toneless ha-ha-ha chuckle followed by a derisory click of the tongue that annoyed Julia so much she wondered why she didn't slam the phone down again.

'You did your best but it wasn't fucking good enough. Now you can *pay*, Julia fucking Grant.'

She felt the first shudder of fear. I know that intonation. 'Who is this?'

'You mean, you really don't know?' he taunted.

She was certain now that it was Smith but she needed time to think. 'Will you stop wasting my time. I cannot conduct a conversation with someone whose name I don't even know.'

'Ah, but you do know it,' he said. 'Extremely well. And it's you wasting my time. I need those bucks. And I need them fucking fast so I can get out of this goddam country. As far away as I can fucking get.'

No wonder I didn't recognise his voice, she thought. In the past he had always spoken to her with respect, and hardly ever a swear word.

She had to think quickly. First she pressed the record button. Then she reached for the red telephone at the far end of her desk, cursing Wendy for always putting it there when she dusted, instead of next to the cream one where she could reach it. Lying awkwardly across the polished mahogany surface she dragged the instrument towards her while still holding the receiver of the cream phone in her left hand. If she could stall him long enough to contact Paul.

'Damn!' Her thigh slipped on the slippery surface and she only just managed to grab the receiver as the whole thing hurtled off the desk with the weight of her falling body. A pain ripped through her knee but miraculously she still had the receiver in her hand. She dragged the cord of the red phone with her foot until the instrument was almost near enough to reach over and dial the number.

'Bad language won't help you, Julia.' The disguise had been discarded and the voice was now unmistakable. Oh yes, she had heard it often enough. But even without the disguise he sounded different. More in control than he ever was before. Not like a hunted criminal at all.

Careful what you say now, she told herself firmly, in case he subsequently tries to accuse you of harbouring him. Don't forget he's on the run.

Despite her awkward position on the floor she was sure that if she could manoeuvre one of the receivers under her chin she could punch out Paul's number on the red phone. In his sporty Honda CRX he could be at the house in fifteen minutes. Smith had her phone number so he would know her address too. The sooner she got hold of Paul, the better.

But the phone list was on top of the desk on the far side, and her knee was throbbing with pain.

'You're not answering me, Julia. I told you, I'm in a hurry.'

'Where are you?' she asked. It was a long shot. He was hardly likely to tell her, but it was worth trying before she spoke to Paul.

Sam Smith laughed. 'All in good time, clever clogs.'

She stopped breathing. Clever clogs?

'If I call the police,' she said, breathing again because lots of Lancashire people used that phrase, 'if I call the police they'll trace your call. Is that what you want?' They couldn't, but Smith wasn't to know that.

'You love your daughter, don't you?'

'Look, I've no idea what you're on about, but just leave my daughter out of this.'

'How can I?'

'What do you mean?'

'I mean that if you don't give me the dough by eleven o'clock on Monday morning I won't be responsible for what happens to your darling precious beautiful Nicola – oops, sorry, it's Nicky, isn't it? And she sure is beautiful.'

'You're mad. I haven't got that kind of money.'

The walls of the room began to sway towards her. Nicola? He called my daughter Nicola.

'Oh yes you have. And you're lucky I'm not demanding a million. Charles Grant and his son Simon sold that chain of estate agents for a packet. When they died you inherited the lot. I know, Julia.'

'But I can't touch it. It's all in trust for Nicky.'

'Lucky Nicky.'

Her head began to spin. 'I'm going to phone the police,' she said calmly.

'You have a beautiful home, Julia.'

'What?'

'I don't like the wrought iron gates, though. Your balls could get hung up on those long sharp spikes. But the cobbled driveway is fucking classy. I like the gables and the old slate roof too. And the back garden's so secluded. Lovely roses . . . '

She heard the rasp of his breath. Excited staccato beats that made her want to throw up.

'But it's nothing compared to the inside, is it, Julia? Now that's something else. Especially the Persian carpets and the Queen Anne stuff in the dining room. Must be worth a bomb.'

A noose tightened round her neck. It was him! He was in your house last night. He killed Duke. The voice inside her head almost drowned out Smith's next words.

'You haven't forgotten where you came from, have you, Julia? You were shit lucky. You wouldn't miss a miserable two-fifty grand.'

He sounded so smug. I should be in command of this conversation, Julia told herself, yet from the moment it started he was the one with the upper hand.

'Your threats are not frightening me,' she said, finally managing to tuck the receiver firmly under her chin so that one hand was free now to dial the police. Or Paul, if she could dredge his direct number from her memory. 'So if you don't mind — '

'Not so bloody fast. I haven't finished talking yet.'

'Well I've finished talking to you.'

'I don't work alone, rich bitch. I have good friends, as you must know by now. You love Nicky, don't you? She's a lucky kid. Just like you, Julia. Lucky. She has everything she wants. Me mates tell me she looks real cute in her school uniform. Blue skirt. Pink blouse. Little blue beret. You must be very proud of her. But I can tell you she looks even cuter in the white frilly skirt she wears to the Sonya Lake dance school. Almost as good as you do in that see-through nightgown of yours. Nice set-up those little ballerinas have there. Big hall, all those airy windows — '

Oh God. Cheadle High Street. The blue Volvo?

'And Julia. Just in case you're tempted, don't tell the police about this conversation. They wouldn't understand the special thing between us, would they? Be sensible. Don't tell anyone. Not if you love Nicola. Sorry. I mean Nicky. And not unless you want certain interesting facts made public. A very juicy piece of news about Manchester's top defence solicitor. Yes, Julia, I could tell the authorities a thing or two. I've never seen the inside of Styal Prison but they tell me the women there have a pretty cushy life.'

Julia fought for breath.

'What facts?' she managed to say, her voice a mere croak. Smith is no fool. If he is my brother he would know I would not give him a quarter million quid to stop him revealing that I am the twin sister of a convicted murderer, as ghastly and as gruesome as that is. Or to stop him having the sordid details of my childhood sexual abuse splashed across the media. But what else is there that he might know, if he is my brother? It must be something far worse than that . . .

'You know. You know.' He paused. Then he said, 'Now don't forget. Monday morning. I'll be in touch to tell you where to leave the money. In tens and fifties, Julia. No fuckin' twenties.'

'What facts?' she yelled into the phone.

'That you killed your foster father. And that's just for starters.'

- 24 -

Julia put down the receiver. She heard the click as it slotted into place. Funny how I've never noticed that sound before. Almost like . . . what? A gun?

Still sprawled on the carpet she lifted the receiver up, then put it down again. Yes. It was just like the click of a gun being cocked. Or how she imagined it would sound.

Like a puppet without strings she picked herself up from her ridiculous position on the floor. She put both telephones back on the desk, then sank into her chair and rubbed her painful knee.

A gun?

She flicked her eyes to the ceiling. Don't be ridiculous, Julia. Do what anyone under threat would do. What any competent solicitor would do. What every mother in your position would do.

Phone the police.

Or should it be Paul first? He would get things moving faster.

She yanked the red telephone towards her. She could also ask Paul to organise that trace facility. BT would set it up immediately they got police authorisation.

But first things first, Julia. Tell him you need protection. Tell him why and don't get side tracked.

She grabbed the receiver and started to dial.

Then she stopped.

104

Fool. Idiot. Imbecile. Are you out of your mind?

She banged down the receiver then pressed her palms over her ears as every syllable of what Sam Smith had said came screaming back to her inside her head:

You killed your foster father. And that's just for starters.

Don't tell the police. Don't tell anyone . . .

She rubbed her eyes, hoping this would make her see more clearly. The whole episode had a nightmarish quality to it, as unreal as the fragments of recall from her past. Fragments of a little girl alone, of horror, disgust and fear. Fleeting fragments of love and warmth and closeness. Fragments of loss and longing . . . of chocolates . . .

And now? Jumping in and out of her brain but refusing to be caught was a new bizarre fragment that his ridiculous unbelievable words had triggered. A fragment that for a fleeting moment connected to a thread in her brain but leapt away immediately. A fragment that terrified her.

How could she believe him? He was just trying to frighten her. It couldn't be true. The last time she had a foster father she was only ten years old. You can't kill someone when you're ten years old. Oh, he was so much cleverer than she had thought. Stupidly she'd let him know about her amnesia. He was using that knowledge. He knew she wouldn't know if he was telling the truth or not.

But what if he *was* telling the truth. Maybe she had done something bad. Something wicked. Something far worse than just lying there allowing that foster father to molest her because she so badly needed to be loved and wanted. Far worse than possibly being the sister of this poor clever depraved man whose life had gone so wrong . . .

How would she know when she couldn't remember?

She needed to hear it again. Not trusting herself to press the right sequence of buttons for a playback on the new answer machine, she yanked out the Olympus tape, slotted it into her Sanyo recorder and pressed the rewind button. The tape whirred.

You love your daughter, don't you, Julia?

Oh yes. It was real all right. And sounded even more menacing the second time around.

She pressed the fast forward button, then the play button again.

. . . and Julia, just in case you're tempted . . . Don't tell the police. Don't tell anyone. Not if you love Nicky . . . And not unless you want certain interesting facts made public . . . I've never seen the inside of Styal Prison but they tell me the women there have a pretty cushy life. *You killed your foster father and that's just for starters.*

The words drummed in her ears like a CD that's stuck: Don't tell the police. Don't tell anyone. You killed your foster father. And that's just for starters. You killed your foster father. And that's just for starters —

Don't tell the police. Don't tell anyone —

He was mad. Demented. Insane. It wasn't only his escape he and his accomplices had planned so meticulously. It was this. All these lies.

She ran the tape back to zero then tidied her desk and put the chair back in the kneehole. It was as though she was looking down from a great height at someone else doing these things. Everything seemed to be happening in slow motion although she was trying desperately to hurry.

To tell? Or not to tell?

How clever was he really? How many spies were working with him? Would he really know if she told the police?

Of course he would. He and his spies would see the results of her telling. And if anything happened to Nicky . . .

From his positive tone of voice, there was no doubt in her mind that Smith would tell the police that she carried criminal responsibility for her foster father's death, whether it was true or not. But what if it was? In English law the age of criminal responsibility begins at ten. The police would undoubtedly investigate. They would question her. There would be enormous difficulty in remembering the facts that might help to show her innocence, but the police being the police would inevitably leak details of the investigation to the press in order to smear her since by virtue of her position she was a constant thorn in their side. This would spell the end of her career. The end of everything —

But I can't remember.

A gun? Yes. You'll need a gun. He shot Duke. He shot Sergeant Scott.

No. For Christ's sake, Julia Grant, you're a lawyer. Try to behave as though you're advising a client under threat. You wouldn't advise a client to get a gun. If Paul knew what you were planning now he would tell you that you were behaving without caution or judgement. And so would Ben. I know they would. But they don't know the half of it. Neither do I. Yet. Oh, if only I could remember . . .

Get a gun from where?

Moss Side, of course. All your clients in Moss Side have guns. Or they know someone with a gun. Joe Sagoe. He would lend you one. Or Charlie Kuma . . .

Stay calm, Julia. And stop talking to yourself. You have a day and a half to think this out before you have to hand over a quarter of a million quid that you haven't got.

There must be a way around it. Someone will be able to help.

Don't tell anyone. Not if you love Nicky. Not if you want to avoid being taken in for questioning and all the detrimental publicity that would follow . . .

Don't tell Wendy. Don't tell Nicky. Don't tell David and Jess. Don't tell Ben. Don't tell Linda. Don't tell Sonya Lake. Don't tell Miss Haydock or anyone else at St Mary's school. Don't tell Paul.

There was no one she could tell. Not one sodding soul. No one she could trust. No one to help her.

No one.

Then it hit her.

The white frilly skirt. The ballet school. The big windows . . .

He knows where it is. He followed me there. He saw me leave Nicky there.

You fool, Julia Grant.

She looked at her watch and ran down the stairs. How long since you put the phone down? Where was he phoning from?

Handbag. Keys. Hurry, woman. Behave naturally. If Wendy sees you like this she'll start asking questions. Take a deep breath.

'Wendy, do you think you could be a darling and wait here till I get back. I've got someone coming to replace that lock.'

'I was staying anyway,' Wendy said softly. 'Aren't you a bit early for Nicky? I could fetch her if you like. Then I could tell her the terrible news. It would save you.'

'No!' She covered her mouth with her hand. 'I'm sorry, Wendy. I didn't mean to shout. I must go myself. I promised.' She heard her voice rising again.

Behave naturally.

Seconds counted, but as she opened the front door something stopped her dead. Something that made her realise that Wendy was the only person who she could even vaguely confide in and the knowledge made fresh tears spring to her eyes. 'I . . . I don't know what I'd do without you, Wendy.'

Wendy hurried to Julia and put her arm around her shoulder. 'I'll go down to Margaret's quickly and get one of the puppies. Just as soon as I've — just as soon as I've dug the hole.'

Julia nodded speechlessly. She glanced at the clock on the wall. She had to go now.

She pulled away from Wendy's comforting arm and steadied herself against the door. 'Forgive me, Wendy. I've got this thing about blood and dead bodies. I couldn't have looked at Duke again. I couldn't have buried him myself. I don't know why I'm like that but I am. I can't help it.'

'Julia, don't torture yourself. At least you and Nicky are unhurt and nothing seems to be missing — except that little photo and I'm sure I'll find it. Please try to relax.'

Julia fled down the steps to her car. At the gate she almost collided head on with Sergeant Bennett's black car. He jumped out and apologised profusely.

'I've just come to tell you we've secured the right to occupy the empty house opposite. The team's moving in shortly. They'll have a fine view of the house and garden and the road.'

'As long as nobody sees them,' she said. 'It's most important.' Paul had moved fast.

If Bennett noticed the panic in her voice he did not comment but merely nodded and smiled. 'Please continue to tell us of any vehicles you're expecting,' he said.

"Yes," she said, her mind miles away in Cheadle. She revved the engine and he reversed to let her through. If he knew what she was doing he would also regard her actions as lacking caution and judgement, she thought as she drove out into the slow moving Wilmslow traffic. She turned right at the Blue Bell garage then put her foot down as far as the law would allow and headed for Cheadle.

- 25 -

Sonya Lake patted Nicky's shiny blonde topknot. 'She's working very hard, aren't you, Nicky?'

Nicky looked up at her teacher, her eyes brimming with adoration.

'Off you go then, and change your shoes,' Sonya said. She turned to Julia. 'As you know, Mrs Grant, they normally move into Grade One at age six. But this child is exceptional so I've decided to promote her to Grade Two. With one or two extra lessons she's perfectly capable of catching up, though she'll have to work hard.'

Julia's eyes misted over. 'That's wonderful,' she said, wishing she could share this news with Simon, 'and you really think she's up to it?' She remembered how Jessie's insistence on two hours practice a day had put her off the piano.

'Nicky's very single-minded,' Sonya said, dropping her voice to a whisper, 'and she's different from the others.'

'Different?'

Sonya blinked her kohl-rimmed eyes and lifted her hands, letting her fingers float down gracefully, like autumn leaves from a tree. 'It's an almost indefinable quality but when you see her dance you'll understand how it sets her apart. She'll go right to the top.'

Peeping through the glass doors during the final ten minutes of the lesson, Julia had only had eyes for Nicky and hadn't compared her to the others. Preoccupied with keeping an eye on the car park for a pale blue Volvo, she had also been agonising over whether or not to tell Paul what had happened. Smith had already demonstrated how capable he was of carrying out his threats. With X number of accomplices who'd already acquired an intimate knowledge of the pattern of her life and were presumably still watching her every move, Smith would soon know if extra police were drafted in to guard her, and he would know

109

why. And what would he do then, she had asked herself. Her career and her whole life would be at stake.

'Has she always been exceptional?' she asked Sonya. 'I mean, when did you first know?'

'Right from the start,' Sonya said without hesitation. 'Her grace. Her musicality. Her line. The way she uses her head and her arms. Oh, it's what makes my job so exciting.'

'I knew she was keen, but I had no idea . . . '

Julia's voice drifted off as she watched the mothers waiting at the door to shepherd their befrilled offspring out of the school. Sonya stood aside to let the next class enter the hall. 'Look,' she said, her face all aglow, 'why not stay and watch one Saturday. You'll see for yourself what I mean.'

'I'd love that,' Julia murmured, trying to sound like an ordinary mother with nothing but the shopping and cooking to think about.

After the goodbyes she led Nicky to the car, holding her hand extra tightly. She double-checked the central-locking and scanned every corner of the street before she edged out of the car park.

Crawling along Cheadle High Street she glanced in her rear-view mirror. Does he really have all those accomplices and spies, she wondered. Yes, of course he does. His escape proved it, so I have no choice but to give him the benefit of the doubt.

She stopped at the traffic lights. Interesting facts? Murder? She was still afraid to put into words the first bizarre memories the sight of him had triggered. But now the new, even more frightening, images that had flashed across her mind this morning were something else.

How would she ever know if these memories were real. Maybe her imaginings would turn out to be like the testimonies of witnesses who swear they've seen something that is later proved to be entirely false. While she was preparing his defence, Smith never even hinted at a possible connection. Not even when they laughed about their birthdays being the same. The whole thing could be a complete fabrication on his part.

Could she risk telling Paul any of this? Did she really want to make it easier for Paul to apprehend him? Wouldn't she prefer it if Smith succeeded in escaping to another country? His destiny had recast him into a different being. It was too late now for change. There was no future for them as . . . She was too cowardly to even utter the words side by side in her mind. And anyway, if she went to the police and he got caught, he would carry out his threat.

But it was time to push aside these outlandish thoughts. These silent conversations with herself were becoming too frequent, interfering with her work and with her relations with her daughter. She glanced at Nicky, so excited at being promoted to Grade Two and the extra lessons she'd be having that she hadn't once mentioned Duke. Hopefully she would accept the substitute Poodle puppy before she had time to suffer too much anguish over her adorable golden Labrador.

As they drove into Hillside House Nicky said: 'Is Duke back, Mummy?'

She stopped the car. Now, she said to herself. Tell her now.

But the words would not come. By the time she had closed the garage door Nicky was racing through the rose garden towards the kitchen and Julia had to run to catch her up. Duke would have bounded up to meet them by now. Tell her, for God's sake. Now. Before she sees the puppy.

Without warning, Nicky stopped. She looked back at Julia, her eyes clouded with doubt.

'Mummy, where's Duke?'

Just then Wendy appeared at the back door with the puppy in her arms. 'Nicky, look what Mummy's got for you,' she said.

Nicky's eyes widened in disbelief as she focused on the ball of wriggling fluff.

'Can I hold him?' she asked, her voice trembling with excitement.

'Of course you can,' Wendy said.

'What's his name?'

'You must choose.' Wendy held the puppy out to Nicky.

'Is it a boy or a girl?' she asked, cradling it in her arms.

Wendy smiled. 'She's a girl.'

'Then we'll call her Duchess. That's what you said Duke would be if he was a girl. Duke and Duchess.'

Now, Julia told herself. The puppy will quickly take Duke's place. 'Nicky, why don't you let Wendy give Duchess some milk while you and I go upstairs. There's something I want to talk to you about.'

'Oh, but Mummy, I want to play with Duchess. Hey, I wonder what Duke will say. Did he come back from his walk, Wendy?'

Wendy's eyes sought Julia's help. 'Not yet,' she said, prising the puppy from Nicky's arms, her eyes averted from the child.

Julia led her daughter through the kitchen, past Duke's basket with its wet-dog smell and its chewed-up blanket that once was Simon's picnic rug, into the hall and up the stairs to Nicky's yellow playroom where she kept her books and her toys and played her solitary games when it was too wet to go outside.

'Darling . . .' Julia said softly, leading her to the sofa, recognising the need to be more gentle in her approach than ever before, desperately wanting to say it so that Nicky understood he was gone forever, but also so that she was not too hurt by his going.

'What, Mummy?'

'Duke. Duke has gone away.'

'When is he coming back?'

'Nicky darling, he isn't coming back.'

'Why?'

Slowly Julia shook her head.

'Mummy? What's wrong? Mummy! Is he dead?'

Julia nodded, alarmed at the extent of Nicky's reaction, at the velocity of the torrent of tears. 'He had an accident. My darling, I'm so sorry.'

'Oh, Mummy — I want Duke to come back. I don't want Duchess.'

Take her in your arms, you fool. Wipe her tears away. Hold her, like other mothers do. Comfort her. Cry with her . . .

She hesitated and the moment was gone. 'We must take great care of Duchess. She'll be missing her mother,' she said.

Nicky stopped crying. She tilted her head to one side. 'Poor Duchess. I'll be her mother. Will she sleep in Duke's basket?'

Julia lifted her off the sofa. The desire to take her in her arms was overwhelming, but as usual something held her back, something that always stopped her making the physical contact until the moment it would have seemed natural had passed.

'I know, Mummy. Kitty can also look after Duchess. Let's take her to Kitty.'

- 26 -

With Nicky totally absorbed in Duchess, Kitty and the kittens, Julia had her first real opportunity since Smith's phone call to contact Paul, even if it was only to tell him about Duke. Alone in her study, her silent debate with herself still resulting in no clear-cut result, she wondered whether there was any real basis for her fears. Who is Smith, she asked herself, besides being a psychopathic murderer?

I am desperate to know, but I do not want to know.

And yet I think I know.

But whoever he is, Smith is no fool she told herself for the hundredth time. And he would know that merely claiming publicly that I was his sister and that I was abused by our foster father would not be enough to end my career. And certainly not bad enough for me to dish out a quarter of a million quid to him. And not bad enough for me to obey his ridiculous command that I should not tell the police or anyone else. He would know that I wouldn't buy that. So he has concocted this grotesque accusation that I killed my foster father — our foster father? — believing that I would do everything to keep it quiet, and knowing that because of my amnesia I can't afford not to believe him.

Filled with a mixture of revulsion and fear she went back once again to the other side of her argument: your brother died just before you were adopted and yet you so often have this strong awareness that he's still alive, and you keep dreaming of him on that impossible mountain. Is this only a manifestation of your deep longing?

No. If that was all it was why did I have such a violent reaction at Strangeways when I first saw Smith?

She stood at the window, looking down at the garden. Nicky was lying on the grass, her head level with the puppy's head. How adorable they both looked. So precious and oh, how short-sighted she was to think she could fight this alone. Somehow she had to seek help but at the same time discreetly enough to keep Smith from talking, and keep Paul from getting his hands on Smith.

With her mind made up she picked up the phone and dialled Paul's number. She listened to the ringing tone.

He'll think I've gone mad, she thought. I could tell him about the break-in, and Duke, and the phone-call. And of course his threat to Nicky. But then I'd have to tell him everything or he wouldn't understand. But there's no way I can tell him only one little bit of that because Paul is Paul and he'd get it all out of me and I couldn't handle that.

In her heart she refused to believe that what Smith had told her was true, but his bizarre words had lit little embers in her memory that had given her the weirdest feeling there was a possibility it could be true. So she reminded herself that the last thing she wanted was Smith landing in the hands of the police and causing her professional and personal downfall. Paul's phone was still ringing. She could put it down now and he would never know.

Too late.

She jumped as she heard his voice and said the first thing that came into her head.

'I have a persistent headache, Paul. Could be a cold coming on. It's going round the office. It wouldn't be fair to see you tonight. And I'd be a dead loss anyway. I'm really sorry.'

'Julia, are you sure you're okay? Remember, I told you earlier I couldn't get away at all today. Much as I'd love to see you.'

'No, I'm fine,' she said quickly. 'Apart from the headache.'

'Good,' Paul said. 'Have a hot toddy and go to bed early. And give Nicky a hug from me. If I can't manage tomorrow night I'll see you both next week.'

'Oh, by the way, Paul . . .'

She breathed in deeply, filling herself with courage, realising the need to at least go half way in appeasing Paul if just one whiff of this reached his ears. This is it. Now or never and it has to be now. 'I was wondering . . . Well . . . on second thoughts the tracing facility would be a good idea after all.'

'Good thinking,' he said.

'You never know. Smith just might try to contact me. I wouldn't put it past him. I don't think he'd dare try the office. But if he rang here I could press the BT alert button. Maybe help you track him down,' she said, crossing her fingers.

'I'll organise it now. Are you absolutely sure you're all right?'

'Yes, of course I am.'

'Well, don't forget, Julia. I'm here if you need me. I'd be with you now if I could. Take care.'

Julia hung up.

Coward.

Her only consolation was that she had been able to keep her voice reasonably calm. She would never press that alert button to enable them to trace Smith's calls. Not if she wanted Nicky to stay alive and not if she wanted to remain a practising lawyer.

She screwed up her eyes. And yet it was a comforting feeling that she would have a safety valve, just in case things went badly wrong.

Really? she asked herself.

Coward. Re-dial Paul's number now. Tell him. Tell him about being followed. Tell him about Duke. The break in. The phone call. The threat to Nicky.

Her hand quivered over the re-dial button.

But if Smith really was who she thought he might be, she could also be endangering her own brother's life by telling the police. How could she do that? Maybe if he were given a chance . . .

Her head reeled with the incongruity of her thinking, the inconsistency. Julia Grant, are you crazy? You know damn well the behavioural pattern he has demonstrated is typical of a psychopathic killer. He is now showing his true colours. He has become a different person. You are a lawyer. A sensible, intelligent, law-abiding citizen for heaven's sake. He's a killer and the police must be told. No matter who he is. Or what he says he knows you did, that you damn well can't remember . . .

She picked up the phone again. Willing herself to keep going this time, she pressed the re-dial button.

'Paul, there was something else — '

'What Julia? Tell me, for God's sake.'

She chewed her fist. She knew she had to do this before her courage evaporated, before she weighed the odds in favour against the dangers of saying nothing.

And then, before she could change her mind, it all came bubbling out.

She told him about Duke barking. The open door. Duke dead. The phone call. The demand for the money. The threat to Nicky if she didn't pay.

But nothing, not a word about the other threat.

Paul was strangely silent, though she sensed he was coiled up like a snake about to strike. He asked no questions until she was finished, and then he said, calmly and in his most officious superintendent's voice, 'Ignore the money bit. They all try that one on. We'll add an armed contingent to the men already in the house opposite. Video cameras will record every exit and entry, relayed to my office. When he phones again, press digit one and let me know immediately what he says. He's played right into our hands this time.'

She was amazed at how calm he sounded. She felt breathless after her confession, but there was one more thing she had to say and say it she had to. Now or never. No matter what Paul's reaction was. No matter what it did to their friendship, even though she knew it was a preposterous demand to make of a police officer.

'Paul. Can I trust you not to make Smith's phone call and what he said public knowledge in the force. Not even to your right hand men, in case it leaks back to Smith.'

- 27 -

Julia lay on top of the duvet. She'd been relieved when Wendy insisted on staying to do the night-time rituals. Supper. The dishes. Bathing Nicky and reading her a story. Settling the whining Duchess in Duke's smelly basket, swaddled in an old pink baby blanket Julia had kept in a plastic bag all these years.

The house was quiet now. Wendy at home, Nicky asleep and the puppy finally silent. She gazed at the row of mirrored wardrobes that reflected so enticingly the view of the river and rolling grasslands of The Carrs. The right side was hers and the left had been Simon's. Over the years she'd expanded into his side, except for one cupboard which she kept locked, the section containing his personal things, like his gold watch and his ring, things that for the first few years she had often looked at and touched so that she could feel that he was there in the room, next to her.

With a sudden urge to feel him close she retrieved the key from her dressing table drawer and unlocked the cupboard. Groping under a small pile of silk scarves for his ring, her fingers met with something hard and cold.

Simon's gun.

A war souvenir his father had given him. She'd forgotten all about it. He had never licensed it, so when Simon died she had left it where it was because she hadn't known what else to do with it.

Gingerly she ran her fingers over the ugly grey metal. The cold hard lines of the weapon brought it home to her how alien the thought of killing another person was.

But what if there were no other way of preventing Smith from hurting Nicky? Because in the end it was going to be up to her to ensure the safety of her daughter. And right now getting hold of two hundred and fifty thousand pounds seemed an impossibility —

No, Julia. There must be other ways. Anyway, there's no ammunition.

But one of your gun-toting clients would have some . . .

As though someone else was in command, she opened the Manchester A to Z. With the square magnifying glass Simon had used for stamp collecting, she zoomed in on the labyrinth of Moss Side.

Are you crazy, Julia? said that annoying inner voice. To think of going on your own into the heart of Manchester's notorious gangland area?

Oh, shut up. There's nothing I wouldn't do to protect my child.

Nothing?

117

Quickly she dismissed the negative arguments that flooded her mind. She could jeopardise her career, yes, but instead she paraded the more tangible arguments in favour:

Avril Scott was an armed policewoman, with a support team close by, and look how easily he finished her off and got clean away. Even a plain-clothes man sitting on your tail twenty-four hours a day wouldn't stop Smith if he was determined.

Yes, I know. But I have to do it, and anyway, I've been into seedy areas before. I'm perfectly capable of taking care of myself.

Or was she? Those self-protection classes would have to be fitted into her agenda very soon. As a back-up to the gun, if nothing else. No. Instead of the gun would be better.

Wouldn't it be great if I could ask Paul to help me, she mused. He had once been head of the firearms team. He had a rifle and a pistol locked up at the Altrincham Rifle Club range, he had told her. Not long ago he had boasted, modestly of course, about the row of trophies in his flat that she really ought to come and see. He could teach her how to use it.

What a crazy thought, Julia. You really are losing your mind. Why are you being so obsessive? Why can't you be like other women? Perhaps it's because other women have led ordinary lives so they don't need to be obsessive. Oh, how I bloody well wish I could lead an ordinary life . . .

On a piece of paper she scribbled the name Charlie Kuma. The letters had a wobbly look as though she'd written them in her sleep. Charlie had been pretty clean lately, but he owed her one and she was sure he wouldn't blab. She had forgotten the name of the street he lived in with his girl friend, but was sure she could remember how to get there. Joe Sagoe, who lived in the same road, would have been a safer bet. He never opened his mouth. But Avril Scott had been shot outside his house so it was likely he'd be picked up for questioning. It didn't take rocket science to work that one out.

She tore off the piece of paper and slipped it into the A to Z ready for tomorrow, necessity blanking the part of her brain that was screaming Stop.

SUNDAY

Julia sped down the narrow twisting tree-lined road, past Styal Prison and on towards the airport where a myriad lights gleamed like glow-worms on a misty riverbank. Swinging north on to the M56 a sudden shower steamed up her windows and drenched the car with spray from thundering lorries. She kept going, carried on straight into Princess Road, then slowed down as she reached Moss Side, just short of the city.

Charlie Kuma lived with his girl friend at the opposite end of Joe Sagoe's street, a long row of terraced Coronation Street houses somewhere between Claremont Road and Moss Lane East. She would recognise Joe's house. Joe had a macabre sense of humour and nobody could miss his house, unmistakable bright red painted brickwork with its peacock-blue front door, and black skull and crossbones. She'd have to watch out though, in case the police were still staking out the house.

Round and round the wet deserted streets she drove, searching for a familiar landmark. Down a side street she glimpsed a police van. Keep moving, she told herself. The police are wary of anyone cruising around in Moss Side, stopping or doing anything out of the ordinary. You don't want to get picked up on suspicion of drug dealing, or prostitution . . .

Freddie Pye's Scrap Metal. Charlie's house was somewhere near here. Damn. A dead-end. New concrete bollards blocking the road in three directions.

Out of nowhere a skinny youth appeared on a bike, water swishing from the tyres, his ebony skin glistening in the rain. As he circled the Merc his head swivelled to watch her with his muddy, red-rimmed eyes. He could throw a brick through her windscreen and nobody would even stop and stare. He skidded to a halt next to the car, leaned on his handlebars and looked at her. A moment later he unzipped his yellow anorak and plunged his hand into the inside pocket. A drug dealer. God, do I look that desperate?

Relax your face muscles and reverse again, she told herself. Keep your movements slow and controlled. Avoid eye contact.

When she looked in the rear view mirror again, the dealer had gone. So that's how they did it. On bikes they could nip between bollards for a quick getaway where cars hadn't a hope.

Take your time now. It can't be far.

West Indian Sports and Community Centre. God of Prophecy Church. It all looked familiar, yet the seedy, deserted look of the area seemed to have worsened. Boarded-up houses. Overturned bins. Dogs poking around in mounds of black bags. Sodden piles of waste paper. Alleyways clogged with refuse. Broken windows stuffed with bits of cloth . . .

Then another row of grey concrete bollards.

Where are you, Charlie Kuma?

There was still an eerie absence of anything on the streets, yet Julia had a feeling of being watched, as though any minute now a row of thugs would emerge from the faceless houses.

Turning the next corner she saw a police van blocking the road. Four police officers stood next to a house with a peacock blue door that had to be Joe Sagoe's. Doing the fastest three-point turn she'd ever done, she shot into the next side street.

This is madness, she said to herself, her heart almost beating out of her chest. Not a chance now of trying to get to Charlie's girlfriend's house; the other end of the street would be blocked off too. Besides, getting nicked carrying an unlicensed gun was the quickest way of losing her practising certificate. Her livelihood.

Unlawful possession of a firearm. How would I plead? Reasonable Excuse? It would depend on whether the court approved of the motives. What motives? Somebody is threatening to kill my daughter, Your Honour. Who is threatening to kill your daughter, Mrs Grant? I'm not at liberty to say, Your Honour. It is not an answer simply to show that the weapon was carried for self-defence, Mrs Grant. There is a reasonable excuse only if the weapon is carried to meet an immediate and particular threat . . . But, Your Honour . . .

Well, that's that then. No ammunition, so get the hell out of here.

Some other weapon will have to do. Scissors, kitchen knife, razor blade, acid.

She felt a rush of bile to her throat. 'No!' she screamed out loud.

She quickly looked around to see if anyone had heard her, then drove on. She stopped at the next corner and let out a huge sigh of self-disgust. It is an offence to carry any weapon in a public place, don't you know, you depraved woman. And it doesn't have to be a machine gun or a flick knife. Even a piece of household cutlery in your handbag or a baseball bat under the car seat, makes you guilty of possessing an offensive weapon. The plain fact of the matter, Julia Grant, is that you can never hold a weapon with the specific intent of using it in a defensive fashion. And you should bloody well know that.

Except . . .

Except in a situation of complete surprise. In a life-threatening situation if a weapon comes to hand and you use it to defend yourself then you've got reasonable excuse.

Julia was like a lioness with the preservation of her cubs uppermost in her mind. She thought of Wendy's home-made floppy velvet hats, with long hatpins stuck in the front to stop them flying off your head in the wind. You just happen to have one on the back shelf of your car.

Well, I'd never actually use it, would I? No, of course you wouldn't. But it would be there, wouldn't it?

She glanced up at the house on the corner, grasping for anything distracting that would strangle her sick thoughts before they got beyond control. Wind howled through the broken windows. Perhaps there were children huddled in its damp, unsheltered corners, cold and hungry, deserted and unloved. I should be at home with Nicky now, playing the Swan Lake music and watching her dance, just like I promised. Not driving around Moss Side deliberately trying to break the law.

The rain came down with a hissing roar that made the street seem even more desolate. She flicked the windscreen wipers to extra fast, released the hand brake and, keeping a wary eye open for police cars, she crawled slowly down the street. What made me think I could ever use this gun, even if I could have got ammunition from Charlie K?

To what evil madness is Sam Smith driving me?

Back on Princess Road, she headed south. No harm had been done, thank goodness. The only purpose the gun would have served was as her own personal psychological crutch. But thankfully common sense had whipped away that crutch leaving her . . . What?

Afraid?

Me? Julia Grant. Afraid?

Gradually her foot eased off the accelerator, until she had slowed almost to a complete stop and her eyes had become mere slits as she wrestled with her conscience.

Rubbish. You're getting soft. Remember Joanne Perkins? Duke? Avril Scott?

You need that ammunition and you need it today.

She looked in her rear view mirror. No pale blue Volvo. No police car.

So it wouldn't hurt to have one more go at finding Charlie Kuma.

* * *

Charlie's wife lived in the Gooch Close area, in one of the newer houses on the site of demolished Victorian terraced houses. Charlie had told her he sometimes went back there when he'd had a fight with his girlfriend.

I could be there in five minutes, Julia said to herself, pressing her lips tightly together as if this would stop any further debate.

At the major intersection with Gooch Close, the lights turned red. She cursed her bad luck. They could jump you here, even in broad daylight. This was the most dangerous area of Moss Side, where rival gangs shot and knifed each other to death in the war for the control of the illegal drug trade. Ahead of her, making the newer modern houses look like rabbit hutches, an ancient church towered majestically into the rain-darkened sky.

As she waited, a youth with a back-to-front navy blue baseball cap sauntered towards her. She threw her handbag on the floor and checked the door locks. She watched him sidle round the back of the car.

122

The lights were still red.

The youth kicked the bumper, then slunk up to her window and glowered at her, hunching his shoulders as the wind blew the rain into his pale, pinched face.

'Sod you,' he shouted, showing his yellowed teeth.

The lights changed. She let out her breath and turned sharp left, foot flat down, tyres screeching. The nearside wheel hit an empty tin, sending it clattering down the street.

She parked the car outside Charlie's council house. She was glad the rain was keeping most people indoors.

She got out and hit the remote. The locks clunked and the alarm lights flashed. Two men with hair shaved at the sides and sticking up on top like petrified stalagmites materialised from nowhere. They stood watching her, then walked on muttering to each other and looking back over their shoulders.

She turned up the collar of her raincoat. 'Into the Lion's Den,' she muttered, dodging piles of dog dirt on the pathway to the house.

Charlie's wife opened the door, one child clutching her skirt, another on her hip.

The smell of unwashed nappies, cabbage, mould and cats wafted through the door. Julia made an effort not to breathe. Behind the woman she could see a steep narrow staircase with two steps missing.

'Is Charlie here?' Julia asked.

Charlie's wife laughed, a short hollow sound that echoed down the bare passage. A cigarette stump dangled from her bottom lip.

'Come in. Ya'll catch ya death out there.'

Digging her nails into her palms, Julia followed her into a tiny dark room on the left. Wallpaper hung down in tattered strips from the damp walls. The woman kicked a pile of newspapers off a straight wooden chair in front of the boarded-up window.

'Sit here,' she said, then lowered herself onto a filthy, sagging armchair. It was the only other furniture in the room besides two old maroon motor car seats, their yellowed foam innards protruding like lumps of fat from a slaughtered pig.

Julia felt the nausea rise in her throat. 'Where is he?' she asked.

The baby looked at her with eyes as round and brown as pennies. Vomit dribbled down its mouth on to its mother's stained and creased dress.

'Haven't laid no eyes on the bastard all week. Maybe he's . . .' The woman shrugged.

Julia waited quietly. She wasn't going to give up now. Everyone knew everything in a neighbourhood like this. People talked. Someone would know where Charlie was.

She forced herself to smile at the woman. 'You must have some idea.'

The woman crinkled up her big dark eyes, as though trying to weigh up why Julia should want to see Charlie. 'Could be with that bitch.' Her top lip puckered. 'Could be at Sweet Cherry. Bout eleven tonight,' she added surprisingly quickly.

Julia felt her heart beat faster, felt a bead of sweat trickle down her chest. Sweet Cherry was one of the most infamous clubs in Manchester, in the centre of the red light district of Moss Side, where once the middle class elite had luxuriated in their Victorian mansions.

There's no way I could walk into Sweet Cherry, she told herself. Not now. Not at eleven o'clock tonight. Not ever.

Just then the baby brought up all the milk it had consumed, and another toddler came tumbling down the steep narrow staircase.

The woman leapt to her feet and picked the screaming child up by the arm.

'Now look what you done. You and your smartarse car.'

Julia stood up. 'I'm sorry,' she said, and let herself out.

Three surly youths were walking towards the Mercedes SLK. She ignored them as she climbed nonchalantly into her car.

'And when you find him tell him his brats is hungry,' the woman yelled after her.

On the next corner Julia stopped the car. She opened the window, letting the rain spatter on her face as she breathed in deeply. She looked back towards Charlie's house, biting her lip until it hurt. That wasn't a home. It was just a place to keep off the streets.

A tall slinky man with plaited hair, an embroidered waistcoat and thick gold chains around his neck, came out of a nearby house. He glared at her as he unlocked his shiny new BMW. 'Lookin' for someone?' he asked.

She shook her head, double checked the locks and drove off into the rain. Informers are always on the lookout for a quick payoff, she reminded herself. The police force is super-alert around here and I'll have to leave soon or I'll find myself picked up for questioning. If ever Paul got wind of it . . .

As she turned into Princess Road, Smith's words rang in her ears.

Don't tell anyone. Don't tell the police.

She was glad she had told Paul the bones of Smith's call. Yet now, as she headed back to Wilmslow, she was even more convinced it was still only her and Smith.

- 29 -

By the time Julia drove up to Hillside House she was terrified that something might have happened to Nicky in the hours she'd been away. She glanced at the empty house opposite, reassured when she saw a hazy face at the window.

Wendy met her at the door.

'Is Nicky okay?' She heard the tremble in her voice. Did ordinary women feel this terror whenever they left their children?

Wendy closed the door. 'She's in her bedroom,' she said calmly.

Julia's stomach scrunched into a knot. 'So early?' she asked.

'Don't know if she's asleep yet, but she's in bed. Had her tutu on earlier. Said she was going to dance Swan Lake but she took it off in the end. Don't worry. She's been fine.'

Wendy's voice was soothing, though her words were tinged with reprimand. 'Had her tea half an hour ago,' she went on. 'She and Duchess together.'

'Together?'

She smiled at Julia's dismay. 'I put a mat on the floor and they both sat on it. Shared their food.' She lowered her eyes, still smiling, and Julia knew there was more.

125

'And then?' she asked.

'Well, Duchess is so soft and clean . . .'

'Oh, Wendy. That puppy's not in Nicky's bed, is she?'

'I told her. Nicky, I said. Just this once. And only for half an hour. You see, that's about how often it — well, I don't think it's properly trained yet, is it? She wanted Kitty and all the kittens as well but I told her they were quite happy in their box in the utility room.' Wendy glanced at her watch and pulled a wry face. 'I said it was too early to go to bed but she said Duchess was tired.'

Oh, what the hell, Julia thought. What does it matter if the bed gets wet. I left Nicky alone again when I was supposed to have spent all day with her. And what about Wendy? She should be out with Alan. The poor girl hardly ever sees him. I must make it up to both of them, she told herself.

She took off her jacket and dumped her handbag on a chair. 'Any calls?' she asked, hoping she sounded as though she didn't really care.

'Just the superintendent. Twice.'

'Any others?'

'It rang once while I was in the utility room,' Wendy said. 'When I picked it up and said hello I heard a click. I'm sure he'll ring again.'

Yes, I'm sure he will, Julia thought. He hadn't even told her yet where he wanted her to hand over the money and time was getting short.

'Thanks for staying so late, Wendy. Oh, I almost forgot. I'll be leaving at seven tomorrow morning. I have to see to some financial matters before I go to court.'

It wouldn't be a five-minute job either, she thought as she ran up the stairs. To get her hands on two hundred and fifty thousand pounds.

No, Simon. I don't want the trust revoked . . .

And as if it were yesterday that terrible night at Withington Hospital exploded into Julia's mind —

Gripping the metal frame surrounding his broken body and wondering why this ghastly thing has happened to the man she's grown to love, the man she's not given enough to, and now it is too late. Seeing the pleading in his eyes, straining to hear his voice. Not believing he can actually be dying, fighting to keep away the tears and the pain of impending loss.

Hearing his voice: 'Please, Julia, let's get Ben to execute a deed to vary the trust. It's what Mum and Dad would have wanted, if they'd known . . .'

Telling him firmly, though inside she is crumbling: 'No, Simon. I don't need the money. I have my job. I earn enough for my needs and for Nicky until she's eighteen. Natalie and Charles were right to leave it all to Nicky.'

His voice getting fainter: 'They were so thrilled that she was a girl. Please, let me see her again – '

Taking the baby from the carry cot, holding her up as tears roll down his cheeks. Watching him drift off. Stroking his brow, pressing her hand into his. 'Simon, darling, I love you and I always will.' The first time she has ever told him this and not even knowing if he can hear her.

The nurses sending her home at three in the morning. The phone ringing minutes later to say he's had a massive haemorrhage and will not last the night. Rushing back to the hospital, the baby in the carry cot, tearing through the rain-drenched streets at ninety miles an hour, blinded by tears, screeching at the top of her voice *No No No* until she almost collapses at the wheel –

Julia pushed the memory from her mind. Now was what mattered. The present, not the past. The money Smith was demanding was probably more than the bank would lend her, but she had to try. If that failed she'd be forced to ask Ben to help since he was the only other trustee.

But after Friday night she was hardly in a position to ask Ben for any personal favours. From now on their partnership would continue on a strictly business basis. Besides, there'd be too many questions and she couldn't risk getting trapped into telling him why she needed the money.

For a moment she stood outside Nicky's room, her teeth tightly clenched. She would have to work out which was the greater risk: not paying the money and risking an attack on Nicky, with the added risk of life-shattering, career-ending media headlines . . . or confiding in Ben.

Getting the money, but running the risk of him telling the police she was being blackmailed. Which would amount to the same thing.

It was ludicrous to even ask herself the question.

She could do neither.

But somehow she had to get the money.

Tip-toeing into Nicky's room, her eyes lingered on her daughter. She would die if anything happened to her. The thick lined curtains were closed and although the night light was still on she could see no sign of Duchess. Gingerly she lifted the sheet, and there she was a snowy white bundle moulded in the space between Nicky's chest and arm.

The puppy had been a stroke of genius. Nicky had adored Duke but his muddy paws and slobbering jowls had not exactly fed the child's need for make-believe motherhood and cuddly companionship. Whereas already Duchess was filling the roles of playmate, baby doll, sister and anything else for which Nicky felt a burning hunger, and had miraculously dulled the pain of losing Duke.

The abandoned tutu and the pink ballet shoes lay on the chair next to the bed. The Swan Lake CD was on the pillow. She touched her daughter's cheek, then gently prised the warm, floppy puppy from its nest. For a moment she held it close, breathing in its puppy smell. She closed her eyes as she stroked its fluffy coat. No wonder Nicky loved it.

She carried it to the basket in the kitchen and covered it up. Then she changed her mind. She picked it up again, pulled out a chair and sat down at the old oak table with the puppy on her lap. With Nicky in bed so early, the house seemed outlandishly large. In the window she could see its silence and its loneliness stretching down a long bare tunnel to nowhere. She cradled the puppy in both her hands. She was desperate to tell someone, to share her ordeal with some other human being. Maybe if I do, she thought, it would help to sort it out, help me to decide what to do.

But there was no one she could tell.

Before going to bed she thought she really should return Paul's phone calls. But Paul was the most perceptive man she knew and might detect in her voice guilty traces of this afternoon's escapade. He would ask where she'd been and why. Better to wait till tomorrow. By tomorrow she will at least have become more used to the ghoulishness of having roamed around Moss Side on her own looking for ammunition, and would be better able to tell the necessary lie.

Gently she lowered the puppy into Duke's basket, then dragged herself upstairs. Half an hour after getting into bed she sat up with a start, her book across her chest, the bedside light still on. She could hear Nicky's voice but not what she was saying, and there was another sound.

A scraping scratching sound. Something being scraped against metal.

She got out of bed and stood at the window. A cool breeze sent a shiver down her back. What does an old Volvo sound like in the middle of the night, she wondered. Would I recognise it in this eerie yellow light, or would it look like all the other cars that pass this way?

She ran to Nicky's room. The light from the passage threw a beam across the bed.

'I'm cold, Mummy,' Nicky said when she saw Julia. 'Where's Duchess?'

The scraping noise was louder here.

'She's tucked up in her basket, darling.'

She walked to the window. She pulled the curtain back and held her breath as she scanned the garden. The breeze rustled the trees. And then she saw it, an overhanging branch scraping the metal gutter.

She hurried to Nicky's bedside as though someone was right behind her. On a sudden impulse she pulled back the bedclothes and slipped in beside her daughter. 'Go back to sleep, my love. You'll see Duchess in the morning.'

'I wish you would always sleep with me, Mummy.'

It's strange having another human being so close to me, Julia thought as memories of long ago snaked into her consciousness.

My brother's arms. His warmth. His voice soft and soothing. The accusations. The separate rooms. The cold and the crying. And then the creaking floor, the chink of light, the sickly smell of chocolates, switching on the lamp, the weight on the bed . . . the hands . . .

A little whimpering sound jolted her from the jagged memories. Nicky was crying. 'What is it, my darling?'

'I want Duke, Mummy.'

Slowly, inch by inch, she placed her arm around her daughter. She snuggled closer. Soon the crying stopped. Why have I never done this before, she wondered, letting the warmth flow between them, listening to the slow, even breathing.

And to the scraping noise outside.

Would Smith try breaking in a second time? Could he pull it off again with the house across the road bulging with armed police, their instruments of detection beamed on every corner of this house?

Goose pimples stole across her arms and without rationalising her thoughts she made up her mind.

She kissed Nicky's forehead, then crept out of bed.

She peered at her watch.

Ten o'clock.

The timing was perfect.

Half an hour to get Wendy installed over here.

Half an hour to drive to Moss Side. And meet Charlie at Sweet Cherry.

- 30 -

Julia drove slowly down the dimly lit street, her eyes flicking left to right, watching for anything suspicious. Lights flashed behind her and the next moment a black Audi came alongside her and hooted. Hardly breathing, she pulled into the curb.

'Think you own the joint, eh?' the driver yelled, then moved on with a look that epitomised the futility of mindless road rage, but nevertheless sent Julia's pulse racing.

Sweet Cherry was in the basement of an old Victorian house set back from the road about fifty yards away. That much she knew. It would be sensible to walk from here rather than leave her car in full

130

view of patrons who might be anyone from clients to police. She got out and locked the car.

Walking past a graffiti-covered house, its walls flush with the pavement, she heard a woman scream. She looked up at the chinks of light in the boarded-up building. There was absolutely nothing she could do to help. She walked on, feeling the agony of abandoning someone in need.

The twisted blackened wreck of a burnt-out car lay half across the pavement. Fumes of smouldering rubber stung her nostrils. A group of Rastas with long matted hair and bubble hats stood laughing and gloating and puffing at their cigarettes. As she walked past the wreck, their eyes glinted like chips of black ice.

She quickened her pace. A minute later she was outside Sweet Cherry.

As she stepped through the door, Paul's words flashed into her mind. 'When I was an inspector I often had to go into shady third-rate clubs,' he'd told her once, 'and they'd say, Hello boss. Wanna a piece o' chicken? But I tell you what, you had to watch yourself or you'd get a knife in your back. I've been in there and my hair has curled up at the ends.' All right for you, Paul Moxon, Julia thought. You're six foot tall and rippling with muscle, trained for the job.

Cautiously she ventured down the dark, uncarpeted stairs. A smell of mould and rot took her breath away. A group of leather jackets leaned on the crumbling banisters. Three or four wolf whistles pierced her ears.

'Show us ya legs, lady. Right ta the top.'

She pressed her shoulder blades together and carried on.

Beyond the door the beat of Reggae throbbed. She lifted her chin and walked in. She had to look as though she was used to doing this.

She made her way across the threadbare carpet embedded with years of food and drink and heaven knows what else. It felt as though her shoes had Bluetack on the soles.

Here the smell was worse. Stale beer. Bodies. Tobacco. And the heavy unmistakable aroma of cannabis.

Everyone in the room stopped talking. She looked around. No

Charlie Kuma. She glanced at her watch. Five to eleven. There was one empty table near the bar.

The barman's eyes narrowed with suspicion. Whispering something to two women slouched over the bar counter, he slowly took the cigarette from his lips.

'What'll ya have?'

Gingerly she sat down. The chairs were filthy too. 'I'm waiting for a friend,'

'Chicken patty? Pasty?'

'No thanks,' she said. They only sold food to get a licence to stay open late. It could be a week old for all she knew.

She peered around the room. Two bare light bulbs hung at each end on greasy strands of flex, lighting up the peeling walls stained yellow with nicotine.

At the next table a short, thickset man sat drinking beer from a can, tapping his foot in time to the music. He moved his chair closer to hers. Flicking his ash on the floor his eyes moved slowly down her body.

'Not seen you in here before.'

She crossed her legs. These were the people of the night, a different breed of people, the dregs of the community. They would stay here till daybreak. Take whatever they could. Whenever they could. However they could.

She edged her chair away. 'It's my first time,' she said, looking pointedly at her watch. Charlie's wife had not really known he would be here. She'd give him another five minutes, and then she'd go.

'Stood you up, has he?'

Julia shook her head, but said nothing. She turned her back to the man and faced the bar.

The two women pointed at her and laughed, their hips swinging to the beat of the music. The taller one stepped towards her, put one hand on her hip and cocked her head sideways. 'What business you got here?'

Everyone was staring at her now. One man stood up and pushed through the tables towards her. His fingers curled around a thick gold chain hanging over his embossed satin jacket. 'Looking for somethin'?'

132

Julia looked at her watch again. 'I'm waiting for a friend.'

'Oh, yeah.' Gold Chain took another step towards her. Someone turned down the music. 'What you doin' in here?' he said.

The man at the next table moved closer too. 'You heard him. Why you here?'

And then she saw him, walking to the bar with that mop of wild, woolly hair.

'Charlie.'

He swung round. 'Julia! Hey man, it is you. What you doing here?'

Gold Chain quickly slunk away.

She gulped with relief, hardly able to speak because of the fear in her throat. 'Looking for you, of course.'

'I ain't done nothin'.'

'I know.' She liked to think the hours she'd spent counselling him had something to do with that, though she wasn't naive enough to think he'd never go down the same road again. She flashed him what she thought would look like a smile of approval. 'I just want to talk to you.' He pulled out a chair and sat down next to her.

'How d'ya know where to find me?'

'I went to your house. Your wife said you'd be here.'

'She's not my wife no more. Them kids ain't even mine.'

'I'm here to ask a favour.'

He looked at her with screwed-up eyes and lips flattened in a line. 'You in some trouble then?'

'Yes. But I'm hoping you can help me.'

'Tables turned, eh, Julia?' His eyes burned with curiosity. 'I'll help you. If I can.'

Charlie was one of those criminals she suspected only did what he was doing because he knew no other way to make a living. Not a breath of viciousness in him. A bit like Joe Sagoe. A rogue. A criminal, yes. But in a strange way, charming with it.

'Can we go somewhere private?' she asked. 'Everyone's looking at me.'

'No wonder, Julia. You stand out. You're different. Your skin, your hair, your clothes.' He looked approvingly at her cream jeans and sweatshirt. 'And they're curious, this lot. They wanna know why you're here.' He lifted his eyebrows. 'But don't let 'em bother you. They won't do nothin'. How can I help?'

Just then someone turned the music up. Just as well, considering what she was about to ask him.

She leaned towards him. 'I need ammunition.'

He sucked his lower lip. His eyes flicked away from her, then flicked back again, and in that moment she saw a ray of hope.

'D'you know where I can get some?'

He stared vacantly across the room.

'You must know, Charlie. All your friends have guns.' And so did he, she was sure.

His eyes darted back to her, then down to the floor. Staccato movements, following the beat of the music.

'Charlie? Please. I'm not going to kill anyone, I promise, but I need to have it.'

His jaw moved sideways as he ground his teeth together. She saw the shifty look she'd seen before in scores of criminals' eyes. I'm mad to throw myself on his mercy, she told herself.

And then she thought of Sam Smith. He would stop at nothing to get what he wanted.

'Charlie? Where can I get some slugs?'

'I dunno,' he muttered, still looking at the floor.

'Please,' she said, watching every flicker of his eyelids. 'I'm not trying to catch you out. Honest. You know you can trust me.'

He shook his head. 'Sorry, Julia.'

'Someone is threatening my child, Charlie. I need it, just to scare him off.'

He shrugged, and she wondered if he'd guessed who it was that needed scaring off.

'Look, Charlie. I've helped you in the past and I'll help you again.' She could hear the desperation mounting in her voice and vowed to stay calm.

He shook his head again.

She breathed out and closed her eyes. What now? Just get up and walk out? Come on, you can do better than that. 'Then just tell me who else I can ask,' she said, hoping this would make him weaken.

He glanced at her, looked down again.

Oh God. He really isn't going to help me . . .

Then slowly he looked up. His chin sank onto his chest, and in that split second she knew she'd won him over.

She moved her chair closer. If I have to, I'll go down on my knees rather than lose him now. 'Please, Charlie, it's terribly important.'

He put his head in his hands, baring his teeth. He'd always done that when he was struggling for the right words. Julia waited, not moving, listening to the drum beats inside her chest. Charlie glanced up at the ceiling and then raked his thick square hands through his hair.

'Okay,' he said. 'I'll try. What's the gun?'

Quickly she opened her handbag. After one look he nodded. From her jeans pocket she took a bundle of tightly folded notes and pressed them into his hand. 'I'd rather nobody else knew about this,' she said.

'No worries, Julia.'

She looked at him and smiled. She put her hand in her pocket again, raised her eyebrows and kept her hand there until she was sure he'd seen the gesture.

'Can't promise,' he said. 'But be here same time tomorrow night. Okay?'

Monday was always a bad day and this week it would be extra bad, especially with the Longdale murder trial starting on Tuesday morning and so much preparation still to do. She thought of Nicky. 'Yes,' she said. 'Tomorrow night.'

She took a tissue from her pocket. Charlie frowned. His hands reached out towards her and then quickly he withdrew them. That's incredible, she thought, seeing Charlie's eyes misting over. I do believe he would like to comfort me, if only he knew how.

'Look, Julia. You done good for me. You want some sod killed, you tell me, okay?'

'I don't want anyone killed. And I would never get you involved.' She smiled. 'But thanks all the same.'

'For Chrissake. I bet you don't even know how to use that fucking gun.'

'I told you, I don't want to kill anyone. Just scare them off. But — ' She clutched at the loose material of her sweatshirt. 'Could you show me how to use it?'

He stood up and walked her to the door. 'I'll show you tomorrow night,' he said.

Outside in the street Julia tilted her head backwards, letting the rain run down her face, letting it soak her hair and her clothes and mix with her tears.

MONDAY

Leaving the Mini idling, Wendy leapt out and opened the gates to Hillside House, wincing as the metal scraped against the round polished cobbles. In the last few days ordinary sounds like this had made the nausea even worse, especially this early in the morning.

As she ran up the front steps, Julia was at the door to greet her. 'Would you mind closing the gates please, Wendy. I've got the kettle on.'

That meant — I want to talk to you, Wendy thought as she hurried down the drive to do as she'd been asked. Something must be wrong. Usually Julia was happy to have the gates left open to drive her swish red Merc out once Wendy had arrived. And tea with Julia this early meant serious business. She wondered what she had done wrong. She felt part of this family, always had, right from when her mother had been housekeeper to old Mrs Grant. She couldn't imagine being dismissed. Maybe Julia had just received the phone bill and seen the huge number of calls to Alan. She couldn't know how much trouble she was having with him and that keeping in touch by phone was vital, especially when she was as desperate as she was now. It was time she bought a mobile phone but they were so expensive and she was saving all her spare money for the furniture, once Alan agreed to a house. If he ever did.

'Sit down, please, Wendy.'

She sat down at the kitchen table and watched Julia stir her sugarless tea. She noted the dark circles under the eyes, no doubt a result of working late last night. She envied the way Julia could always look so chic in spite of her long straight hair and never going to the hairdresser. And the way she could wear the plainest dress as though it came from those catwalks on the telly.

At last Julia looked up. The skin was taut across her high cheek bones and her big blue eyes wide open, almost as though she was purposely removing all emotion from her face. 'I'm worried, Wendy,' she said. 'Crime is increasing in Wilmslow. Houses like ours the target. Youngsters on drugs looking for small, expensive items. Money. Jewellery.'

Wendy nodded. Poor Julia. Obviously upset, but it was impossible to tell what she was really thinking. A strange woman. So cool. But then, in her job she must be able to keep a straight face, even though she dealt with things far worse than dead dogs. She remembered the day Julia got married to Mister Simon. The reception was here at Hillside House, when Mr and Mrs Grant were still alive, flowers everywhere, a big marquee in the garden. Not once did she see Julia touch Simon's hand. Or kiss him, not even when they were dancing. She was like that with Nicky too.

Julia put down her cup and took a deep breath. 'So from now on, Wendy,' she said, slowly like, as though she had all the time in the world yet wasn't quite sure what she was going to say, 'we must all take extra precautions.'

Wendy nodded. She could see Julia wasn't finished, and it was obvious she needed to talk. So she poured another cup of tea while she waited for her to carry on. She wanted Julia to feel she was here for her because there didn't seem to be anyone else she could talk to so openly, except perhaps the superintendent.

'You see, that break-in has brought home to me how vulnerable we all are,' Julia said at last. 'Nicky will have to be guarded even more carefully than she is now.'

'But Julia, she's never out on her own.'

Julia shook her head. 'No, Wendy,' she said. 'I don't mean that. I mean we must never take our eyes off her. Not for a single moment.'

Wendy stared at her. 'I can understand you being worried. But when she's not at school I'm always with her. Nothing will ever happen to Nicky. I can promise that.'

But Julia wasn't listening. 'We can't afford to take any chances. From now on we'll keep the gate closed, the outside doors locked. Nicky must never, never be out of your sight.'

Wendy gulped. 'But she's never on her own as it is.'

'I know, Wendy.' Julia's voice softened and for a moment she actually smiled. 'But there've been some dreadful incidents recently. I've written to Miss Haydock about extra precautions at the school.' She pointed to a sealed white envelope on the table.

Wendy squinted at Julia. The kids at St Mary's were never allowed out of the grounds. And with that new high fence, all this seemed a bit over the top. Duke's death was a tragedy, but this was not like Julia at all.

'And if you go shopping, please don't leave Nicky in the car. I want you with her every moment. I want you to hold her hand.'

Wendy felt a surge of pity for her employer. She had everything that money could buy, yet this one break-in seemed to have got to her in a big way.

But who was she to argue? A little extra care and attention wouldn't be any hardship, though she wasn't sure it was a very healthy move. Children needed some space of their own. That's what Julia had always said in the past, and one day, if she was lucky, that's what Wendy would like for her children too.

'Nicky's dressed and ready to go,' Julia said. 'She's upstairs with Duchess.' It seemed as though she was trying hard to smile, sort of forced, like everything else about her this morning. 'But don't drop her off too early. And park your car as near the gates as possible. And walk with her until you hand her over to one of the teachers.'

'Sure. Don't you worry. Anybody touches her they won't know what hit them. I don't have a black belt for nothing, you know.'

Wendy couldn't believe she'd actually said that. Her black belt status had never been discussed before but she'd always known instinctively that Julia felt her precious only daughter was in the best possible hands. So why not rub it in, if it helped to make Julia feel safer.

She reached over the table and pressed her hand on Julia's. For a moment she thought she saw a tear in the corner of her eye, but she must have been mistaken. Julia Grant wasn't the crying kind. She was as tough as they make them, like she had an invisible shield to hide her feelings.

'I'm thinking of doing that self-protection class at the fitness club you told me about,' Julia said as she stood up to go. 'Oh, and Wendy, you might wait outside the school for a few minutes after you've dropped her off. Just to make sure she's safe.'

Wendy watched the kitchen door swing backwards and forwards on its springs. She couldn't bear the thought of a life like Julia's. On her own. Scared stiff. Bringing up her kid without a father.

As soon as she heard the front door close she reached for the phone. She might catch Alan before he went out on his first plumbing calls, and then on the way back from dropping Nicky off she'd pop into Boots for the pregnancy test. Just to make absolutely sure.

- 32 -

Paul looked up from his Monday morning pile of mail. Most force problems were well sifted before they reached his desk but he still needed to know about them. And operational planning and policy decisions were not things that could be hurried.

'Sit down, Kevin. The trace on Julia Grant's phone. Anything come up yet?'

'Nothing, boss. You'll be the first to know. But shouldn't we cover her office phones as well?'

'Smith knows there'd be her PA to go through first so he's more likely to try her home number. There's nothing private about that. She dishes out cards to every blasted criminal she sees. Besides, she's hardly ever in the office.'

'And her mobile?'

'Too often switched off. And for some reason she doesn't make it public.'

'Right, boss.'

Keeping his promise to Julia, Paul had decided to keep to himself the details of Julia's phone call on Saturday night. Normally he would relay such information to Kevin who would plan his strategy accordingly. While acknowledging her request that no one else should be told in view of the potential danger to Nicky if indiscriminate vigilance were openly exercised, in the light of Avril's murder he hoped to intensify the hunt for Smith and step up discreet protection for Julia, although it was difficult to know what more to do without her permission. Several times he'd been on the point of organising her phone to be tapped, but each time something held him back.

He'd been shocked by her revelations. The audacity of the man incensed him. To twist the likes of Joe Sagoe round his little finger not only to fix his escape but also to track every detail of Julia's life. To have entered her home undetected, shot her dog and then demanded two-fifty grand or he'd harm Nicky. That made his blood boil.

'By the way, boss, Sagoe swears he wasn't driving the van. They were wearing masks so the witness could have been mistaken. Unfortunately he's not the only grossly fat man in Manchester.'

'Damn.' Paul rattled his fingers on the desk. 'What about prints?'

'Gloves.'

'Of course.' Paul's lip curled with rage.

'Sagoe's still in custody at Greenheys, boss. Can't hold him any longer without a charge. Says it was coincidence Smith was near his house when Avril was shot. Says he hadn't been home for days. Could be true. But he's always a tough nut to crack. Never says a word.'

'Well, if we don't get a confession today, we can always pick him up again. Tell me as soon as you hear anything.'

Just then Paul's phone rang. 'I'll get back to you later, Kev.'

Kevin walked to the door. 'I'll be at the incident room, boss.'

Paul nodded then picked up the receiver.

'Morning, Sir.' It was Ann Forrest's voice, secretary to Bill Brownlow, Assistant Chief Constable, Crime. His immediate boss.

'Morning, Ann.'

'He wants to see you, Sir. Can you come up?'

Paul looked at his watch. Eight-thirty. Strange. His regular meetings with the ACC were always at nine.

He groaned at his overflowing in-basket, then drained the last drop of cold coffee, wondering what was on Bill Brownlow's mind. He knew the ACC well and had an uncomfortable gut feeling of what it might be about.

He made for the stairs. Walking to the top floor would be good exercise and also give him a chance to formulate his reply to his boss.

The door to Ann's outer office was wide open, as usual. She smiled. 'Go on in and take a seat. He's on the phone, but won't be long.'

Paul dropped his shoulders, knocked gently and walked in.

- 33 -

The Assistant Chief Constable motioned Paul to sit down. He was still on the phone, his back to the window, his face in darkness. Paul always felt at a disadvantage coming into this office with the glare of the light, and sometimes the sun, full in his face.

Through the window he could see Old Trafford cricket ground, the distinctive redbrick pavilion, the immaculate oval surrounded by tiered stands. Beyond it lay the vast suburban criss-cross of Stretford and Sale, with Cheshire's emerald green hills rolling into the distance.

He glanced at the ACC's solemn face, the astute brown eyes, the broad intelligent forehead. The experienced cop with a good dry sense of humour.

The ACC put down the phone. 'How are things, Paul?'

'Not bad, Sir.'

'Anything further on Smith?'

'No joy yet. But it's early days.'

Bill Brownlow pursed his lips. Like everyone else in the force it was obvious he was not only saddened by Avril's death, he was enraged.

Paul ran his forefinger under his collar. 'But if I've got nothing in forty-eight hours, Sir, I'll begin to worry.'

The ACC looked long and hard at Paul. In that instant Paul knew he'd been right. Bill Brownlow knew about Julia.

'Paul, I hear whispers that your involvement with this is more than professional. Are the whispers correct?'

Paul looked straight into Bill Brownlow's eyes. He had always appreciated the direct approach. It was the method he himself employed. However, he didn't run murders any more. Normally he wouldn't be dealing with such a case. His job entailed decision making and co-ordinating at a high level and was mostly administrative. He had

142

two detective superintendents reporting to him. As detective chief super in charge of operations, his was essentially the watching brief, unless something catastrophic happened. On the big scale, Smith's escape and the murder of a police officer were hardly in the catastrophic category. Prisoners did sometimes escape, and sadly officers were vulnerable to attack, but clearly Bill would know that as far as Paul was concerned personally, Smith's threat to Julia and his killing of Avril had put this case well and truly in the catastrophic category.

'Yes, Sir. They are.'

It never ceased to amaze Paul how everybody else always seemed to know more about your private life than you did. Until this weekend he had never formulated his relationship with Julia, had never considered her his woman. From the start he'd known there were too many professional variances, although she attracted him more than any woman ever had.

'What is the position, Paul?'

'Well, first of all, Sir, if I'm involved with a case in which Mrs Grant also has an interest, then my dealings with her are at a professional level.'

'I'm sure they are.' The lines on Bill Brownlow's forehead deepened. 'But you work on opposite sides of the fence, Paul.'

'Not really. I'm doing my job, she's doing hers. She's very good at her job and I have a great deal of respect for her, although I can't say the same for all the criminal solicitors I know. But at the end of the day we both want to see justice done.'

Put on the spot like this, he was surprising even himself with his impromptu appraisal of his friendship with Julia.

'Yes, but there's a difference, Paul, isn't there? Say you have a man you consider guilty of an offence. You've put together evidence and the Crown Prosecution Service has decided there's a case to answer. Mrs Grant might be representing that man, and it's up to her to see if she can get her client off. However, my question was not in fact relating to your professional relationship with Mrs Grant, as I'm sure you realise.' His eyebrows lifted, indicating that it was now over to Paul.

Paul cleared his throat and did his best to relax the muscles in his neck. 'I've known Mrs Grant for some years, Sir, but our – our relationship, as you refer to it, is by no means consolidated.'

'I presume you mean that your intentions are serious but that Mrs Grant's are not.'

The ACC was a shrewd man. He didn't miss much. 'That's about it, Sir. She's – '

'Playing hard to get?' A touch of a smile softened one side of Bill Brownlow's face.

This whole conversation was putting ideas into Paul's head. Wasn't it about time he made a positive move to put their friendship on a more intimate level?

'Not exactly. I see her often. We have outings together. Concerts, picnics with her daughter. If I could, I'd . . . well . . .'

Paul thought his boss was going to finish this sentence for him too, but instead Bill Brownlow brushed his moustache with his fingers and straightened his face. 'What I have to consider now, Paul, is whether someone else should take over the major responsibility for the recapture of this man. It could go back to Kevin Moorsley.'

Paul was pleased he had his reply on the tip of his tongue. 'Sir, it still is Kevin's case. But I know this man Smith. I've been involved with him for years and I'm not going to let him slip through the net again. And even though I am emotionally involved, to a limited degree, I would ask for the opportunity to continue on the case.'

'Emotions are very powerful things, Paul. You're angry about Avril Scott. You're concerned about the safety of Mrs Grant, doubled the surveillance on her home, put a trace on her phones. We don't know what will happen next. You might have to do certain other things that could be hurtful to her. It's difficult to make professional decisions during a time of emotional stress.'

'I know that, Sir.' The ACC didn't know the half of it.

'Say for instance, Paul, that someone dear to you has been murdered and I'm in charge of the case. It could be that the suspect wouldn't be treated as fairly as he might be, because my strong emotions would be involved in the decision making.' He paused, lowering his head but keeping his gaze fixed on Paul. 'Have you made professional decisions regarding Mrs Grant only because they were necessary?'

Paul felt his anger rising. 'Yes, of course they were necessary. We have a duty to protect the public.'

'Or did you make them because you were being over protective towards her? The two things could clash, you know. I'm not saying they do. But they could. And your concern could become greater as Smith becomes more desperate. We both know you make decisions to protect what is most important to you. And they might not always be the right decisions as far as your job is concerned.'

Paul drew himself up in his chair. 'It's unthinkable that I would let my involvement impair my professional judgment, Sir.'

'Okay, Paul. I accept that. Carry on with the case.' He leaned towards Paul. 'But, I'm relying on your professional ability and judgment. You'll know when you're getting too involved. And that is the time you'll come and see me.'

'Yes, Sir.'

'We understand one another, Paul?'

He had a sudden image of Julia. Her flowing blonde hair, her smile. Her intense blue eyes. Her calm well-modulated voice with its velvety tones. Her vulnerability in spite of that tough outer facade . . .

'Right on the line, Sir.'

Paul walked slowly down the stairs to his office. He sat down at his desk and wiped the perspiration from his brow. He needed to see Julia. She was the number one known contact. He wondered fleetingly whether Bill Brownlow had been right, whether his obsessive concern for Julia was potentially obstructive. He knew only too well that it was the classic conflict the ACC had alluded to. It was important to recapture Smith without delay, but equally important to him that Julia and Nicky were not exposed to danger. Especially now, with all the added complications.

He picked up his phone and dialled Julia's number at Lloyd Grant.

- 34 -

Julia rested her elbows on her desk, her head in her hands. A quarter of a million pounds was a huge amount of money. Money she didn't have. She reminded herself that there were only two ways she could try to raise it, a bank loan or the money held in trust for Nicky. Both had little chance of success.

John Cartwright had been bank manager to the Grant family for many years, but getting a further loan on top of the massive one she'd recently raised when they opened another Lloyd Grant branch in Longsight, would be a tricky one. No amount of Cartwright's smarmy charm could mask the fact that he was bound by rules and regulations, and yet Julia with her faith in human nature couldn't help hoping their long association just might dip the weights in her direction.

She dialled his number. 'I'm afraid he's not in yet,' his secretary said. 'Can I help?'

'It's a personal matter,' she replied. 'And very urgent. A matter of — I mean, could you please ask him to ring me as soon as he arrives.'

She gave her the numbers and rang off. It was five past nine. Smith had said he wanted the cash at eleven. Even if Cartwright phoned back in time there was only the slimmest chance he would lend her the money and getting it by eleven would be well-nigh impossible. Smith had not phoned with instructions for the pay-off. He wouldn't risk phoning the office. He'd guess she'd be in court by ten, so how on earth would he arrange the rendezvous? And would she have to hand over the money to a man with a red carnation in his lapel at the top of the Town Hall steps or leave it in a litter bin behind the Bridgewater?

She tipped the entire contents of her personal file onto her desk and dug out the papers relating to the funds held in trust for Nicky.

Trusts were not Julia's line of business. Never had been. But one thing she did know was that trusts were watertight: the money could not be paid out to Nicky before her eighteenth birthday. Unless . . .

Unless what? Perhaps I could ask Ben, she thought. If I can ever bring myself to speak to him again. He might think of a legitimate loophole to release the money. But only as a last resort, because then she'd have to tell him why she needed it so desperately and she couldn't take that risk. He — even more than Paul — was capable of prising from her the monstrous event in her childhood that Smith accused her of, that even now, after twenty-six years, she still could not remember, and most of the time doubted it could ever have happened.

Her phone rang. She grabbed the receiver, willing it to be John Cartwright. It was her personal assistant.

'Yes, Linda?'

'There was a call for you, Julia. I didn't get his name but he said he couldn't hold on and would you phone him back. Said it was important and you'd know what it was about. Shall I get the number for you now?'

'Give me the number, please Linda, and I'll get it myself.'

Surely it couldn't be Smith, boldly giving a number to ring him back. But who else would not have given his name? She took a large swallow of her tea, then dialled.

'You thought I'd forgotten, didn't you, Julia?'

The lean bearded face with the piercing blue eyes that were so alien yet so familiar swam into her vision. 'Look,' she said, closing her eyes tightly. 'It'll be difficult to get my hands on the kind of money you're demanding. If you still want to proceed with this madness you'll have to give me a little more time.'

It wouldn't do to try to talk him out of it, she told herself. I must keep him thinking he will get what he wants, that he has me in his power. If he thinks he's losing control there's no knowing what he'll do. Even if he is who I think he might be, as far as he's concerned it's obvious there is no love lost between us.

She heard a long sigh followed by short rasping breaths. 'Don't fuck me around, Julia. Where's the loot from Grant Estate Agents? I don't want it all. Just a measly fucking two-fifty grand. Don't you think I deserve it?'

She had no idea how to answer that. And what would Paul say if he knew what she was doing? Even she knew it was madness but what else could she do?

A noise like a tidal wave roared through her ears. I must cool it or he'll sense how powerless I am, and use this to add to his strength.

'You're crazy,' she said. She no longer cared about the decorum she normally maintained between solicitor and client. 'I told you, it's tied up in trust for my daughter.'

'You're a lawyer for fuck's sake. *Do* something about it.'

Perhaps I can appeal to the other side of his unhinged personality, she thought.

'I need time,' she said, toning down her anger. 'Certain procedures have to be followed. You must be patient. It might even be impossible to obtain the money from this particular source. I don't know yet.'

'Then it's fucking time you did.'

'Look, Sam —'

'I'm not taking any bloody excuses.'

'It's only just gone nine o'clock. Most banks don't get going until around ten. I've phoned once but —'

'Don't give me that crap. No excuses. Just the money. I must get out of the country. I didn't have your luck, Julia. And to refresh your memory —'

'It does not need refreshing,' she said. 'Listen. If you give yourself up now you'd have a far better chance of leniency. I'll help you. I promise.'

Is this me speaking? Help him? When I don't even know for sure who he is.

'Don't make me laugh, rich bitch. Don't insult my intelligence. With a quarter million smackers I can go anywhere. Be anyone. Do anything. Why would I choose to rot in Strangeways?'

'In the end you won't have a choice,' she said evenly. His burst of laughter told her she was wasting her time. If only John Cartwright would phone back . . .

She had a sudden thought. 'Will you hold on a few moments.' It was taking a chance but she had no option. She had to try everything.

'Don't try anything funny, Julia. You know what'll happen, don't you?'

She pressed the mute button. 'Linda,' she yelled down the passage. 'If Mr Cartwright phones please tell me at *once*. Don't let him ring off, whatever you do.'

As she got back to Smith she heard a distinct running-out-of-patience sigh. 'I'm doing everything I can to get the money,' she said, glad that he couldn't see the look of despair on her face.

'Okay,' he said. Then silence. 'One week today, Julia. Not one sodding minute longer. And that's more than you deserve. '

She breathed out slowly. One whole week. But I must not become complacent. A week could flash by in no time at all.

'I'll phone you every day to remind you. And remember, Mrs Smartarse Solicitor, if you breathe a word to anyone I'll know about it and you won't like the consequences. And I forgot to tell you. Just in case I run out of money to phone the police about what you did, I've written it all out, put it in an envelope with a stamp on it all ready to post if I have to, and oh, how thoughtless of me, I almost forgot to ask how Nicky is.'

Julia dug her fingernails into her scalp. 'She's — '

'No. On second thoughts, don't bother,' he said. 'When I saw her this morning she was just fine. I thought she was going to be late for school but the little yellow Mini arrived just in time. My mates were right. She looks real cute in that blue skirt and pink blouse. Lovely school, St Mary's. Pity 'bout the high fence and the barbed wire, though. Makes it look like a fucking prison, doesn't it?'

Julia opened her mouth to speak but he had gone. She replaced the receiver, and when a moment later it rang again, she almost leapt off her chair.

'Another call, Julia,' Linda said. 'DS Moxon from Chester House.'

'I'm due in court at ten and I haven't even opened my mail yet. Tell him I'll ring him this afternoon.'

'He's been holding on. Says it's urgent.'

'Okay. Put him on.'

'And Ben's free now,' Linda added quickly. 'He wants to see you before you go. About the Longdale case.'

'Thanks.'

She took a few deep breaths, inhaling slowly and letting out the air even slower, until she felt so light-headed she was ready to lie down on the carpet and go to sleep until this whole ghastly nightmare had ended. The thought of talking to Ben so soon after Friday night made her shudder, but she'd have to break the ice some time in order to ask him about the trust. She rubbed her neck and shoulders with her fingers, pressing the small painful balls of muscle until they felt like steel nails digging into her. She still had to sort out the urgent mail and give Linda instructions about what to do with it. Everything else could await her return, whenever the hell that was going to be. It's time Mark, or even Caroline Ross took over some of my workload, she thought. She's been with the firm three years now. Can never be faulted on a point of law but shuns a relatively simple bail application in a magistrate's court. Damn her.

She picked up the receiver.

'Hello, Paul. Sorry I didn't get back to you last night.'

There was a slight pause while she listened to him breathing. She knew that Paul only did that when he wanted to impress on her that he would not be inclined to take any of her excuses. 'I understand,' he said. 'But we have a lot to talk about.' His voice was cool and businesslike. And then it softened. 'How are you?' he asked.

'Fine,' she said, with equal restraint, 'apart from missing Duke.' She was far from fine and didn't think she ever would be again. Never before had she been so confused. On the one hand, she told herself, I know Smith should be apprehended as soon as possible, but on the other . . .

'I know you're in a hurry, but I wanted to remind you that BT have re-programmed your home phone with the Malicious Call intercept mechanism. If Smith phones just press digit number one and the call will show up on BT's computer.'

'And by the time you get there Sam Smith is five miles away.' She hadn't meant to sound sarcastic, but Smith was far too clever to fall into such a simple trap.

'We can set up hidden cameras in the booths he uses. If he phoned often enough a pattern could emerge. We'd then have the booths watched. Of course he might have a mobile.'

'No, he hasn't. I could tell it was a public phone he was calling from. Anyway, all this is academic,' Julia said. 'He might use different call boxes every time. We don't even know if he'll phone.' She crossed her fingers. Am I obstructing the law?

150

'We have to try everything, Julia. He has killed a policewoman.'

She heard the tone of exasperation in his voice. 'I know and I'm really sorry, Paul.' She paused and glanced at her watch. 'I must go now.'

'Julia, I need to see you. What about tonight?'

'Oh, I'm afraid I'm tied up tonight.' Her date with Charlie Kuma was only at eleven, but she couldn't take a chance on Paul leaving in time for her to make a ten-thirty start for Sweet Cherry.

'I'll call you tomorrow,' she said.

'We need your help, Julia.'

'Paul, I —'

'Please. This won't take a moment. If you know of anything that might lead us to Smith, I want you to tell me. And the names of any people who might have information. You will tell me, won't you?'

Julia's thoughts ricocheted from one corner of her brain to the other. The less I say the better, she thought. I've already told him enough to make Smith carry out his threats if he finds out. If I could just get the money quickly and pay Smith off, all this would be over. He could leave the country. And disappear from my life forever.

'I'm sure you already have all the names,' she said.

'And Julia, I don't have to spell it out. But you're a prime target.'

But she refused to let him finish. 'It's only the money he wants, Paul.'

'For Chrissake don't give him any money. Don't think you know this man, Julia. I've been dealing with people like this all my life.'

'Paul, I must go. I could meet you at lunchtime tomorrow. If not, then maybe at six-thirty or seven . . .'

'Six-thirty at the Addy,' he said firmly. 'Better than the five minutes you call lunch-time, sitting on those dreadful plastic chairs in the court coffee-room.'

'Okay. I'll ring you if I can't make it.'

She put down the receiver. It was almost nine-thirty. There was still nothing from John Cartwright, so as much as she hated the idea, she would have to talk to Ben. And not just about the Longdale case either.

Julia knocked and walked in before she could change her mind. In one hand she held the trust papers, in the other her briefcase.

Ben glanced up without meeting her eyes, then looked down at his desk.

'You wanted to talk about the Longdale Trial,' she said. 'It begins tomorrow.'

'Refresh my memory.'

There was clearly to be no apology. He sat unsmiling behind his desk. There were none of the usual Monday morning pleasantries, no offer of coffee and clearly no intention of even mentioning Friday night. Julia wished he would. It would clear the air.

She put down her brief case. 'Very briefly then. Jane Longdale sexually abused by her grandfather since she was nine. She's seventeen now. When he goes for her again she picks up a knife from the kitchen table and . . . '

Julia steadied herself on the corner of Ben's desk, grasping the wood as if it was a lifeline and she was drowning.

In the absence of any comment from Ben, she carried on. 'If the jury isn't satisfied that she had the necessary *mens rea*, they must acquit. But even if they decide she did have *mens rea*, provocation may still be a defence to the charge of murder.'

She stopped for a moment, took a deep breath and then carried on. 'His continued sexual abuse caused the girl to have a sudden and temporary loss of self-control.'

She kept her eyes riveted to Ben's face. His lips were tightly pursed. He was looking at the floor.

'It's simply a question of whether Jane was sufficiently provoked,' she went on, pushing aside the images that were intruding with increasing lucidity. 'In my opinion she was. Counsel agrees. The old man's continual advances were unwanted, disgusting and degrading. She's a sensitive, intelligent girl. There was no period of contemplation between the grandfather's final act of abuse and Jane's blind act of desperation. The facts of the case speak for themselves. Any reasonable person in like circumstances would have done the same thing.'

'That's for the jury to decide,' Ben said, still not looking at Julia. 'And there's no need to get so bloody worked up about it.'

She took a long, slow, deep breath. She'd expected his attitude to be cool after Friday night's fiasco, but not outright hostile.

She waited a few moments but there was no change in his attitude. Clearly this would not be a good time to ask him about altering the terms of the trust, but time was not on her side, she knew he was seeing a client in London tomorrow and might be away several days. John Cartwright's decision could take days rather than hours. Her seven days grace could vanish before she could blink an eye. No. I must have my back-up ready, she thought. I must ask Ben now.

'Can I speak to you about a personal matter?'

She saw the lines around his mouth tighten. He must think she was going to bring up Friday night. Slowly he slid the cap on to his gold Parker pen and looked up but not at her.

'Sit down,' he said.

'I know we've never discussed this before . . . ' She cleared her throat, angry with herself for behaving like a suspect who has just been picked up for questioning. 'But as co-trustee of Nicky's trust fund, I would like you to co-operate with me over the question of varying the terms of the trust.'

'Co-operate with you?'

His laugh was bitter, though relief was written all over his face.

'As I recall, Julia, those funds are to be released to Nicky when she's eighteen.'

'We could change the original terms of the trust if — '

'If Nicky were eighteen? Yes, at her discretion of course. But Nicky is not eighteen.'

Julia wanted to scream. 'I know. But something urgent has cropped up.'

'Oh, really?'

'I need two hundred and fifty thousand now.'

'There's no need to shout.'

153

'Well, don't look at me like that. I have twelve years to reimburse the fund before Nicky turns eighteen.'

She thrust the sheaf of parchment in front of Ben. 'Read it,' she said. 'It states clearly that Nicky's grandparents hereby hand over to the three trustees two million five hundred thousand pounds, the net proceeds from the sale of their estate agency business. Charles and Natalie never intended all the money to go to Nicky. You know it has provision to be extended to any other grandchildren.'

'And I don't need to remind you,' Ben said icily, 'that there were not any other Grant grandchildren. Nor will there ever be.'

Julia bit her lip. She and Simon had dreamt of two more.

Ben handed the papers back to her. 'Well, that's the nuts and bolts of it,' he said. 'Apart from the twenty pages of admin rubbish about how we were to invest the money.'

'Could there be a loophole?'

'Because you want the money?'

Her instinct was to walk out now and never come back. But in one way she couldn't really blame him. Her request must seem bizarre. 'I will forget you ever said that. I want to borrow some of it for a very good reason,' she said, fighting to stay calm. 'And I want to pay it back before she's eighteen.'

'Of course. Defaulting trustees always do.' He leaned back in his leather armchair and half closed his eyes. 'Am I hearing you right? A quarter of a million! What on earth for?'

She had thought hard about an excuse that Ben would buy. 'I'm afraid it's . . . personal,' she said at last, knowing how lame that sounded.

'Why can't you tell me?'

'It's a very private matter.'

'And you expect me to break Simon's trust in me to appease some personal whim of yours?'

'It's very important.'

'Okay,' he said, with the same look of petulance Julia had seen on Friday night. 'I think I know.'

For a moment she had a sinking feeling that the game was up. That somehow he had found out about Smith's phone call. But there was no way he could possibly know. She had told no one but Paul. And even he didn't know it all.

'Please, Ben. Please. One day I'll be able to tell you why. But not now.'

'You amaze me. I never thought I'd see the day when you'd let a man like Moxon make you do things you know are wrong. And if you think I'm going to go along with this ludicrous unethical plan so that you and your fancy policeman can — '

She didn't wait for him to finish. Blocking her ears, she fled blindly to the door, necessity making a new plan of action burst crystal clear into her mind.

- 36 -

Pausing just outside the swing doors of court number five, Julia held her mobile phone away from her ear as she imagined Cartwright's grey eyes drawing together with customary precaution.

'Two hundred and fifty thousand, did you say, Julia?'

'Yes, John. Sorry I can't explain right now. I've a case coming up in court in a few moments and I'll have to switch off my phone, but I must have the money by Friday at the very latest.'

For a fleeting illusory moment she thought he was going to say yes. A picture flashed into her mind of stuffing a great mound of notes into a bag and staggering out of the bank. What does a quarter of a million pounds look like in bank notes, she wondered. Did she have a big enough bag? How heavy will it be?

Wishful thinking, Julia. John Cartwright does everything according to the book and he hasn't even asked yet why I need the loan. And if he knew the reason he'd be on to the police even before I ring off.

'In view of existing loans with Hillside House as security,' he said in his usual non-committal tone, 'I don't want to raise your hopes. I'll ring you in a couple of days to arrange a meeting.' And then, in the same light tone, he added, 'Of course, Julia, I'll need to know the reason for the loan and how you intend to repay it.'

155

'It's vital that I get this money, John,' she said quietly. It was important that her bank manager should not sense any panic in her voice. 'But I'm afraid I simply must go now. Duty calls.'

She turned off her mobile and stuffed it into her handbag. She almost wished he'd said no straight away. Now she would have the agony of waiting as each clock-ticking day took her closer and closer to next Monday's deadline.

- 37 -

The courtroom was filling up. People all around her talked in hushed tones. Julia sat down on the far right of the bench and took a file from her briefcase. She would only need to be on her feet for a few minutes, since all she'd be asking for was an adjournment for four weeks and bail for her client.

But at ten past ten there was still no magistrate. Right now the Longdale murder trial was opening in court number one at the Crown Court. She'd told Geoff Atherton she'd be a bit late, but this was ridiculous. Besides, she should also be in court number two where the dreaded Buchan case was continuing.

She stared around the banana yellow walls of the courtroom trying to ward off the growing sense of alarm that was threatening to swamp her. I'm a normal, intelligent woman, she told herself, yet I feel so impotent. Most women have mothers and fathers, husbands or boy friends, someone they can ask for advice. I have nobody. I suppose I could go to David and Jessie. In theory my adoptive parents are the only family I have, apart from Nicky. They still love me, in their quiet, undemonstrative way, but I haven't time to drive to Southport. And if I did, they wouldn't understand my dilemma. I could phone, but that would be even more difficult.

Jessie . . . the conversation would go, if you have five minutes to spare I'd like you to tell me what you think I should do. Well, you see, there's this client of mine. He's as guilty as sin. He thought I would get him off but the jury thought otherwise and now he's got life imprisonment. Then he jolly well deserves it, dear, Jessie would say . . .

156

No. It would never work. Talking to Jessie would only upset her. And David would go straight to the police the moment he thought someone was gunning for her or his darling Nicky.

And who else is there? Someone I could really trust . . .

Ben? In theory, yes, but no chance now.

Wendy? Sweet and helpful and knowledgeable about how to deal with young children. Physically super tough but a little vulnerable perhaps. And no guarantee she would not tell Alan.

Paul?

Yes yes yes!

But he's a policeman.

So what now, she asked herself? As each day dawns those little embers of my memory are continuing to ignite, to skitter around the core of Smith's bizarre accusation, only to fizzle out before I can grasp them. But despite my ongoing amnesia it is perfectly clear to me that Smith is convinced I will give him a quarter million quid to keep quiet about killing my foster father. I don't even remember the man's name. How I wish I could remember. How I wish I knew what I should do.

It's a bit like being lost in the middle of Paris on that enormous roundabout with about ten roads leading off it and not knowing which one is which. You know exactly where you are. You know what you're up against. You know that one road will get you out of Paris.

But you have no idea which is the right one.

- 38 -

As Julia walked down the rat infested stairs she regretted not asking Charlie to meet her somewhere else, anywhere rather than Sweet Cherry. But at least this time he was waiting for her when she arrived.

'There's a room at the back,' he said. 'Let's go.'

The small dim room was even more foul smelling than the main room. Charlie kicked the door closed, then shoved a chair against it. On the one rickety ring-marked table were two glass tankards of ripe-smelling beer that mingled with the putrid stench from the mildewed floorboards to produce an aroma like nothing Julia had ever smelled before.

'Thought you'd like a Red Stripe while we talk business.'

'Thanks.' she gave him an anxious smile. 'Have you got it?'

'Course I have. Sit down.' Charlie's lips tightened across his teeth in a slow smile as he took a small cardboard box out of his anorak pocket and handed it to Julia.

She tensed her muscles to stop her hand from shaking. She took a sip of the lukewarm beer, letting it swirl in her parched mouth before it slid down her throat like warmed-up honey. She opened the box, then reached in her handbag for the gun.

'You haven't a clue, have you, Mrs Solicitor?'

She shook her head and handed the gun to Charlie with the brown plastic handle facing him. 'Never point a gun at anyone,' she said, forcing a laugh as it slipped into his palm.

Charlie grinned. 'It's all right. The safety catch is on. Ready? Okay. Now, hold it like this. To release the magazine, press that button just behind the trigger.'

She did as she was told. Is this really me, she wondered.

'Good. Now load the magazine. Press that button and yank it out. Now slot the slugs into the end of the magazine and push 'em down. Come on. You do it now.'

She pressed the button and pulled out the oily magazine. One by one she inserted the bullets, sliding her fingers over their cold gleaming noses as they slotted in.

'Okay. Now flick up the safety catch with your thumb, slide the magazine in at the bottom end of the butt, and ram it home till it clicks.'

'Is that it, then?' she whispered when she'd finished.

'Yeah. Nothing to it. But you'll have to practice, Julia. You may need to do it quickly. Good. Now let go the slide. There you go. Loaded and cocked.'

'What? No. I can't have a cocked gun in my handbag.' She almost dropped it on the floor as though it was a scorpion about to whip its lethal tail into her finger.

Charlie took the gun from her. 'Okay,' he said gently, as if he were speaking to a child. 'When there's a cartridge up the spout, do it this way. Hold the hammer back with your left thumb, pull the trigger and let the hammer come slowly back into the uncocked position.'

'Oops! It jumps.'

Charlie smiled. 'You learn fast, Mrs Solicitor. Okay. Now, because there's a bullet in the breech, push up the safety catch. And that's it, except for firing it.'

She breathed out. It was hard to believe she was going through with this depraved charade when she had no intention of ever using it — well, only if Nicky were in danger. And only into the air as a deterrent.

'Hold it with both hands,' Charlie said. 'Right hand firmly round the butt, left hand overlapping the right.'

'It feels awkward.'

'It won't when the time comes.' He looked at her and raised his eyebrows. 'And don't forget. It kicks up when you shoot.'

'Does that mean I must aim lower?'

'No, don't aim too low. But don't shoot at the head. Anything above the head and you've missed. Hold it steady. Look down the barrel. Make sure the front sight fills the space of the notch, if you've got the time. If not, just point and shoot.'

She looked up at the blackened ceiling then down at the filthy floor. Is this just another bad dream, she wondered. My primary weapon should be to go to the police, or reason with Smith, as I've done in the past. Persuade him to give himself up.

A picture of Nicky flashed into her mind. Nicky with her smile so like Simon's. Nicky with her love for anything and everything that is alive and breathing. My precious daughter.

TUESDAY

Standing sideways in front of the hall mirror at Hillside House, Wendy arched her back and pushed her stomach forward. Although it was prudent at this stage to keep her pregnancy hidden, she was dying to see some outward sign, but there wasn't the slightest bulge and even her breasts looked much the same, although in the shower this morning they had felt tender to the touch.

She smiled at herself in the mirror. Nicky was at school. Duchess was a curled-up ball of fluff in Duke's basket. The housework was finished. This was the moment she'd been waiting for, though she hadn't expected to feel so frightened. Frightened, but at the same time more excited than she'd ever felt in her life.

With trembling fingers she unwrapped the Boots packet and read the instructions. Taking the portable phone from its cradle in the kitchen she went into the bathroom. How incredible that in only three minutes she'd know for certain whether or not she was carrying Alan's baby.

Staring at the spot where in three minutes the blue line would appear if she were pregnant, she wished Alan were here to share this fantastic moment. She tried not to imagine what he would say if it were positive. He might say nothing, and just never turn up again. That's the way he was. He hated complications.

He'd be at home now, on his lunch break. Irresistibly her hand was drawn to the phone. She dialled, her smile fading as she remembered how her mother had always blamed her for the break-up of her marriage. 'Your father was fine till you came along,' she used to say. 'He couldn't stand your bawling. That's when he started going down the pub and drank himself to death.'

She heard the ringing tone. Should she tell him about the baby first, or the house? A little two-up two-down cottage was all they'd need . . .

'Alan? Oh, I'm so glad I've caught you.'

'I'm just on my way out. I can't stop.'

If she could keep him talking the blue line would appear and she could tell him the good news straight away. 'I won't keep you a minute, Alan, but you know what we were talking about the other night. Well, I thought if we bought a little house together, I have quite a bit saved.'

'Wendy. For God's sake give over. We're fine as we are. Anyway, some poor sod's house is flooding and I must go. Will I see you Friday?'

Without another word she pressed the off button. She'd never done that to anyone in her whole life and she couldn't believe she'd just done it to Alan.

With slow jerky movements and a sinking feeling that seemed to drag her insides down into her legs she picked up the tester.

- 40 -

Julia was thankful it was only a two-minute walk from the Law Courts to the Mark Addy. She loved this walk. Often she would stroll over the bridge towards the Salford bank and gaze down at the River Irwell. She would imagine it flowing past this very spot in the Victorian days, when what was now the pub had been thronging with people waiting for the river bus. But there was no time for day-dreaming today.

With a glance at her watch she hurried through the quaint silver-domed entrance. Running down the steps into the long narrow room with its arched red brick ceiling she hoped he would still be there. The light from the full-length windows overlooking the river dazzled her eyes. It took her a moment or two to spot him.

He was sitting in one of those cubicles separated by wooden partitions topped with coloured glass squares. As soon as he saw her he stood up and ushered her to the seat beside him.

'I'm sorry I'm late,' she said, still out of breath. 'It's been one of those days.'

It took another few moments to adjust to the subdued red lighting in the cubicle. Julia wondered why Paul had wanted to see her. His eyes were shuttling from one side of her face to the other as though there was something he was looking for but couldn't find.

'How's Nicky?' he said at last.

'Fine.'

'Good. The usual?' She nodded, then watched him stride to the bar.

What is it about him that always makes me feel as though my heart is missing a beat, she asked herself. The smile? The energy?

She turned away and gazed around the pub. Groups of sleek-haired women in expensive black outfits were laughing and chatting to men in well-cut charcoal grey suits. She envied those women. They appeared not to have a care in the world.

Paul put a glass of white wine in front of her. 'It's a bit smoky here,' he said. 'We could go outside.'

She curled her fingers round the stem of the glass and gripped it tightly. 'Let's stay here,' she said. After her day of exposure in the courts she liked the feeling of mock privacy the cubicle gave her.

'You look as though you've had a lousy day,' he said.

She slowly shook her head. It would be impossible to discuss with Paul the intricacies of the cases she was dealing with.

He reached out and laid his hand on her shoulder, giving it a gentle squeeze.

'I find it very hard to deal with crimes as awful as this, Paul. It makes me want to —'

'Cry?'

'Yes.'

He moved towards her. She thought he was about to wrap his arms around her, but he didn't. 'Talk about it,' he said. 'It'll help.'

She dug her nails into her palms. 'I'm representing a man accused of raping his six-year old step-daughter, and it's . . .'

'Yes,' he said. 'I know the case. It must be hard for you.'

Her handbag was lying on the seat between them. Something made her touch it. With her fingers she traced the outline of the pistol. She had felt like a criminal rushing back from the court to the office and getting it out of her locked top drawer. She could never take it with her to court but at all other times she made sure she had it with her.

'And he definitely did it,' Paul said.

Julia pursed her lips and looked straight ahead.

He dropped his shoulders with a sigh. 'Sorry. That wasn't fair. But sometimes you must know.'

'Yes. Often I think I know. But I'm human. I could be wrong. Sometimes they are telling the truth.' Julia could still see the accusing fingers of the social workers when she'd done little more than put her arms around the boy next door and it had seemed even Jessie didn't believe her. 'But what if your mother or father or brother is arrested for a crime they didn't commit? Some cranky witness makes it seem like an open-and-shut case. You'd want them represented by a solicitor who approaches the case with an open mind, wouldn't you? One who doesn't assume they're guilty? And who — '

'Julia, calm down. Yes, you're quite right. I would,' he said.

For a few moments he said nothing more. He picked up his glass, took a gulp of his beer, put the glass down then turned to face her. 'But the Longdale case is quite different, isn't it? Jane Longdale has admitted her guilt.'

'Guilt?' She closed her eyes, then opened them again and this time she looked straight into his eyes. 'Guilt?' she repeated. 'Don't you mean she has admitted killing her grandfather?'

'Killing is murder.'

'Yes. But for years he sexually abused her, for God's sake. On the day she killed him she was driven to a state where she lost her self-control. Something inside her snapped.'

'Julia, you're shaking. What's wrong?'

'I'm sorry. Both these cases have really got to me. I don't know why.'

'I wish I could help you to relax,' he said, in that concerned, caring way he sometimes had of speaking. He lifted her glass and handed it to her.

A Mozart concerto was playing softly in the background. Paul was staring at her now in a way that made her want to forget all the professional differences she was convinced would always be between them.

He was watching her closely. 'Come on,' he said. 'Let's go outside.'

Without waiting for her approval he picked up their glasses and led the way to a table on the patio overlooking the river.

163

'This is better,' he said. 'Now we can talk.'

'Sounds serious,' she said. For a moment she wondered if he was going to talk about them, their friendship, but then she knew by the way he pursed his lips that he was not.

'It is, I'm afraid. Very serious. Bob Bennett says you're still refusing to have anyone in the house or garden. Why?'

She gazed at the river. It was easier than looking at his eyes. 'I think you know that already. Besides, you have the house opposite crawling with cops.'

'Julia, please look at me.' He held her arm. 'I'm concerned for your safety but I'm equally concerned about capturing Smith.'

A piece of polystyrene foam bobbed over the undulating surface of the river, diffusing the muddy reflections of the concrete buildings on the opposite bank. She watched it disappear beneath the bridge, fascinated by the knowledge that it would reappear on the other side. Why was I foolish enough to think that being with Paul this evening would make Smith disappear from my mind?

She turned to Paul at last. 'You mean I could be the bait?'

'Don't worry,' he said. 'Nothing will be obvious.'

He was looking at her with his eyelids half closed, as though he thought there was something she should have been telling him, but wasn't.

'Julia.' He twisted in his seat until he faced her, then rested his hand on her arm. 'Smith's threats may seem to you like the normal histrionics of a condemned man, and what he did on Friday night and his demand for a quarter million pounds merely further manifestations of his rage. But believe me, I can not afford to overlook them. Remember Avril Scott?'

She kept her eyes down. Her fingers found her handbag. Again she traced the outline of the gun. 'What he did to Avril would surely have been on the spur of the moment.'

'Exactly,' Paul said. 'So you can't ignore the man or his threats. He's a madman. He's seeking revenge for something he feels his solicitor owes him. So let's be honest. Increasing surveillance would increase our likelihood of capturing him. Has he phoned you again?'

164

'No.'

He moved his hand up her arm to her chin, forcing her to look at him. 'So you'll agree?'

She shook her head. Further words choked in her mouth. She still had no way of knowing whether what Smith had said was true. How comforting it would be to be able to tell Paul who she thought Smith was. To share her fear with him. To tell him about Smith's terrifying accusation which he had uttered in such a direct manner that she was in no doubt that he would, if forced, tell the police and she would be taken in for questioning with all the repercussions that would cause. But this was all wishful thinking.

'Julia. I must make sure you're safeguarded. Purely as a member of the public, you understand. Nothing to do with your relationship with me.'

Relationship? He'd never used that word before.

She sipped her wine. 'Paul,' she said at last, 'if Smith did approach the house again, and if he got one whiff of the kind of highly sophisticated armed presence you're contemplating, he'd be off like a shot. But goodness knows what he'd do next.'

Paul sucked air in through his teeth, his eyes flicking from left to right. 'You know damned well he should have gone down for the Dunn rape. He's rotten. There's hatred and rage in that man. He could do it again and that's why I'm so worried.'

She watched the quick rise and fall of his chest, sensing the power beneath his anger. He has fire in his belly, everyone always said about him.

But she had made her point. That was enough. If she carried on protesting Paul would begin to wonder why. 'I think you should leave things as they are,' she said. 'And hope that Smith doesn't spot anything suspicious. We all know he's no fool. He must be fully aware that his threat in court would not be ignored. He knows how you guys work. But anything above the norm would make him smell a rat.'

'Right. A compromise. Nothing at your house yet, but increase cover at the house opposite. Smith won't see a thing but we'll be ready for him. Okay?'

165

'Okay,' she said, and then, forcing lightness into her voice, 'Oh, I nearly forgot to tell you. I'm going to one of those self-protection classes tomorrow night that you're always on about.'

'About time. But you look too tired to go prancing around in a gym. Look. I've an idea. Pack a bag on Saturday, for you and Nicky. We'll go somewhere for the weekend. Well, don't look at me as though I've suggested a trip in a Russian spaceship.'

'I can't, Paul.' She picked up her handbag and stood beside the table, ready to go. 'Anyway, you have a big case on. Surely you shouldn't leave town.'

'I'll choose a hotel nearby,' he said, standing in front of her. 'I'll have my mobile phone and my bleeper. We all need a break.' He took her arm. 'I would drive behind you,' he said, 'but unfortunately I have to go back to the office now.'

'I'm fine, really. And I'd rather you didn't, anyway.' Silently they walked out of the pub.

Without warning he bent down and kissed her cheek. Neither of them said another word but something had changed.

* * *

Julia drove home bewildered, her thoughts zigzagging between Paul and her dilemma with Smith. She pressed the CD play button. Perhaps the poignant notes of the clarinet concerto would steady her nerves. Deciding not to take the bypass, she came off Kingsway, then took the far quieter old A34 to Wilmslow. Quieter, but better lit.

When the exquisitely beautiful slow movement started, she turned up the sound. Mozart must have been in love when he wrote this, she thought, completely forgetting for the first time in more than three days to look in her rear view mirror.

- 41 -

Wendy spooned the batter straight onto the hot plate on the Aga. When little holes appeared on top she turned the pancakes over. She filled the kettle and put the honey and the butter on the table. When Julia finally arrived home she'd at least have her favourite snack to eat.

She picked up the phone then put it down again. If she didn't do it soon Julia would be home and she would have missed her chance.

Today should have been the happiest day of her life. She wanted to tell Julia, but Julia might not want her to carry on working in her condition and she needed the money. She wanted to tell the whole wide world. But although she was ecstatic about the baby, she was also frightened. It was really important now for her and Alan to have a house. She remembered her mother telling her how patient she'd always had to be. 'Men don't like to be pushed into things,' she had said. 'They like to think it was all their idea.'

But like a bird frantically trying to build a nest in spring, Wendy didn't think she could be patient. She wanted her house now.

'Men!' she said aloud. But inside she was shouting I'm going to have a baby. I'm going to have Alan's baby!

- 42 -

On the dashboard a red light flashing. Jesus, these old Peugeots were nothing but fucking trouble. But they were a doddle to steal and what a great feeling to be right behind the SLK, close enough to see the shape of her head and that beautiful long blonde hair.

You needed a good fifty yards to get up enough speed to zoom up behind her. Force her into the curb. Or better still into a wall. Not too fast. You don't want to hurt her. But only a frontal impact would inflate the airbags and pop open the doors, and Christ, here he was, having to keep twenty yards behind her in case some other bastard nipped in ahead of him. You needed a pretty empty stretch of road otherwise you would have all the busybodies slamming on their brakes and offering to be witnesses.

He glared at the back of her head. It was her own fucking fault. He'd told her he would speak to her every day on the phone. He was sick of that cocky bitch at the office telling him Mrs Grant was in court, and that silly little bitch at the house saying 'and whom shall I say called?'

So he would have to see her in person. He had no other choice. He had to keep up the pressure. A slow dripping tap that would finally make her scream for mercy and fall at his feet with the money in her hand. He grinned. He would get that money one way or another. He had to. And he'd be killing two birds with one fucking stone. At last he would be getting his own back.

This airbag plan. It was a long bloody shot. Joe had done it with a Mondeo and it'd worked a treat. The surprise element was vital. Trouble was she'd be shit scared and might do anything. But he had to make sure she got the message that he wasn't just fucking around. Just in case she thought he'd eased up.

Handforth traffic lights red. All cars in front of the Merc flashing their left indicators. Great. Lights changing to green. Nothing behind him. Cars ahead turning left and a fantastic stretch of open road ahead. Jeez, his best chance coming up, for sure.

Approaching the dip. Still nothing behind.

Let the gap widen. Slowly does it. Let her get ahead. Not too much.

Timing vital. Speed at least seventy to make it work. Force her to accelerate just before Dean Drive intersection and hope like hell the Peugeot's got the guts to do it.

The point of no return . . .

Now.

- 43 -

Paul picked up the phone. Even though he spent so little time relaxing at home these days it was still necessary to leave the phones switched on.

'Hang on, Kev. I'll turn off the telly.'

In one continuous series of movements he hit the sound on the remote, punched the no-hands button and slammed the receiver back on the wall, grabbed his beer from the work top and turned down the gas where one thick piece of rib-eye steak was sizzling under the grill. Only then did he sit down and glance at his watch. Must be important for Kevin to be phoning him at home.

'Okay, Kev. Shoot. What've you got?'

'Nothing, boss. Absolutely sweet bleeding nothing.'

Paul gulped his beer and wiped the foam off his lip. He banged the glass down on the table.

'Except one thing, boss.'

'What?'

'Stolen car. Old turquoise Peugeot. Missing from a building site near Dukes 92 Lock on the Rochdale Canal.'

Paul clenched his teeth. 'Smith?'

'Just a hunch. Think he'll try again?'

'Damn sure he will.'

'Well, I'll get back to you if anything more comes in.'

'I'll be here. Keep in touch, Kev.'

Paul opened the fridge and took out another ice cold lager. He snapped off the top and watched it cartwheel across the white floor tiles. And then he changed his mind and poured the entire contents down the sink.

Gazing out over the tree-lined car park, he remembered the way Julia had looked at him tonight at the Addy. Shyly at one moment, sadly the next, and then, amazingly for someone so traumatised by events, sexily! At first he'd thought he was imagining it. It was so unlike Julia that it had taken him a moment to realise she was actually giving him the most positive signals since they'd met, although it wouldn't surprise him if it were entirely unconscious on her part. She had turned to him, her eyes half-closed, her body swaying towards him but stopping short just before she touched him. He wondered what had happened in her childhood to make her so afraid of physical contact. She gave unstintingly of herself to help others in need. Sometimes she gave an inordinate amount of time to a client she believed innocent in the hope of rehabilitating him, but seemed afraid to seek help for herself.

He turned up the grill and took the M & S salad from the fridge. If only she were here now. She would like it here. So much more compact than her huge draughty old house. Even though these luxury flats were converted from an old Victorian house, the pristine bathrooms, white Formica tops and ceramic floors would seem like heaven to Julia after the ancient fittings and creaking wooden floors of Hillside House.

Julia . . .

He turned off the gas and slid the steak onto a plate. He tossed the salad, grabbed a knife and fork and flopped down on the sofa. God, he needed this weekend break as much as she did. When he'd left her at the car park he'd had the feeling that with a little more time she might have agreed to the weekend away. Maybe if he just pitched up on Saturday afternoon with his overnight bag on the back seat of the CRX, she would weaken. Especially if Nicky was given a chance to voice her opinion.

With one mouth-watering piece of meat on his fork he looked at the phone on the wall. No, he thought. Any further attempt at verbal persuasion might merely annoy her, even put her off altogether.

Action was what was needed now.

- 44 -

Lulled by the romantic notes of the clarinet Julia suddenly realised there was a car right behind her. She saw the lights first, blinding her in the rear view mirror. With her pulse racing she put her foot flat on the accelerator to get away from him and yanked on the steering wheel to try to turn into Dean Drive, but it was too late, he was almost on her. She saw the curb racing towards her. His lights filled the mirror and then she heard the crash.

Her car leapt forward. Hit the curb. The airbag came at her like a wild animal. The central locking system clunked as the door locks released.

A pain shot through the back of her neck.

A thumping noise. Running footsteps . . .

And then the door was yanked open and he was there, his eyes leering at her. Weaving backwards and forwards until he was almost touching her, coming closer and closer . . .

'Don't touch me.'

'Not touching, Julia. Just looking. You ought to be more careful. Stopping so suddenly like that. Look what you done to my car.'

She thought of frightening him with the gun but realised he would grab it and she'd be the one pleading for her life.

'I told you I'd phone every day, didn't I? But I can't fucking phone if you're all over the goddam town all bloody day and all night! Can I, Julia?' he yelled.

She didn't answer, grateful that he didn't also know her mobile number.

She stared at his face and realised that something had changed. She hadn't seen him since that final day in court.

The beard had gone!

She was looking into a smoothly shaven face which in spite of the scars on his cheeks made him look years younger.

And absolutely different.

He moved closer. The floppy velvet hat Wendy had made for her, complete with its glinting hatpin, was on the back shelf of the car. There was no chance of reaching it. A few cars came past but not one even looked like stopping.

'Great music, that,' he said, cocking his head to one side. 'Love to stay and listen but must be off now.' He looked around furtively. 'Haven't time to chat. Lovely chats we used to have in Strangeways, eh, Julia? Still dreaming about that twin brother of yours?' And then his eyes lit up. 'Nicky musta done well at school today. All smiles when she came out until the nanny dragged her into that yellow Mini and I couldn't see her any more. Well, be seeing ya. Only six days to go . . .'

- 45 -

Propped up against a pile of velvet cushions on the sofa in the drawing room, Julia sipped the hot sweet tea Wendy insisted she have for shock and nibbled on a delicious pancake spread with butter and honey. Wendy was spoiling her as usual.

'It happened so quickly,' she said. 'I was nearly home. The clarinet concerto was still playing —'

'So loudly,' Wendy interrupted, 'that you couldn't hear the other car.'

'Only when it was right behind me. I saw the lights first, in my rear view mirror. Thought he must be drunk or high on drugs. Put my foot on the accelerator — '

'But you were too late.'

'He forced me into the curb. Crashed into me.'

'You could have been killed,' Wendy said, hands over her eyes.

'I felt a shooting pain in the back of my neck and then . . . '

Julia pressed her hands into the sides of her head. Screwed her eyes up tightly. This was what Smith was doing to her. Even making her forget what he himself laid down so emphatically. She'd actually been about to tell Wendy what happened next.

'Drink your tea,' Wendy said.

Julia opened her eyes. She looked at Wendy and shrugged. She still didn't know how she'd managed to drive home. 'I'd better report this to the police,' she said, 'and then I'll go to bed.'

'Did you get his number?' Wendy asked.

'Did I hell. But I think it was a . . . Oh,' she said, stopping herself just in time. 'Silly me,' she added quickly, holding her hand to her mouth. 'I don't even know what make it was. Or the colour.'

'You should take a few days off,' Wendy said, frowning. 'See the doctor.'

Julia struggled to her feet. She had to show Wendy she was perfectly all right. 'I'll be fine in the morning. It'll be another busy day so I'm going to need a car while mine's being repaired. I'm lucky the damage is very slight. They could fix it in a couple of days.'

'If you drop your car at the garage tomorrow morning, I'm sure they'll lend you one,' Wendy said. 'Lucky the Merc garage is on your way to work.'

- 46 -

Suspended half way between sleep and consciousness the sounds of the night were amplified in Julia's aching head. The east wind. An owl. The traffic. The distant roar of aircraft taking off. The ancient water pipes crackling as they cooled down. And the scraping noise again.

What is real and what am I imagining, she wondered. Is someone breaking in?

She climbed out of bed and reached for her handbag, took out the pistol and cocked it, just as Charlie Kuma had shown her.

Slowly she opened the curtains. The trees, lit by yellow street lights, cast long shadows on the lawn like a row of giant butcher knives.

Simon's toy black cat on the windowsill flashed its emerald eyes. Silhouetted against the loops of condensation at the bottom of the windowpanes, it looked as though it would pounce at any minute. The time on the radio alarm clock in bright red luminous numbers said two thirty-five.

She felt a sudden coldness on her back. She whipped round. Lattice shadows on the wall criss-crossed the portrait of Simon, moving ever so slightly and making him look as though he was about to step out of the frame, alive . . .

> . . . *Another aircraft long ago roars into the sky. A long-legged bird flies into the engine. The plane plummets to the ground and bursts into flames. She smells the smoke, feels the heat. Feels the agony of yet another loss . . .*

To banish the scene Julia fled down the passage, careering from one wall to the other, the pistol cold and heavy in her hand. Reaching the top of the stairs, she sat down on the top step and closed her eyes.

Chinks of memory exploded in front of her like a pop video, two seconds a scene, but in a new, almost logical sequence that filled her with horror and then with a sadness that felt as though it would rip her apart. The smooth shaven face loomed in front of her, reminding her that she had not yet checked the seldom-used dining room after Friday night's break-in. A few paltry household items were not what Sam Smith had been after, but she had a sudden urge to see for herself what he had seen, and to imagine what might have gone through his head.

She tiptoed down the stairs and into the long narrow room on the ground floor. The twelve chairs were lined up alongside the mahogany table like soldiers on parade. She stood at the sideboard, the very spot where on Friday night Sam Smith must have stood, and shivered as she touched the gleaming polished wood. She turned away, then double-checked the rest of the house. Sam Smith had taken nothing but she sensed his presence everywhere.

She was half way up the stairs when she realised what was missing. She retraced her steps to the dining room and stood once more at the sideboard. The oval silver frame with the photograph of Nicky, identical to the one on her office desk and the miniature that had disappeared from the top of the fridge — the one David and Jessie said looked so like Julia as a child — was gone.

WEDNESDAY

Daylight had just begun to spill from the edges of the curtains when the phone rang. Julia had already showered and dressed and had swallowed two Paracetamols for the excruciating pain in her neck. She'd had one hour's sleep.

She recognised his voice and answered in her most polite solicitor's tones. 'You're wasting your time phoning so soon. You know I can't possibly have raised the money yet.'

'I said I'd remind you every day, rich bitch. You should be grateful I'm taking such an interest in your welfare.'

She moved her head from side to side, trying to ease the pain, then decided it would be better to keep it absolutely still.

'You're not very talkative this morning, Julia. Still upset about last night, are you?'

'You're mad. You could have killed me.'

'I'd be fucking daft to kill the goose that lays the golden eggs.'

'If I'd been injured it might have made it more difficult for me to obtain the money.'

'Crap. I know you'll get the money. I know why you'll get it. And so do you.'

She felt the tendons in her neck tighten.

'But I won't wait forever, Julia, dear. Oh, and by the way,' he added softly, 'say Hi to Nicky for me. That's one real cute little kid.'

Julia gripped the table. The way he was speaking now was sending images hurtling into her mind that made no sense. How can a grown man's voice resemble that of a small boy's, she asked herself.

'And don't tell the filth, Julia.' His voice was back to normal. Deep and cold and filled with hatred. 'You're thinking about telling detective bloody superintendent fucking Moxon, aren't you. Well, don't. And I'm sure you know how much the filth love cold cases.'

Paul yawned and glanced at his watch. Far below him the sleeping city was beginning to come to life. The low golden sunlight glinting on windows. Pigeons on roofs, rustling their feathers. Cars queuing up at traffic lights. It was a long time since he'd spent a whole night at the office. He'd only intended his spur of the moment visit after Kevin's phone call to be a short one, and he was amazed he'd actually managed to doze off for a couple of hours.

He pulled the phone towards him and punched memory recall. He hoped he would catch Julia before she left for work. When she was driving she almost always switched off her mobile. She said it was dangerous to talk and drive a car safely. Mozart enabled you to think and concentrate on driving at the same time, she always argued, smiling smugly as though anyone who didn't do this was really missing out.

It rang once. 'Julia Grant. Hello — '

'Thank God I've caught you.'

'Paul what's happened?'

He had never heard her sound so frightened. 'No problem,' he said. 'It was great seeing you yesterday. Just hoped we could meet again after work today.'

'I'm sorry. I told you. I've got this self-protection class tonight.'

'Of course. It slipped my mind. What about afterwards?'

'I haven't been sleeping well. I need an early night. I'll ring you later in the week.'

'Okay,' he said. 'Don't forget Saturday, will you.'

'Paul, I must go.'

'Sure you're okay?'

'Of course I am.'

'Ring me if anything goes wrong. Anything.'

'I will. Thanks for calling.'

'Bye . . .'

Paul felt a bit idiotic, but he'd just needed to hear her voice and make sure nothing had happened after he'd left her yesterday. He heard a familiar knock and swung round as Kevin Moorsley walked in.

'Anything from the Malicious Calls Bureau, Kev?'

'Nothing, boss. Why?'

'Don't know. Just a gut feeling he has contacted her.' He raked his fingers through his hair. He should be telling Kevin everything, instead of allowing Julia to influence his normal course of action. 'And if he has, why didn't she press the number one digit?'

Kevin shrugged.

'I want him, Kev, and I want him now. This is one of the finest forces in the country. What's wrong with us? Why can't we nail him?'

'We've done everything, boss, but there's ef-all to go on.'

'Step up surveillance, Kev. Do the pubs again. Get on to Ken Riding and Bob Bennett. Tell them the situation has worsened. Tell 'em to get their arses into gear.' He paused and took a deep breath. 'But remind them that discretion is of the utmost importance.'

Kevin gave Paul a look of puzzlement and exasperation. 'Yes, boss.'

'And let me know the instant that old turquoise car is spotted.'

- 49 -

Wendy let herself in and went straight to the kitchen to put the kettle on for their early morning tea. She patted Duchess then picked her up and took her out into the kitchen garden for a few moments. Duchess obliged and Wendy picked her up and took her back to her basket.

'Feel like a coffee, Wendy? You look done in.'

Wendy whirled round, surprised to see Julia down so early, especially as there was no sign yet of Nicky. And just look at her. As right as rain after her smash last night. Not even a sign of her sore neck and the trauma she'd been through. 'Oh, no thanks,' she said. 'Maybe tea. I couldn't face coffee.'

'You should see a doctor,' Julia said quietly. 'You don't need to suffer, you know.'

Wendy bit her lip to stop the tremble. 'I'm fine,' she managed to say, then turned away as tears welled in her eyes.

'No, you're not,' Julia said. 'Something's wrong. Isn't it?'

177

At the first heave of Wendy's shoulders Julia rushed to her side. 'Sit down, Wendy, and tell me all about it.'

The knot in Wendy's throat tightened. This was it. She'd been daft to think she could hide it from someone as clever as Mrs Grant.

Julia took two mugs off the hooks. 'You're pregnant, aren't you, Wendy?'

Wendy nodded slowly.

'Oh, Wendy, dear! How far?'

Wendy shrugged. 'Haven't a clue. Couple of months.'

'Does Alan know?'

'I haven't told him.'

'Oh, but you must. He'll be thrilled.'

'He'll kill me. He won't even move in with me. Won't hear of buying a house. He might dump me altogether if I told him.'

Julia sat down next to Wendy and poured the tea. 'He's going to find out sometime.'

'I know. If you could guess so easily, so could he.' Wendy suppressed a smile even though she felt so close to tears. 'But every time I bring up the subject of marriage he says why do we need to get married? Oh, Julia, what shall I do?'

'Wendy, having a child is the most wonderful thing that can happen to a woman.'

Wendy felt her eyes filling up again. 'I know. And I love Alan. I want to live with him. I don't want to bring up a child without a father.'

Julia sipped her tea. 'Lots of people do,' she said quietly.

Wendy smiled sheepishly. She was always putting her foot in it, as her mother used to say.

'But I'm sure Alan will be thrilled,' Julia added, with such a knowing, kind smile that Wendy wanted to hug her. 'I wish I could stay and talk to you, Wendy, but I must go now. The sooner I take the Merc to the garage the sooner I'll get it back. Take care. And tell Alan soon.'

Wendy walked outside with Julia and closed the gate after she had driven out, relieved to see that the damage to that beautiful car was indeed not as bad as she had thought it would be. Poor Julia. Lately she had been looking kind of sad. It wasn't just the break-in and Duke's ghastly death, she was sure, or even her accident last night. But something more than that. Like something deep inside her was weighing on her mind.

She was glad she had a busy morning ahead. Now that Julia had made it sound so easy, she could hardly contain herself until twelve o'clock when Alan would be home and she could phone him with her news.

At last the moment came. Nicky was safely in school. She'd done the vacuuming, put the laundry on and cooked the thick vegetable soup for tonight.

Alan's sister Dawn answered the phone. Each second she waited for Alan made her resolve grow weaker. After hanging up on him yesterday he might not even agree to talk to her.

There he was at last. 'Hi. What's up, Wendy?'

'Nothing. It's just . . . I thought maybe I could see you today.'

'I'm busy. What you want to see me 'bout?'

'Remember what we talked about the other night? The house. Well, you see . . . there's something else you should know.'

'Oh, give over, girl. Don't you ever know when to stop.'

She heard Alan's impatient sigh. Maybe she should just blurt it out, now, on the phone, but she couldn't. The words wouldn't come.

'Look, Wendy. I've been thinking, well, maybe we shouldn't see each other for a while. I've a hell of a lot of work on. You might see things in a better light if you have a bit of a change. Like you always say, a change does you good.'

'No. You've got me wrong. I don't want a change. Alan, it'd be much easier to talk if you were right here.'

'But I'm not there, am I? And I gotta go. Look, I'll ring you in a coupla weeks. See how we go. Okay?'

- 50 -

'My name's Mike. I'm a professional martial arts instructor and this is Daniela, my assistant. It's impossible, ladies, in a one-night self-defence course, to learn to defend yourself in all situations, so I'll concentrate on a few basic things you can practice and use straightaway.'

He was over six foot and perfectly proportioned, with thick straight black hair and dark eyes. Julia felt that not only would Mike be fearless, he'd be a good teacher. Daniela was small and shapely, rather like Wendy. Both were dressed in white tracksuit pants and T-shirts and looked like adverts for multivitamin pills.

'It's the shock of being attacked that hits women first,' Mike said. 'Some take two or three seconds to get over the initial shock. Others, thirty or forty. Some are paralysed right through the attack. So it's a good thing to practise with your partners. Just say to them grab hold of me here, please, darling, and rough me up a bit.'

Partners? She wondered how Paul would react to such a suggestion. It might be fun if nothing else, and she hadn't had much of that for a long time.

'It gives you confidence,' Mike went on. 'Makes you realise you're not helpless, as so many women imagine they are. My wife has actually dropped me to my knees with just so much as a tap when I wasn't expecting it.'

He paused while they all laughed.

'Yeah. Amazing, isn't it? But true. You see, at rest you only breathe in and out sixteen times a minute and it's hardly noticeable.'

You're right, Julia thought. But it sure is noticeable when someone isn't breathing at all. Like when I stood over Simon's bed and saw the glazed look in his eyes and knew he'd stopped breathing altogether. And like when . . .

She could feel her eyes rolling back. She tried to stop the unconnected train of thoughts but for an instant they insisted on blocking everything else, making little sense but sending a chill down her spine.

The chocolates. The sickly smile. The voice in her ear . . . the blood . . . and then the other voice . . . his little hand holding hers. Hurry, Julia . . . come with me . . . run . . .

'But in a confrontation situation you need more oxygen,' Mike explained, panting and making his stomach go in and out. 'So if someone's got hold of you, the time to hit him is when he breathes in. And when I say hit, I don't mean *bang*. All you need is this.' He gently tapped the lean area of his stomach. 'And down he'll go.'

Mike smiled at each of the women in turn, a motley collection ranging in age from about seventeen to over fifty, from really skinny to seriously plump.

'Okay. First a brief run through tonight's programme, starting with last-resort tactics. Someone taps you on the shoulder and wants to know the time. You don't want to break his jaw and drop him to the ground, so these are only for when you know you're going to be physically attacked.'

'But how do you know?' Julia blurted out.

'When someone comes within your own personal space and you feel physically threatened by his presence. Look. Stretch your arm out and bend it up, then draw a circle round yourself from the point of your elbow. That's your own personal space. If someone's in that space, they're going to attack you. Or make love to you,' he added, grinning. 'So don't wait for them to grab you. Just go for it.'

He beckoned a well-built teenager just in front of him. 'One example,' he said. 'You're walking through Sainsbury's car park. Turn that way, please, will you, and start to walk.'

The girl walked, and Mike walked a good few paces behind her.

'Are you feeling physically threatened?' he asked her.

'No.'

'Right. Now start walking again.'

This time he walked a couple of inches behind her. 'How about now?'

'Yes! Oh, hell, yes,' the girl said, grabbing the back of her head with both hands and starting to run.

'So there you go,' Mike said. 'Nobody walks that close unless they're going to physically assault you. Right. After that, posture. Your body tells the person whether or not you're open to attack. Yeah? Two dogs facing up in the street. Glaring at each other, growling. And the first one to lose that posture is the loser. Animal instinct. And everybody's got it.

The problem is, we're too civilised and most of us have lost it.'

Julia wondered whether her body reactions told Smith she was open to attack, and whether he would know when she was ready to attack him.

What the hell is happening to me, she asked herself. How can my thoughts be so deliberately outside the law? And would I really hurt him if I had the chance, knowing there's a possibility that . . .

Mike's voice filtered back. 'After that there'll be balance. And listening to your senses. And combating fear, which is the most important part of this course. Yeah. Does anyone know why you get frightened?'

No one answered.

'Is it something to do with adrenaline?' Julia asked.

'Right. When you're under threat, your body releases a massive amount of adrenaline. I can make adrenaline go into my body so all the hairs on the back of my neck stand up. Controlled adrenaline rush. You can learn to do this. Adrenaline rushing into your body can either make you go for it, or it can paralyse you.'

'Fight or flight,' Julia said.

'You've got it. Fight or flight.'

Mike reeled off the rest of the manoeuvres on the programme. 'And last of all, hands-on training. One at a time. Fighting me. As though you're attacked in the street. Yeah? It's the climax of the course.'

The women smiled apprehensively. Julia kept her eyes glued to Mike. Yes. This is what I came for. Then I can throw away that gun.

'But first some examples,' Mike said. 'A girl of fifteen walks her dog in a park. A man asks her the time. She looks at her watch. He grabs her, drags her into the bushes and rapes her.'

He paused. No one said a word.

'Next. Pervert preys on mums. He phones you. Says, I'm outside the school, waiting for your daughter to come out.'

Julia bit her knuckles.

'You okay?' Mike asked.

'Yes. Thanks. I'm fine.'

'Sure? Right. So what do you do? It's three o'clock. Your daughter comes out at quarter past. Your first reaction? Phone the police. And then? Get your car out the garage? Or run straight down to the school?'

'Run,' said a thin redhead on Julia's left. She'd told Julia her name was Georgia, but had clammed up when Julia asked about the mass of purple bruises on her arms.

'Right. But be careful. This guy's watched you for a week. Watched which way you go to the school. Yeah.'

Julia clasped the tops of her arms.

'So what should you do?' Georgia asked.

'Phone the school. Tell them you've had a malicious phone call. Please don't let Sarah go until I pick her up. Nobody else. Not even a policeman.' Mike looked at each of them in turn, making sure his words were sinking in.

Julia tried to equate Mike's fictitious attacker with Smith. Something was wrong. Something in the back of her mind she'd been trying to fathom out ever since his first call on Saturday. And with a jolt of recognition she knew what it was.

Smith doesn't attack children.

His record showed he has never attacked a child. He'd even told Julia in Strangeways how much he liked them. He'd seemed to empathise with them. So why had he said Nicky might be harmed if Julia didn't do what he asked?

During the brief silence that followed, a sudden movement dragged her eyes to the green swing doors that led to the tea room.

- 51 -

Sam smiled to himself. Anybody could walk into this dump. Nobody even wanted to see a fucking membership card. Nobody even looked at you as long as you appeared to have a purpose. And did he have a purpose.

He strode across the lobby. Climbed the stairs two at a time. He'd already sussed out the entire layout, whistling through his teeth when he saw the almost deserted showers down the corridor on the right. You never know, he thought. Could come in handy.

At the top of the stairs he leaned on the railing to get his breath back. He knew she was in the main exercise area. After following her into the building he'd peeped once or twice through the swing doors and seen the women's antics. What a joke. She'd never surprise him with any of those fancy moves. Unfit or not, he knew how to take care of himself. Especially against a woman.

He walked over to the green swing doors again, his ancient trainers squeaking on the polished tiled floor. This time all the bitches were picking up their bags and walking towards the door. He stood behind a pillar and watched while they all trooped into the restaurant. Well, he had all night. They'd be drinking tea and yakking their heads off like all bitches do. He could wait. It'd be worth the wait to scare the living daylights out of her when she finally came out of this joint. That's what she needed, the cocky bitch.

Scaring to death.

Mike clapped his hands. 'Right, ladies. Let's get down to the serious part of the training, and this will culminate in a full-scale assault on each of you in turn. But first, a few preliminary moves. Imagine you're being attacked. You really let fly. Bang. And don't go like this . . .' He closed his eyes and hit out wildly. 'You must focus. It's no use if it doesn't work. There are only two possibilities. Work. Won't work. Okay? Again.'

To each of them Mike offered himself for mock attack. When it was Julia's turn she lashed out at him.

'No, you're not hitting hard enough. Make a good tight fist. Don't worry about the damage you might do.'

She hit him again.

'No. It's still half-hearted. Does anyone play tennis? If you don't take that arm back there'll be no power in your shot. So bring that shoulder in behind your punch.'

She punched him in the stomach, really hard. Sam Smith. She saw the surprised look in Mike's eyes.

'Okay, excellent. And now the groin.' He paused for effect. Several of the younger girls giggled. 'Hitting a man in the chest won't do any real damage. If he grabs you by the hair, lift your right knee straight up between his legs, then whip the lower bit of your leg up so the flat of your foot hits his groin at a hundred miles an hour. He'll soon let go of your hair . . .'

Mike's voice grew faint as Julia's mind drifted to the mammoth task of borrowing money to pay Sam Smith. If John Cartwright refuses I'll be forced to go behind Ben Lloyd's back and carry out my unthinkable Plan B . . .

'Next,' Mike said. 'Attacker grabs you round the neck. You must turn your head towards him so his fingers are no longer on your windpipe. Turn it away and he'll break your neck. And drop your right shoulder. That way you can see what you're doing, because then you're virtually looking at his crotch and slipping out of his grip at the same time. So you punch it repeatedly until he drops. If he's wearing tight jeans you'll know exactly where to go.'

It sounded so easy, Julia thought. If I could perfect these moves I definitely wouldn't need a gun, or a hatpin. She felt a sour taste in her mouth and a wave of disgust that she had ever contemplated a weapon of any kind.

'You can also go in from the back,' Mike said, his face dead serious. 'And if you get one of the two round objects, that's perfect. Snatch as hard as you can and try to rip it off his body. But you're doing two things here, ladies, because you're also going to smash his face in. Why? Because he's going to go down so fast he hasn't time to put his hands out, and his face will hit the ground first. Most effective.'

Julia glanced at Georgia, who looked back without a smile, her lips tightly pursed, her red eyebrows almost meeting in the middle.

'Sorry to sound so crude,' Mike said, 'but it's best to tell you straight so you know exactly what you're doing. And when that happens to a bloke there're two things he wants. First his mum. And when he knows his mum isn't coming, all he wants to do is die.' A smile at last.

While they practised the mock movements, Georgia whispered to Julia, 'Will you have the guts to really do this stuff?'

'I can't wait,' Julia said, laughing.

'And now, a most important point,' Mike said. 'If an attacker comes up behind you, scream as loud as you can. Scream. And for most people, it's enough'

After a final refreshment break Mike changed into his combat uniform. Loose white cotton pants with white V-neck top and, of course, the black belt ready for the final hands-on session. Julia smiled to herself. Wendy would die of surprise if she could see me now.

She watched Mike's eyes move slowly from one woman to the next, as if to assess their physical ability to defend themselves. 'I'm going to assault you for real,' he said. 'Fight back as hard as you can. Think of it as the worst possible attack that could ever happen to you. Your life is in danger. You could end up in a pine box. And remember. There's no scale from one to ten. Every time it's ten. He grabs you. Ten. He's still got hold of you. Ten. Groin, chin, ribs, eyes. It's all got ten on it.'

He looked across at Daniela. 'For us, Daniela and me, it's different. We'd kill with a ten. We have to scale down to a five or a four, a tap or a knock. But not for you ladies. You ladies are tens. Right. Now, go for it.'

The stocky teenager was the first one up. Mike stood facing her, unrecognisable with padding all over his body, a box over his genitals, and a protective mask held in place by a strip of mutton cloth wrapped around his face with only narrow slits for his eyes and mouth. A pretty frightening sight.

The attack was for real, all right. The girl gave it all she had. At the end of the two-minute bout she was puffing and panting and red in the face.

And then it was Julia's turn. Daniela prepared her with white arm pads, knee and shin-guards that Velcroed round the backs of her legs, soft white boots and boxing gloves. She felt her heart begin to thump. As Mike came towards her, faceless and fearless, a metamorphosis took place. Instead of the mask with slits Julia saw piercing blue eyes . . . coming closer and closer . . .

In a voice that was not hers she screamed, a long, loud, blood-curdler that echoed round the room.

Sam Smith recoiled, then renewed his attack. She screamed again.

Why are you doing this to me? Why have you driven me to this?

Two minutes had seemed like an eternity when the other women were fighting, but for Julia it was not enough. She kicked, punched, boxed whatever part of Sam Smith's long muscled body she could reach. Not one move resembled any of the carefully rehearsed modes of defence they'd spent more than three hours perfecting.

Finally, she kicked him in the groin. Then she turned and ran.

There was a stunned silence as Daniela led her away and removed her protective clothing. Mike stood up, glanced at her but said nothing.

When the last woman had defended herself, Mike took off his mask. Breathing heavily he dished out the relevant criticism and advice to each of them in turn.

When he came to Julia she looked at him sheepishly. 'Sorry, Mike.'

'You did great. You had the right idea. Look after Number One. That's you. Never mind him.'

'And remember,' he said to them all, 'your face shows your fear. If your lips have gone white and your eyes are wide open and the pupils have gone small, he knows you're petrified to death. That's what he's looking for. It gives him power when he sees you're scared.

'And now a final word. The best alarm is your lungs. You heard Julia's scream. Not a little scream, a good, loud ear-piercing scream.' He winked at her. 'It'll stun him as much as it stuns you, and that's when you start your attack because that's when he's at his most vulnerable. A rape alarm's a good idea too, by the way. Round your neck on a piece of string. No use if it's in your handbag.'

Handbag. The gun in my handbag. Useless after all, Julia thought.

'Now, most important of all,' Mike said, 'have you the confidence to go out there and defend yourselves?'

Julia looked him in the eye.

'Yes!'

- 53 -

Sam climbed out into the rain, slammed the door and kicked the ancient Rover he'd nicked last night. 'What a heap,' he muttered to himself, cursing the broken wipers, the wonky steering and the measly quarter tank of petrol. But a cinch to steal, and better than the trashed turquoise Peugeot. He glanced at the Polo she was driving tonight, parked a few cars away from his. He grinned to himself. He'd come out tonight with no plan of action and it was a one-off chance that he'd tried the door handle and found to his amazement that the Polo was not locked. After that it was a doddle to make sure she would not be able to start it.

Pulling up the collar of his coat, he headed for a tree on the edge of the car park. According to the notice in the club entrance, the self-protection course was due to end about now. He was prepared to wait all night, rain or no rain. Essential to keep the pressure on or he'd never get the money.

Being wet and hungry always took his mind racing back to Ada. Staying on with her had been better than running away and getting caught and locked up again. Better than having no one at all. It was the day she had two of them together that brought it to an end. On his thirteenth birthday for fuck's sake. He couldn't even put up with one – but two . . . Oh yes, she had it coming . . .

He refocused on the main door, waiting for Julia to appear.

And there she was at last. Running. No umbrella. Looking quite different with that hat pulled down her head.

He watched in fascination as she flicked a remote at her car.

Nothing happened. No flashing lights. No release of locks.

He held his breath as she opened the door and tried to start it, kept trying to start it and finally got out and locked the car with the key. Jeez, she's going to walk, just like he hoped she would, though if she had any sense she'd phone the jerks who lent her a car with a fucked up central locking and alarm system.

A ten yard start. When she moved, he moved in step and in the shadows. Saw her stop at the lights, finger the hat, push the damp strands of hair from her eyes.

Across the roundabout. Over the bridge and up the hill. Speeding traffic. Muddy spray. To frighten her, he'd have to surprise her, like last night with the Peugeot. If she stuck to the main roads he'd have a problem.

But there she was, crossing the road, turning off into the shadows of a little one-track road that twisted down to The Carrs.

Julia was already half way down the hill when she noticed the lights in all the cottages in Old Road were already out. Damn these early birds, she thought. She should have rung for a taxi. She quickened her pace and it was then that she heard the footsteps behind her.

Already her private space felt invaded. A controlled adrenaline rush, Mike had said, but this one was entirely involuntary. And so was her full-blasted shriek that pierced the Wilmslow silence.

Only now did she glance behind her. It was him all right. In her space. Blue eyes bulging. Act quickly, she told herself. Show no fear. That's what Mike said. Show she was in command.

She spun round and like an automated robot she whipped the hatpin from her hat and stuck it into the bit of his body straight in front of her. Almost in the same movement she shot her right leg towards his groin.

As he crashed to the ground she hurled the hatpin into the bushes at the side of the road and started to run.

Oh my God! What have I done?

- 55 -

Sam Smith lay for a few seconds in the foetal position, writhing with pain, doing his best to control it but not having much success. He could still hear that window-rattling scream. It was just the way Ada used to scream and he hadn't heard a sound like it for twenty-three years. He wasn't surprised when he saw a few lights go on in one or two of the cottages. The whole town must have heard that scream.

He was lying in the middle of the road so the first thing to do was get the hell of out here. Crawling on his hands and knees he slunk into the shadows of the bushes on the far side of the road where he could wait until the lights went out again and the pain had subsided.

'I'll get her back for this,' he hissed. He hated anyone getting the better of him. Julia Grant had hurt him. Hurt his pride too. Taken him by surprise when it was he who'd meant to surprise her.

As soon as possible he would have to get to his car and bum an icepack, a bed and some grub off Joe Sagoe.

* * *

Joe Sagoe poured the jambalaya into a bowl and sprinkled cinnamon over the top. He turned off the Primus and, with a wooden spoon plucked from the debris on the floor, he dished the food onto two enamel plates. He shoved one towards Sam, then sat down on an empty beer crate and began eating.

Ever since Sam had pushed open the skull-and-cross-bone door and collapsed onto the old beanbag in the corner, the delicious aroma of one of Joe's famous stews had been tantalising him. He looked at the jambalaya now, turned away and closed his eyes.

'So? What you waiting for?' Joe said.

Half lying, half sitting Sam clutched himself between his legs. Now that he actually saw the food, red, glistening, spreading all over the plate, he was not hungry any more.

'You can tell me what happened, Sam. It won't go no further than them four walls.'

Sam groaned. To tell him that Julia Grant had stuck a hatpin in his gut and kicked him in the balls would be worse than admitting he'd been caught jumping out of a window.

'Took you by surprise?' Joe said, grinning, leading Sam on.

Sam threw him a filthy look but said nothing. Joe laughed out loud. 'You wanna watch it when you're messing around with these classy dames,' he said, shovelling in another load of jambalaya. 'You never know what they'll do. Mind you, Julia Grant's smart as well as classy. Gotta a lot a time for her. Wouldn't never have no other lawyer unless like last week when they couldn't raise her on the phone.'

'She was like a wild cat gone mad.'

Joe looked straight at Sam and sucked in his lips. 'We want our money, Sam. If she ain't gonna play ball, better you get the dough some place else. Frank and Stringer don't work for peanuts. And don't forget. You owe us for the passport too.'

He piled in another spoonful. 'Reckon she'll cough up?'

'Too right she will. '

'Oh yeah? Then why this? And that?' He pointed to Sam's stomach, then to the bit lower down. 'What happened?'

Sam leaned forward, trying to ease the pain. 'The bitch had a fucking hat on. With a hatpin.'

A big grin spread slowly across Joe's bloated face.

'You musta got too close.'

Sam looked down. He couldn't bear to meet Joe's gaze.

'No kidding,' Joe said, pulling his face straight.

'I only meant to make her so shit scared she'd hurry up with the cash.'

Joe wiped his hand across his mouth and laughed, his thick, bushy eyebrows raised. 'So what now?'

Sam shrugged. A spasm of pain doubled him up again.

Joe hurled his empty plate at the piled-up sink and swivelled round to face Sam. 'Know what? You oughta see a medic.'

'Got any more jokes?'

'Puncture wounds is bad news. See nothing on top. Gradually goes bad underneath.' He squinted at Sam. 'If you get real sick you can't stay here. Not if there's gonna be a dead body to cart away. Sorry, mate. I ain't riskin' another pick-up. I suppose you got a stolen car sitting on the road for all the cops to see.'

'Cool it, Joe. It's in the third street down. Anyway, this is nothing.' He pointed to his stomach. 'Soon be okay. I got nowhere else to stay. And don't forget I'll cut you in five grand and maybe a bonus too.'

At the mention of the money Joe's face softened. 'Tell you what. Might be able to get some antibiotics from Shukler. He's just turned over a Boots Chemists delivery wagon – got more of the stuff than he knows what to do with. Let's watch the late Granada news first, then I'll bob down and see if he's in.'

Dominating the room from the middle of the greasy green wall of the kitchen, the television set was the only respectable piece of equipment in the house. Joe's pride and joy. He flicked the remote.

'Hey!' Sam said, managing to smile for the first time since he'd staggered in half an hour ago. 'Look at that!'

It was his own face, magnified and distorted. Must be the shot they took when he was arrested as a suspect in the murder of Joanne fuckin' Perkins.

As Sam's bearded face vanished off the screen it was replaced by Detective Chief Superintendent Paul Moxon, sitting poker-faced at his desk, appealing for witnesses to report to Stockport police station where an incident room had been set up to deal with the murder of the policewoman.

Joe stood up, hands on hips. 'That's it,' he said, talking over Moxon's voice. 'See that filth? They're gonna close in on you, mate, and I got my own skin to take care of. Already spent two fucking days inside 'cause of you. Told 'em nothing but I don't want no more trouble.'

With that he hit the off button and pointed to the kitchen door.

'I'm real sorry, mate,' he said. 'I'd help you if I could. But you'll have to go. Don't forget to take these. My brother's shirts and stuff.'

He tossed the plastic bag with the clothes at Sam, strode to the door and held it open.

Sam knew when he was beaten. He struggled to his feet. Shuffled out, eventually found his car and sat slumped at the wheel.

Fuck Joe Sagoe.

This whole thing was Julia Grant's fault. She'd betrayed him, just like all the other bitches he'd ever known. And now she'd done this. If it weren't for her, he'd never be in this shit. If it was the last thing he did, he'd make her pay for it . . .

He shook his head. What was he thinking about? Right now she had something he wanted, something he couldn't get from anywhere else, something he needed even more now than he had before. Not just for his escape pay-off to Joe and the others and to make a new life somewhere far away, but to cross the fucking channel and see a foreign medic. He'd already phoned a mate about a lorry leaving Stockport every Tuesday night at midnight bound for the French coast. It would cost a packet but when he got the cash it would feel like peanuts.

He dug in his pocket for the screwdriver. His whole body ached but he couldn't stay here much longer. He was used to being rejected, thrown out of houses. He'd always been leaving somewhere. Orphanages, foster homes, prisons. He didn't care. He didn't belong anywhere. Or to anyone. Nobody mattered except himself. Sam Smith.

So, where to now?

The pain in his head was getting worse. Worse than the pain between his legs. And much worse than the slight pain in his stomach. He tensed his hands on the steering wheel until he felt he could snap it in two.

The engine roared into life. Bitches. Whores. What had they ever given him? Sod them all. They all deserved to die . . .

He thought of Ada. Already he could smell the brandy and the cheap perfume. Feel the pain of the cigarette searing his flesh.

His mother. Nameless, faceless. If he knew who she was and where to find her he'd have killed her long ago for leaving him to the mercy of all the other bitches. And every other one he'd ever known followed in quick succession. He put his foot on the accelerator and swung out of the side street.

He slowed down at the next intersection. He could hide up in that derelict building he'd seen in Castlefield near Dukes Bar, the night he'd picked up the Peugeot. Just until the pain eased. But he'd have to ditch this useless Rover before venturing into the city. If only the fucking banging inside his head would stop —

As if from nowhere a girl appeared from behind a wall. Her long blonde hair blew across her face as she stepped towards the road.

The light caught her face.

Ada!

The pain moved to the front of his head.

Ada smiled. He jammed on the brakes.

Leapt out of the car.

Saw her eyes widen.

Saw the smile turn to fear.

THURSDAY

Paul followed Kevin down the muddy lane. He saw the trail of footprints cordoned off. Saw the trail overlapping it as though something had been dragged behind the owner of the shoes.

Stepping over the blue and white police tape, Kevin uncovered the half naked body. 'Forensics are on their way, boss.'

'I hardly need to know any more, do I? The body's in exactly the same state as Joanne Perkins' was.' He turned away, but not before he had sickened at the row of burn marks running up both the girl's arms and across her cheeks, presumably from a lighted cigarette. And the knife wound that almost certainly had finished her off. 'Do we know who she is?'

'Not yet, boss. But any girl hanging around the Alexandra Park area at midnight is usually after only one thing.'

'Witnesses?'

'None. No murder weapon either.'

Paul looked around the litter-strewn enclosure. 'I want to see Forensics' report soon as possible. Just to make doubly sure.'

'Think it was Smith?'

Paul turned to the body. 'Who else? Pattern of burn marks on the thighs, the arms, the hands. Same angle of cut in the chest. Nipples missing . . . ' He twisted his head away.

'And the hair too, boss.'

'For Chrissake —'

Paul forced himself to look at the blood-encrusted strands draped around the girl's fragile shoulders except for a two inch gap where the hair had been hacked off to bare the neck. 'Anything under the nails?'

'Nothing obvious. Didn't put up much of a fight.' Kevin glanced uneasily at Paul. 'Sorry I called you out, boss. But it's one I didn't think you'd want to miss.'

'You did right.'

Nodding to the uniforms on duty at the scene, Paul climbed into the Honda and buzzed down the window.

'I want surveillance in the house opposite Julia Grant's intensified.'

Kevin gave Paul a puzzled look. 'We've already done that as far as we can go, boss. Wouldn't it be better to have the men closer? In her garden and her house? And twenty-four hours personal?'

'No chance of that.' Paul banged his fist on the steering wheel.

'There's got to be some reason, boss. But what? Something we don't know about but I'm damned if I can begin to guess what it is. In your wildest dreams you might even think she might be protecting him.'

Paul turned the key in the ignition and the CRX roared into life. 'I'll be at Chester House,' he said, winding down the window. 'Let me know what happens.'

'Yes, boss. I didn't know you liked Smarties,' he said, pointing to the large multi-coloured box lying on the passenger seat.

- 57 -

Julia eased the Polo into the visitors' car park at Chester House and made sure the car was locked this time. The call-out mechanic had fixed the problem in five minutes, but she'd be glad when she got her own car back tomorrow. Paul's early phone call, asking her to come and see him about extra security in view of the early morning murder of a prostitute in Moss Side, enabled a smooth passage through the gate.

She walked slowly towards the entrance. He had said he was too tied up to leave his office, but felt it was imperative the situation was discussed. Julia felt she could not refuse.

At the enquiry desk she spoke to the clerk. 'I've come to see Mr Moxon.'

'Your name, please?'

'Julia Grant.'

The receptionist spoke briefly to Paul's secretary, then smiled at Julia. 'Mr Moxon will see you in about ten minutes. I'll give you an identity badge. Please take a seat. Someone will be down for you shortly.'

Julia sat down on the edge of a chair in the reception area.

Five minutes passed.

Paul had seemed certain the murder was Smith's handiwork. So the fugitive was becoming more desperate and in theory she would have to do something more to safeguard Nicky, just in case. She couldn't think what more could be done, but she might suggest they post a couple of discreet plain-clothes at the school, discreet enough not to be noticed by Smith and his spies.

The thought that so far Smith had never harmed a child nagged at her. Did this mean he never would?

Ten minutes.

It was only after she had put the phone down this morning, shaking with the shock of the news of the latest murder, that she realised Paul would undoubtedly tell her that not only was Nicky not sufficiently protected, but neither was she. Armed only with a sparse knowledge of self-protection that when first tested had resulted in nothing more than a scream and a kick to the groin, plus a gun she was ethically and morally incapable of using, and a hatpin that judging by Smith's subsequent nocturnal activities had proved totally ineffective, she would be inclined to agree with him. And he would expect her to give him some kind of explanation of why she had to continue not risking letting Smith see any evidence of police protection.

This would not be easy. If she only told him about her possible relationship to Smith but not what he'd threatened to reveal, he would probably say, Okay, big deal, Julia, you can't choose your family. Being Paul, he would ask a few pointed questions and the next minute she would be cornered and would find herself telling him about the sexual abuse from her foster father. He would be disgusted. Maybe even sympathetic. But he would know that these two facts alone, if publicly revealed, were certainly not enough justification for her to risk Nicky's safety. And he would probe further for a more feasible reason.

So she was back to square one. She could not tell him anything.

Fifteen minutes.

She wanted to believe that what Smith claimed she had done could not possibly be true. But what if it were? She desperately wanted to know but at the same time she couldn't bear the thought of knowing. And yet she couldn't deny that each day a tantalising trickle of memories was gradually and haphazardly returning random pieces of the puzzle slotting in yet still not revealing the full picture.

Twenty minutes.

Be realistic, Julia, she told herself. Forget all that. There's only one thing you have to do and that is to prevent Smith telling the authorities.

How?

By giving him the money, of course, Dummy. That was priority number one and it would solve everything: ensure Nicky's safety and prevent her own ruination. Simple.

There was still time to abort her visit. Don't tell anyone. Don't tell the police . . .

Oh God. What am I doing here? I should have made an excuse not to see Paul.

She leapt from her seat, plucked the identity badge from her lapel, mumbled an apology to the clerk and fled through the big glass doors and out into the car park.

As she fastened her seatbelt her phone rang.

'What happened, Julia? They said you just left.'

'I'm sorry, Paul. I had an urgent call. I'll ring you later.'

Half a minute later it rang again. John Cartwright's secretary. Could she be in his office at nine o'clock?

Her spirits soared. If his answer were yes, everything would be solved.

- 58 -

Julia parked near the Royal Exchange, cursing as a sudden downpour drenched the city. With her hat down over her eyes and every muscle tense, she ran across the cobbles into St Anne's Square.

'Please take a seat, Mrs Grant,' said the clerk at the reception desk.

Dutifully she sat down in one of the armchairs arranged around a small table covered with today's morning papers. What she really wanted was to walk straight in to John's office. She didn't want one of his plausible excuses. Didn't want the final blow wrapped up in his flowery language, or delayed a minute longer. If his answer was no, she wanted it straight so that she could put Plan B into action without wasting any more precious time.

The killing of the prostitute in Moss Side in the early hours of the morning hadn't made the national papers yet. It wasn't in the Metro either, and the Manchester Evening News first edition was only due out at noon, when inch high headlines announcing the sickening murder would be all over the city. She closed her eyes and into her vision swam a picture of the girl. She would be slight, with straggly dyed blonde hair. What was left of her thin underfed body would be half-clothed, burned, mutilated, with certain parts missing. And if her eyes were still open they would be wild with fear . . .

Somehow Julia would have to stop any more of this carnage.

Only a quarter million pounds to get Sam Smith out of the country could do this. Or he had to be put behind locked doors again. But the consequences of this alternative were not worth thinking about.

She stared at the panelled wall in front of her as though it were a movie screen. She saw Paul snapping on the handcuffs. Saw herself standing in the dock, the headlines proclaiming her monstrous genealogy and the crime she had committed.

She hadn't spoken to John Cartwright since he'd called her on Monday morning. The days were flashing by in what seemed like hours. If his answer were negative, she'd have no option but to go for Plan B. She clenched her fists and took a deep breath. You can't do it, Julia, she told herself. No self-respecting lawyer would contemplate such an act of forgery. And if John Cartwright is any kind of a bank manager he'll give you the money now if only to prevent such despicable malpractice. Crimes came in all degrees of despicability, she reminded herself. She still couldn't believe what she'd done to Smith last night. Everything had been automatic. The scream. Blindly thrusting the hatpin into the nearest part of his body. Right foot flying to his crotch. Running till her lungs were exploding. Stopping to get her breath back so the policemen watching from the empty house wouldn't be suspicious. Opening the gate. Walking as sedately as she could to the front door.

As though nothing had happened.

Shaking her head in disbelief she dug into her handbag and found the crumpled foil-backed card of Paracetamol. Her neck was still painful from Wednesday night's jolt. Her muscles ached from her assault on Mike. She pressed out one capsule and managed to swallow it just as John's secretary appeared.

'He'll see you now, Mrs Grant.'

She knew his office well. Opening up a second branch of Lloyd Grant had been her brainchild. She'd set up the bank loan, using Hillside House as collateral. She'd made all the financial arrangements. Apart from adding his signature to the papers, Ben had left everything to her.

'Julia. How nice to see you again.'

John Cartwright's smile was smooth and practised. His slow, gushing voice gave nothing away but was laden with a degree of false sentimentality that made Julia shiver.

She returned his smile with her equally practised poise, confident it did not reflect one iota of her inner turmoil.

From the front of his large, black, polished desk, empty apart from the blank computer screen and a gold pen and pencil set, he pulled out a chair for her. In all the years she'd known him she had never seen him appear even half as busy as she always was.

She sat down, put her handbag carefully on the floor, then placed her hat on top of it to hide the tell-tale shape of the gun.

'Well now,' John said. 'About your request for a loan.'

It was something about his tone that made her certain of his answer.

He cleared his throat, the way someone would if they were nervous about what they were about to say and had an idea it might not please the listener. 'I don't have to tell you that in order for the bank to lend you two hundred and fifty thousand pounds, and of course, this applies no matter who we're dealing with, we would need security.'

Get on with it, John. Just say it.

'Now, under normal circumstances your house would provide that security more than adequately.' He scratched his florid cheek with a perfectly manicured nail. 'But because of the existing charge on the house we would need to look . . . elsewhere.'

She sensed that somehow he knew just how desperate she was and was trying to be as gentle as possible. Could she afford to sit here another ten minutes to hear what she almost certainly already knew? Damn. Had that second branch of Lloyd Grant really been necessary? The extra staff were eating up most of the profits so far, leaving Ben and her scarcely better off than they'd been with only one branch.

John Cartwright stroked the fold of skin beneath his chin. 'But notwithstanding the question of security, you still haven't told me for what purpose the money is required.'

It would be useless to plead. She could invent something now but in order for the loan to be agreed, John would demand an income and expenditure account. Or proof in writing of her ability to repay.

All of this she knew, so why was she even sitting here? Just another of her ill-thought-out, inconsistent, illogical actions kindled by Sam Smith . . .

'Would you like some tea, Julia? You look a little — '

'No thanks. I'm fine.' She dropped her shoulders and lifted her chin.

'I'm sure you're aware that if the decision were in my hands alone, I would . . .' His voice drifted off and he looked at her with raised eyebrows almost as though he thought she might be the one to provide the solution. 'I'd like to help,' he said at last, 'and I'm sure we could work something out, but — '

'But without adequate security and clear reasons for the loan,' Julia butted in, 'you would turn down my application. Right?'

'I'm afraid so.' He didn't even hesitate. So why all that farting around when he could have come straight to the point?

Mumbling that she had to be in court, she grabbed her hat and her handbag. Before John was out of his chair she had covered the space between his desk and the door and was out of the room.

'Plan B,' she said out loud as she ran into the summer downpour, heading for the office, leaving the car in St Anne's Square and not caring who heard her or who saw the wild look in her eyes.

Ben was in the lobby when she burst in through the door. He stared open-mouthed at her dripping clothes.

'Why the hell didn't you take a taxi?'

His unexpected appearance threw Julia into confusion. She pulled off her sodden hat. 'It's like this every June, isn't it, but it always catches me out.'

He fidgeted with his hands as though he was embarrassed at her reply.

He'd not been due back from London till tomorrow. Julia knew that before putting Plan B into operation she must grasp this one last unexpected opportunity his early return was presenting.

Her skin chilled as he turned and walked towards his office. She was unable to stop herself. She ran after him. 'May I talk to you?'

He drew in his breath as though he was going to say something, then silently led the way. Julia declined his offer of a seat. If she hesitated for one more second this final chance might be lost.

'Ben, I want to make an advance of capital out of the trust fund. For the benefit of Nicky.'

She was used to his poker-faced expression. There was seldom any sign before he made decisions. But this long pause was unusual.

For one unbearably sweet moment she had one of her visions of it all happening. Borrowing the money from the trust. Handing it to Smith. Smith somewhere in South America, her ghastly secret forever locked away. Nicky walking happily to school, playing in the park . . .

'I thought we'd been through all this.'

His voice was non-committal, without the undertone of bitterness so obvious on Monday. She waited but he said nothing more.

Okay, Julia Grant. It's up to you to plead your case.

With one hand she leaned on his desk.

'Since last talking to you, I've taken expert advice.' She paused. How she hated having to lie to him. How she wished things could revert to the easy professional relationship that had existed between them until last Friday night.

'Go on,' he said, his eyes distant, yet with an underlying look of . . . what? She didn't know, even though she knew him so well. Disgust perhaps.

'Right. Well, I believe now's the time to provide for Nicky's school and university fees. The trust contains provisions under which we're allowed to do that, doesn't it? Pay for her education?'

'Yes. That is so.'

'So. I'll take out two-fifty thousand now and get the education brokers to do the necessary.'

'Julia? You look terrible. Why don't you sit down? Take off that wet jacket.'

She shook her head. She needed this to be over now.

He sighed, took a step towards her, then seemed to change his mind and walked to the far side of the room. 'The situation is crystal clear,' he said. 'This trust is watertight. We have two and a half million sitting there with Melbourne Kennedy which they've invested in stocks and shares for the benefit of Nicky and she's going to get it when she's eighteen,' he said, swinging round to face her.

'You mean you're turning down my request?'

He pursed his lips, looked down at the floor, then back at the rain spattering on the window.

'Why, Ben?'

'Because it's a damn rotten idea. Reducing the trust fund when Nicky's only six. When her present school fees come easily out of your earnings. When the income the trust is earning now would undoubtedly cover future school and university fees even if they trebled. Are you losing your marbles, Julia?'

She stared at him in disbelief. 'I shouldn't have to beg for something that is Nicky's by right. I should be able to have money from that trust for any reason I think fit. I'm the child's mother, for God's sake. I should be able to — ' She put her hands over her face. She was fully aware of her own irrational and unprofessional behaviour.

'Why? What's got into you, Julia? What is all this about?' He walked towards her.

She edged backwards. 'I've already told you why.'

'Nicky's education? I'm supposed to believe that. That's rubbish. And why didn't you tell me this on Monday, for God's sake? Why the big secret when you first mentioned it?'

She blinked her eyes and, as she did, another vision loomed. Not a tall, lean, emaciated wraith, grey of countenance, desperate to wreak revenge by dragging her into the quagmire of his own pathetic life, but a small knobbly-kneed child with a shock of blond hair flopping over big blue eyes, whose body had warmed hers when only one threadbare blanket had left her shivering in the night . . .

'Why should I always tell you . . . everything?' she said, confused by her own ping-pong thoughts.

He walked back to the window, hands thrust deep into his pockets. He stood watching the rain, then swung round to face her again.

'I think it's time you took a holiday. I don't know what's come over you. I'm not quite sure why I have to spell it out to you like this, but the settlement was made by Nicky's grandparents with Simon, you and me as trustees, under which Nicky is to have the capital when she turns eighteen. And they chose the age of eighteen for good tax reasons, didn't they, Julia, rather than twenty-one or twenty-five. They got expert advice. She can't have it under eighteen, unless it's for some exceptional need. As you damn well know.'

Julia rubbed her eyes. Oh yes. It's an exceptional need, all right, but nevertheless she felt very foolish. This is what Sam Smith is doing to me, she thought. Forcing me to search for loopholes which I knew before I started did not exist.

Plan B then, is all I have left.

'You know I've always been very close to the Grant family,' Ben went on, almost as though he were seeking atonement for his outburst. 'At school with Simon, shared digs at university, best man at your wedding, carried his coffin . . .'

He breathed in deeply, then cracked his knuckles one by one. 'And now,' he said quietly, 'I'm your . . . your partner.'

He walked to his desk, leaned on his hands so that his eyes were level with Julia's and it was impossible for her to look away.

'I know what's going on,' he said.

She gripped the desk. He can't possibly know. He's just saying that. Nobody knows except Paul and even he doesn't know everything. Damn. Why didn't I think this whole thing through properly. Ben knows what goes into my bank account every month, knows what Nicky's little private school costs. If I was going to tell lies about wanting money, I should have thought of something more immediate than education. I knew he wouldn't buy this, but what else is there?

She forced her face to remain expressionless, her hands to be still. 'You know Nicky has to have the best education. Simon wouldn't have settled for less. It should have been a discretionary trust.' Aware that her voice could be heard through the thin dividing walls, she repeated more quietly, 'A discretionary trust, under which the trustees make up their minds as they go along about what's going to happen for the good of the child.'

'But it's not a discretionary trust, Julia. So forget this wild scheme, this whatever it is you're planning with Moxon. Okay? Forget it.'

- 60 -

Julia sat down at her desk. She was on her own now. Completely on her own. She'd been foolish to try. Jealousy makes people say and do things quite out of character, and she should have made allowances for this. She should also have thought of something more plausible than school and university fees. She looked at her watch. She was due in court five minutes ago but she'd just have to be late. This was priority number one.

It was a good thing the shares were registered in a nominee name of the stockbroker. It saved signing a lot of share transfers when time was vital, and all that was needed now to instruct their broker to proceed was a letter signed by them both.

By herself.

And by Ben.

She swivelled round to face her computer.

Dear Fred,

*Ben and I have decided to raise two hundred and fifty
thousand pounds out of the trust. Please, at your discretion,
sell sufficient to raise that money.*

*With education costs rising so rapidly we have decided it
would be better to provide for Nicky's education without
further delay, so we authorise you to proceed immediately.*

She paused. That's all very well, but what should Melbourne Kennedy do with the money? Ordinarily it would be paid into the firm's Client Account.

She pressed the delete button, then started again.

Dear Fred,

*Ben and I have decided to raise two hundred and fifty
thousand pounds to pay for ~~Nicola's~~ Nicky's education.*

*Ben and I have agreed that I will make the arrangements for a
dedicated insurance policy through a reputable firm of brokers
that deal with school and university fees insurance.*

*So please credit the money to my private bank account by
inter-bank transfer as we don't want to get this confused with
our Client Account.*

She read it over, made a few changes, added a suitable ending and printed it out. She was counting on Fred being so busy that he would not dig too deeply into the reason, which now that it was in writing seemed flimsier and more ludicrous than ever, but with time running out there was nothing else she could do. How long, she wondered, would it take to sell those shares and get the money?

She picked up her phone and dialled Fred's direct number.

He answered after the first ring. 'It's Julia Grant, Fred. How are

205

things?'

'Fine, Julia. How can I help?'

'Just some information, please. I'm a bit out of touch. What's the Stock Exchange account date these days? I heard the rolling settlement had come down.'

Last time she'd had any dealings it was ten days, and that was ages ago.

'It changed some time ago, Julia. It's three days after instructions now.'

She thanked Fred and put the phone down, cursing her lack of foresight. Damn, if only they'd kept ten percent of the trust money in cash.

Three days. But it would be three working days. Today was Thursday. Sam Smith's deadline was Monday. Oh God. One day short.

She clamped her teeth together. One day short was better than no money at all. She signed the letter then tore off a small piece of paper from her pad.

This was the point of no return.

BWA Lloyd, she wrote, pressing down with the pen the way Ben always did.

She wrote it again. She wiped her cheeks with the back of her hand.

Forgive me, Ben. I'll explain as soon as it's safe to tell you.

She looked at the signature from every angle. Yes, it was a perfect facsimile. Before she could change her mind, she pulled the letter towards her. Next to her own name she signed BWA Lloyd, folded the letter and placed it in an envelope. On the front she wrote:

Mr F Kennedy. Melbourne and Kennedy. Personal and Confidential.

She sealed it and put it in her handbag. She would deliver it herself on her way to court.

This is for you, Nicky. For us. Our future.

She put on her hat and stuck the pin through the fold-up front, took the pistol out of her handbag and locked it in her desk drawer.

She felt sick and dizzy but strangely content. Now all she had to do was stall Sam Smith for one extra day.

61

Kevin Moorsley looked across the desk at his boss. His face was taut and he knew what that meant.

'Let's take Sagoe in again, Kevin. Bang him in cells at Stockport.'

'What are the charges, boss?'

'Further investigations. Smith shot Avril near Sagoe's house. That's enough for me. And don't tell me I'm grasping at straws.'

Kevin sighed. 'We got nowhere with him last time.'

He stood up and walked to the door. When the boss said nothing it meant there was no point in arguing. But as he well knew, sometimes the seemingly haphazard hunches of DCS Paul Moxon triggered the solution to the most insoluble of crimes.

62

My lucky break, Julia thought as she put down the receiver. Joe Sagoe. The one person who might have news of Smith, his physical condition and where he was hiding, asking for me, rather than the duty solicitor. She hadn't risked going to Sagoe's house in case it was still under surveillance, so this was a golden opportunity.

She removed the pan of soup she'd been heating for her supper, then dialled Wendy's number. If only the girl would move into Hillside House instead of sharing that tiny flat with her friend, she wouldn't have to drag her out at all hours whenever she had to see clients urgently.

But, as usual, Wendy didn't mind. 'I'll come straightaway,' she answered cheerily. 'Is Nicky asleep?'

'Out for the count,' Julia told her. 'You should have seen her and Duchess. Up and down the stairs like tornadoes, the two of them.' She glanced at the fluffy bundle in the basket. 'I reckon a bomb wouldn't waken this little Poodle now.'

'Sometimes I could murder that puppy,' Wendy said. 'But then I don't know what Nicky would do without her. I'll be there in five minutes.'

Julia put down the phone. A sudden movement at the window made her jump. It's my own reflection, for goodness sake – hair awry, eyes staring, behaving like a fugitive. And no wonder. After what I did today.

'Smith has done this to me,' she said aloud.

She shuddered at the thought of what she'd done to him. Why the hatpin, she asked herself. The scream and the kick in the crotch would surely have been enough. Or she could have used any one of the counter-attacking moves she had just learned from Mike. Come to think of it, Smith didn't lay a finger on me, even though he was invading my space. Maybe he needed to talk to me, to seek my help . . .

Julia's knowledge of anatomy was limited to what she had learned at school, supplemented with other scraps, haphazardly gleaned as necessary to help her with murder cases and others where bodily mayhem had featured. The hatpin must somehow have missed all his vital organs, yet three inches of steel must have done some damage, even though it had come out of his lean sinewy stomach without a trace of blood.

Joe Sagoe just might have seen Smith. It was a long shot. He hadn't phoned today as he promised he would. She needed to know what state he was in. She hadn't analysed this need, but she knew she wouldn't rest until she'd discovered what had happened. His silence meant either that a public phone was now too risky, or that he was ill. But if he were ill, if she really had injured him, he would hardly have been capable of rape and murder.

But by all accounts he had done just that. Which meant he was alive and well.

And just waiting to make his next move.

She had to know for sure. And Sagoe just might be her man.

A high-pitched grunt from Duke's basket made her start. As she bent down and stroked the Poodle, she thought of Duke, his golden coat, his rain-wet smell, his adorable head drooping over the basket as he followed her every move with those loving brown eyes.

Last week Duke was still in that basket.

She closed her eyes. Duke in his basket, when our world was still normal, safe and happy. When Nicky and I could do whatever we liked. When my longed-for brother was the stuff that dreams were made of, to be fashioned in any name or guise I chose. How that world has changed. How I wish I could turn back the clock. But Wendy will be here in a minute and must not see me like this.

She wiped her eyes. A memory flashed . . .

Somewhere. Long ago. Holding back her tears.

If you two little brats don't stop bawling this minute, I'll give you both something to cry about . . .

You two . . .

She wished she knew how it was that she remembered some things and not others, and why events were so out of sequence. Are some memories mere imaginings, she wondered. How can I be certain where reality leaves off and fantasy begins?

- 63 -

Julia took the shortcut through Bramhall into Stockport, crossed the Buxton Road into Hillgate, turned into Edward Street and parked her now immaculate red SLK outside the police station.

She ran up the steps and pushed through the heavy swing doors. At the reception area a uniformed WPC, who she knew well, greeted her.

'I'll tell the custody sergeant you're here, Julia.'

Julia thanked her and sat down to wait. She had a sudden crazy urge to nip upstairs for the latest low-down in the Incident Room before she saw Sagoe. Nonsensical, of course, she told herself. And sufficient to have you thrown out of the police station for transgressing the parameters of your job . . .

The WPC caught her daydreaming eye and smiled. 'PC's on his way to take you down,' she said.

Minutes later a member of the custody staff beckoned Julia to follow him downstairs into the custody suite. He stood in front of her at the door, keyed in the security code on the lock and entered.

She walked up to the broad desk and took her file and notepad from her briefcase. Without being asked for it, the custody sergeant presented her with the cumbersome custody record for her client. She spread it in front of her and checked off, almost automatically, the clinical history relating to his arrest: time, reasons, health. She looked up at the custody sergeant's square, jovial face and wondered why he seemed to extract so much satisfaction from his job. 'It says here he's been arrested for murder times two and assisting an escape from lawful custody,' she said.

He nodded and raised an eyebrow. 'Correct,' he said, and I've just called Mr Moxon to come and explain the situation and give you disclosure.'

He looked up at the sound of footsteps approaching from behind Julia. She swung round, drop-jawed, and found herself looking into Paul's eyes. She was momentarily speechless, shocked to find that Paul was becoming personally involved in the enquiry at this level.

Paul flashed a barely perceptible smile. 'Disclosure, Mrs Grant?'

Julia followed him along the corridor to an interview room, only then noticing that Kevin Moorsley was walking alongside her. The din of raised voices coming from the cell area almost drowned the cacophony of tinny radios all broadcasting different versions of the seemingly same mindless music and made any conversation impossible. Julia tried not to breathe in the smell of urine and disinfectant, though she had to admit Stockport was like a hospital ward compared to some police stations. Jeyes Fluid would make a fortune if they could improve the aroma, she thought.

Once inside the interview room she rediscovered her voice. 'Mr Moxon, what a surprise to find you here.' She glanced at Kevin Moorsley and nodded as he pulled out a chair for her at the grey metal table dominating the room.

'The feeling is entirely mutual, Mrs Grant. With your involvement with Smith I would have thought you would decline to act.'

'For Mr Sagoe?' she cut in, making a deliberate show of opening her handbag and putting the packet of Dunhill Extras on the table, together with matches. Sagoe will have had everything taken off him except something to read and his cigarettes, but he wouldn't have a light. She had given up the weed years ago, but offering him one of hers might make him relaxed enough to answer her discreet question about how Smith had stood up to her impromptu attack. An interview between a client and his solicitor is privileged and its contents cannot be used in evidence, but if their conversation *were* overheard the consequences would be dire. She looked around quickly for evidence of bugging, though she doubted Stockport would stoop so low. There was the usual microphone on the wall above the table. Behind her the tape-recorder was still and silent. A small panel controlled the ventilation system, a merciful refinement in this windowless room. Nothing else. She was safe.

She smiled at Paul. 'You won't mind, I'm sure,' she said at last, 'if I feel free to be the judge of that decision. Anyway, let's get on with it, shall we? Disclosure.'

'What do you want to know?' Paul asked.

'I would have thought that was obvious.' Julia was now entirely immersed in her role as solicitor for this suspect. Paul Moxon became just another police officer trying to put away just another of her clients. Very well, she thought, if he's got the ammunition to do it, fine. If he hasn't, he's up against Julia Grant.

'So?'

Paul leaned forward, his elbows planted on the table in front of him, hands raised in the air and clasped together with overlapping fingers. 'One: Sagoe is a known associate of Sam Smith. You probably knew that anyway so I'm not going to give you chapter and verse on this.

'Two: eye witnesses to Smith being sprung from the prison van gave a description of an accomplice who fitted with Sagoe. Before you ask, none will be able to ID Sagoe because the offenders were masked, but it was the general height and build we were interested in, you know, one of those things you can start to build up a picture from.

'Three: one of my officers was shot dead, as you know full well, not more than a hop, skip and jump from Sagoe's house, which she was staking out. And then a prostitute gets killed in the neighbourhood and the MO is pure Smith. We're not saying Sagoe was in on it but it fits in with Smith being there because of his connection with Sagoe.'

Julia watched his face closely. He had a look of steely determination. He was obsessed with re-capturing Smith. 'But you've already hauled Sagoe over the coals and let him go, so what new evidence have you got that warrants another arrest?' she demanded.

'The killing of the prostitute was only last night,' Paul said. 'We haven't asked him about that yet.'

'And you can't reasonably expect to either, surely?'

'Worse things have happened,' he said. 'A young girl from his community viciously killed by a man he's brought there, you never know . . .'

Julia took a deep breath, wincing at the smell of stale cigarette smoke wafting up from the tin wastebasket which, judging by its odour, was nothing but a giant ashtray. 'Well, if that's it, I'd like to have a word with him, please.'

'Coffee?' Paul asked. 'It'll only be a MaxPax, but better than nothing.'

Julia's face softened. 'That would be nice.'

'Kev, MaxPax for Mrs Grant, if you don't mind, and wheel in Sagoe on your way back too. If I'm not mistaken it's milk, no sugar.'

Moorsley obliged without a murmur, closing the door behind him.

Still watching the door, Paul waited a few moments, then switched his gaze back to Julia.

'Don't do this, Julia. You know you've got a conflict. And you know I'm right. There's enough there to go at, and if he played his cards right he'd come clean and we can do a deal with him.'

'But you want me off the scene first, don't you, because you think I'll be harbouring some interest in favour of Smith that would make me advise against doing a deal.' She shook her head. 'Frankly, I'm disappointed, Paul. You've got a hunch, maybe even a good one, but it's some way off being damning evidence. I don't have a conflict. And I also think you know exactly how I'm going to advise my client. Naturally if he wants to confess, I won't stand in his way.'

Paul looked pleadingly at Julia, then lowered his eyes.

'Paul, don't ask me again, please. Let's keep this professional.'

'No,' he said, then looked up slowly. 'I want to see you afterwards.'

'You mean — '

'Nothing to do with this case.'

'I must get home. Wendy's baby-sitting.'

'Just for a few minutes. Please. It's important.'

Only moments ago he'd been the tough efficient policeman. And now?

Heavy footsteps echoed along the corridor, a sense of urgency in their staccato beat.

'That'll be Kevin bringing your client down. We'll do this by the book. See you afterwards, away from here. I'll wait at your car.'

Julia nodded her agreement as the door flew open.

'Boss,' Moorsley blurted. 'It's Sagoe. You'd better come right now. Custody Sergeant thinks he's dead.'

* * *

Julia thanked the PC for escorting her to the door. She had hung around for a few minutes to see if there was anything she could do to help, but in the end had asked to leave. Paul had said he had wanted to see her, but that was before the shock news of Sagoe's death. There'd be no chance of that now so the sooner she got out of here the better.

She shivered as she walked out into the cool night air. Poor Joe. He'd never looked healthy as long as she'd known him, but at least he had no family left to mourn him since his brother was killed.

She stopped abruptly at the top of the steps as the realisation suddenly hit her. Now I'll never know whether Smith was badly injured or not, she whispered to herself, until he makes his next move. There's no one else to ask. He could be here now, in this road, waiting to follow me in whatever car he has just stolen . . .

Her legs felt stiff and leaden. She looked both ways and then once more before going down the steps. She stopped again. And although there was no traffic in sight, she hesitated. Finally she crossed the street and ran to her car. She was just about to unlock the door and jump in when she heard footsteps behind her.

- 64 -

As Paul bounded down the steps he took the two tickets from his pocket in readiness. He had wondered all week how to persuade her to spend some time with him, and the Royal Northern College of Music concert advert on the canteen wall had provided the perfect answer.

'Tomorrow night. Back row seats. All I could get. Programme nothing but Mozart,' he blurted out as he skidded to a halt beside her.

Like a frightened kitten she jumped when she heard his voice. He quickly took her arm.

'All your favourites,' he said, smiling and holding up the tickets.

'Oh, Paul,' she said, sounding as though she was about to cry.

She was flicking her head nervously from left to right. A few people were walking past and it seemed that she was scrutinising each one of them.

'Is this what you wanted to see me about so urgently?' she asked.

All at once Paul realised how frightened she was. She had worked hard at appearing unconcerned at Smith's threat, but now she was like a bird that has flown into a room and can't find its way out.

'You need a break,' he said. 'All this is too much for you.' He held her arm. 'And there's something else wrong too. What is it, Julia? Has Smith been in touch with you again?'

'Paul, nothing's wrong. I . . . I'm just . . . I'm missing Duke.'

'Yes, of course you are.' He moved closer. 'But please come tomorrow. We can meet at the concert hall if you're working late.'

'Paul . . . '

'What?'

'What about Sagoe?'

'A heart attack, I think. And I must go back quickly. I'd hoped you'd come to the flat for a coffee. I've something I want to give you. It'll have to wait till tomorrow. After the concert.'

'I didn't say I'd come.'

'You need to relax, Julia. Mozart. All your favourites. Please?'

He pulled her towards him, surprised when his fingers felt her ribs through her flimsy blouse.

'Yes. All right,' she said. 'But only if Wendy can baby-sit.'

'Quarter past seven. In the foyer. Quick drink first.' He opened the door for her. He held her gaze and then she was gone.

As he ran across the road he watched her tail-lights disappear.

A thread, he thought, as he charged back up the steps. A fragile thread. But it's a start.

- 65 -

Nothing moved on the Rochdale Canal. Nothing but the murky green ripples splashing against the slimy walls. He heard footsteps echoing on the towpath. Stopped. The footsteps stopped.

He held his stomach, dug his fingers in to stop the pain. He looked over his shoulder. There was no one there.

Must lie down soon. Somewhere. Anywhere. Christ. All the fucking buildings were boarded up. Must get to Dukes . . .

Blue and white police ribbon. Must walk faster.

Under Deansgate. Water swishing over the lock. Lock 91. Thirsty. Dukes Bar not far now.

Under the railway bridge. Water dripping. Drip drip drip. A train squealing on the rails.

Must lie down. Must get to that derelict building opposite Dukes Bar. The one with the tower. Blackened with age and fire. No windows left to board up . . .

At last. Lights. Hanging baskets full of flowers. Chairs outside. Sounds of laughter. Jeez, he could smell the beer. Taste it. Feel it trickling down his cracked throat.

He jingled the coins in his pocket. Enough for half a pint. Maybe some fags and matches too? No. Not a hope. Must conserve the funds for petrol and vital phone calls.

He stood drinking near the door. Safer there, just in case. Two more gulps of beer. Felt like angels pissing down his throat.

215

Damn. Too much. Hand over mouth. Quickly. Out the door. Over the bridge. Up three steps to the cobbled car park. A dirty white Fiesta. Abandoned?

Keep going now. Under the dripping archway and there it is, oh God, how beautiful, it could be the Ritz, a pigeon perched like a statue of liberty on top of the sagging roof, stumbling over hollyhocks, piles of rock, rubble, plastic bags, ancient rusty pipes and twisted metal. Falling on the floor. Vomiting at last.

He drew his knees up to his stomach. Pressed out the last two buttons from the foil pack Joe had given him. Washed them down with the few remaining drops in the small plastic water bottle, thankful he had a spare one in Joe's survival bag.

Drip drip drip. Water from nowhere into puddles on the floor. Only it wasn't a floor any more. Weeds growing out of it. An old boiler with a shiny tube going through the charred bricks.

Julia Grant did this. Must pay her back. For fuck's sake, how? Think. How?

The wind howled, blew dust in his face. He pulled a piece of black plastic over his head and slid into blessed oblivion.

In his sleep he heard a siren.

Was it dawn or was he imagining the light in the gaping holes that once were windows?

He opened his eyes wider. Saw bits of wire hanging from the blackened rafters, the piles of rubble. Shivered. Drew the plastic closer. He had often seen this building from Dukes Bar but had never thought it would be home.

REVENGE. He saw the word scorched in the wooden rafters, cut by flames belching from his wound. Never intended touching the child or hurting her in any way. Only to frighten the bitch into giving him the cash.

But things were different now.

He held his swollen stomach. Never thought it would come to this. It was okay walking down a street, going in a pub, taking a chance. But not okay to see a medic with all their fucking forms and questions.

He felt the square edges of the passport in his pocket. All he needed was the brass. And the bitch had all that, only she was hanging on to it. Hoping the filth would get him before she had to cough up. So far nothing he had threatened or done to her had made her see sense. By now any other broad would have thrown the lucre at him. Take it, they would have screamed. Anything for peace. For safety. For silence. But not Mrs Solicitor fucking Grant. She thought she could out-think him. Wear him down. Make him give himself up.

Well, she was fucking wrong.

Nothing Ada had ever done had surprised him as much as that hatpin. He'd hardly felt a thing. No blood. Nothing to worry about at first except the indignity. And the pain in his balls.

But now it had changed.

The pain gnawed. The buttons had made no fucking difference. He adjusted the plank under his head.

Pain. All his life he'd had pain. Not just from Ada but long before when he'd first fled from it into the night, sirens screaming, frightened, cold, running, feet bleeding, sleeping on stones, running . . . running . . . running . . . Away from the blood and the terror . . .

He knew how to tell pain to go away. Ada had taught him that. Otherwise he'd never have survived. So do it now, for Chrissake.

Tell yourself you have no fucking pain.

He licked his lips. What he wouldn't give for that John Smith's he'd left on the windowsill at Dukes.

A scuttling near his feet. He jerked his knees up and wrapped his arms around his ribs.

He'd had rats for playthings when they used to come up through the holes in the caravan, when Ada locked him in for hours and hours. The games had always been evenly matched. He'd be sitting on the floor, dead still, watching the rat until it was right next to him. Then he'd shoot his hand out like a chameleon catching a fly and grab its tail.

He'd hold it firmly. Watch it wriggle and squirm, wetting itself with fright. He'd always given it a chance. It could have bitten him any time it liked, but it never had. And when it was worn out and shit scared and its hair was standing up straight with lack of food and water, he'd let it have it.

First a blow to the head to stun it. It would stagger a bit then flop over. Its eyes would close. Then they'd open and look at him like it wanted to say something. It would squeal. Oh yeah. It would squeal okay. Just like he had. Yelled and squealed and cried and pleaded, only no bastard had shown him any mercy. Now it was the rat's turn.

The next step was a lot of fun. The only fun he ever had. Out would come his flick-knife, the one he'd nicked off old Bert when he hadn't let him warm his hands on his miserable old fire when Ada had taken his coat off of him for coming home late. It was a long time since he'd had a flick-knife of his own.

One jab on either side of its spine usually made the legs go berserk. After a few minutes it would stop and just lie there looking at him. He always took the front legs off first, laying them next to the rat like two crutches. It looked so stupid with only two legs.

He took his time over the back legs. First there were the smaller, more interesting bits. Like the ears . . .

The room – the whole dilapidated space was starting to revolve.

He closed his eyes. Breathed in deeply. He knew what was coming.

First there was nothing. Just blackness. Then jagged flashes across the big red screen. And those white marble sculpted shapes coming and going like the intestines of a rat when he'd slit its stomach and tried to push them back inside.

The scuttling noise again. The waves of dreamy relaxation. He knew the signs.

And then, from nowhere it came. Leaping into his head. A plan.

A brilliant plan.

He forced his eyes to open.

Julia.

Thought she was so tough. But she wasn't. She would scare easy. Not the usual bullshit. He'd tried all that crap and none of it had worked. But now he knew how.

It was all different now.

First he'd frighten the shit out of her. One step at a time. Like with the rats. Leave her to stew and then . . . Wham! A shame, really. All her fault. Now he had to go the whole hog. Put the bitch through hell and back again until she paid up. Scare her to death.

Must get to a phone.

He tried to move. His eyelids drooped. He forced them open but they closed again. His head slid slowly down. Tomorrow, he murmured. Tomorrow I'll begin.

FRIDAY

66

Julia sat at her desk paging through the files for the day's cases, seeing the words but not their meaning. If I don't hear from Smith before I go to court, she said to herself, this will prove conclusively that he is ill.

Or even dead.

She gulped the cold black coffee. No. Not dead. Please, not dead . . .

In this cat and mouse game the element of surprise would be high on his agenda. If he could make me think he was dead I would begin to relax and thereby increase my vulnerability. Well, I'm ready for that.

'May I come in?'

Before she could object, Ben walked in. He pulled up a chair and placed it on her right, far too close for her liking.

He looked at her and squinted. 'You look terrible, Julia.'

Her efforts to cover the circles under her eyes with the Max Factor Lasting Performance she kept for emergencies had clearly failed. 'I didn't sleep last night,' she said.

'You look as though you haven't slept for a week. What the hell is wrong?'

She pressed her thumbnails into the ends of her fingers one after the other. She looked down at the dents and watched them slowly disappear. Why is he behaving as though nothing unusual has happened between us? Was that barbecue fiasco only one week ago? Has he forgotten everything?

She edged away from his encroaching arm. 'Nothing,' she said. 'Nothing's wrong.'

'Well, I'm glad you've at last decided to take a sensible attitude about last Friday night. We must have a chat and see what we can sort out.'

His smugness made Julia feel quite sick. How the hell have I worked with him for so long and never noticed before how bloody insensitive he is?

220

She scraped her nails against her teeth. He had once been a friend, a confidant, a trusted colleague. He seemed so distant now. In fact everyone Julia knew was distant these days. There was not one person she could really talk to — not even Paul — or even Wendy now, so wrapped up with her pregnancy.

I desperately need his help and all he can think of is making a bloody pass at me.

'You could do with a rest, Julia. Why not take a few days off?' He reached for her hand.

She snatched it away.

'Sam Smith's threat getting to you, is it? Even though you said it wouldn't. He's sure been having a field day. A cop, and now another prostitute.'

She turned away and shook her head from side to side as though this would make her see more clearly.

'At least he's proved he isn't interested in harming you, Julia. I thought you'd be his number one target, but you were right all along. He was only reacting on the spur of the moment like so many of them do. So why don't you relax?'

A rash of goose pimples erupted at the tops of her arms. She wanted to scream. She didn't need this. She stood up and turned to face him.

'If you'll excuse me, Ben, I don't want to be late for court.'

He gripped her wrist. 'For God's sake, Julia. Sit down. You're in no state to go to court. Look at you. Caroline or Mark will fill in for you. I'll drive you home.'

She threw the files into her briefcase, switched her phone through to Linda and marched past him, her lips tightly closed, her eyes blurred with the tears she was determined would not fall.

As she slammed through the reception office Linda shouted after her. 'There's a call for you, Julia. It's — '

But the crash of the banging door drowned the rest of Linda's words.

67

With little space between the magistrates' bench, the court clerk and the solicitors' bench, Julia felt more than ever before as though the two rows of seats for the public were right on top of her. As usual she pretended they did not exist. The yellow walls, the dull brown and beige of the carpet, and the spider web of lights hidden in the latticed ceiling did nothing to alleviate her sensation of entombment.

She opened her file. Signalling discreetly to her client, she scribbled him a note, something she'd just thought of that she wanted him to emphasise in the witness box. She tore the page from her pad, folded it, stood up and began walking towards the glassed-in dock, when a movement in the public gallery caught her eye.

A man was looking at her, his eyes . . . .

She held on to the side of the dock. Without showing a flicker of recognition, she handed the note to the dock officer, returned to her seat and made sure her face was still in repose.

The one thing she didn't want was to give him the impression that she knew he was there. In a courtroom she'd become over the years rather like a poker player. Even when someone said something of major significance, which nobody else picked up on, she would never immediately jump on it or show that she'd been given a little gold coin. She would quietly store it away. She would then start to develop an argument, which appeared on the face of it to have no relevance to that little gem she'd just been given. And because she'd developed an instinct for not giving herself away, she'd become like a millpond: nobody could read her emotions or the way she was thinking, and she would not release herself from that state until her final speech, letting go the passion as she brought out one point after another, everything that had been lying quietly under the surface.

Those years of practice were paying off now.

The bastard: he wanted her to see him.

Don't react, Julia. He's deliberately trying to wind you up. Do nothing. Don't look at him and he'll think, well Christ, did she even see me? Or, did she see me and is she so clever that she's playing me at my own game?

She could tell the police right now that he was here in this court. They would catch him. Word would get out to his spies like wildfire. Nicky would be in danger and he would tell the whole world . . .

But like a snake creeping into a warm basket, curiosity overcame. And she couldn't stop herself looking up again.

He was gone.

She leapt to her feet. Saw the magistrate's pursed lips.

'Do you have a problem, Mrs Grant?'

'I'm sorry, Sir. I thought I just — '

Her hand flew to her mouth.

Anyway, it couldn't have been him. In spite of having shaved off his beard, the man was hardly going to walk into a public courtroom, knowing the whole of the Manchester police force was out looking for him. Not unless he was demented or intent on suicide, and she knew he was neither of those. If she went blabbing to the court that she'd just seen Sam Smith.

'Yes, Mrs Grant?' the magistrate said patiently.

'Sir, I would like to ask for a short stand down. It's entirely my fault, Sir. It looks as though I've left half the contents of my file somewhere, either in the advocate's room or the canteen, I imagine. Very silly of me, but I really will need them.'

'We're wasting time, Mrs Grant, but we'll retire for a few minutes until you're back.'

She careered up the steps, through the swing doors into the main corridor, quickly scanned the rows of black vinyl seats, glanced through the plate glass windows overlooking Crown Square, and skidded round the corner to the lifts. Not one lift even on its way so she started down the stairs. Stopping on Level 2 she looked down over the balcony at the open-plan ground floor. No sign of him.

Down one more flight and the cream walls with matching cream floors seemed to suck her into their blandness. It was like trying to run in a dream.

He couldn't have got far. He must be somewhere in Crown Square, so get moving, she told herself. This could be your only chance.

Nodding at Security she almost collided with the bank of potted palms, pushed through the swing doors then yanked open the heavy glass door and stopped at the top of the long flight of stone steps that swept down to Crown Square.

He was nowhere in sight.

It was strange that no one else had seen him. With his face all over the media every person in Manchester must know what he looked like. Or had nobody recognised him without the beard?

She ran around the square, peering at everyone. She would have to get back. Maybe she had superimposed his face on some innocent onlooker. She'd done that before. It was something she was rather good at.

If the person she'd seen was Smith then the hatpin could not have done much damage. But if it was *not* him . . .

She began the long walk back up the steps. Embarrassed. Frustrated. Disgusted. More isolated and more alone than ever before. She re-entered the court room, suddenly realising she had no papers with her that could be flourished to justify her earlier departure. 'Sorry about that,' she muttered breathlessly to the clerk, 'I'll have to make do without the documents – can't find them'

- 68 -

Julia finally got to the office at five-thirty. With a mug of coffee in front of her, she dialled the Hillside House number. Wendy had agreed to baby-sit while she went to the concert with Paul tonight. She'd said Alan was out of town on a big job and she hadn't even wanted to go for her usual Friday evening hairdo.

Nicky answered. 'Hiya, Mummy. Paul was here. Are you coming home now?'

Julia smiled to herself. He was full of surprises. It was some time since he'd just popped in to say hello to Nicky on a Friday evening. 'I told you I'd be late tonight, darling, but I'm glad Paul came. What did you two do?'

'He brought me Smarties. And a pink frilly scrunchie for my ballet bun. And a book about horses. And another book about a little girl who goes to London to dance in the ballet.'

'You lucky girl.'

Lucky? Julia suddenly had a painful twinge in her chest. Even though Hillside House was being guarded as though it were Fort Knox, should she be going out yet again, when Nicky was theoretically in potential danger? Out all day, every day, at work, in court, visiting prisons and police stations. Shouldn't she grasp this one opportunity to be at home with Nicky?

'And Mummy, he said he had a surprise for us tomorrow. What d'you think it'll be?'

'I don't know, darling. But if we knew, it wouldn't be a surprise, would it? Now be a good girl and go to bed early. Don't forget it's ballet tomorrow, and *The Wizard of Oz* in the afternoon. Tell Wendy I won't be very late. I love you.' She put down the phone. Wasn't that just like Paul. An extra effort to make a quick visit to Nicky and still be at the College of Music by seven fifteen. Amazing.

Something stirred in Julia as she resumed her work. I have this strange feeling. I'm not certain what it is, but in spite of what happened today, in spite of my feeling of isolation and disorientation, for the first time in a very long while I feel . . . what? A warm glow. A pleasurable anticipation of the hour and a half of Mozart?

Hell, no. It's much more than that. It's a feeling churning inside me that makes me want to run and do cartwheels and laugh, and forget all about Sam Smith. Is that possible, she asked herself. Surely not.

At six-thirty she put the files she needed for the weekend into her already bulging brief case. After a quick wash she changed her plain white shirt for a yellow silk blouse and put a thick gold chain inherited from Natalie round her neck.

Still managing to keep the image of cartwheels and blue skies in front of the gathering clouds, she stood at the mirror in the office cloakroom. Ben was right. I do look terrible. A touch of dark grey eye shadow, matching smudgy eyeliner, a flick of mascara and an extra coat of coral lipstick made a slight difference.

At the last minute she unlocked the top drawer, checked the safety catch and put the gun in her handbag. With her black suit jacket slung over her shoulders, she locked the office doors, then drove to the College of Music, the warm glow almost blotting out the blackness of her fear.

- 69 -

Paul was waiting just inside the doors. Wearing a yellow silk scarf tucked into the neck of a cream shirt under a sleek navy blazer, he stood out amongst the motley crowd of eager Mozart lovers.

'Good timing,' he said as they walked across the foyer to the bar. 'What'll you drink?'

Julia smiled at him, and the glow seemed to spread right to her toes.

'Dry white with ice?'

He carried the drinks to a table where they could watch the entrance to the concert hall.

'Same taste in colours,' he said, staring unashamedly at Julia's flimsy blouse.

She sipped her wine. 'Yes. It's a happy colour, don't you think?'

'You always look good, no matter what you wear.'

'How d'you mean?'

'There's a sort of classicism in your choice of clothes. It never seems to follow the trends of fashion, yet you always look just right.'

He was so serious. It wouldn't do to laugh. Yet what he said made Julia's glow intensify. 'Thank you,' she said. 'But I can assure you it's quite unconscious on my part.'

'Just one of your many natural talents, eh?'

* * *

At the interval Paul hurried out to join the coffee queue. With the music still in her ears and the same feeling of euphoria that was keeping the dark clouds at bay, Julia watched him standing there, tall and straight against the wide, high expanse of the foyer.

He put the coffees on the table.

226

'Penny for them,' he said.

'That was fantastic. How can music be so beautiful and yet so sad?'

With his arm touching hers throughout the first half, the magic of the music had made her curiously aware of a oneness of soul and body. She had a vision of the music flowing not into two bodies but into one. She became conscious of this as being part of the experience of listening to the music and it took her by surprise.

Paul smiled and sipped his coffee. 'The passion comes from the heart of the composer, as you've so often told me, but I'd say that tonight it was the clarinettist who gets the Oscar for making this concerto set one's heart on fire.'

'Well, well, well,' she said, shaking her head in amazement, 'I think I really have succeeded in converting you.'

'Mmm, up to a point, yes,' he admitted. 'And I'll always think of you when I hear the clarinet concerto. But I still go for a bit of old Glenn Miller, Whitney Houston, or Carly Simon,' he added dreamily.

Under his breath he began to sing softly. '*I get along without you very well* . . .'

She saw pain in his eyes and wondered why. These were very old-fashioned tastes in popular music. 'I'd like to hear it some time,' she said. 'I like most music. And I'll tell you a secret. I get a kick out of pop concerts too.'

Paul's eyes opened wide. 'You do? So do I!'

'That's amazing. Don't you love the way it makes everyone into one big happy family – for a few make-believe hours?'

He stared at her, nodding. 'We'll have to go together some time.'

Strange how she'd always thought there was little to warrant their friendship becoming any deeper than it was. That it was the things they did not have in common that were the stumbling block to their friendship. A feeling of weakness mixed with enchantment swept over her, banishing all thought of the very real differences they both knew existed.

Last night he'd said he wanted her to go to his flat for a coffee. But that was last night. She could not presume that the invitation would stretch to tonight as well, but she desperately hoped it would.

'Come on,' she said. 'There's the gong. Let's go back in. It's the 21st piano concerto now. What a treat!'

They took their seats. Julia closed her eyes and felt the swirling darkness closing in. Frantically she opened them again, and let her arm drift closer to Paul's.

- 70 -

Apart from the impressive row of shooting trophies on the mantelpiece, just looking around Paul's neat, compact flat told Julia very little about the man. In the entrance hall a mirror, a small black table, a potted palm. A stark white Formica kitchen. Habitat furniture with black varnished wood, straight lines, cream cushions. A rambling plant whose huge perforated leaves were advancing on an enormous TV, CD and DVD player, and what she suspected was a powerful and sophisticated two-way radio.

'My furniture's all in storage,' Paul said. 'I bought this place fully furnished. The house in Hale was too big after Jane and Tandy left.'

Julia sat down in the easy chair he had indicated. 'Who's Tandy?'

'My daughter.' He paused. 'She's eleven now.'

'You didn't tell me.'

'You never asked.'

'And Jane?'

'We were divorced five years ago. She lives in Australia. Married again.'

'I'm sorry.' To hide her confusion she looked around the walls.

A Van Gogh print, a couple of Lowry's industrial landscapes, a small oil painting of Old Trafford cricket ground. No photographs of Jane, though. Or of Tandy.

Paul shrugged. 'No need to be sorry. It was over.'

'I mean Tandy.' She'd have been about Nicky's age when she left, Julia thought. 'You must miss her.'

'Very much.' He flicked a switch on the CD player, filling the room with Carly Simon's rich deep voice. It was the song he'd mentioned in the interval — *I get along without you very well* . . .

He looked down at Julia as though uncertain of what to do next, his arms limp at his sides. Then he knelt down beside her, took her hand in his and remained absolutely still and silent, staring into space, his eyes glistening with what looked suspiciously like tears.

When the song ended he moved away and sat on the sofa facing her.

'Julia. Has Smith tried to contact you again about the money?'

'No.' She hadn't expected this. She sensed the effort he'd made to break free from the spell the music had woven around him.

'Frankly, I'm surprised. And I'm worried.'

'About me?'

'I wish you'd agree to more protection. It doesn't make sense.'

'I have to carry on with my life.'

'Of course. But just remember, he's still out there.'

'Has nobody seen him?' she asked, wishing she knew for certain whether her sighting of him in court this morning had been reality or hallucination. Reality, she hoped. For if she had injured him badly enough to lead to a serious medical condition, then by law she should be telling Paul what she'd done.

Paul shook his head. 'I was so certain Sagoe would lead us to him.'

'Must you spoil a beautiful evening,' Julia said, desperate to avoid any pressure from Paul, and suddenly fearful that the gun would suddenly burn its way out of her handbag and reveal itself.

'The doctor said that even with medical treatment he'd have died. A massive heart attack just waiting to happen.' He looked straight into Julia's eyes. 'There was in fact a mix-up with his medication. By the time the omission was discovered it was too late.'

Julia was amazed that Paul was volunteering this news. 'Jesus, all along I knew you didn't really have a good reason for bringing him in . . . but why are we talking about this now?'

She wondered what on earth had possessed her to come here to Paul's flat. He was a cop, she was a defence lawyer; nothing could change that. They'd never agree in a hundred years on the big issues that confronted them daily in their jobs.

Grabbing a small black stool he put it right in front of Julia and sat astride it, his eyes level with hers. 'I didn't get you here tonight to talk shop, please believe me. My intentions were far more dishonourable, or hadn't you noticed that despite the fact we're on opposite sides, I'm very . . very, fond of you?' His voice had an unfamiliar tremble. 'And I suppose it's because I am that I've been going almost insane with the thought that you are the main target of the most wanted man in Manchester. That makes you my responsibility, and you're snubbing my attempts to protect you.' He put a hand on her thigh and looked into her eyes. 'And that, Mrs Grant, really pisses me off.'

Julia knew without a doubt that any further legal discussion was over for tonight. She watched his hands move, tentatively. Inching further along her thigh. Oh God. She had long wondered what it would feel like when he finally touched her. Would she be afraid?

She stood up suddenly, and so did Paul. He pulled her towards him, not roughly, but like an upset child in need of comfort. For a few moments she held herself stiffly, feeling waves of dizziness as his cheek pressed against hers.

No, I'm not afraid, she told herself, but it's not anything like I thought it was going to be. I can smell his after-shave. Feel the stubble on his chin. I can even hear his heart beating. It's strange, being close to him like this. Unbearably exciting, but at the same time so comfortable.

But not now. Not when her world was turned upside down. She had to finish things and didn't want to draw Paul in. This had to be done by her alone, or their chance of happiness together would be lost forever.

What am I doing?

Gently, ever so gently, so that he couldn't possibly think she was recoiling against him, she pulled away. 'You'll probably think I'm an awful tease,' she whispered, her face still close to his. He tucked her hair behind her ears and smoothed it down the nape of her neck with fingers so delicate they could have been stroking a child.

'Am I to take that as an instruction to back off?' he asked.

'I have a horrible feeling that if I don't go now, I may not go at all.' She looked into his eyes. She could feel a heat rising through her body as they slowly moved apart. 'I must go now. I can't keep Wendy any later.'

At the door she hesitated. She remembered what he'd said outside the police station last night and wondered what it was he had wanted to give her. There was still time to change her mind. Wendy would wait up all night if she needed to and often did.

'I hate you driving on your own so late. I'll follow you home.' There was an unusual gruffness in his voice that he attempted to camouflage by a discreet little cough.

'I'm fine,' she said in a whisper. 'There's nothing to worry about.'

'That is debatable. Nevertheless, I'll be behind you.'

He put his hand in his pocket and held up a shiny Yale key. 'Put this on your key-ring. You never know when you might need it.'

'Your key? Is this what you said last night you wanted to give me?'

He nodded. She shook her head.

'No, Paul.'

'Please.'

She turned the key over in her fingers. It had been purchased recently. 'Paul. You know this is impossible, don't you.'

'Nothing is impossible.'

'It would never work.'

He put his index finger vertically against her lips.

- 71 -

Turning right into Kingsway at the Tesco clock tower, Julia saw that it was nearly midnight. She had kept Wendy far too long. Increasing her speed on the bypass, she switched on Radio Piccadilly and was startled to hear Paul's voice in the middle of what was obviously a recorded appeal, since in her rear view mirror she could clearly see his CRX behind her.

' . . . last seen wearing grey flannels, white open necked shirt, grey trainers. He is armed and dangerous. He should not be approached, but anyone with information about his whereabouts, or who thinks they may have seen him, is requested to telephone Stockport police station on this number . . .'

Julia flicked off the sound, hopefully banishing her guilt with it. She

231

considered what she liked most about Paul. His kind, gentle manner. His smile. His willingness to listen to someone else's point of view. His dark brown eyes that tonight were so sad. His devotion to his daughter. And to Nicky. The way he listened to music . . .

* * *

Wendy was in the family room, still watching television when Julia walked in. 'I'll be down in a minute,' she said, then ran upstairs to Nicky's room. She sat down on the edge of the bed and gazed down at the flushed face of her daughter, surrounded by its halo of unruly curls, so like one of Botticelli's angels, she thought. She bent down and lightly kissed the dewy forehead, breathing in a blend of Pears soap and puppy smell, then tiptoed out and closed the door softly.

Wendy's film was just ending when Julia came downstairs. 'Any calls?' she asked, pretending not to be interested one way or another.

'Two,' Wendy said crossly. 'And both times he put down the phone when I answered.'

Julia shivered. 'Some crank, I suppose.'

'I think you should be ex-directory.'

'I have to be available for my clients. You know that, Wendy.'

Just then the phone rang. Julia rushed to the entrance hall to answer it. 'Hello — '

'Julia?'

'Oh. It's you.'

'Well, don't sound so disappointed. I've only rung to make sure you're all right.'

'Yes, fine. Thanks for escorting me home. And for a lovely evening.'

'Thank you,' he said.

'I'm sorry about . . . well, I didn't mean to . . . you know.'

'My fault,' he said. 'I wanted to say . . . '

'Paul?'

'I wanted to say — well, just that I'm sorry too.'

'Why?'

'I think you know why.'

'Do I?' She waited.

'Never mind,' he said. 'We'll have tomorrow.'

'Paul, I can't go with you tomorrow. I told you. I'm taking Nicky to *The Wizard of Oz*.'

'Goodnight, Julia. Sleep well.' And he was gone.

'Obviously wasn't that crank again, was it?' Wendy asked.

'What? No, it was Paul. He followed me home. Don't you worry about the crank, Wendy, he'll soon get tired of it. Will you have some tea before you go?'

'I've put the kettle on.' She looked at Julia and frowned. 'There was a picture of that murderer on the telly again tonight.'

Julia kept her eyes on the screen. It was amazing how the media had latched on to this case. 'Oh, really? How did he look?'

'No different. Blond hair. Mean eyes. Beard. You should know. You've seen him often enough.'

Twice she'd seen him lately. Or was it three times? And every time he'd had no beard. 'Yes,' she said, still looking blankly at the telly. All his records showed him with a beard. He didn't grow it and cut it off and grow it again and cut it. No one had seen him without that beard. Not as far as she knew.

But I have, she told herself, and I should have told Paul. I should ring him back now. Her silence appalled her. If she told him they could do a Photofit of him clean shaven, put that on the telly instead. But then Smith would know she was talking.

Wendy brought in the tea. 'It's frightening, really,' she said. 'Like you said last week, they look quite ordinary, murderers. No different from anyone else. No tails. No horns. No slimy scaly skins. Yeah. Frightening.'

SATURDAY

Sam wasn't sure what had woken him. It could have been Ada yelling but was probably a siren or an early train. Or even a rat squealing. Straining to lift his head he peered through the cobwebs. The bare windows framed a grey sky splodged with ink-dark clouds. It was still too early to try phoning Julia again. He might even decide to give it a miss and let her wonder what he would do next.

He felt as though nails were sticking into every inch of his body. Even moving his arms was excruciating, but if he didn't get cracking soon he would stiffen up even more. Besides, he'd been here long enough. It would only be a matter of time before someone saw him coming and going and recognised him in spite of no beard. If that abandoned looking white Fiesta was still in the car park he could head for the hills right now, before it got too light.

He sat up. The pain knifed through his stomach. He needed something to wrap around it, to hold it in tightly. Peering through the gloom he saw amidst the piles of cardboard and rusty tins a length of old mutton cloth, filthy, but it would have to do.

Once on his feet, the dizziness subsided. Moving around was clearly what he had to do. No more of this feeling sorry for yourself, Smith. Gritting his teeth he walked a few steps, then stopped and bent over from the waist.

'Don't let go now,' he said aloud. 'Not with the first, the one and only glimmer of hope in all your life within your reach.'

The pain is the enemy. A red fiery ball. An army of soldiers in every corner of my body. At a signal they will march to the centre. At another signal they will charge. They will conquer the enemy. They will throw the red fiery ball out of my body and I will watch it sail through the caravan window, flying through the sky getting smaller and smaller

234

The patches of sky were becoming lighter. A siren grew louder, then faded. Kneeling down on the uneven earth, he wound the rag around his stomach as tight as he could and tied a flat knot. Then he closed his eyes.

Get on the alert, you bastards. Now. March. Good, you're nearly there. Charge. Grab the enemy and throw him out.

He opened his eyes, and there it was. The red fiery ball flying through the air against the pale dawn sky. Over the canal, over Dukes Bar, fading until it disappeared beyond the city skyline.

He smiled through his tears. It had worked, as it always did if he concentrated hard enough. The pain was gone.

From Joe's survival plastic bag he changed into a pair of clean jeans and one of the khaki shirts Joe had kept after his younger brother had died in Northern Ireland. Leaving the dirty clothes for the rats, he walked under the archway towards the dusty white Fiesta.

- 73 -

It was the not knowing that Julia could no longer stand. She'd been awake all night wondering if he was alive or dead and whether she'd hear from him today or not. Have I sunk as low as he has, she asked herself.

Exhausted even before the compulsory game of hide-and-seek with Nicky and Duchess, she'd finally taken them both down to the family room to watch the Saturday TV for children. Alone at last, she picked up the phone next to her bed and dialled Martin Bedlow's home number, hoping he had not already left for the hospital.

'I'm sorry to disturb you so early, Mrs Bedlow, but could I speak to Martin? This is Julia Grant.'

'Oh yes, Julia. Martin's often spoken about you. Hold on and I'll get him.'

Although an orthopaedic surgeon, Martin was the only doctor Julia knew well enough to ask about puncture wounds without risking

235

awkward questions. He'd been a contemporary of Simon's and Ben's at Manchester University. In the heady days after they'd all qualified and embarked on their lives as working professionals she'd seen a lot of him and his first wife: night clubs, opera, pop concerts, dinner parties, weekends at the Lakes — it had been a non-stop merry-go-round of social activity.

She'd lost touch after Simon's death, so she'd never met his second wife.

'Julia. Great to hear your voice. How are you? Nothing wrong, I hope.'

'I'm fine, Martin. But I need your help with a case I'm working on. Not exactly your field but . . . '

'Fire away. If I can't help I'll ask someone who can.'

Julia wished she'd rehearsed the questions, put them into order in her mind. 'Well, if someone were stabbed in the stomach with - with say a hatpin, what condition would this person be in? That is,' she added cautiously, 'if he could not get medical attention.'

'I presume then, that he's on the run,' Martin said quickly.

Damn. 'Yes,' she said. She couldn't risk saying more.

'It would depend on the length and condition of the hatpin. We give injections into stomachs these days and they don't do any harm.'

'Three inches. A bit rusty.'

'Hmm. Below the belt?'

'Yes.'

'Without seeing the patient I can't be accurate, you understand that, Julia. But the hatpin may have punctured the bowel in several places and from these tiny puncture wounds there'd be a bit of leakage into the peritoneal cavity, like a perforated ulcer.'

'And what would happen then?'

'The body would try to close up the wounds, but would probably eventually fail. Then general peritonitis would set in.'

'How long would he keep going?' Is it really me asking these questions, she wondered.

'Hard to tell, Julia. Depends on his general health.'

'Thin. Wiry. Pretty fit.'

'In that case, he'll do quite well. Four, five days. Possibly ten. Maybe more.'

Oh no. What have I done, she asked herself for the hundredth time.

'How will he feel?'

'Feel? Up and down. Not too bad at first. Then some local pain and tenderness. Afterwards there'll be bowel obstruction. Nauseous. Just a bit at first. Thirsty. But if he drinks he'll bring it up. Eventually he'll get weaker, with gradually increasing pain.'

'And how will he look?'

'Initially, quite normal. Depends on his immune system. Later he'll look drawn, pale, jaundiced. Pinched from dehydration because nothing will stay down. If fever sets in he'll be flushed, lose weight, have difficulty in walking. Septicaemia will set in. In the end he'll collapse and become comatose. He'll look bloody awful then.'

'That bad?' She could feel her skin contracting as though she'd been immersed in a bath of icy water.

'Well, imagine a case of untreated appendicitis. It's a slow, nasty process.'

A rush of darkness swept across her vision. 'How slow?'

'Depends again how fit he is.'

She'd stuck the hatpin into him on Wednesday. God, how could she have done it? This was Saturday. Day four. Yet it seemed much longer. And damn it, Martin was still not telling her exactly how long.

She hung on to the edge of the bed. 'And then?' she asked, barely able to breathe.

'You mean, if he still gets no treatment?'

'Yes.'

'Almost certainly he will die.'

- 74 -

Wendy blinked at the early morning light streaming in through the window. She wished Janey would stop talking.

'Should have come with me to the King William,' Janey said, 'instead of moping all by yourself just because Alan didn't want to see you. Then

237

you wouldn't be so grumpy now.'

'I wish you'd shut up and let me sleep another five minutes. I was baby-sitting, wasn't I? I couldn't have gone to the pub if I'd wanted to.'

'He didn't waste any time, you know.'

Wendy opened her eyes wide. 'What?'

'He was with that Gloria woman. Blonde skinny one. Tall. You know.'

Silently Wendy reached for her gown, her hands trembling as she rushed to the bathroom. In five minutes she was dressed and into her car, her mind finally made up.

It was only a short drive to Alan's sister's house in Handforth. A bit early for a Saturday but if she didn't go now she'd never catch him. She parked the Mini outside Dawn's and rang the bell, still numb with shock. Now that she was here, what on earth was she going to say?

Alan answered the door. He was dressed, but his hair was uncombed and he hadn't shaved. 'Wendy, what the hell you doing here? You'd better come in.'

He took her into the front room and closed the door softly. She sat down on the sofa and he stood looking down at her, hands on his hips.

'What's up?'

'You were with Gloria last night.'

'Shh. They're all still asleep.'

'At the King William.'

He walked over to the window and opened the curtains. 'So what? She was on her own. So was I. We're old friends. What you expect me to do? Ignore her?'

The numb feeling was wearing off and Wendy felt the first signs of panic. 'Are you in love with her?'

'You nuts? Look, she means nothing to me. I was working late as it turned out. I dropped in for a pint, took her home and that was all. Wendy, don't look so bloody miserable. Anyway, I still think we shouldn't see each other for a few weeks. Maybe after a break you'll calm down a bit. Okay?'

Wendy closed her eyes. It was now or never. She had nothing to lose. He'll probably kick me into touch, she thought in a torment of unhappiness, but he's got to know some time.

'I'm pregnant.'

'What?' He held his hand to his throat, fingers spread wide. 'You sure?'

'Positive. I did a test.'

'How far?'

'Two months. I think. Maybe three.'

It was as though she'd hit him in the chest and knocked the air out of him. He just stood there and stared at her with his mouth wide open. His jaw moved from side to side but he didn't say another word. Then he looked at his watch.

He spoke softly. 'Look, I got a call-out just before you came.' He walked over to her, gently took her arm and saw her to the door. 'I'll be in touch. Take care.'

Wendy drove home in a daze, trying to figure him out. He could have said something. She'd expected him to rant and rave, but he took it so calmly, and she hadn't the faintest idea now whether he was angry or not.

Or even whether he cared a damn.

- 75 -

Julia and Nicky arrived early at the dance school. While Nicky went to put on her tap shoes, Julia joined the group of mothers behind the glass doors, some waiting to fetch their children from the pre-primary class, others delivering their children to the next class.

A young, thin, harassed-looking woman standing next to Julia smiled. 'I'm Sandra's mum. You must be Nicky's mum,' she said, peering at her. 'I never seen you before, but you look just like her.'

Julia did her best to return the smile. 'No, I don't often come in, but I'm being allowed to watch today.' She laughed awkwardly. 'A special treat,' she hurriedly explained.

The woman looked impressed. 'Wish I could watch.' She looked lovingly at her dark-eyed child whose hand she tightly held. 'You got a job then?'

'I'm a lawyer.'

'Really.' Sandra's mother's eyes opened wide. 'Shocking all these burglaries. Rapes and murders and stuff,' she said. 'That monster with the beard. Even hanging would be too good for him.'

Julia nodded half-heartedly. What would the woman say if she knew who the monster really was? Or really might be. And what would she say if she knew Julia was negotiating to give him a quarter of a million pounds to keep him quiet and get him off her back?

She felt sick. She wished the class would start, then the woman would stop talking.

The pre-primary class had just ended. Sonya, her dark hair in a sleek bun, greeted Julia with a dazzling smile and indicated the row of wooden chairs along the wall.

And she was right. From the very first bar of music Julia could see that there was something magical about the way Nicky moved that was different from all the others. Looking so cute in her gathered net skirt, she wished Simon could see her now.

'Four steps soft. Three stamps and one clap. Big smile please. Hands behind backs. Heel close, heel close. Three claps, feet together,' sang Sonya above the sound of the piano.

After half an hour of lively tap, the children changed into their pink ballet shoes for the part of the class Nicky always said she loved the best.

'Fairies can't be seen,' Sonya said, leading them into a circle. 'They can't be heard either. I don't want to hear a single sound but I want to see magic fingers sparkling. Now, feet in first position, arms nice and round. Three slow demi-plies. Now zip up your legs. Feet together. Up on your toes. Spin round with arms up . . .'

Julia watched mesmerised as the graceful fairies were transformed into witches. 'Catch the bat. Into the pot. Grab the spider.'

After that it was point and close, point and close to a lively waltz, and finally the promised pony races.

'It's the team who do it best, not the fastest,' Sonya said. 'Two ponies at a time. Trot, gallop and o-ver the jumps.'

At the end of the class Sonya waited for Julia at the door. 'I'm glad you came, Mrs Grant. She was better than ever today. But I've been having second thoughts.'

Julia felt her smile fast disappearing. What now, she wondered.

'For a few weeks we'd like Nicky to come to extra classes on Tuesdays, four till five-thirty, just until she catches up with the others. It's only fair to her. I'm engaging a new young teacher, Dominique, a brilliant dancer. Nicky will adore her.'

Nicky tugged at Julia's hand as Sonya carried on. 'Apart from ballet and tap, Dominique will also concentrate on musical interpretation, so important at this stage.'

At last Julia found her tongue. 'I'm sorry. Tuesday's are out of the question.'

'Oh, Mummy. Please.'

Julia dragged her fingers through her hair. 'Four till five-thirty . . . I'm afraid I just can't get away in time to bring her. Perhaps some other time.'

'Please, Mrs Grant,' Sonya said quietly. 'It's not every day we get someone like Dominique. Or Nicky.' She patted the child's head. 'Can't someone else bring her?'

Nicky looked up, her big blue eyes wide with expectation.

'Mummy, Wendy can bring me. Please. Say yes.'

'Yes, of course. I'm sorry. I wasn't thinking. Wendy can bring her. Four o'clock, you said?'

Nicky flung her arms round Julia's waist. 'I knew you'd say yes, Mummy.'

- 76 -

Floating at least ten feet above the seat of his car, Alan swung into Manchester Road and headed for the city. The call-out could wait. This couldn't. He'd told them to turn everything off at the mains so they'd be fine for another hour.

Wow! This was the weirdest feeling he'd ever had. He would never have believed he could become such a great big softie, but he couldn't help it. His baby. Growing inside Wendy's smashing little body.

Zooming past the University and the BBC, he turned off Oxford Road and parked near the G-Mex Centre, watching the sun glint on the glass roof and thinking all the time of running his hands over the swell of Wendy's belly, the swell of his baby. Come to think of it, she did have a slightly more rounded look to her than usual.

After a brisk walk he found the Register Office in a smart modern building near the Manchester Evening News, tucked in a leafy square between the law courts and Deansgate. What a rat he'd been to her lately. It would serve him right if she walked out on him, so the sooner he did this the better.

He was first in when they opened at nine. The receptionist directed him to the Superintendent Registrar's office on the first floor to give notice of marriage and apply for a licence. Apart from a few tricky questions when it came to surprising Wendy for her birthday, it was plain sailing. She must not feel pressurised, the charming Registrar warned. And Alan laughed. 'There's no danger of that.'

'Good,' she said, with an empathetic smile Alan felt sure was genuine. 'I'll show you the marriage rooms now, and you can choose which one you'd like.'

Twenty minutes later he was running down the stairs two at a time with the appointment booklet in his hand. The Gold Room. Tuesday afternoon. It was lucky you needed only one clear day's notice, not including a Sunday, so Tuesday was perfect. He would ask her to meet him somewhere. Then, just like in the movies, he'd whisk her away and get married. The most perfect birthday present he could give her.

Oh, he couldn't wait to see her face.

- 77 -

Julia was clearing the lunch dishes when she heard the sound of a car in the driveway.

Nicky and Duchess had their noses pressed to the hall window.

'Mummy. Quickly. It's Paul. Can he come with us to *The Wizard of Oz*? Please.'

Julia unlocked the door and watched Nicky fly into Paul's outstretched arms. As he held the child tightly to his cheek, she tried to

242

analyse the strange feeling this sight aroused in her.

He smiled at her over Nicky's head. 'Well?' he said. 'Are you two ready to go?'

Nicky tightened her arms around Paul's neck. 'Yes, 'course we're ready, aren't we, Mummy? Is this our surprise, Paul?'

Julia glared at him. 'Paul. I promised Nicky we'd go to *The Wizard of Oz*. Besides, there's the puppy. And the kittens.'

Paul cocked his head to one side. 'Come on. We can all go to *The Wizard* another day. We can't waste such good weather. And I'm sure Wendy would take care of the puppy and the kittens.' He looked into Nicky's eyes, bigger and bluer than ever as she stared back adoringly at him. 'How about it, Princess? Shall we all go to White Pool Farm? They've got horses.'

Nicky looked open-mouthed from Paul to Julia and back again to Paul, then flung her arms around his neck and kissed his cheek.

Paul grinned at Julia. 'Looks like that's settled, then, doesn't it?'

Julia couldn't help wondering if he were using Nicky to force the pace between them. Second only to her beloved ballet, horses were the unrequited passion of her daughter's life, and Paul knew that. Then with a pang she remembered his daughter Tandy and the way he'd listened to the Carly Simon song. Maybe he needed a temporary substitute for his daughter, and who could blame him? Nicky loved him. He loved her. And perhaps that was all there was to it.

She led the way into the house, still not certain what to do. So far there'd been no call from Smith. A good sign or a bad one? She hardly dared put her thoughts into words. According to Martin Bedlow's prognosis, Smith was unlikely to be able to phone her, let alone execute his threats.

Yet yesterday morning I saw him in the court.

Her chest tightened. Smith needs the money, must be desperate for the money, now more than ever. I know he won't let go without a fight.

She sighed, collecting herself as she tried to push Smith, the murderer, from her mind. Because that's who he was. Just a murderer called Smith trying it on. He's nothing to do with you, Julia, so stop worrying about him. He won't have been badly injured. She still had a few days grace and in any case she couldn't get her hands on the money until Tuesday. There was nothing to stop her going. She looked back at Paul's and Nicky's expectant faces.

'I'll throw some things into a bag,' she said, grinning broadly, for what else could she do. 'Then I'll phone Wendy. Can you wait ten minutes?'

- 78 -

Nestling in picture-book rolling countryside, White Pool Farm was a small unpretentious hotel Julia felt certain must be the Peak District's best kept secret. Clearly Paul had chosen it with Nicky in mind. Besides a paddock full of ponies, with children's rides supervised by the owner's daughter, there was a virtual menagerie of animals. And at bedtime she'd struggled to prise her daughter from the playroom.

'You're very quiet,' Paul said as they sat enjoying a coffee and liqueur at the bar just off the dimly lit lounge.

She smiled. He had the same intense look she'd seen last night at his flat. She hoped she wasn't betraying her sudden awareness of their unaccustomed intimacy. I should have let Nicky have dinner with us, she thought.

She'd always considered him attractive, in the way you'd admire a charismatic world figure, like Nelson Mandela. There was about his bearing and his manner a quality not many women, or men, would fail to find appealing. But how strange that after knowing him professionally for . . . what? ─ four years ─ she'd only just become aware of his powerful sexuality. Perhaps this was an inherent quality that all men of this calibre possessed as part of the total package labelled "charm". And she'd just been too provoked by their professional differences to appreciate that underneath all that police toughness there was this gentle being, this fiercely attractive man.

Last night at his flat he had aroused in her a variety of responses. Not only the conflicting realisation that in spite of the fear, the stirrings she felt were extremely pleasurable, but a far deeper need that if indulged in at this stage could make him impossible to resist, and thus

244

place her in a hopeless situation. It's weird, she thought. Even though I'm frightened by this new and unexpected feeling of wanting him to make love to me, I also want to be near him all the time. Share things with him. And I also desperately want, need, to tell him . . . what? Yes, dammit, about what happened long ago. Unburden the mantle of horror and guilt that began to envelop me from the moment I first saw Smith. Guilt that in just the last couple of days has begun to encompass an even more frightening dimension as the seeds of Smith's ghastly accusation have begun to sprout tentative tendrils of almost clear recollections of a scene so violent that what Smith had said could almost be true. But surely this was merely a manifestation of Smith's cunning, that by planting a seed it would undoubtedly germinate in her fertile mind . . .

She sipped her coffee. How cruel fate was. How ironic that in her present situation, this tug of war going on in her mind, Paul was the last man on earth she could confide in. It was doubtful she would have the strength to satisfy the one need without fulfilling the others. It wouldn't be long before, as a natural progression of falling in love, she would find herself telling him everything.

Paul signalled to the barman to refill their cups. Then he turned back to Julia.

'Well, Julia. Aren't you going to tell me what's on your mind?'

Under his intent gaze her bones seemed to turn to water. He had that all-knowing look that shouldn't really have surprised her. After all, he hadn't risen to the rank of detective chief superintendent for nothing. She had a feeling he knew exactly what she was thinking.

The longer she kept silent, the deeper she felt the invading flush redden her cheeks. She stirred her coffee. How can you be shy at the age of thirty-six, she asked herself, when every day you deal with complete strangers who seek your help. When every day you stand up in front of learned magistrates defending those strangers with what everyone told her was such ease and eloquence.

But somehow this was very different. She thought of the night to come. She twisted her stool to face him, trying her utmost to look relaxed yet afraid of committing herself to what she knew would be an irretrievable step.

'Julia . . .' His voice was low and soft. 'I think I know what you're going through.'

'Do you?' she asked, pressing her hand to her mouth.

Paul's intuitive powers were legendary, but he couldn't possibly know who she thought Smith might be, or about the fleeting childhood memories that had begun to haunt her. Or perhaps they had been haunting her for years, without her realising it.

And least of all could he know about Smith's terrifying accusation and how this had since driven her every discordant move.

Paul might think he knows, but he can't possibly know about the daily phone calls. Or my witnessing Joe Sagoe's arrest while frantically reversing my car. Or that weighing down my handbag is an unlicensed gun with ammunition supplied by Charlie Kuma, a convicted criminal. Or that on Monday morning Smith followed Nicky to school. That on Tuesday night he rammed my car and on Wednesday night, in fear and desperation, I plunged a three-inch hatpin into his intestines. Nor could he know that I forged my partner's signature to pillage money from a trust fund. And that a clean-shaven Smith sauntered unmolested into the Manchester City Magistrates' Courts and I did nothing to alert the police . . .

So how the hell can he possibly know what I'm going through?

He edged closer to her. 'When Sam Smith threatened you in court, you thought nothing of it? Right? But damn it, Julia, since then he's committed two more murders. He's dangerous, for Christ's sake. You must be scared out of your wits. It would be unnatural if you weren't, and there's something so odd about it, I wish I knew what it was.' He clenched his fist into a tight ball. 'And the bastard could be anywhere.'

Julia shrugged with what she thought was convincing nonchalance, wondering just how long she could keep up the façade. She wouldn't put it past Smith to have followed her here, except that according to Martin he'd be in no fit state to be swanning around these remote Derbyshire hills.

Unless he'd managed to get medical attention . . .

Yet Smith might even at this moment be on his deathbed. Perhaps he'd already died. On the other hand Martin may have exaggerated the effects. I must not underestimate Smith's strength, she warned herself. Or his determination and his capability of carrying on in circumstances few people would tolerate. She took a deep breath. Whatever made me think that? Is it because I am made of the same stuff as he is?

Paul gripped her arm. 'Is there anything you want to tell me, Julia?'

She looked straight into his eyes. She had to say something, just to keep the questions at bay.

'I still think Smith means to get the money, but surely he'd have made another move by now. And, well, he hasn't.' She stopped. It would be unsafe to say any more.

Paul's eyes narrowed. 'He may be saving you for later. You do realise, don't you, that you bear a vague resemblance to Joanne Perkins, or maybe it's just the hair.'

Julia felt the air rush from her lungs. 'Can we change the subject, Paul? I'm more than capable of looking after myself, especially after that course in self-protection.'

He gave her one of those lopsided smiles of his. 'Sorry. The idea of coming here was to get away from it all, to help you to relax. I promise not to mention it again tonight. With one proviso.'

Julia held her breath. 'And what's that?'

'That you promise to let me know immediately he contacts you again.'

She wished she wasn't being forced to go so far outside the system. Because for Nicky's sake, and for Paul's and her own, his request was unthinkable. The last thing she could afford to do was make it easier for Smith to fall into the hands of the police.

'Okay,' she said. And mentally crossed her fingers.

With one hand he lifted her chin while with the other he traced the outline of her lips. 'I'd never forgive myself if anything happened to you,' he said.

But she barely heard him. She was remembering last night. Remembering his hand on her thigh and how much she had wanted more.

'We both know what's happening, don't we Julia.' He pushed a strand of hair off her cheek.

She looked down and smiled, not meeting his eyes. Oh yes, she thought. It's happening all right. On these two bar stools in a remote hotel in the Pennines. For the first time in my life it is happening. It was never like this with Simon. Simon broke through my fear, but only because of his extreme kindness and gentleness, not because of an explosion inside me that is not like anything I've felt before. Already I am way beyond the point of reason where I might have sat back and said don't do this, Julia. Make sure you know what you're doing, Julia. I am powerless to stop. My newly awakened body has taken over. Everything else has ceased to exist. Even Sam Smith.

Paul had been watching her. He's reading my body language and my thoughts as though I'd spoken them aloud, she thought.

'Let's go,' he said.

He helped her off the stool and led her briskly up the stairs, not looking at her and not saying another word. For the first time Julia knew what it meant to walk on air. But in spite of the urgency each moment appeared suspended in time, giving her the chance to etch it on the screen of her mind to recall later when she might doubt this night had ever happened.

Paul walked straight to the door of his room, which was adjacent to the one Julia shared with Nicky. As he put the key in the lock he stopped. His shoulders sagged. He glanced down at her and frowned.

For a long moment he stared at her, then took a deep breath. 'You'd better go to Nicky, Julia.'

'I'll just see if she's all right,' she said, hardly recognising her own voice. She unlocked her door and slowly pushed it open. She winced as it creaked.

'Mummy, where've you been? I had a horrid dream.'

Paul's fingers tightened on her hand. In the light from the passage she saw Nicky sitting up in bed.

She looked at Paul. A pain shot through her as if a vital part of her body were being surgically removed without an anaesthetic. Still gripping his hand, she twisted away.

'It's all right, Nicky. I'm here now, darling.'

She didn't dare look at Paul again. 'I'll see you tomorrow,' she whispered. 'At breakfast.'

'Julia . . .'

As though tearing it away sinew by sinew, she withdrew her hand and quietly closed the door.

SUNDAY

The mist swirling, the voice . . . Come with me, Julia, echoing around the craggy hills . . . the rocks receding . . . yes . . . one more glimpse . . . the loss more agonising than usual . . . holding on . . . fading . . . fading . . .

Gone!

Julia opened her eyes. She was panting, as though she'd been running. In the first dim light of an early mid-summer dawn, she was surprised to see Nicky curled up beside her. Gradually the objects in the room took shape. The yellow and white curtains, the carved uprights of the four-poster bed, the tall gilt-edged mirror, the oak-panelled walls, the yellow daisies on top of the chest of drawers . . .

Where am I?

Then she remembered.

The hotel.

Paul.

She could still feel his hand on hers but had no idea whether four minutes or four hours had passed. She closed her eyes again. She imagined him lying in his bed about twenty feet away, nothing but a single wall between them.

From somewhere inside her head a voice was saying, Go to him, Julia. Go.

Nicky was fast asleep. The door would be locked. Paul's room was right next door. She would hear if Nicky called her . . .

Go!

She wriggled off the bed, tiptoed to the bathroom, switched on the light and saw a face she hardly knew: skin flushed and taut, eyes wide open, sparkling.

With lightning speed she splashed herself all over with cold water. She pulled on her clothes then brushed her hair, letting it fall in straight

250

loose tresses down her back and over her shoulders.

With the key in her hand she crept silently across the thick gold carpet to the door. For a moment she stood and listened, then she was in the passage outside his room. She knocked softly, then ducked two steps sideways. There was still time to go back. He had told her she should be with Nicky —

But his door had opened.

'I wanted you to come,' he said, guiding her into the room, 'but I never thought you would. Nicky?'

Her heart thumped wildly against her ribs. 'She's fast asleep. What time is it?' she asked, feeling ridiculously nervous.

'Just after three. Is she likely to wake again?'

'Normally she never wakes up. I'll hear her if she calls. I don't think these walls are very thick.'

She walked to the window. The curtains were still open and she breathed in the fresh smell of the night. The moon lit up the farmhouses on the distant hills, a full moon, which according to farmers often heralded an improvement in the weather. It also explained why there was a soft dreamy quality to the air. Was it possible to pick up the broken threads, she wondered.

'Did you sleep?' she asked.

'You kidding? Did you?'

'It was mostly dreaming,' she said, and for a moment the smudged images returned.

'Of me?' He had come up behind her and was touching her shoulder.

She shook her head. She had never dreamt of him, she who was such a dreamer.

'Who?' He turned her round to face him.

She had told him before about her recurring dream. 'My brother,' she said, separating him in her mind from Smith, for in her dreams he was always faceless. 'The usual dream.' And she was glad Paul had the sense not to ask her any more. Not now, when all she could think of was him.

He moved a step closer. 'You know what?'

251

'What?'

He dropped his arms to his sides. 'I feel like I'm on my first date. Excited as hell but don't know how to go about it.'

'Me too.'

She closed her eyes, then quickly opened them, half-expecting not to see him there at all. He reached for her hand, held it for a moment, then let it drop as though still not certain what to do. Slowly he smiled the wistful half-smile that crinkled up his eyes. The one that at first she hadn't really noticed, but lately seemed fashioned especially for her.

'I have for years, you know.'

'Have what?'

'Loved you.'

Everything inside her was dissolving, including her neck and her knees and everything else that was holding her up. 'You're kidding.'

'Uh huh. Ever since, well, ever since I first saw you.'

'But you didn't even like me then.'

'Oh yeah?' He grinned, then swept her up and carried her to the bed. He sat her down with her legs dangling over the side, then knelt down on the carpet facing her. 'You don't know much about me then, do you?' he said.

He touched her hand. Something made her pull away.

'Julia?'

She shook her head.

'Relax,' he said. 'And tell me what it is you're afraid of.'

No. Don't answer that, Julia. Say nothing.

'All right,' he said, 'I just want to look at you. Please. May I? Look at you?'

Her mouth was dry. She felt her body stiffen. She nodded.

He frowned but made no move to touch her.

Then slowly, tentatively, she ran her fingers through his hair, stroking the little tufts of silvery grey just above his ears. 'Mind if I look too?' she said, her sudden boldness surprising her almost more than it surprised him.

Slowly, carefully, as though he was unwrapping a precious piece of china, he began unbuttoning her blouse, never once taking his eyes off

252

her face.

'Paul . . .'

'Shh.'

He pulled her to her feet. For a long time they just stood, holding each other, hardly moving. He did not attempt to touch her but she could feel his warmth reaching out to her.

She kissed his shoulder. With an anguished groan that came from deep within him, he held her closer.

'I don't want this to end,' he said.

'Neither do I,' she whispered as he gently eased her down.

From then on there were no separate movements, no separate words, no separate feelings. Everything that happened was part of one single work of art, strung together like a symphony that encompasses every nuance of sound, rhythm, passion – and every emotion in the human spectrum.

* * *

For a long time afterwards they lay still, their breathing gradually returning to normal. Julia was the first to move.

'I didn't know it could be like that,' she said, without any embarrassment or fear.

He trailed his fingers down her cheek.

'I want to spend the rest of my life making love to you,' he said.

She closed her eyes.

'You're crying,' he said.

'Not crying. Just . . . so happy.'

'I'm happy too, that it was so good for you.'

'No,' she said quickly. 'It's not just that.'

'What then?'

'I can't explain. It's just everything. Being together.' She didn't know how to tell him that no man had ever made her want to make love. Had ever made her feel so unafraid, not even Simon. That there was in his lovemaking – in their lovemaking – a dimension she had never dreamed existed. A dimension that embraced every atom of her being.

'Why did we wait so long?' he said.

'I don't know.'

'You've always seemed so frightened. Do you want to tell me why.'

Slowly she shook her head.

'Okay, it doesn't matter. Another time will do. And I don't want to chase you, but do you know what the time is now?'

She looked up. Daylight was flooding through the window.

He picked up her clothes, then sat on the bed and watched her getting dressed.

She slipped into her shoes and bent to kiss him. 'Nicky will be awake soon. I'll see you at breakfast.' She walked towards the door.

'Julia?'

She stopped and turned to face him. He was standing by the bed, staring at her, his mouth open, a look of torment in his eyes.

'Paul, what is it?'

'Are we . . . I mean . . . do you . . .'

'What?'

'No,' he said, 'it's nothing. You must go to Nicky now.'

- 80 -

Julia watched the sun pour life into the huge yellow flowers on the curtains as she waited for Nicky to wake up. Tiptoeing to the window, she felt like standing on top of those stark Pennine hills and shouting out loud:

I'm in love with Paul Moxon.

She had to tell someone. Not Nicky, not yet. But who would understand how after one night of passion she could be so sure she was in love? Or were these overwhelming sensations just masquerading as love? Would David and Jessie approve, she wondered. They were always asking if she'd found someone new. For Nicky's sake, they said, it would be nice.

Well, *nice* it certainly would be. But would it work? A criminal defence lawyer and a policeman? Nobody more than the two of them knew the extent of the conflicts that combination could spawn in a mere twenty-four hours, let alone in a lifetime together.

A lifetime. Is that what I want?

And anyway, who said anything about a permanent relationship? All that sentimental talk about wanting to spend the rest of his life making love to me was just —

'Mummy. Come and look at this.'

Running to the bed she flung her arms around Nicky: she couldn't help herself. 'Look at what, darling?'

Nicky's eyes opened wide in surprise. 'Nothing,' she said. 'I just wanted to hug you. And here you are. Hugging me.'

'You little monkey. I would have come without that little trick.'

They laughed and Julia pulled her out of bed and danced with her around the room.

'Wendy hugs me. You never hug me, Mummy. Why?'

'I'm hugging you now,' she said, squeezing Nicky tight. 'Come on. Let's get in the shower, then we'll go and have breakfast with Paul.'

'Do you think he'll play hide-and-seek with me?'

- 81 -

It's strange being so close to Paul, Julia thought. Yet not alone with him. He seems to have a permanent smile on his face, more in his eyes than on his lips, which deepens every time he looks at me. I suspect that I have a similar look on my face. In fact we probably look like two smiling Cheshire cats that have just polished off a bowl of cream.

At the next table a man was reading a Sunday tabloid. Julia heard the paper crackle as he turned the pages over and when she looked again she found herself staring at a large colour photograph of Smith. SMITH DOES VANISHING TRICK was the headline.

She followed Paul's gaze. He had seen it too.

She scraped some butter onto her toast. The photograph emphasised the blond beard and the blue convex eyes. Only Julia knew how dramatically his appearance had been transformed, revealing a far sharper jaw line than the beard suggested. The police must surely have guessed that he might shave his beard. She looked away. Oh how I long

255

to be released from the tyranny of secrets, she told herself. It's ridiculous to put myself through this agony. Smith must have had a blood test when he was arrested. I could easily have one now. A DNA test would prove almost beyond doubt whether we are twins or not. Paul, I imagine myself saying, won't you be a darling and arrange for me to have a DNA test. And if you don't mind, could you please ask Forensics to compare it with Smith's DNA . . .

Impossible.

She clenched her jaw until it felt as though her teeth would crack, but this was not enough to stop the barrage of thoughts invading her mind. The truth of it is that I'm still afraid to know. The proof would make it irreversible. Never again could I hide behind my doubt. Would I be able to face Paul again? Look him in the eye and say I loved him?

'Come, Princess,' Paul said to Nicky when she'd finished her last mouthful of scrambled egg. 'Let's all go for a walk.'

Paul led them down a shady path, dappled with sunlight filtering through the trees. All three holding hands, with Nicky in the middle, made Julia feel she was in another dream, a dream she didn't want to end. They stopped and listened to a blackbird, marvelling with heads tilted upwards at the sweetness of its aria. Just then Paul's mobile phone rang, shattering the magic.

He walked a few paces away. Several seconds later he turned to face Julia and Nicky.

'I'm sorry, job calls, I'm afraid. We'll have to leave.'

It took only minutes to pack.

Along the way home Julia gazed longingly at the grandeur of the hills. One day we'll come back, she thought, as they sped past the *Cat and Fiddle.*

'Next time we have a spare hour or two we could drive down Goyt Valley,' Paul said, as though sensing Julia's thoughts. 'All this beauty on our doorstep and we never take the time to see it.'

At Hillside House he took Julia's bag inside. 'I'm sorry it ended so abruptly,' he said. He gave them both a swift kiss and Julia a lingering look. 'We must do it again some time,' he said.

Julia smiled, although she was closer to tears.

He opened the car door. 'What'll you do now? It's a bit of a let down for you both.'

'Maybe drive to Southport,' Julia said, with sudden inspiration. 'It's ages since we've seen David and Jessie.'

'I'll get someone to accompany you,' he whispered, glancing at the house where Bennett's men were stationed. 'Don't worry. I'll make sure you won't see them. But they'll see you.'

'Okay,' she said, knowing that in this one instance there was no point in arguing.

'Ring me when you get home. Or if you need me — for anything.'

'I will,' she said. She grasped Nicky's hand and waved as he drove off.

- 82 -

Sam Smith had four big things on his mind.

Number one was controlling the pain.

Number two was how to keep hiding the fucking Fiesta. He couldn't leave it on the road. Someone was bound to report what would look like an abandoned car. There was no way of getting it to the derelict barn, so the churchyard at the cross roads it would have to be. A chance he'd have to take.

With one hand he gripped his stomach. With the other he took the photographs from his trouser pocket. They were getting creased from looking at them so often. Pity he'd had to dump the silver frames. He looked at the small one first, then the large one. If he did that quickly they seemed to come alive. She was so beautiful. If he looked at them for long enough it helped to keep the pain away. They took his mind on a long backward journey . . .

He'd been lucky to even find the barn. The map Frank had scribbled on a Manchester Evening News shortly before the escape had long since been lost. But no fucking problem. He'd just closed his eyes and there it was in front of him, plain as daylight, every road, every sign, every tree and every landmark. As soon as he'd coaxed the fucking car to the top of the hill and looked down over the moors, he'd known that he was home. Sometimes his photographic memory was a blessing.

This old barn was only marginally better than the burnt-out building at Castlefield. He had to huddle in a corner to escape the blasts of wind that rushed in through the cracks. When it rained he got pissed on from hundreds of tiny leaks, and the mod cons were non-existent. But he could see for miles around. Spot anyone looking for him.

His third problem was money. There wasn't much petrol left in the Fiesta, and up here in the middle of nowhere there was no chance to steal another car. The nearest phone was at the *Cat and Fiddle*, two or three miles away. So he had to leave enough money for petrol and the second phone call because without that the whole plan would fall to pieces.

Number four, and the one he'd spent the whole weekend working on, was how best to play his masterstroke.

- 83 -

David and Jessie's retirement flat overlooked the sea on one side, with a view of Royal Birkdale on the other. It had seemed ideal when they first moved in, though this time Julia sensed that something was amiss.

After lunch, while Jessie and Nicky were making tea, she asked David if everything was all right.

'If only you and Nicky would visit us more often.' He pressed his fingers into the small of his back. 'I don't drive any more, and I can't play golf because of this crippling sciatica.'

'You could walk gently on the beach,' Julia suggested, just as Jessie and Nicky breezed in with the tray.

Nicky's eyes lit up. 'David, will you walk with me on the beach? Please. We could look for shells.'

David's face creased into a smile. 'I'll be very slow, sweetheart, but yes, that would be grand. Let's have our tea and then we'll go.'

Later, when they were alone, Jessie said: 'You look tired, Julia. You've been overworking again.'

'No more than usual,' she said, her hard-to-believe almost sleepless night still vivid in her mind.

'Then something else is wrong. I can see it in your eyes. Is that why you've come?'

'Not wrong. But something's happened and I'm not sure what to do about it.'

'You've fallen in love.'

Julia grinned and slowly nodded.

'Oh Julia, dear. Tell me all about it.'

'Not much to tell, really. It's only just struck me that he's rather special.'

'Who is he? When can we meet him?'

'Not so fast, Jessie. Nothing's been discussed.' She stood up and walked to the window. The tide was low and she could see David and Nicky walking hand in hand in the distance. 'You see,' she said. 'He's a policeman.'

Jessie lifted her eyebrows. 'Oh.'

'A detective superintendent. You'll have seen him on the telly this week.'

'In connection with that murderer who escaped?'

'Yes.'

'Very distinguished looking. Handsome. Dark.' Jessie smiled, pressing her palms together. 'That him?'

'Yes.'

'He looks wonderful.'

'Oh, he's that all right.' Julia took a deep breath. Having to explain it to Jessie brought the reality home to her. 'But we sit on different sides of the legal fence, Jessie. It would be . . . impossible.'

'I didn't think that word existed in your vocabulary, my dear.'

'We're too fundamentally different in our moral outlook.'

Jessie gave her adopted daughter a long steady look. 'What about love, Julia? The chemistry between two people is a powerful thing.'

Julia couldn't help herself blushing, not only because Jessie was so accurate but also never before had Jessie expressed anything to her of such an intimate nature. Was this what happened when one grew older? Inhibitions melting away to reveal the real person underneath all the restraints that protocol demanded of the young.

'I know,' she said. 'But how can it really be love unless you love everything about that person?'

'No two people think alike about everything. There are bound to be differences. And you know what? Those differences might bring a bit of spice into your life when other pursuits become less important.'

Julia smiled. Jessie hadn't even been able to tell her about the birds and the bees, let alone allude to anything concerning love and sex. But she wondered if that was what was wrong with David and Jessie. They were too much alike, so possibly there'd be little to stimulate conversation, now that he was too old for golf and she had stopped playing in the orchestra.

'And don't forget respect,' Jessie went on. 'You may not agree with everything he does, Julia, but if you respect him and he respects you, the marriage — or the living together — will work.'

'Jessie, I didn't know you were such a philosopher.' Or so broadminded, she thought.

Jessie laughed. 'Well, you know what they say: older and wiser.'

'But wait a minute. Nobody's said anything about marriage. *Or* living together. He's been married before. He might not want to repeat the experience. And it's not part of my future plans. Although . . . Nicky does need a father . . .'

What would my real parents have said if I'd come to them today, Julia wondered. 'Jessie?'

'There is something else. I thought there was.'

'No. Not really. But . . . what was my real name? Before you and David adopted me.'

Jessie blinked her eyes. 'You've never ever asked me that before.'

'No. I didn't think you'd want me to.'

Jessie shook her head. 'I often wanted to tell you . . . everything.'

'Everything?'

'Well, you know, who your mother was and — ' She looked towards the window, then back at Julia. 'And about your twin brother.'

Julia felt the blood drain from her head. 'What about my brother?'

Jessie closed her eyes and shook her head again. Julia flung herself down at her knees. 'What happened to my brother? Why did he die?'

'Do you really want to know this,' Jessie asked slowly, 'after all these years?'

Julia saw Jessie's daisy-papered walls float towards her, wobble, then recede. 'Oh yes, I do,' she said, struggling to steady her gaze. 'More than anything in the world.'

Jessie sat forward and rubbed her eyes. She looked as though she was going to change her mind, hesitated, then took a deep breath. 'David always said that when your memory had fully recovered we should tell you. But it didn't recover. And we never found the right moment. We didn't want to upset you any more than you'd already been upset. And anyway, we had no idea where your brother had been taken.'

'Taken? So he didn't die.' Julia leapt up and walked to the window. She clenched and unclenched her fists. So it is true. No longer is he a faceless wraith disappearing over the top of a dream mountain. He is somewhere on this earth. I did not imagine it. I knew it. All along.

'Did you see him?' She stared out of the window, every muscle in her body tensed up like a violin string waiting to be plucked.

'No,' Jessie said. 'Thank goodness I didn't. That would have made it worse.'

'Did you know his name?'

'Nicholas,' she said.

She swung round to face Jessie. 'Yes. Nicholas! But why couldn't I remember it? I tried. God, how I tried. I couldn't remember anything about him. It was all a blank, until — '

'Shock does that to people's memories,' Jessie said. 'The psychologist told us that when something awful happens that's too much for you to bear, nature helps by blanking it out. But subconsciously you did remember.'

'How?'

'You called your daughter after him.'

Julia felt as though she'd been winded. 'Yes,' she said, flopping back into the chair. 'Of course. And I remember Simon's surprise when I was so certain it should be Nicola, when I rejected all the names he'd suggested.'

'And I got goose pimples when you told me her name. I knew it wasn't just coincidence.'

There it was again, thought Julia. No coincidence. Just a chain of links going back through a sea of mists . . .

'I was so glad,' Jessie said, 'when you started calling her Nicky.' She bit her lip. 'But even then it didn't seem right to tell you about Nicholas.'

Ironic, wasn't it, Julia thought. Each not wanting to hurt the other.

'And my mother and father?' she asked, holding her breath, fearing that to move even slightly might break Jessie's train of thought.

Jessie looked away. 'I wish I could tell you something good.'

'Go on, Jessie.' She moved to the edge of the chair.

'Your mother took you and Nicholas to the church.'

'Which church?'

'St Mary's. In the centre of Manchester. The Hidden Gem?'

'Yes,' Julia said, hardly breathing. 'I pass it often.'

'She gave her babies to the nuns. The nuns took them to the Touchstone orphanage. They didn't even know what day the babies had been born, but by the look of them they took a guess they were two days old, so gave the date as the 15th December.'

Julia's heart beat faster. 'Where is my mother?'

'No one knows.'

'And my father?'

'The nuns told the orphanage they thought he was someone important. Someone whose name had to be protected. An MP, or a judge. But they were only guessing. The nuns thought she was from a good family. She said her name was Victoria King. She was about sixteen, they said. And very beautiful. Now you know as much as they did.'

Julia's head was spinning. She had an irresistible longing to visit the church. She would go tomorrow. She pictured the frightened young girl, weak and exhausted from the birth of her twins, going furtively up the steps of St Mary's and handing over the two tiny babies. 'She must have been desperate,' she said. 'Oh, Jessie. My brother. Nicholas King. Alive after all.'

'What do you mean, after all?'

'Even though they told me he was dead I always felt he was still alive.'

Julia looked up at Jessie's face, so torn with remorse. 'Don't feel bad, Jessie. It's my fault. I could have asked you any time.' Julia stood up and moved over to Jessie, and without thinking she put her arms around her. But Jessie gently pushed her away and turned her head towards the wall.

'You don't understand,' Jessie said, her shoulders shaking. 'I'll never forgive myself. And I don't know why you haven't already asked me.'

'Asked you what?'

'Why we didn't adopt Nicholas as well.'

A silence fell. Julia sank back onto her knees in front of Jessie. 'Okay. Tell me now. Why?'

'There are so many excuses. I couldn't have lived with myself if I hadn't made those excuses over and over again to justify our unforgivable omission.' At last she looked at Julia. 'I said we had no idea where he'd been sent, but I'm sure we could have found out if we'd tried. All we knew was what we were told. That to begin with he was taken to a special unit for boys who had . . . who were naughty.' She turned away again. 'Not just naughty, but unmanageable and wicked. They told us he'd done something terrible.'

'What?' Julia shouted. 'What terrible thing did he do?'

'I don't know. They didn't say, but they did tell us there were marks of horrendous physical abuse on his body, old scars and severe new wounds too — and ghastly wounds on you as well — so they would bear that in mind and he would be treated accordingly, especially because of his young age. But because of the violence of his behaviour, he was not offered for adoption.' She wiped the tears from her eyes, stood up and lurched over to the window. 'We should have insisted. We should have taken him. We could have helped him, loved him. We know that now. We would have been a happy little family, the four of us together. Oh, the poor little boy . . .'

Julia was hardly listening. She flopped back onto the carpet. She gripped her trembling knees. Pieces were slotting into gaps like the reversed film of an explosion.

> *A line of images. Some blurred, others clearer than they've ever been. The lamp. Mr Spencer's head. There! I've even remembered his name. The blood. Everywhere. The pain. Shouting, running. Flashing lights. Sirens. Hurry, Julia, come with me . . . running, hiding, crying, sleeping, waking, cold, running, the stars, the rain . . . running . . . and then . . . Nicholas disappearing . . .*

She screwed up her eyes. If Smith is Nicholas — God forbid — this proves he was just trying it on, to get the money out of me. Twisting it around, trying to make me believe that I had picked up that lamp and crashed it down on Mr Spencer's head. But embellishing it grotesquely by saying I had killed him, because he knew my memory of my childhood was almost non-existent. When all the time it was he who had wounded Mr Spencer with the lamp, though he could easily have thought he had killed him. I can remember now, seeing the huge man lying on the floor, blood everywhere. But Mr Spencer couldn't have been killed otherwise Jessie and David would surely have been told about such a serious crime.

And why do I have this feeling that one last piece is missing?

She held her breath. What if Mr Spencer was killed and the authorities had just wanted to spare David and Jessie the sordid details . . . And how would the police have known who it was that struck him with the lamp. Maybe it was her. Maybe the police just assumed it was Nicholas because he was a boy and she was a girl . . .

She had to know. She had to find out who it was.

'They said he was . . . unreachable,' Jessie said. 'That's what they called him. Unreachable. You'd both been covered in blood when you were eventually found. Full of gashes and bruises, they said. And suffering from loss of blood from the wounds you both had. You had lost your memory. The only thing you knew was that you had a brother. The people at the orphanage, where you were always cared for in between the times when you were fostered, told you Nicholas was dead because they were sure you wouldn't come to us without him if you knew he was alive. You'd been inseparable they said. And, oh God, we let you go on thinking he was dead.'

Tears were streaming down Jessie's cheeks now, yet she seemed determined to carry on. 'But that wasn't all. We were selfish. All the years we had tried for a baby it was always a girl we'd wanted. It was cruel to separate you. You were miserable without him. You had panic attacks, alarming changes of mood and you were clearly depressed and did some really strange things. Talking to your brother. Talking to yourself, you never stopped doing that. We even had a social worker check you out. She said there was nothing wrong with you that time wouldn't cure. She told us to ignore it and you'd soon forget.'

Julia shuddered.

The social worker. The little boy next door. Throwing my arms around him, crying with happiness, sliding down to the ground clutching him and kissing his legs, thinking he was Nicholas . . . the accusations . . .

'Most little boys are naughty,' Jessie went on. 'It's normal. Even you were naughty, Julia. They say clever children are the worst. Nicholas would have grown out of it, I'm sure. He'd been grossly abused, provoked into doing whatever act of violence it was that he did. But we didn't have much money. We wanted everything for you.' She wiped her eyes. 'Our little girl. At last.'

Julia joined Jessie at the window. She stood as close to her as she dared. 'What happened to him in the end?' she asked. Her hands were bunched into fists to stop them trembling.

Jessie gripped the sides of her head. Julia prised her hands away. 'Tell me, Jessie.'

'I have no idea,' she whispered.

More tears streamed down her face. Julia put her arms around Jessie and held her tightly. And for once her adoptive mother did not push her away. 'There's no excuse for what we did. And I just wish we'd told you everything.'

'It's my fault. I could have asked you any time. And then I could have searched for him.' She handed Jessie a tissue.

'You were always searching for him. I used to cry when I saw you at the bottom of the garden, talking to an imaginary child. And in bed at night telling him a story, laughing for the both of you at the funny bits and crying if it was sad. We robbed you of your brother, no matter what he was. I never forgave myself for that.'

Julia stood beside Jessie, feeling a rush of warmth. She wished she could comfort her. They gave me so much, she thought. Where would I have been now if they hadn't adopted me? 'Oh, Jessie. Stop blaming yourself. I'll find him.'

Jessie's eyes lit up. 'We could help.'

'No, Jessie dear. I must do this on my own.'

MONDAY

Julia gulped down her coffee, and with the emergency make-up kit she kept in the bottom drawer of her desk, she attempted to make herself look human. After her electrifying weekend, followed by three gruelling hours last night at Bootle Street police station sorting out a businessman who'd been arrested on a drugs charge, and after four days of the suspense of still not hearing from Sam Smith, she knew she looked grim.

But that was only on the outside. Inside it was far worse: a bizarre mixture of elation and terror, and total bewilderment. Who hit Mr Spencer on the head with the lamp? Was it Nicholas or was it her?

Did Mr Spencer die?

But all these questions are academic, Julia thought. If Sam Smith is not Nicholas.

Elation? Because today she was in love with Paul Moxon. Today she had a big new juicy case. Today she had a brother called Nicholas King who did not die twenty-six years ago. And today, theoretically, she should no longer be afraid, since this was the fourth day in a row with no phone call from a man called Sam Smith.

Like a rat after a feast of poisonous bait, he might at this very moment be slowly rotting to death, she thought. In pain, lonely, sad, bitter at the futility of his miserable life so difficult to separate from her own. And when they found his body, or even before that, she would be driven by remorse and guilt to tell the police how on the spur of the moment she defended herself with a hatpin — yes, a hatpin — when her life was being threatened by — who? — this twisted man who was trying to settle a score.

'Alive,' she said aloud, just as Linda walked in.

'Just a reminder,' said the ever watchful Linda, dropping a pile of files on Julia's desk and handing her another mug of steaming coffee, 'that tomorrow you're duty solicitor at Manchester Magistrates'.'

Julia raised her eyes to the ceiling, and took a grateful sip of coffee.

She'd have to work all hours to clear today's workload. Her diary was grossly overbooked. Her wealthy new client was appearing in court at eleven-thirty and that would throw her schedule completely out of kilter. But if she wasn't there with him he'd simply get another lawyer. It was a big case. And if she didn't stick herself to it like glue at this stage, her ability to prepare it later on would be seriously prejudiced.

With her files under her arm Julia popped briefly into Ben's office. She avoided his personal questions with nods or shakes of her head, and their schedules were re-arranged with Mark and Caroline doing their bit, and even the staff at the Longsight branch chipping in. Afterwards she made a few phone calls, sorted Saturday's mail, and called Linda in again.

'I'd like you to do something personal for me, please.' She kept her eyes down as she spoke. 'Look up the phone numbers of organisations that trace missing people. Salvation Army, DSS, but there are many others you could try.'

'If you give me the date of birth now,' said Linda, 'the DSS can find the National Insurance number straightaway.'

Still avoiding Linda's gaze, she pretended to scratch in her top drawer. 'I'm not sure of the date,' she said. 'Just get me the numbers, please Linda. I'll work on it myself when I get back.'

When Linda had gone she shovelled everything into her briefcase and grabbed her raincoat and umbrella. As she slung her handbag over her shoulder, she felt the pistol slam against her hip. Just as well, as she'd never have got past Security with it in her bag. She unlocked the desk drawer, shuddering as her fingers touched the cold metal. With Smith either dead or dying, she thought, squeezing her eyes tightly shut, I have no more need of it. This weekend I will drive up into the hills and throw it into the depths of the Goyt Valley reservoirs.

She had just locked the drawer when the phone rang. She almost didn't answer it, but decided it could be something regarding her new drugs case. Or Geoff Atherton about the Dennis Magg trial that was opening at the Crown Court in a few minutes time.

It might even be Paul . . .

She picked up the receiver. 'Julia Grant speaking.'

'You thought I'd forgotten about you, didn't you, Julia?'

'What?' A mixture of relief and fear flooded through her. Had Martin Bedlow been completely wrong?

'Don't waste my fucking time, Julia.'

'And don't waste my time either. I'm due in court in ten minutes.'

'Shut up, rich bitch and listen. First. No more fancy ideas about going to Chester House and blabbing your mouth off. We know you got the hots for that piece of shit but you better say nothing to him. I'll know if you do, Julia. So far you've been very sensible, so don't spoil it now. And in case you've forgotten, this is Monday, so where's my fucking cash?'

Julia sank into her chair. Like a big wheel at a fair ground, two names chased around her brain. Sam Smith. Nicholas King. Sam Smith. Nicholas King . . .

'My money, bitch.'

'I haven't got it yet. You'll get it tomorrow.'

'Speak up. I can't hear you. I want it right now. Like we agreed. And to remind you – a hundred grand in tenners. The rest in fifties. None of them fucking twenties. Okay?'

She had to think straight. He'd be in no fit state to retaliate if he were ill. He sounded a bit rough, but there was no way of knowing what this was due to.

Think, Julia.

Okay. There was a time when I had complete control over Sam Smith. When I could manipulate him. When he trusted me. *You're the only person* — or did he say woman? — *the only woman I've ever met that I can trust. Help me, Julia. Please help me . . .*

But things were different now. The pretence was over.

Does he know that he might be Nicholas King? Did he ever know?

Think, Julia. A more effective strategy is for you to show weakness, to show compliance. Convince him that you're going along with his demands. Convince him that he's got you exactly where he wants you. That he's in control.

'I'm terribly sorry,' she said quickly. 'I haven't got it yet. There was a technical problem. Completely out of my hands. I'll have it all tomorrow. Really I will.'

He was breathing heavily but that could be due to anything. Maybe he'd managed to get hold of some antibiotics and was completely cured. 'Tomorrow,' he said at last. 'And that's my absolutely final word.'

'Where do I meet you? What time?' she asked, maintaining her tone of capitulation.

'I'll let you know tomorrow, don't worry.'

'I have a full diary tomorrow. I'm duty solicitor. Why not tell me now?'

'So you can tell the cops? Ha. You know, Julia, I understand you far better than you think I do. I know so much about you, you thick bitch. Even things you didn't tell me. I know everything.'

She held the phone away as another blast of raucous laughter almost deafened her. With little or no retaliation from her now, he was clearly gaining confidence.

'I even know just what you're thinking at this very minute.'

'How could you possibly know, you scum.'

She regretted the derisive word as soon as she'd said it. Let him think he's in control, for goodness sake. If he panics he might do anything.

'Oh, Christ, we have so much in common, Julia.'

'Look, I'm afraid I have to go now. I can't be late.'

'You see, Julia, I understand how you think because I'm also a twin.'

'What did you say?'

'You heard me. You see, all twins have the same problems.'

'You never told me before that you were a twin.'

Nicholas?

'Never tell everything all at once,' Smith said, clearly relishing the sound of Julia's fear. 'Always keep the best things for last. Or, shall we say, second-last. You should know that, Mrs clever fucking solicitor.'

'Sam, I'm very busy. I'll have the money tomorrow, I promise. Have you ever tried getting a quarter million pounds in cash out of someone else's trust fund? It hasn't been easy. Let me know as soon as possible where and when to meet you.'

And with that she slammed down the phone. Wondering where she was getting all this self control, she punched in the number for Melbourne Kennedy and asked for Fred. She closed her eyes tightly until she heard his voice.

'Hi, Fred. Sorry to bother you so early.' she said jauntily. 'But regarding the stocks we asked you to sell, we'd rather like to have everything tied up by tomorrow morning first thing if you don't mind.'

'Julia, I am sorry. I meant to ring you. It's doubtful. A bit of an administrative hiccup, but definitely on Wednesday.'

Wednesday. Oh my God —

She mumbled thank you then put down the phone.

She looked at her watch. Geoff Atherton would be wondering where she was. She forced herself up, checked that she'd locked the top drawer, gathered up her handbag, briefcase and umbrella, and rushed through the door, cursing the abysmal summer weather.

- 85 -

Dodging the clumps of duffel-coated photographers hanging around the court entrance, Julia pushed open the smoky glass doors, surrendering her handbag and briefcase to the X-ray machine as she floated in a daze through the metal detector.

Number two court was crowded to capacity. With no time to go to the cloakroom she screwed up her raincoat and floppy velvet hat with its shiny new hatpin Wendy had replaced when she saw the old one was missing, and shoved them and her dripping umbrella underneath the bench.

Geoff looked relieved to see her. She smiled back vacantly.

'All stand,' the clerk of the court said.

The judge sat down in his maroon leather chair. The dock officers led in Julia's client, stony-faced, neat and clean in newly pressed grey trousers and a sports coat.

'Are you Dennis Magg?' the clerk of the court asked.

'Yes.'

'Sit down, please.'

Prosecuting Counsel rose to introduce himself and Atherton as Counsel in the case. As they politely discussed housekeeping issues before the jury was empanelled, Julia glanced at the clock above the door to the jury room. It was ten-fifteen, less than half an hour since Sam Smith had phoned, and she was no nearer a solution. It would be impossible to get hold of a quarter of a million pounds in tens and fifties by tomorrow, when she'd be here in the Crown Court for most of the day, and at eleven-thirty on her feet in the Magistrates' when her new drugs client was charged. And at five-thirty a client to see in her office . . .

'Will the defendant please stand.'

The clerk of the court read out the indictment.

'Are you guilty or not guilty?'

'Not guilty,' Dennis Magg said.

She could walk out now. Geoff would understand . . .

The panel of potential jurors filed in. After the clerk of the court read out their names, those chosen walked obediently to their seats.

Julia stroked the tendons in her neck that felt as if they were standing out like thick hemp ropes. Something inside her was telling her the time had come to throw caution to the wind and tell Paul everything. Including where she would be meeting Smith to hand over the money. They would apprehend Smith, put him in custody, and that would be that.

Are you crazy, Julia Grant? The first thing he would do is shoot his mouth off. She would be taken in and questioned. Paul would walk out of her life forever and The Law Society would without a doubt stop her practicing —

And she didn't dare think of what would follow.

And what about his accomplices?

Well, he might be bluffing. Joe Sagoe's dead. There could be others, but it just isn't feasible that they'd still have allegiance to Smith after what happened to Joe.

Of course it's damn well feasible. Someone saw me go into Chester House and they are probably still watching me at this very minute.

Geoff caught her eye and frowned. I must be a sight, she thought, with my hair wet and straggly, and if he thinks I look as though I haven't a clue what's going on he'll be dead right.

She glanced at the defendant. But instead of the dark pock-marked face of Dennis Magg all she could see was the lean sharp face of Sam Smith with his slightly protruding eyes, glaring at her and shouting I'll get you, you fucking bitch. You'll pay for this . . .

The members of the jury read one at a time from the card in front of them. 'I swear by Almighty God that I will faithfully try the defendant and give a true verdict according to the evidence . . .'

. . . I understand how you think because I'm also a twin . . .

Prosecuting Counsel described the crime, then the judge addressed the jury – the usual fireside chat about what their job was going to be for the duration of the trial: the judge would be in charge of matters of law, the jurors in charge of fact . . .

Julia's mind continued to reel. Completely ignoring the proceedings, she gazed up at the latticed ceiling, only vaguely aware of the prosecutor's opening speech. She had already agreed it in advance. The lifestyle of the poor pathetic dead girl: looked older than her years, parents divorced, played truant from school, unemployed, stayed out overnight, friends unemployed . . . Prosecuting Counsel rumbled on . . .

Think, Julia. Think back to those interviews with Smith at Strangeways. What did he tell you? There must be something you missed.

Geoff tapped her on the shoulder. He couldn't find his bundle of post-mortem photos, did she have a spare set? Her papers were arrayed in a set of a dozen or so ring binders in front of her, each minutely indexed along the spine. She reached mechanically for one of them, turned to a divider and produced the photos that Counsel was after, barely aware of what she was doing.

Counsel asked for the first witness. The usher led him in and gave him the bible. 'I swear by Almighty God that the evidence I shall give shall be the truth, the whole truth, and nothing but the truth.'

The truth. What is the truth? – Will somebody please tell me . . .

The proceedings dragged on. Julia gritted her teeth. How much more of this torture could she endure? She had to know. She had to find out. Nicholas King was the only one who would really know what happened that night.

She turned and beckoned to her Counsel. 'Geoff, I'm really sorry, I'm going to have to leave. I'll get the office to send one of our juniors over to cover while I'm away. I'll be back as soon as I can after my case at the Magistrate's.' He looked at his watch, but before he could enquire what the problem was, she turned towards the judge, bowed discreetly and after grabbing her raincoat, hat and umbrella she walked noiselessly towards the exit. She was vaguely aware of her client staring at her as she walked past the dock, but she was beyond seeking his permission or approval. Once outside the courtroom she ran along the concourse, pushed through the swing doors and flew down the stairs, grabbing the handrail as she almost tripped and fell.

She looked around the square. She didn't know which way to turn or what to do next, but there was no way she could stay in there until eleven-thirty. She had to think. She had to work things out, before she lost her mind.

- 86 -

Ben Lloyd paced the floor of his office. Each time he'd tried phoning Hillside House over the weekend there'd been no reply. Even Julia's mobile had been switched off. When he had seen her briefly in the morning she'd looked tired and haggard.

He stopped to watch the rain lashing the street. Would it never stop? This was supposed to be summer. He glanced at his watch before starting to pace again. What a fool he had been to behave the way he had the previous Friday night. He'd been even more thoughtless in denying her a sympathetic ear over borrowing funds from the trust. Her desperation for the money had made him suspicious, and lately, whenever he suspected Paul Moxon of having anything to do with her, something inside him would snap.

Forcing himself to sit at his desk he went through evidence he'd collected from a witness, but nothing succeeded in blotting out the vision of her that occupied his mind. He resumed his pacing. The frustration was killing him. He buzzed Linda. 'When's Julia due back?' he asked in what he hoped was a casual tone.

'If her trial runs, I don't think she'll be in much before half four.' Linda said. 'And a client to see at five-thirty.'

'Could you ask her to see me first, Linda, before she calls anyone or sees anyone, okay?'

He stood at the window, thinking again about the trust. He had no idea what had made him imagine her appeal had anything to do with Paul Moxon. In his blind jealousy he hadn't even had the courtesy to listen to her properly. He'd behaved like a prize idiot. Time to try and make up.

Striking out blindly from Crown Square, Julia ran to the Gartside Street car park, got into her car and sat there in the dim light, hands on the wheel, rigid as she tried to think things through. It was the only place she could think of where she'd be completely alone. Sometimes she did her best thinking in the car, but today not even listening to a favourite Mozart concerto helped to clear her mental log jam.

Think, Julia. Think.

Okay, okay, but I'm almost certain he's never said anything before about being a twin.

She always made copious notes when she took instructions from her clients, and Smith's case had been no different. It helped her construct a three dimensional plan in her head – what the prosecution witnesses said, what her client's response was, then she would try to link this matrix with other defence evidence, whenever available. An eye witness, an alibi, a forensic expert.

Every killer has a motive for murder, and Julia had soon found the underlying psychological cause. In Smith's case, assuming he would admit the killing, he despised his foster mother, Ada, the deserted wife turned alcoholic prostitute, not averse to leaving him at the mercy of her more depraved clients. In the early days of her questioning, she could see that if he transferred his hatred for Ada and his desire for revenge onto his victim . . . Bingo – diminished responsibility could have begun to look like a real possibility. And perhaps there was another causative factor too, she had thought, but quickly she had blocked that out too.

She remembered the day she'd begun to make real headway with him. She could see herself now, entering the big prison gates, smelling the stale cigarette smoke in the lift. Sam Smith's piercing blue eyes staring at her across the interview table.

'Now we need to go through this bit again, Sam. Step by step. When you had the scuffle you came at her with the knife. Why?'

'I had to protect myself. I'd never seen these people before. None of them till I went to that pub. She'd already had a go at me. She was crazy. I took the knife out my pocket and held it up, just to frighten her. I didn't mean to hurt her.'

'Was the knife pointing down, or towards her?'

'I didn't actually stick it in her. But when we fell over it might have gone in. Just a slight nick. Someone else must have found her after I'd left. Someone with a knife like mine. Someone who hated her. I didn't kill her. I didn't. Honest I didn't.'

'And the cord around Joanne's neck? Perhaps you accidentally pulled it just a bit tighter when you'd only meant to frighten her.'

'I told you, Julia. We'd been fooling around. She was teasing me like. Laughing. You know. Joking. Some girls, they dig that sort of thing. I didn't tighten the cord round her neck. I just played with it. Like I might have nicked her with the knife by mistake but someone else did all those other things. After I left.'

'What about the cigarette burns on her pubic area? Did she have those when you were fooling around? Or did you do them?'

'I don't remember seeing no cigarette burns.'

'Oh. So you did see her with no clothes on.'

'I didn't.'

'So you didn't see the criss-cross cuts on her thighs?'

'I told you, I didn't. I saw none of that stuff . . . '

'Oh, this is ridiculous,' Julia said out loud as his image faded. 'This is getting me nowhere.' Her hands were still gripping the wheel and she looked around the car park to see if anyone had observed her. Damn. In spite of being able to remember the interviews almost word for word, so far nothing she'd recalled had helped one iota to determine anything that could give her a clue to him being a twin. She was almost sure he'd never even hinted at it.

Anyway, thousands of twins are born every year. It's nothing very unusual. She looked at her watch. She'd better get over to the Magistrates' Court quickly for her bail application, and then head back to the Crown Court or Geoff would give her hell.

Half way out of the car she stopped as a babble of noises rattled and clanged in her ears.

She slid back onto the seat as a swarm of images flew around her head – a far clearer sequence than she was used to seeing.

The hairy hands, the stubbled chin. The broken lamp. Blood. Calling out the name Nicholas — that is new too — and his voice urging, Run Julia, run. Like I've seen it before but look at this. It's changing. Wet. Cold. nightgown soaked. No shoes. Feet bleeding. Long grass. Taking off his pyjama jacket and putting it over both our heads. Arms and legs entwined. Faces touching. Beyond us voices getting closer. In a circle. Dogs. Sniffing. Don't let them take you away, Julia, he says in my ear. And I can see his neck, see the swan. The swan. I must stay with the swan. As long as I can see the swan I'll be safe . . .

Followed by darkness. Except for one little recollection that pushed its way into this melee of memories . . . "*I took the knife out of my pocket,*" he'd said. Knife in his pocket . . . Knife in his pocket . . . Oh rubbish, she told herself. Every little boy has a knife in his pocket. Nicholas had always had one in his. And then a sudden flash, in a forward time warp, the word TOUCHSTONE. Roaring in her ears.

Julia snatched a handful of tissues from the box on the floor of the car and held it to her mouth, bending over as convulsion after convulsion shook her body.

88

When Julia finally burst in through the office door at four-thirty, Linda came to meet her, her smile fading as she saw Julia's face.

'Julia? You're as white as a sheet.'

'I'm fine. I just haven't had time to re-do my make-up and I've had nothing to eat.' She took a deep breath, as though she'd been swimming under water and had to come up for air. She was still wondering how she'd managed to conduct her business at the Magistrates' and then stay looking even half intelligent during the rest of the all-day session at the Crown Court. 'I'd love a coffee, though,' she said. 'Have you got my messages?'

'Ben wants to see you first. It sounded urgent.'

Julia couldn't face anyone right now, least of all Ben. 'Tell him I'm – tell him I'm tied up.'

'Right. I'll get your coffee. Oh, by the way, that list you wanted is on your desk.'

'Thanks, Linda. I'll study it tonight.'

The search was hardly necessary now, Julia murmured to herself. She was still trying to keep everything dark in her head, trying not to embrace what she'd just remembered. The swan. The Touchstone. There, they were both too strong to be dismissed but she had to be firm. She had to carry on. They were vital clues but they had to be verified.

So far, today had been a disaster. She'd even lost the bail application for her new drugs client. And there'd been no time yet to pop into the Hidden Gem, something she had promised herself she would do today.

Hearing a tap on the door, she looked up to see Ben walking towards her.

Quickly she opened a file on her desk. 'I'm terribly busy, Ben. Can't it wait till tomorrow?'

He walked round the desk and stood beside her. 'You look ill, Julia. Surely you can tell me what's wrong.'

'You don't look too good yourself,' she said, trying to smile. 'We must both be overworking.' She closed the file. 'Okay, but please make it quick. I'm really pushed for time.'

He cleared his throat, then edged closer until he was almost touching her.

'I'm sorry I was so hasty about the trust,' he said. 'Just tell me what you want. I'll talk to Fred Kennedy first thing tomorrow morning.'

Julia gaped at him. She could feel her eyes widening to the limit. As though they were going to pop clean out of her head.

'What's wrong? I thought you wanted the money in a hurry.'

'It's . . . too late,' she said, in the squeaky voice that always manifested itself when she was under stress, but which she never recognised as her own.

'You look terrified. Too late for what?'

'I mean . . . '

'Julia?' He grasped her shoulders. 'What the hell is going on?'

She tried to pull away. 'Nothing,' she said. 'I just don't need it any more.' Later I can explain, she thought. If he wants to dissolve the partnership, he can. I won't care what happens then. I'll have paid Smith. He'll be safely out of the country, keeping his mouth shut, starting his new life.

Abruptly Ben let her go. 'So what was all that fuss about needing the money so urgently?' His voice had hardened.

Right now all she had to worry about was getting through tomorrow. She remembered that the pistol was still in her desk drawer, and she'd have to get it out before she went home tonight.

'I've thought about it since,' she said, improvising as she went along. 'I was over-reacting. I wanted the best for Nicky. But I see now that it's far too soon to be committing the funds in that direction.' Too damn right, she thought, it was a daft proposition from the start. But oh how calmly I am lying. And he looks as though he believes me. 'If you'll excuse me, Ben, I'm busy. But thanks all the same.'

She punched in Linda's internal number. 'Linda, have you got my messages now? And Mrs Jackson's file, please.'

She stood up and leaned on the desk. In spite of the practised play-acting, her hands were shaking.

Ben stared at her. 'You need a couple of days off. We can all cover for you.' He had pity in his eyes and Julia hated anyone to feel sorry for her.

'I'm absolutely fine,' she said, lifting her chin. 'Anyway, I had a break at the weekend.'

'Oh! Really. Where did you go?'

'Paul Moxon took us to White Pool Farm.'

Ben's mouth opened as though someone had hit the back of his neck. Without a word he turned and marched out of Julia's office.

89

Julia found she had a magical twenty minutes to spare between dealing with her messages and her interview with Mrs Jackson. She made a quick decision – crazy, but she had to do it.

Taking nothing with her, not even her handbag, she left the office. She ran down Deansgate and into Brazennose Street. Glancing at Lincoln's accusingly sober face with its metallic stare, she darted through the leafy square with its picture-view of the Town Hall's soaring tower. And then, like some shrine beckoning her, there it was:

The Hidden Gem. She stood rock-still and gazed at the church in awe. She had hurried past it hundreds of times, never dreaming it was here that she and her brother had been thrust into the nuns' arms by a frightened young girl, who'd told them nothing but her name.

Approaching through the covered archway between Brazennose and Mulberry Streets, her heart began to beat faster as she visualised the frantic young mother, unable to see for the tears filling her eyes, hesitating, then finally walking up the four stone steps, holding tightly to her swollen breasts the newly born babies.

At the top of these steps Julia stopped. She looked down at the mosaic floor of the porch, at the words *Ave Maria* in blue letters that Victoria King must have read in those last few moments of being a mother.

She pulled open the stained glass door. She let her fingers linger on the brass handle, which Victoria King had grasped as she steeled herself to enter the church, comforting her babies as they cried.

She stood just inside the door listening to the organ music playing softly in the background. She smelled the incense, gazed at the rows of gleaming onyx marble pillars, the life-sized marble statues and the altar where two tall slender candles in twisted brass holders flickered in the dim light. Exactly as Victoria King had seen them . . .

'Can I be of assistance?' a soft voice said behind her.

She spun round. The nun had clear, pale skin and the kindest deep indigo eyes that smiled as she spoke.

'No thank you,' Julia said. 'It's all right. I was just looking. I hope you don't mind.'

'Is this the first time you've been to our church?'

'No, but, well, it's a long story, and I so much wanted to — wanted to find out . . . '

'Come, my dear. Let's sit down over here.'

Holding Julia's arm the nun led her to a pew at the back of the church, and before Julia knew what was happening she had poured out the whole story. 'I've come because it's the only place I know for certain that my mother has been. But I can't help wondering what made her choose this place.'

'Even in those days this was a well-known church,' the nun said in hushed tones. 'The oldest post-Reformation Catholic foundation in the city. The doors are open every day, all day. And even if she'd left her twins in the porch outside, she'd have known they'd be found immediately because every day there's Exposition of the Blessed Sacrament. People from all over Manchester and far beyond use it.'

'So she wouldn't necessarily have lived here in the city?'

'She could have lived anywhere. The buses have always come into Deansgate and Albert Square.'

Julia looked into the nun's kind eyes. 'Do you think she'd have been — very poor?'

'No. Not at all. In those days, in certain circles, it was still not socially acceptable for a young girl to have a baby out of wedlock. The higher the social position of the family, the higher the disgrace would have been perceived. She may still have been studying, or promised herself in marriage to some other man. There are so many possible scenarios it would be impossible to guess.'

She took Julia's hand. 'But one thing we can be certain of, my dear. The abandonment of her babies was an act of desperation. She will have felt that there was nothing else she could do. Your mother was a very brave girl, who must have suffered a great deal but did what she did in order to give you and your brother the best possible chance of a good life.'

A good life? Perhaps for only one of us, Julia thought.

For a few moments they sat in silence while she soaked up the atmosphere which for the young Victoria King must have been so painful. Here, perhaps on this very spot, she had given away her babies, never to see them again.

Julia thanked the nun. She marvelled at the compassion she had shown to her, a complete stranger. She wished she could have stayed longer, but she had an appointment to keep.

Outside the church everything looked normal. But for Julia it would never again be the same. In front of her she could still see her mother. She is placing the two babies into the arms of the nuns. Then she is turning and pushing through the stained-glass door, her eyes blinded with tears, her breasts bursting with milk. Out into the city streets. Alone.

TUESDAY

90

It happened without warning, as it always did. First it was just the hills moving in the dawn sky. Then the ground beneath him undulating like a silent slow-motion earthquake, with the sound of the wind and the beating of his heart muffled as though he were plunging deep into the ocean.

And then the floating sensation, the one he always got when Ada called.

He heard her voice again. Shrill and demanding. 'Sam!'

He would have to go in the end. Maybe she'd give him a drink. She might also give him food, and then he wouldn't have to steal those three-day-old sausage rolls from the corner bakery . . .

And there she was, grasping his wrist and dragging him to the caravan, her straggly blonde hair flying in the wind, her voice rattling through him.

'I told you to come, you scumbag.'

He felt the pain of the cigarette sear his stomach. He screamed, then quickly, before she burned his arms, he began the ritual. It was great the way the pain melted away. And if he didn't actually look at the burn marks, he could swear he'd been making it all up in his head.

He watched the two bodies, slippery with sweat, making disgusting slapping noises. Her eyes were closed. She was yelping like a dog and digging her claws into the man's back.

Sam lay quietly, feeling sick, knowing what was still to come. Knowing the caravan was locked and he couldn't get out. When the man had finished he got up, kicked Sam in the head and then turned him over. Sam lay still, his eyes tightly closed, his face screwed up, making the pain go, waiting, waiting until the man had gone. And when he had gone he heard the voice in his head. And very quietly, so that Ada would not hear him, he slid the knife out of his pocket and thrust it deep into her back.

Slowly his vision cleared. His body felt so good that he sat up and looked through the open door, focusing on the bleak moors beyond the barn. Dark burnt heather close by, then dark green and grey, then pale grey meeting the dark grey of the sky. Fading to nothing. Life was like that, he thought. In the end it fades to nothing. Sometimes he wondered why he bothered. It was all going to end anyway.

He reached for the plastic water bottle. He could finish the lot, but knowing what that did to him lately, he tilted it slowly so that only a few drops touched his tongue.

His clothes were a mess. Hung on him like a scarecrow's. The last of the precious clean clothes, the ones Joe had given him before he'd thrown him out, were still in the plastic bag, being saved for the big moment.

Julia. How people changed. He didn't trust her further than he could throw her now. Yes, okay, she promised she'd give him the money today, but he didn't believe her any more. It was her lies that were forcing him to do this. He didn't want to do it, but there was no other way. Nobody cared about him, so why should he care about anyone else? So far, nothing he'd done to frighten her had made her see sense. Mrs fucking solicitor thought that if she kept him waiting long enough he would just walk away and forget the whole thing. Then she could walk away too.

He'd have done things differently if she hadn't stuck that hatpin in his guts. This whole fiasco was her fault. He could keep the pain away for a day or two longer but he wasn't fucking ignorant. He'd die if he didn't see a quack soon, but he needed big money for that. Needed it now. She said she'd have it today but he couldn't trust her any more . . .

He was all set. And he knew exactly what time the children came out of school.

He sat as still as a statue. Conserving his energy. He watched the sky change from grey to pink. Soon he was floating just above the floor of the barn. He didn't have long to wait now.

- 91 -

Julia opened her eyes, remembering with a surge of excitement that exactly two days ago at dawn, she'd been with Paul in his hotel room. With each hour that went by, with each new stab of fear, she realised how much she needed him, and yet the crazy thing was that despite what Jessie had said, she knew it was wishful thinking to imagine it could ever work.

How she'd have loved to have had dinner with him last night. But she couldn't have eaten a thing and he'd have wanted to know why. And now today loomed before her like a sheer mountain face, without a comforting ledge in sight. Duty solicitor. Smith's phone call. Smith's deadline for handing over the money. Nicky's extra ballet class . . .

Touchstone . . . Swan . . . Who is Smith? Who hit Mr Spencer with the lamp? Was it me or Nicholas? Without positive proof you have to give him the benefit of the doubt . . .

She clamped her hands over her ears, trying to shut out her inner voice which was becoming more intense and more intrusive each day. Thank goodness nobody else could hear it. It was a form of talking to herself that was making her increasingly suspicious about her mental stability, but without anybody to confide in, who else was there to talk to?

She swung her legs over the bed and dropped her feet into her slippers. Tiptoeing to Nicky's room she peeped in, then went downstairs to make the tea. She patted Duchess, put the kettle on and took a bowl of milk to the utility room for Kitty. With a steaming mug in front of her she sat down at the kitchen table. Okay, Julia. Think logically.

Right. Smith. He was abandoned. Shoved from pillar to post. Real date of birth unknown, but someone will eventually have picked a date because the system says, well, you must have a date of birth. The same thing went for his name. He could have gone through life with this name, Sam Smith and this date of birth that everyone accepted, and it could all be fictitious.

She put a slice of bread in the toaster and waited for it to pop up. If I wanted to, I could call myself Madonna. Born on April the first. And if I said it often enough it would get written down in records. The information the police have on criminal records is what you tell them, apart from exceptional circumstances where they do a thorough investigation into a person's antecedents. What's your name? Sam Smith. Your date of birth? Let's have a set of your fingerprints. Fine. So right from the age of thirteen, when he was first arrested for burglary, he got fingerprinted, and the name and date of birth were whatever he told them they were.

The toast popped up. She spooned a dollop of marmalade on top of it. She felt sick and frightened but knew she had to eat. He had said once that he was into astrology or she'd never have told him her date of birth. Perhaps, after she'd eaten, this trembling would stop. She took a bite of toast, then pushed the plate away. She sipped her tea, staring into space.

Think. Close your eyes. Think about that day at Strangeways when he chatted about astrology . . . the smell of fresh paint . . . his eyes . . . their voices . . .

'They all told me you were the best. You're real smart the way you suss things out, aren't you, Julia.'

'It's my job.'

'It's no wonder you're such a good lawyer.'

'Why do you say that?'

'You got all it takes. You can do anything. Remember things. Think of lots of things at the same time, and you're always like . . . unruffled.'

'How do you know all this?'

'Ada used to tell fortunes too. She taught me how the stars affect people's personalities. I could tell you lots more about yourself if I knew when you were born. When were you born, Julia?'

'December.'

'What date?'

'Fifteenth.'

'I knew you were a Sagittarius. Have a look.' He points to his file.

To please him she pulls it towards her and spreads it open on the table. 'What an amazing coincidence,' she says, smiling. 'Same as mine.

286

Fifteenth of December.'

She opened her eyes, broke off another piece of toast and forced it to her mouth, trying desperately to remember the year of his birth. It was not something she normally bothered about. She didn't need to memorise a client's date of birth unless it was relevant to some legal aspect of the case, because she knew she could always find it in his file if necessary. She'd only remembered the 15th December bit because it was the same as hers, but she hadn't registered the year. Or did she deliberately forget it?

But even he doesn't really know when he was born. Or what his real name is. Not everyone has a nice cosy label attached to him from birth to death. There are loads of people whose identities are false.

She poured another mug of tea. She heard a whimper and bent down to stroke Duchess as she climbed sleepily from the basket. All I have to do is get his file out. And check his year of birth.

She studied her face in the kitchen mirror. The oval shape. The widely spaced, round blue eyes. The broad forehead. She turned, squinting to get a side view of her eyes, and stopped.

Why did no one ever tell me they are far from deep set, she asked herself. To know the truth. To know the whole ghastly truth might be so awful that I might not want to go on living. Perhaps the same protective mechanism that made Sam Smith forget that he had cut off Joanne Perkins' nipples is still protecting me. Yesterday, sitting in the car, suddenly remembering, was bad enough. It was better when I knew nothing about him or my past. Now, apart from one detail I'm unable to pinpoint, one excruciating detail on that fateful night that keeps eluding me, everything seems crystal clear. How I wish Jessie had not told me he was still alive. Or that his name was Nicholas King. Or that he'd done something so wicked that he had to be sent to a special place for evil children. Nameless and faceless as he's been all these years, I could have spent the rest of my life dreaming about what he might have been.

But now it is all different.

Now I want to know, she told herself. But also I do not want to know. For so long I've waited to find him. Wanted to find him. Loved him. Now I don't know what I feel. Fear, disgust, sorrow, pity, love, remorse . . .

She bit into her knuckles. Her teeth made deep indentations in the skin. It was the only way she could stop herself from screaming.

- 92 -

Whenever Julia was duty solicitor she liked to go really early to the office — essential in order to clear her backlog before she was due in court. But this morning there was a far more pressing motive and she didn't know how she kept her foot from pushing the accelerator straight through the floor of the car.

Forced to stop at St Peter's Square traffic lights, she couldn't help marvelling at the unfamiliar silence and the wide-open spaces normally so clogged with people and traffic. In her state of heightened sensitivity she looked around, surprised to feel her heart pounding. The classic dome of the Central Library. The soaring tower of the Town Hall. The majestic Midland Hotel, a rich golden brown in the early morning light, all with their own unique beauty, she thought, and yes, I'm a part of this great city. In my own small way I help to make it function . . .

The lights turned green. She put her foot down and crossed into Peter Street. There'd be no one else in the office at this unearthly hour. Not only would she empty her basket, she'd have time to work out a plan of strategy in case she failed to persuade Smith to wait just one more day. But there shouldn't be a problem, she told herself. Up till now he's been surprisingly amenable to the delays.

She gripped the steering wheel. But first things first.

First I will dig out Smith's file from the archives.

It may not give me the answer I want. It won't provide the final cog in the wheel of uncertainty. But it will go a long way to completing the circle of doubt.

- 93 -

Wendy sat down with her glass of milk, her second today. Even though

288

this was the most miserable birthday of her life, she still had to think of her baby.

There wasn't even anything more to do. The housework was finished, the dishwasher stacked. Nicky was ready for school and was playing hide-and-seek with Duchess. With Julia at work till goodness knows when, the day ahead was not one she was looking forward to.

There wasn't even a card from Alan. Nor had she heard from him since that degrading scene on Saturday. She'd certainly finished that off with a bang.

When the phone rang a moment later she hoped Julia had left the answer machine on. Nobody ever wanted her this early in the morning. But after three rings she picked it up.

'Happy birthday, Wendy.'

'Alan!'

'Look, I can't talk now, but you know the big car park above WH Smith in Stockport? Well, meet me there at four this afternoon. Near the stairs going down to the shops in the pedestrian street. Okay?'

Oh hell. Julia would kill her. 'Alan, I'm sorry, I can't get away.' She could hear him breathing hard. It was her birthday. He might never ask her again.

'Well, on second thoughts, maybe I could manage it. It's Nicky's extra ballet class at four. Would ten past be okay?'

'Yeah, but no later.'

'Right. I'll drop Nicky off and pick her up at five-thirty. Why Stockport?'

'Oh, just a convenient place to meet. Kind of a surprise for your birthday.'

'Oh, Alan.' Tears welled in her eyes. She'd been too hasty in her judgement of him and here he was planning a surprise present for her.

'I must go now, Wendy. See you at ten past four. Oh, and wear something, you know . . . something special.'

- 94 -

It was a quarter to eight when Julia began ascending the steps of the

Magistrates' Court. She still had no idea what she'd do if Smith insisted on having the money today. At every single opportunity she would have to ring Fred Kennedy, just in case by some miracle the money became available after all. But more than that, there was nothing she could do.

She pulled open the heavy swing door, put her keys in the plastic dish, sauntered through the metal detector then headed for the lifts. The confirmation that they'd both been born in the same year, which heck, if she was honest with herself she'd known all along, still didn't prove anything conclusively. Thousands of people were born every day. Even her own birth date was the result of the nuns' guesswork. Of course, there was still the question of the Touchstone Orphanage. Maybe she'd only imagined that Smith had once mentioned the Touchstone, a place she wasn't aware of until Jessie had told her on Sunday that she'd been there when they had adopted her. But hundreds of babies must have been through that establishment, and okay, the evidence was piling up, but it was time she took a pragmatic view, instead of jumping to conclusions.

Brave talk, she told herself as she pressed the button for the third floor. But did any of this really matter? Nicky was far more important. Getting the money to keep Smith from harming Nicky, whoever he was. At the same time, let's face it, if she kept Smith happy he would not spill the beans on her, whether his accusation was true or not.

She punched in the code to unlock the solicitors' cloakroom, consoling herself with the knowledge that everything else today was under control. Wendy to pick Nicky up from school. Take her to Sonya Lake's. Wait for her. Take her home afterwards. Give her supper and wait for Julia's arrival.

It was too early to phone Fred Kennedy, so she went straight up to the Central Detention Centre on the seventh floor, then three flights down in the secure lift to the holding area.

Three or four dock officers were milling around. The other duty solicitor had just arrived. Julia called for the first offender on the long list of overnight arrest cases, a thin lad with pale frightened eyes, bruised knuckles and a cut above his eye.

She motioned him to sit next to her. 'I'm the duty solicitor,' she said informally, trying to put the youngster at ease. 'I'm completely independent. I have nothing to do with the police. I'm here to help you if you need a solicitor.'

He nodded, but said nothing. 'Do you have your charge sheet?' she asked, hoping he hadn't torn it up or chewed it in his nervousness. Extracting it from the pocket of his ripped, bloodstained shirt, he handed it to Julia.

'Wounding with intent. That's serious. Tell me what happened.'

'I was in a fight.'

'I gathered that,' she said, hiding her smile, 'but I'll need a bit more information to represent you properly.'

'This lad, the one who's in hospital, he hit me first. Then he took my money. All my money. My first ever money. My whole week's wages. Me mum's in hospital. They're sending her home tomorrow. Said there's nothing more they can do for her. I'm the only one who can look after her . . .'

Julia listened, biting her lip as she tried to cram as much of the youngster's pathetic life history into the ten minutes she was allowed with him. She had at least eight clients to deal with, and there were bound to be some late arrivals. She advised him hurriedly but reassuringly on his prospects of bail before explaining that he had the makings of a defence. She would need more information and would not have to enter a plea today – that would come later. The young man appeared relieved as a custody officer led him back to the cells.

By nine-thirty Julia had seen the last of her new clients. Since the crown prosecutors invariably got these files last, the cases would not be called on yet. Julia made her way to the solicitor's canteen on the second floor. While having a coffee she could fill in legal aid applications and make calls to verify bail details. It was also a chance to phone Fred Kennedy.

- 95 -

The sign leapt out from the glass doors. A sign Sam hadn't noticed before. Not even when he'd cased the joint last week while waiting for

291

Julia.

'Fuck me.'

He glanced at his watch. Only two fifteen, but where else in or around snooty Wilmslow can you just walk in and take a shower? Well, he'd have to take a chance because being clean and presentable was essential to the plan.

He counted to ten, relaxed his stomach muscles, and sauntered in like a regular.

Turning right he ducked through the door leading to the changing rooms. Mercifully there wasn't a sound from the squash court further down the passage.

Gingerly he pushed open the door to the male changing room, checked for cameras, couldn't see any, and sank down on the bench. He closed his eyes and took a deep breath. From this day on his life would change. He couldn't think why he hadn't evolved this plan at the beginning, instead of kow-towing to Julia Grant's endless excuses.

He hung the precious clean clothes on a brass coat-hook and undressed. Holding his distended stomach he walked into the shower stall and let the tingling jets massage his burning skin. As he was dressing the pain returned. He went through the ritual, forced himself to carry on. What the fuck. He had no other choice.

When he was dressed he checked in the mirror. He stroked the hot smooth skin in the hollows of his cheeks. Christ, he looked terrible, though he did have this strange red flush, as if he'd been on holiday in the Med. What a genius Joe was to remember the razors. Poor old bugger.

Commanding his body to remain upright, he strode through the reception area, glanced at the clock on the wall and walked out into the sunshine. The timing was spot-on.

There were several other cars waiting when he arrived at the school. He turned and parked where he could see the classroom door.

A black Volvo with smoky windows drew up right behind him. A woman in a pink trouser suit got out. With his eyes still on the classroom door he became aware that she was standing next to the Fiesta.

'We spoil the kids today,' she said. 'I always walked home from school.'

The woman went on blabbing. He could smell her perfume through his open window. Why the hell doesn't she fuck off?

Just then he saw the old yellow Mini pull up opposite the entrance.

Sod it.

'But you never know, do you?' the woman said. 'You just can't take a chance.'

Jeez! Why so goddam early, today of all days? Twice she'd been five minutes late and the kid had waited for her at the gate.

At that moment all the classroom doors opened. Out of the Mini stepped the nanny with the big boobs and the shiny dark hair looking quite a dish in a short cream skirt and matching jacket, high-heeled shoes that showed off her muscular legs. He watched her run towards Nicola as though she had a train to catch.

Everything had hinged on that fucking nanny being her usual five minutes late. He started the engine. No point in following them to the house. It would be crawling with the filth. He'd have to come back tomorrow and pray the nanny would be late. Though how he could hang on another twenty-four hours he was damned if he knew. And he'd miss the lorry going to France at midnight tonight.

He gripped his stomach and spoke firmly to his body. When the Mini was twenty yards ahead he moved on. Keeping it in sight he was surprised to see it going straight on, towards Cheadle, driving like a lunatic, the crazy bitch. He glanced at his petrol gauge. Fuck it. He had absolutely nothing to lose.

When the Mini turned in at the Sonya Lake Dance School he swung in behind it. He parked so that he had a clear view of the main door.

'See you at five-thirty,' the nanny shouted as she hurried back to her car and drove off with her tyres spinning.

His heart was beating wildly. This was an unexpected bonus. He settled down to wait.

- 96 -

With an uneasy feeling Wendy drove up the ramp into the car park high above the shopping precinct in Stockport town centre, her eyes scanning the motley skyline for a glimpse of Alan. She bought her parking ticket and stuck it in the windscreen, then hurried to the stairs leading to the shops.

Never let her out of your sight, Julia had said. She should have waited while Nicky had her class, but it would be such a waste of an opportunity when her whole future might depend on seeing Alan today. Anyway, Nicky would be well looked after and she'd be back at five-thirty to pick her up.

In a fever of excitement she watched Alan walk towards her. God, how she loved him. If she couldn't have him she wanted no one, even if that meant her baby never having a father. The way he walked, the way his face lit up as he saw her, it was enough to make her faint with happiness.

'Hi, Alan.'

'You look wonderful.'

She smiled at him, then looked down to hide her excitement. An engagement ring? Like the one he'd given her in her dream last night? She bit her lip. No, don't be silly. That was too much to hope for. It was enough that he'd remembered her birthday. Any little gift would be treasured and it was sweet of him to suggest she help him choose it.

'Ready?' he said.

'For what?'

'A little trip in my car. To Manchester.'

It was just after four and she had to be in Cheadle at five-thirty. 'I haven't the time, Alan. These shops are just as good as the ones in Manchester.' She hated refusing him but right now Nicky came first.

He held her hands and looked down at her. 'It won't take long. Come on. We don't want to be late.'

When Mr and Mrs Alan Seddon walked hand in hand through the glass exit doors of the Manchester Register Office, Wendy still couldn't believe it. The last fifteen minutes had seemed like a dream, and she couldn't take the smile off her face. She'd had no idea a Register Office could be such a romantic venue for a wedding. She had always thought they were drab, dingy places with straight hard benches and faded green walls. Following the Registrar to the stillness of the waiting room, the cool blue of the furnishings had calmed her shattered nerves, and by the time they reached the marriage room she had almost fully recovered from the shock of discovering she was about to be married.

As they stood starry-eyed on the steps overlooking the square, Alan looked down at his bride. 'You look good enough to eat,' he said, and squeezed her hand.

She gazed up at him, happier than she'd ever been.

Glancing through the archway on the right she realised that they were right next to Crown Square. Julia would kill her if she knew she was here, but maybe if she'd seen her standing next to Alan in that lovely gold-panelled room with the gold drapes and the subdued lighting and the yellow and white flowers on the highly polished table, all in her favourite colour, she might relent.

'Where to now, Mrs Seddon?'

She looked at her watch. 'I have to get back quickly, Alan. I must pick Nicky up at five-thirty. But I'll see you later tonight,' she added when she saw his look of dismay. 'After I've finished baby-sitting.'

'Wendy! This is your wedding day!'

She tugged her arm away. 'I can't. Even now I could be late if the traffic's bad.'

He pressed himself against her.

'Oh Alan. Not here. Look, I told you I was busy today. I only agreed to meet you because you said it wouldn't take long.'

'Wendy, nobody gets married and then disappears straightaway. Come on, let's go and have a glass of champers and then we'll go to my place. There's no one there now.'

'Alan, I can't.' She began walking to the car.

'Okay, if this is how we're going to start off let's go right back inside and tear up the marriage certificate in front of the Registrar. Is that what you want?'

'Oh, Alan . . . '

'No? Right. We're going to my place.'

She'd never seen this forceful side of him before. She felt the heat in her cheeks.

She was almost at his car when Alan stopped and turned to her.

'Hell, Wendy, I'm sorry. You'll only be about five minutes late if we leave right now. You know how fast I drive and I know all the short cuts. We'll make it up later tonight. Okay?'

- 98 -

The clock on the Fiesta dashboard flicked on to five-twenty-nine. With one eye watching for the yellow Mini, Sam Smith wrapped his fingers round the door handle and held his breath.

A sudden spasm of pain drenched his body in perspiration. He clutched his stomach and glanced longingly at the bottle of water on the passenger seat. He was tempted, but just imagine if he went to the door and vomited all over the dance teacher.

But as the first child appeared through the doorway, both the pain and the thirst disappeared. There was still no sign of the Mini. Maybe her watch had stopped, and she did have this habit of being a few minutes late picking up the kid. He smoothed his hair and half opened the door, ready to leap out.

He would wait one more minute, until a few more children emerged. The more parents around, the better. The more invisible he would be.

- 99 -

Paul leapt up when he heard the urgent knock.

'First positive lead on Smith, boss,' said Kevin. 'Cleaning woman.

Saw a man who fitted his description leaving a derelict building in Castlefield.'

'When?' Adrenaline pumping through his veins.

'Early Saturday morning. Burnt out building on Rochdale Canal. Opposite Dukes Bar.'

Paul slammed his fist down on the desk. 'Why the delay? This is bloody Tuesday.'

'She'd been petrified that something would happen to her if she told the police.'

'Same old bloody story. So what made her change her mind?'

'Your appeal last night on telly. When she saw the blown up shot of Smith there was something about the eyes that made her certain, although she said he didn't have a beard. Which was the other reason she didn't report it sooner. Said this guy was clean-shaven. And he wasn't wearing grey flannels and a white open necked shirt.'

'Anything in the building?'

'Signs of someone holing up. And would you believe it — '

'Discarded dirty grey flannels and dirty white open necked shirt?'

'You've got it.'

'Any other debris?'

'Not much. Empty Paracetamol pack. Empty plastic water bottle. Must be some good prints on that. I'm waiting for a result any moment.'

Paul's eyes darted from left to right. 'Paracetamol? I wonder why. Nothing else?'

'Nothing much. Oh yes. A dead rat with its legs missing.' He glanced up at Paul, then flipped through the sheaf of papers in his hand. 'But the woman saw him messing around with a white car in Castle Street. And guess what? A white Fiesta was reported stolen in that exact area early Saturday morning.'

'Well, it's not much but it's better than nothing. Let me know as soon as possible about the prints.'

As the door closed Paul sank into his chair. He was exhausted and frustrated. Smith was no nearer arrest than the day he escaped from the police van. There was something that should be giving him a message, but what was it? Paracetamol . . . A dead rat with no legs . . .

He was also frustrated because he hadn't seen Julia since their weekend at White Pool Farm. When he'd phoned yesterday she'd been too busy to talk. She'd even refused his dinner invitation. As he reached for his phone, it rang.

'What's up, Kev?'

'Result, boss. Prints on the bottle are Smith's. And you know what. Sagoe's too.'

Paul made a fist with his right hand and thumped it into the air. 'I knew it. Good work. He's obviously getting careless. Not like him. Wonder why. Keep me posted on the stolen Fiesta. And I want prints from any abandoned vehicles that were reported stolen from anywhere, not just those in the hot area around Dukes Bar.'

'Yes, boss. Anything else?'

'I'm putting firearms on full alert. With Sagoe dead and Smith holing up in that building it means he has no other place to go. Probably no money. He'll be desperate. Put your thinking cap on, Kev. Where d'you think he'd go now?'

'I wish I knew, Chief. Maybe out on the moors . . .'

Paul pressed the off button, waited a moment, then dialled Julia's number at Lloyd Grant.

'We don't expect her in the office at all today, certainly not until late afternoon,' her PA said. 'She's duty solicitor at Manchester Magistrates'. You could try her mobile, though it's usually switched off in court. Do you have her numbers, Mr Moxon?'

'I have them. Thanks.'

Paul swivelled round and gazed at the hazy panorama of Manchester city, remembering guiltily that last night he'd left his Anschutz rifle and his pistol in the boot of the Honda. He shook his head. No matter how tired he was, that must never happen again. He smiled as he recalled the unexpected "poss" he'd had. When Julia couldn't make it for dinner it had been a spur of the moment visit to the rifle club after his stint at the TV Studio. He seldom went these days, but still got one hell of a kick from a perfect score of one hundred.

Ben was relieved to find a parking spot right next to Crown Square. He locked the car then positioned himself strategically so that he would see Julia coming down the steps of the Magistrates' Court. She'd have to walk right past him. He had to talk to her, had to find out what was wrong. She had a frightened, hunted look about her, as though she was desperate for help but had nobody she could confide in. He had never known her like this before and apart from anything else, as her business partner it was up to him to do something about it. Just a quiet little chat away from the office would be best. The office would be out of the question. In that setting she would just revert to her normal crisp business-like attitude with him. What was needed was a strong yet gentle manful approach that would make her feel both protected and cared for, and which at the same time would sew the seeds for her eventual realisation that he was the man to fill the gap in her life, not Paul bloody Moxon.

His luck was in. Only fifteen minutes later she appeared at the top of the steps. She stood like a lost soul in a pose so dejected that he longed more than ever to take her in his arms and comfort her, though this was certainly not on today's agenda. He had learned his lesson and his approach would be far more subtle this time. He watched her hesitate, as though she had been expecting to meet someone who hadn't turned up. She took out her mobile phone and dialled. Less than a minute later she put the phone back in her pocket and walked down the steps, her movements cautious and alert. At the bottom she stopped, as though not certain where to go next. Then, without any apparent purpose, she began walking across the square.

When she was almost opposite Ben, he moved swiftly towards her. 'Julia.'

He was shocked to see the look of fear in her eyes. She carried on walking as though she hadn't even recognised him, almost like a sleepwalker who'd been disturbed, he thought, as he ran after her.

He held her arm. 'Julia, I'll give you a lift. There's something I want to discuss with you.'

'Tomorrow, Ben. I'm in a hurry now.'

'Please, Julia.'

'Sorry. I must go.'

This time he wasn't going to take no for an answer. Holding her arm gently but firmly, he guided her towards the car. 'This is terribly important. It'll only take a few minutes.'

She climbed into the car, sighing deeply as though she was too tired to argue. As they swung into Bridge Street she gripped the edge of the seat.

'But this isn't the way to the office,' she said.

- 101 -

Wendy looked at her watch, cursing the traffic as she finally turned off Cheadle High Street.

Twenty to six. 'Oh no.'

A young woman she hadn't seen before came to the studio door.

'Oh, I was just locking up,' she said.

Wendy's heart beat faster. 'Who are you?'

'Dominique. Sonya's new assistant.'

'I've come for Nicky.'

'Well, I'm afraid all the children have gone.'

'No. They can't have. I'm picking Nicky up. Her mother's in court all day.'

'Oh, you mean Nicola. Well, don't worry. Her uncle fetched her a few minutes ago.'

'Her uncle?'

Nicky had never mentioned an uncle. Neither had Julia. She'd never heard of any relatives at all. And why did this girl call her Nicola?

'What did he look like?'

Dominique shrugged and cocked her head to one side. 'Tall. Fair. Slim. Didn't look well.' She smiled. 'Said he'd been abroad for a few years and was giving his niece a surprise.'

Wendy's insides churned.

'Look, I wouldn't worry if I were you. Nicola was thrilled to see him.

300

They'll be home by the time you get there. Said they were going to play hide-and-seek.'

Wendy raced down the pathway and threw herself into the Mini. Double parking outside the post office she ran to the phone booth and dialled the Hillside House number. When there was no reply she dug for her little red address book and looked up Julia's office number.

'I'm sorry,' said Julia's personal assistant. 'She won't be in the office till tomorrow. She's not on call tonight but you could try her mobile.'

Wendy shoved more small change into the slot. She dialled. An automated voice told her the phone was switched off but if she left a message her call would be returned. Damn.

Back in her car she swung into Cheadle High Street. She looked at the empty seat next to her, as though willing Nicky to materialise.

Uncle? Nicky must have known who he was to have gone with him. Wendy thought she knew everything about the Grant family. There must be family members she'd not heard about. She was worrying for nothing. When she got home they'd be playing hide-and-seek on the front lawn, waiting for someone to unlock the front door.

But Hillside House looked ominously deserted. She glanced at the house opposite. She'd been surprised when Julia had told her only this morning that it was full of armed police trying to combat the recent spate of local burglaries. But they were nowhere to be seen now. She parked in the driveway and hurried to the front door.

'Nicky?' She heard a whine from Duchess, but nothing else. She ran out into the garden. 'Nicky . . . Nicky?'

Back inside she re-dialled Julia's mobile number.

The phone was still switched off. She would have to keep trying until Julia answered.

What now? The police?

But what would she say? That Nicky's uncle had picked her up. That Nicky' had been thrilled to see him. She'd look a fool if they turned up a few minutes later, having stopped off at Macdonald's for a treat.

'Please come home soon,' she said aloud, looking up at the walls.

Duchess shoved a wet nose against her leg. She picked up the puppy and held it close, stroking its soft little head as though it needed comforting. She would just have to sit here and wait. Keep on trying Julia's mobile every few minutes.

And pray.

Ben had to think quickly. Julia's unusual mental state was really alarming him, but in this traffic there wasn't much hope of having the kind of intimate one-to-one conversation that was needed. His apartment, only a few minutes away at Salford Quays, would be the perfect place.

As the car swept past the Mark Addy, Julia took her mobile from her pocket. 'Damn,' she muttered, 'I must have switched it off after my last call. Ben, will you please tell me where we're going?' she said, as she keyed in the code.

'My apartment's only five minutes from here. Much more relaxing than the office.'

Getting no response he laughed awkwardly and glanced at her. She was gawping at him and he realised she had jumped to the wrong conclusion. 'Sit back, Julia, and stop looking so terrified. I'm not going to touch you.'

Just then her phone rang. She pressed the button.

'What?' she whispered. 'Wendy? What did you say?'

Ben turned and looked at her. Julia's face seemed to crumple as she held the phone away from her ear. He pulled in to the curb.

'Julia, for God's sake, speak.'

'She's . . . '

Ignoring the barrage of hooting cars he turned off the ignition and held her shoulders. 'What's happened?'

With an inner strength that over the years Ben had learned to respect, she seemed to energise herself. Wrenching herself free she spoke into the phone again. 'Don't do anything, Wendy. Just sit tight and I'll be there as soon as I can. No. Don't phone anyone. But if it rings take a message.'

Releasing her seat belt Julia threw herself at the door. 'I've got to get home, Ben. Let me out.'

'What's wrong?'

'My daughter. She needs me. Please release the locks so I can get out of here.'

She was like a wild cat, fur standing up, teeth bared, ready to kill if she had to.

Clunk went the locks. 'Don't go, Julia.' He tried to catch her arm. 'Whatever it is, I'll drive you. Julia.'

He watched helplessly as she charged down the road towards the Gartside Street car park, hair flying, feet hardly touching the ground.

- 103 -

The gates of Hillside House were standing open and Wendy was already at the door when Julia skidded to a halt. Wendy took her arm and helped her out.

She closed her eyes and for a few moments she couldn't speak. Then as reality returned she drew herself up straight. 'Any phone calls yet?' she asked, dreading the answer. The frantic detour to the office to retrieve her gun from the top drawer of her desk had only taken a few minutes, double parked and engine still running, but had seemed like a lifetime when every minute counted.

A red-eyed Wendy shook her head. 'Was he really her uncle?'

'Of course he wasn't.'

'Then who? Who? He must have followed me from the school.'

Julia closed her eyes. Twin brother. Uncle.

Nicholas?

Sam Smith?

No!

Through the confused strands of Julia's tangled brain one thing nagged at her — if Sam Smith was Nicholas King then he saved her from a life of degradation by knocking that dreadful foster father out for long enough for them both to get away, but somehow the tables were turned. She got away scot-free. She had all the comfort, the privilege, the kindness and the love. Now he was getting back at her for leaving

303

him alone to rot in the cesspits of homelessness and neglect . . . Oh, if only David and Jessie had adopted him too, no matter what awful thing he did . . .

'Calm down, Wendy,' she said. 'Let's go inside. I'm expecting a call. We can do absolutely nothing until we get that call.'

'But why didn't you let me phone the police? Why not phone them now?' Wendy was shouting with frustration.

Julia put her arm around Wendy. 'Trust me. There are things you don't understand. After we've had the phone call we'll know what to do. Until then we must just sit tight. Let's have tea.'

Wendy filled the kettle, unhooked two mugs and dropped tea bags into them, and only then she seemed to fall apart. 'I don't know how you can be so calm,' she said. 'Most people would be tearing their hair out with desperation. Would at least be phoning the police. Jesus, your child's been kidnapped. What else can it be? And it's all my fault. I don't know what possessed me to go with Alan and get married. Another few days would have made no difference. I don't know why you don't tell me what a useless shit I am.'

'Sit down, Wendy,' Julia said, taking over the making of the tea and adding two spoons of sugar to Wendy's. 'Relax and drink your tea.' The poor girl was distraught.

'When d'you think you'll get the call?' Wendy asked through her tears.

Julia looked up at the ceiling. 'Soon,' she said. And just then the phone rang.

They both jumped as though a bomb had exploded. With giant strides Julia tore up to her study where she could record the call. As she lunged at the receiver she finally made her decision.

The moment she heard his voice she lifted her finger to jab the number one digit, then withdrew it as though she'd stuck it in a furnace. Don't, idiot. BT will trace the call. They will tell Paul . . .

'Ah, Julia.'

'Where's my daughter?'

'First things first. Where's my dosh?'

She had prepared herself for the lie she'd have to tell. Now, more than ever, he must go on thinking he was going to get what he'd requested.

'I have it,' she said.

'In tens and fifties?'

'Yes.'

'Old notes?'

'Of course.'

'Well, well, well. You surprise me, Julia. It just goes to show. You can never know every fucking thing about a person. Even though — '

'Tell me where to bring it. You'll get it as soon as I have my daughter back safely.'

'Safely? Why would I harm her? No, Julia. It'll be the other way around. I'll hand her over when I have the money. She'll be fine. As long as you bring it by nine o'clock tonight. I have an important journey to make at midnight and I can't be late.'

'Okay.' She glanced at her watch. It was seven-thirty. 'Is she all right?'

'She's fine. We're having lots of fun.'

'How do I know you're telling me the truth?'

'You must trust me, Julia.' He laughed. 'Now listen carefully.'

'Oh, for God's sake, just tell me where to meet you.'

'Don't get any funny ideas. Make sure you're on your own, and don't tell the police. You know what might happen if you do.'

'Tell me where.'

'You know the *Cat and Fiddle*? The pub on the Buxton road?'

'Yes.'

'Well, a couple of miles before you get to it, there's a road to the left, sign-posted to Goyt Valley. Just a mile or so up this road there's a gorge. Drop a body down there and no one would ever fucking find it.'

'Where's my daughter?'

'She's in a churchyard. Don't worry. You'll pass it on your way. She's quite safe there. She loves playing hide-and-seek.'

'A churchyard? You're mad.'

'Only kidding, Julia. She's in the car now, waiting for me while I'm talking to you from the *Cat and Fiddle*. Anyway, go down the Goyt

Valley road about a mile. Turn right at the grass triangle. Follow the narrow twisting lane and you come to the old chapel on the corner. Turn right. It goes to a lookout point where you can see right across Cheshire. Fucking tourists all day, going to the reservoir and the ruins of Errwood Hall, but nobody there now. Worst bloody June weather I've known for years. But you don't mind a bit of mist and rain, do you Julia?'

'No.'

'Hell no. But I don't want you to go right up there. I want you to stop just after the chapel, where you see the footpath sign.'

'The footpath sign? But there are hundreds.'

'Don't panic. You can't miss this one . . .'

As his voice meandered on, something inside her snapped, and almost as though it had a mind of its own, her finger moved slowly towards the number one digit.

'Yes,' she said when he'd finished. 'I think I know where you mean.'

'You can't miss the barn. The only one for miles. Be there, rich bitch.'

Now, she told herself, before he rings off. Press it.

'I'll be there,' she said, and stabbed the number one digit.

- 104 -

With Smith's instructions drumming in her ears Julia threw off her clothes and changed into jeans, sweater and strong walking shoes. Into Simon's light and roomy sailing bag she crammed enough old Readers Digests to mimic a large bundle of bank notes. She took the pistol from her handbag, placed it on top of the Readers Digests and clipped the two sides of the bag together. With one flick of a finger she could open the bag and have her hand on the gun. Hopefully the sight of it would frighten Smith enough to hand Nicky over.

Then she put her mind into gear. That's altogether too clumsy. If Smith sees the gun he might shoot me and that would be that.

Quickly she took it from the bag and tucked it into the back pocket of her jeans, pulling her loose sweater over the pocket. She looked at herself in the mirror from every angle till she was certain the weapon was not visible.

In Simon's bookcase, still neatly filed with all his maps and flying charts, she found an ordnance survey map of the Peak District. Desperately trying to remember the exact details of Smith's directions, she marked the route with a red felt-tipped pen. She would put this on the seat next to her for easy reference.

Wendy ran with her to the car, tears still streaming down her cheeks. 'Please. Let me come with you.'

'No, Wendy. I need to be alone. You go home now.'

'I'm not leaving here till you arrive back safely with Nicky.'

'Okay, but make yourself something to eat. If anyone phones tell them I'm working. If Paul phones, tell him . . . oh, anything you like.'

'If I'd stayed with her this couldn't have happened.'

Julia revved the engine. 'It wasn't your fault. We're dealing with a madman. On second thoughts, if Paul rings . . .'

She couldn't think straight. Could Paul get there before I do? BT will have told him about the phone call and where it was from. He could be on his way to the area already, although he won't know anything more. Just as well because if he knew exactly where to go and got there first and Smith panicked, he might hurt Nicky . . .

For a moment she wavered. Paul should be told. But — no, it was too risky.

'No, Wendy,' she said. 'If Paul rings, don't tell him anything. Just say I'm out.'

- 105 -

Julia took the winding sylvan road to Prestbury, cutting corners as she sped towards the old market town of Macclesfield on the edge of the Pennine hills and the Peak District National Park.

She went over everything in her mind, as logically as she could. Yes. Paul will have heard from the Malicious Calls people, guessed it was Smith, been told he was in the vicinity of the *Cat and Fiddle*. But that's all he'll know. I could phone him now. In less than an hour he could be at the exact rendezvous point, even less by helicopter. He'd never do anything to jeopardise Nicky's safety. So what do I have to lose?

But I know Paul. He'll have called out firearms and they're an independent unit who plan their own tactics and make their own decisions. If necessary, they'll be shooting to kill. If that happened they would find that letter on him with all those lies which the police would believe and I wouldn't be able to deny because I can't bloody well remember what happened . . .

There was very little traffic. She was making good time, but she had to decide quickly or it would be too late.

Okay. Imagine you are one of the firearms team. You wouldn't shoot if there were any danger to Nicky. No. But Smith is clearly desperate. Maybe in pain. If he gets the slightest whiff of the police he'll go berserk and might hurt Nicky.

So how can I possibly tell Paul exactly where to go?

Yes. But Smith told me once he loved children.

And for the umpteenth time Julia asked herself why he had let her believe that if she didn't give him the money he would hurt Nicky. This was really bugging her. And when he phoned he had said she was perfectly safe and why would he harm her.

How can I be sure, she asked herself. How can I be sure of anything? If the hatpin had badly injured him, it would be impossible to have successfully posed as Nicky's uncle and persuaded her to go with him. So maybe he was fine after all. Taken anti-biotics . . .

Just after Macclesfield the road began to climb. The lush green countryside disappeared and Julia was out on the moorlands.

Then something made her glance at the passenger seat. She saw the bag with the Readers Digests but there was no sign of the ordnance survey map with the route marked in red.

She pulled over into a handy lay-by and slammed on the brakes. She searched on the floor and on the back seat, in the glove box and down the sides of the seats. It was nowhere. Unbelievably it must still be on her desk.

She glanced at the clock on the dashboard. Damn. There wasn't time to go back. Don't panic, Julia. You'll have to remember exactly what he said.

- 106 -

'Why the *Cat and Fiddle*, boss?'

'I'm damned if I know, Kev. But he's not there now. Buxton have been up there already and found nothing.'

Paul leapt from his chair and started pacing up and down the office. 'Christ. He could be holed up just around the corner from the pub, or bloody miles away.'

'At least it narrows down the area, boss. What about Mrs Grant?'

'I rang the house after we'd heard from BT. Missed her by seconds. God knows where she's gone. Her mobile's switched off as bloody usual.' He swung round to face Kevin. 'And there's something not right. Wendy sounded petrified, and when I asked her to put Nicky on she didn't answer me at first. Then she said Nicky was out too. So you tell me why Wendy was still there.' He stuck both fists in the air. 'Why?'

'One could make a calculated guess, Chief.'

Paul felt a shudder start at the base of his neck and slowly vibrate all the way down his back. 'Don't worry,' he muttered. 'I already have. Goddamit, I should have guessed that once the city got too hot for him he'd make for the moors. Yeah, okay, I know you said he would. But imagine the audacity, to walk into the *Cat and Fiddle* and use their phone.'

'It's probably the only public phone for miles, boss.'

'Damn. I should have applied straight away to the Home Secretary to have her phones tapped.' Paul balled his right hand into a fist and slammed it into the palm of his left hand. 'My instincts at the time were spot on.'

'I didn't know you'd contemplated it.'

Paul nodded. 'But I thought it was too much of an invasion of her privacy. She made a big enough fuss about having the malicious call set up. She'd have hit the ceiling if she found out I was tapping too.'

Paul flicked his eyes upwards as he recalled the ACC's words. The moment you feel your judgement is being impaired because of your relationship with Mrs Grant . . .

'What now, boss?'

Paul sat down and yanked the phone towards him. 'I've got an emergency firearms team standing by,' he said quietly.

Kevin raised his eyebrows. He walked to the door. 'And what if the call turns out to have been perfectly harmless? Surely she'd have phoned you by now if she was in danger?'

Paul picked up the receiver. 'I'll keep trying her mobile till she answers. And there's one other thing I can try. A long shot but I'll give it a go. Meanwhile keep in touch with Buxton and Cheshire, and give Ken Riding a buzz. And Kev, don't move out of the building. If there's action I'll want you with me.'

As soon as Kevin had left, Paul dialled Hillside House, but quickly changed his mind and jammed his finger on the cradle. He would try Julia once more, and then Wendy.

- 107 -

Still in an agony of indecision Julia switched on her mobile phone. Tell him where to go, as long as he promises not to intervene too soon, just be there in case she needed him . . .

But before she could dial, it started ringing.

Mist swirled around the car like smoke forced into a room by a blocked chimney. It was like winter up here in the hills. The ringing went on and on, louder with each ring until the bleak black moors began gliding towards her. Gliding, then receding. Gliding towards her . . .

She pressed the button. 'Hello.'

'Julia, where are you and what the hell's going on?'

'I can't talk now, Paul.'

'Yes you will talk now. You'll tell me exactly what's happening.'

'Please don't interfere. Everything's under control.' She knew she was obstructing an officer in the execution of his duty but she was sure if Paul knew why he would understand.

'You're meeting Smith, aren't you. He's got Nicky, hasn't he?'

'Paul, I know how to handle him. I think he's my . . . '

She stopped herself only just in time.

'I want to know where you are and where you're meeting him. And anything else I need to know in order to make sure Nicky and you aren't hurt. Tell me, Julia.'

'Paul, Smith does not hurt children. He only wants money.' She wished she could be certain.

'Christ, there isn't time to argue about this now. He's got her, hasn't he? He's unstable. He can do anything. You can't take a chance.'

Julia agonised over what would be best. Alone, she could persuade Smith to negotiate, persuade him to give up Nicky and in return promise to give him the money tomorrow. She tugged at her hair. But Smith had said he was going on a journey tonight at midnight so he wouldn't be open to negotiation.

'There are things you couldn't possibly understand, Paul.'

'I do bloody understand,' Paul said. 'I understand that you're at the end of your tether. I've been so blind. You've been persecuted by this bastard since the day he escaped, haven't you? And there's more to it, isn't there? Not just the two-fifty grand. There's something else you're not telling me. Am I right? You've not been behaving logically. What is that something, Julia? What else is he demanding?'

She gripped the phone until she felt it would snap in her hand.

'Answer me, for Chrissake. I thought we had something special between us. And unless you can show that you trust me, I'm afraid it proves I was very mistaken.'

She longed to be able to tell him. Longed to be able to say he's my twin brother, Paul. He stuck his neck out for me. He was only a little boy but he saved me from – oh, how could I ever say it? I love you, Paul, but please keep out of it. You don't understand. He's had a raw deal. His thinking is twisted and warped because of what he's been through. Because of what he did for me. Hitting Mr Spencer on the head with the brass lamp. Getting me away from that house. But now he only wants what he thinks is his due. He only wants the money and he'll vanish out of our lives forever . . .

No. Paul would never buy that. Something in her reasoning was grossly wrong and she wished she knew what it was. It was a weird feeling, fearing and despising someone as much as she did. Despising him for his unthinkable crimes, despising him for his systematic persecution of her, for what he was doing to her now, for what he had made her do to him, for what he was doing to Nicky, and for what he was doing to Paul and her . . .

Yet still loving him . . . heaven help her.

Loving? Yes, and he had loved her too. So where was that love now? It will have died, along with all the goodness that he had, because it could not thrive without the nourishment of a reciprocal love. How let down he must have felt. How bitter. How alone.

She spread her fingers out then clenched her fists. Is he Nicholas King, she asked herself. He must be, although I still have no positive proof. It could have been the power of suggestion when I'd seen his date of birth, yet how can I deny the gut feeling I had when we first met? And the feeling he clearly had too.

And if he is Nicholas King, then I do love him, because I love Nicholas King. I have always loved him. Nothing can ever change that —

'Julia? Speak to me.' Then more softly. 'Speak to me, dammit. Tell me where you're meeting him.'

'I have to go now, Paul. This is my show. He warned me not to talk to the police and he means it. He must not see you. If he does, he just might hurt Nicky.' And blurt out that nonsense about me killing Mr Spencer, she thought with a shudder, which she now knew was a complete fabrication but that wouldn't stop the police acting on the information and dragging her name through the inevitable dirt. And if they shoot him they'll find that letter on him anyway, so at all costs I have to keep them away from him. 'Nothing you say is going to stop me going. Until I have Nicky I want you out of the way. Do I make myself clear? I told you, there are things you don't understand.' And neither do I, she thought, squeezing her eyes closed.

'Oh Christ, Julia,' he whispered. Then he added: 'Be careful. He's armed.'

'I know,' she said. 'But so am I.'

'Julia . . . '

She pressed the off button, started the car and pulled onto the road.

Dark purple clouds swept across the sky. She shivered. If it rained Nicky would be cold, dressed only in the clothes she'd worn for dancing. She watched the road ribboning across the valley, a harmony of bold flowing lines that only nature could have fashioned from such an impoverished terrain. As always the simple grandeur took her breath away.

But now it was scary too.

As it started raining a black crow darted from a ditch, swooped across the windscreen and climbed into the thickening mist. She pressed on with an increasing sense of urgency. Tunnel vision had set in. At the crest of the plateau the wind strengthened. It was even bleaker now, with hairpin bends and fewer stone walls.

She kept her eyes skinned for the Goyt Valley turn-off, but today it was a road with no comforting familiarity. Was that the *Cat and Fiddle* looming in the mist? If it was, she'd come too far. But no, thank goodness, it was another ghostly farmhouse.

A clump of trees, a derelict stone barn, and then the sign: Salterford, three miles, Goyt Valley, four.

She turned off the main highway down the steep, narrow one-way road to Goyt Valley, a gradient about one in five with high grassy banks on either side, a stone wall on top with wire fencing. And on the left, way down in the valley, the Lamaload Reservoir where bodies vanish . . .

Up the hill again, sheep grazing on the banks, past a crumbling building, a lay-by on the left, a Peak National Park notice saying, No Parking Overnight, everything so far exactly as he'd said.

Then at last the grassy triangle.

As she turned right the road plunged down into another valley. Splashing through puddles, up a steep hill, twisting, turning, over a stone bridge with green railings, a cottage on the right, power lines, a derelict farm house.

And there it was. The chapel.

His voice in her ears: chapel, churchyard, turn right, up the hill, footpath sign, broken wall, the stile, the hills, the field and then another stile.

The wind plastered her hair across her face as she struggled to close the car door. Clinging to the stone wall she found her way to the first stile. Apart from the roar of the wind and the crackle of dead gorse beneath her feet, there was a creepy silence. She looked across the field and through the gap of the second stile, as though lining up the sights of a rifle. Dark heather, the pale cream grass, and beyond the valley a black hill. And then she saw it.

The barn.

But there was no sign of Smith. Or of Nicky. Or of the car he must have stolen to get up here.

She had a distinct feeling of being watched and looked over her shoulder. The sudden strong wind had cleared the mist and clouds but there was nothing, though she thought she had heard a noise a bit like a helicopter that came and went like a wave tossed on the seashore, clattering the pebbles.

In this dim light the barn was little more than a shadow, and like everything else today, hardly real. Yet inside that shadow is my daughter, she reminded herself. And a man called Sam Smith.

Or is he Nicholas King?

She stopped. Inside her head she heard her silent scream. How can I be so filled with horror at what might happen to Nicky and to me and my future life if something goes wrong and he carries out his threat, and yet at the same time be bursting with . . . what?

Trepidation? Excitement? Oh God yes, because this will be my last opportunity to ask him those two vital questions.

Checking the catch, she slung the bag around her neck. Two hundred and fifty thousand pounds in tenners and fifties, please. Yes, Mrs Grant, not a problem. The tellers carry that amount around all the time, just in a briefcase.

But what if my bluff fails and he sees the Readers Digests before I can reason with him?

Pushing against the wind, she clambered over the first stile. Her feet sank into tufts of light-coloured grass. Out of nowhere another wispy curtain of cloud dropped down across the sky, shrouding the hills in a greenish underwater light. She hurried towards the second stile. With one leg over the stile, she froze.

Almost hidden by the dry stone wall, standing looking at her, motionless in the eerie light, eyes blazing, was Sam Smith.

Closing her fingers on the catch of the bag she climbed down and faced him.

'Where's Nicky?' she said.

Leaving the helicopter close to the chapel, and using the stone walls as cover, Paul crept round the field ahead of the twelve armed men, his feet sinking silently into the spongy grass. It gave him a strange feeling to be carrying a rifle again, especially one as potent as this. He still didn't know what had possessed him to ask the team leader just before they boarded the helicopter if he too could be armed in view of his close association with the Smith case and the very real danger to himself if Smith should spot his presence. He'd been amazed that Jake had agreed to his request. 'Strictly off the record, Sir,' Jake had said, handing him the Heckler & Koch MP5 sub-machine gun. 'And you know the rules better than I do, Sir.' 'Don't worry,' he'd told his ex star pupil, running his fingers over the black lacquer paint and remembering only too well the unique features of the MP5, a 9mm magazine-fed rifle with a red-dot sight, extremely accurate and a superb weapon to handle. 'I won't use it unless the circumstances are exceptional.'

When he could see Julia and Smith clearly silhouetted against the western sky, he stopped.

'Are you sure he's armed, Sir?' Jake asked, barely whispering to make sure Smith heard nothing.

Paul nodded to the inspector. 'I'm sure. And so is she,' he whispered back grimly, remembering with a shudder that Avril had also been armed. He took a deep breath. There were times when he wished he was still head of the firearms unit, and this sure was one of them. But Jake was in charge and he was not going to let Paul forget it, even though he had once served under Paul. The strategy they would use was entirely up to him and Paul had no authority to intervene. And no authority to shoot.

Paul saw Smith move closer to Julia. Instinctively he tightened his grip on the rifle.

'You look shocked, Julia. What did you think would happen to me when you stuck that fucking pin in my gut?'

'Where's Nicky?' she asked again, in her annoyingly squeaky voice, just when she needed to sound in control.

He shrugged his shoulders. 'Never mind Nicky. She's fine. First things first, Julia. But before I leave you forever, you and I need to talk.'

'Where's Nicky?' she screamed.

'Shut the fuck up. I told you. She's okay. You won't get nothing till you calm down. And until I get my money.'

He stepped nearer. Julia jumped back. Now would have been his best chance for revenge, but he made no further move towards her. Just stood there, clutching his stomach, and panting.

The surprisingly clean shirt, a military-type khaki with two breast pockets, hung in deep folds from his bony shoulders. He had no jacket on but didn't seem to feel the cold. In the weird greenish twilight his eyes looked more than ever like two glass marbles. Julia searched the contours of his pain-wracked face for some feature she might have missed. Some characteristic feature that would confirm that the lifetime of love she'd poured into a being created from the vaguest of memories was justified.

But Smith's face was nothing like it was even two weeks ago, and certainly nothing like her own, she told herself. Though distorted by pain and ravaged by the poison Martin Bedlow said would slowly kill him, she was certain now that it was a face she had never known before.

'Come closer, Julia. Do you like what you see?'

She was speechless.

'In Strangeways you told me you used to dream I'd come back to you. Remember? Well, here I am. Feast your eyes. In a few minutes, as soon as I get my cash, I'll be gone. Into the mist. Over the mountain. Just like in your dreams, eh Julia?'

She stared into his eyes. The doubt crept back. Does he know his real name, she wondered.

'You don't know, Julia, do you? Our mother dumped us. No one knew where we were born. When we were born. Who was born first. Who our mother was. And certainly not who our father was. I reckon the social workers at the Touchstone gave us the first names that came into their heads.'

Touchstone. I didn't even need to ask him. So, is this the final proof?

No, what about the swan birthmark? She wished she could remember exactly where it was. Somewhere on his neck or shoulders, but she wasn't sure. The swan would be the final proof.

'Where will you go?' she asked.

'What do you care?' He leaned towards her. She could see the rim of dark blue that surrounded the paler blue in the centre of his eyes. And the little golden flecks in the middle.

Watch my eyes, Julia, and I'll watch yours. And we'll see the stars float on the moon . . .

Why hadn't she noticed this during the months she'd been interviewing him? Her eyes were blue too and Simon used to tell her she had little golden flecks in them . . . like stars . . .

Smith's knees buckled and his eyes rolled to the back of his head. He grasped the top of the wall. 'Okay. Just give me the cash and let's get this over and done with. You've fucked me around enough as it is. As you can see, I can't afford to wait any longer.'

'Where's Nicky?' Julia said. This time, using every ounce of her will-power, she kept the panic out of her voice. And the remorse too, as she remembered what Jessie had told her. "And fresh wounds on you too", making it clear to her now, even without the swan, that all his ills must surely stem from his brave attempt to rescue her from that monster. He did that for me, she told herself, at the same time convincing herself that his accusation that she had killed Mr Spencer had merely been a fabrication in order to extract from her the money.

She saw the pain mirrored in his twisted face, but in spite of this he pulled himself fully upright, 'Cash first. Then Nicola.'

'How do I know you haven't harmed her? I want her now. And I want that letter you said you'd written.'

He patted the left hand pocket of his shirt and shook his head. 'You'll get bugger all if you don't stop shouting your fucking mouth off. I wouldn't dream of harming my own niece, now would I Julia?'

Niece.

This was how it had been for months. She no longer knew what was real and what wasn't. Slowly she reached out and touched the bag.

Fresh wounds on Nicholas. And on me. From the monster.

Why?

Because Nicholas hit him with the lamp, of course . . .

Her fingers found the catch. What should I do first, she asked herself. Stop him looking in the bag. Or let him know I have a gun. Or tell him the truth, that there is no money yet.

'Go on, Julia.' He was watching the bag. 'I know what you're thinking. Say my name, go on. Like you used to. Let me hear it again. Just one more time.'

Her head began to spin. The dry stone wall waved like a snake wriggling towards her.

Nicholas.

But no way could she say it out loud or even let him think it was in her head, so close to being spoken. Not until she was sure, one way or the other.

She stared at the emaciated figure, so close now that she could smell the decay. For a split second she closed her eyes. All my life I have dreamt of him. Missed him, loved him, craved to be with him . . .

At any moment, weak as he is, he could grab the bag, open it. See there was no money. What a hair-brained idea this was.

I have little time. And no choice at all.

'Well, haven't you a tongue in your head . . . bitch?' He said the word almost as an afterthought, softly, wincing, closing his eyes, as though he didn't want to say it at all.

She glanced at the bag, wishing now that she'd left the pistol on top of the Readers Digests. She should have thought it out properly. How on earth was she going to get it out of her pocket without it looking exactly like she was reaching for a gun in her pocket? It would be impossible to frighten him without him thinking she was going to shoot him.

'Give me the fucking money.'

She slid her hand as nonchalantly as she could towards her back pocket, trying to keep her elbow from pointing up like a chicken wing. She could feel her face contorting with disgust and self-loathing.

And on his face she could see the realisation of what she was doing.

With one hand she reached down to open the bag. At the same time she carried on fumbling in her pocket. If only she'd had time to practice.

His hand touched his belt.

She yanked the pistol from her pocket.

A flash, a shot, or maybe it was two. Then something hit her leg. Smith fell forwards, the force of his fall knocking her to the ground.

My gun must have been loaded after all . . .

But I didn't even pull the trigger . . .

Blood gushed from his chest. Julia sat up, tore off her jacket and covered his shuddering body.

He looked up in surprise, then clawed her down again as his hot sticky blood drenched through to her skin. She held him close, fighting the dizziness, trying to blink away the spots before her eyes.

'Now it's your turn, Julia.' His voice was faint, carried by the wind into the disappearing hills. 'And when you're standing in the dock, remember that what I did was to save my life, just as what you did now was to save yours. That's how things happen. Events catch up with you.

Make you do things you never intended to do. Remember, Julia. I did it to save my life . . . And yours . . .'

His full weight was on top of her now. His fingers were like talons digging into her arms as he clung to her. He coughed. Blood spluttered over her face and head. Then he started laughing. It was the most chilling sound she had ever heard. A laugh, a howl, a cry for help –

She turned her face sideways, pressing it into the ground. She smelled the earth, the blood, the grass. She heard his voice from long ago:

> It's all right, Julia. He won't hurt you any more. Hurry! Take
> my hand. Run . . . Hide here, in the long grass . . .

His fingers slackened. His breathing came in short gasps. Fumbling at his neck she quickly loosened his collar.

And then she saw it.

The swan.

The feeling that overwhelmed her was like a big soft blanket you wrap around yourself when you're really cold. It is more vivid, she thought, and much larger than I imagined it would be when I first remembered it that day in the car park, but unmistakable. It used to be pink but now it's a deep purple. With the twitching of his neck it seems to flap its wings as though trying to fly away. I remember how jealous I used to be, angry that he had a swan while I did not.

'Nicholas,' she said at last.

His eyes were almost closed. 'My blood mingling with yours. Full circle, eh, Julia?'

She felt the slow beating of his heart against her chest. Felt the trembling of his limbs against hers, heard the slow deep gasps for air.

'Did you know straightaway?' she asked. 'That day at Strangeways?'

'Yes . . . and so did you . . . but I knew before that . . . at least . . . I thought I did.'

'How?'

'I was in the public gallery one day. Watching the trial of a mate. He'd told me he had a shit-hot lawyer who was going to get him off. I saw you. I had the strangest feeling that I knew you. But wasn't sure. I often used to wonder where you were . . . and what it would be like to see you again. It was a nice thought. To imagine you just might have been my twin. And then later . . . when I needed a solicitor . . . I asked for you. Still only thinking this was a good idea because you were supposed to be the best. But when I saw you in the interview room . . . close up . . . it hit me. That it really was . . . you. But I saw no future in it. We had grown too far apart. I decided I would not let you know I recognised you . . .'

'But instead you decided to exploit the situation.'

He answered with the slightest movement of his head and Julia had no idea whether this was a yes or a no. Not a coincidence after all, she thought to herself.

'I wasn't quite sure,' she said. 'Until now. Not until I saw the swan.'

'Oh yes . . . you were. You knew too.'

She let this pass. And there were things she had to know. 'Do you remember everything that happened before we ran away?'

Each breath he took was becoming shorter and more shallow. 'Yes — of course I do,' he said. 'Remember how he forced us . . . to sleep in separate rooms? I heard. Your screams. Couldn't understand why Mrs Spencer didn't come to see what happened. Must have been drugged for her pain. Lucky I came . . . into your room when I did. He was beating the shit out of you like a man crazed with anger. You were covered in blood. So was he. The broken lamp had cut his head. Sometimes . . . we do what we have to do. You should . . . know that, Julia. He deserved . . . to die.'

'Die? He died?'

Her heart thumped against her ribs as the horror sank in. So it was me. Not Nicholas. I killed Mr Spencer with the lamp but Nicholas took the blame.

Yet at this very moment another tendril of memory was snaking into her brain. Becoming clearer by the second . . .

Blood . . . pain . . . Nicholas putting her nightgown over her
head . . . Mr Spencer lying on the carpet . . . a blood stain

321

spreading across his shirt like a flower blooming . . .
Nicholas grabbing her hand . . .

His grip loosened.

She held him tight.

His eyes closed. He was still. And Julia felt as though an axe had cleaved her chest in two.

- 110 -

Paul grasped Julia's trembling shoulders.

'Relax, Julia. You're safe now. Smith is dead.'

'Paul . . . ' She turned her face away from him, then quickly asked, 'Where's Nicky?' in a voice he didn't know.

'She's safe too,' he assured her. 'She was locked in the car. He didn't harm her at all.'

He prised her fingers open and lifted her away from Smith. He picked up her gun and Smith's and handed them to the inspector.

'This one's unloaded, Sir,' Jake said, placing Julia's pistol in a clean plastic bag. He hesitated, then handed it to Paul without further comment.

Paul put the plastic bag in his pocket, then tried to wipe away some of the blood from Julia's face. 'An ambulance is on its way to take you to Macclesfield Hospital,' he said. 'Don't talk now. You're in shock and badly wounded.'

She looked down at the hole in her jeans, and for the first time seemed to register some pain.

'Where's Nicky?' she insisted. 'What happened?'

'She's fine. I'll tell you later.'

'Paul —'

'Don't try to talk.'

'Did you hear what he said? About us being . . . '

'I did, but his voice became so faint I didn't hear it all.'

He knelt at Julia's side while one of the firearms team cut away her bloodstained jeans and applied a dressing to her wound. She kept looking at Smith's body, then looking away and shaking her head, murmuring her daughter's name over and over again.

'I'm afraid I'm not going to let Nicky see you tonight,' he said when the dressing was complete. 'She wouldn't understand all this blood. It would frighten her,' he added, with more resentment in his voice than he'd intended. 'She's absolutely fine. She's with a policewoman, waiting for me in the helicopter. I've promised her a ride home in it and she can't wait to take off. You can see her tomorrow,' he said more gently, 'when this mess has been cleaned up.'

She looked at him with large staring eyes, as though she'd been concussed and he was a perfect stranger. She opened her mouth, but no sound came out. Tears rolled down her cheeks, mixing with Smith's blood and the dirt she'd picked up from lying on the ground. Paul tried again to mop it up with his handkerchief, but she ended up looking even worse. Like someone in a horror film.

He wasn't sure whether she was taking in what he was saying, but decided that she needed to be reassured about what had happened.

'I rang Wendy right after I'd spoken to you. I had a feeling you might have recorded Smith's call. She played back the tape of the entire conversation. You also very thoughtfully left the ordnance survey map on your desk. It's a good thing you pressed that alarm button. If we hadn't been here he might have killed you with his second shot.'

He saw the ongoing questions in her eyes. 'We found Nicky in the churchyard. In a white Fiesta we suspected Smith had stolen. I spotted it from the helicopter through a lucky break in the mist. Spotted your car too.'

There was still no response, except an even greater look of fear and confusion, and a widening of her eyes at the mention of the churchyard. 'Don't worry, Julia. Your daughter looked bewildered but totally unharmed when I found her. He must have convinced her they were playing a game when he locked her in the car. She even laughed when she saw me, as though I wasn't supposed to find her. I can't tell you what a relief it was.'

Just then he heard the yelp of the ambulance as it drew up adjacent to the stile. The older of the two paramedics, a stocky dark-haired man with droopy eyes, attended to Julia. The younger one, who was also the driver, attended to Smith.

After a quick examination of the body the younger one stood up. 'No point in attempting a resuss,' he said. 'Another ambulance will be here shortly to take away the body.'

The older man knelt beside Julia and opened the bright orange box he'd carried from the ambulance. He smiled at her. 'My name is John,' he said. 'What's your name, lass?'

Paul quickly intervened, supplying Julia's personal details, what had happened, how long ago, and the calibre of the gun Smith had used.

'I'll put a needle in your arm now,' John said in his soothing voice. 'Just a little pinprick. Then we'll run some fluids through you to make you feel more comfortable.'

Amazed at how quiet Julia had become, and how calm she now looked, Paul watched them fit an aluminium stretcher underneath her. They elevated her leg, put her on the portable heart monitor and checked her blood pressure and pulse. Finally they put another dressing on her leg and fitted a padded splint with Velcro straps to hold it together. While this was going on she looked alternately from Smith's body to Paul, moving her head slowly from one to the other, still without speaking.

'She's as stable as we can make her now,' John said. 'We'll radio ahead to alert A & E at Macc District General.'

Paul walked alongside Julia as they carried her to the ambulance. He asked himself why she had excluded him from her ordeal when she must have known all this could have been avoided if she'd told him what was happening. Seeing her like this on the stretcher brought into stark relief the reality of the last fifteen minutes: the revelation of Smith being her brother, the obvious rapport between them, his own crime of pulling rank and persuading Jake to illegally issue him with a rifle and then shooting Smith instead of leaving it to the team, the consequences of which did not bear contemplation.

'I'm taking Nicky home with me,' he told her. 'I'll tell Wendy she can take over tomorrow while I'm at work.'

He watched Julia until the moment the doors were closed. She was watching him too, but never said a word.

Led by the newly arrived police motorbike, the ambulance set off for Macclesfield, emitting a long drawn out wail that echoed round the hills.

I don't believe it, Paul thought, and ran to the helicopter.

- 111 -

As the ambulance sped through the twisting lanes, Julia wondered if any of this was really happening. For the last twelve days it had become more and more difficult for her to tell whether she was acting sensibly or ridiculously illogically, and where reality had ended and fantasy had taken over. The events of the past hour were still a blur half way between the two. A blur that left her brain numb. A blur that was necessary to blot out what had just happened. Nicholas . . . Nicky . . . Paul . . .

She had searched Paul's ashen face for the man she thought she knew. He had not made one comment about her relationship to Smith. His cool professional manner, except when he spoke of Nicky, was entirely predictable in view of what he'd learned tonight. Though, thank goodness, she thought, he hadn't learned it all. And now he never would.

Then suddenly she remembered. The letter . . .

They would find it. It would be drenched in blood but forensics would decipher it and that would be the end of her. She closed her eyes and let her thoughts wander where they would. She had felt the distance between her and Paul widening as each minute passed. It seemed so ironical, she thought. Her worst secret should in theory be safe now. But even if the letter proved illegible it would still stand forever between them. Paul was the only person left in her life, apart from Nicky, who really mattered. She had watched his face until the moment the ambulance doors closed, waiting for some small gesture, anything that would acknowledge what was between them. Anything that might appease her need for him. She even wished now that he'd reprimanded her. 'Oh, Paul . . . '

325

'Take it easy, Julia,' John said. 'You're going to be okay.'

She nodded. John glanced at his watch, then smiled reassuringly. 'These police escorts sure do straighten out the roads. We're almost there. How's the pain now?'

She shook her head and within seconds a mask appeared from somewhere above her head.

'Mixture of oxygen and nitrous oxide,' he explained. 'Laughing gas to you.'

After a few breaths she felt herself floating off the stretcher. She wished the sickly gas were even stronger. Enough to blot out the horror of the night. Then something swam into her focus. Two foetuses in adjoining sacs of amniotic fluid, the slug-like cocoons curled around each other. Touching . . . touching . . . touching . . .

- 112 -

Julia kept her eyes fixed on the white porous tiles of the A & E cubicle ceiling, still trying to get away from the two foetuses. But it was no good. Even when she closed her eyes they were still there, entwined, linked, entangled . . .

After the paramedics had handed her over and all the usual tests and X-rays had been completed, they told her they were calling out an orthopaedic surgeon. A few minutes later, amongst the mêlée of doctors and nurses, she became aware of a new presence. Someone standing beside her.

'Julia,' a voice said softly. She opened her eyes.

'Martin!' A fresh deluge of tears gushed from her eyes. Martin, of all the orthopaedic doctors that could have been on call.

He placed his hand gently on her wrist and felt her pulse. 'You know, you've been on my mind ever since you rang on Saturday. I had a feeling something was wrong. How do you feel?'

She met his gaze. 'Seeing you here is making me feel one hell of a lot better.' She'd expected to see a look of condemnation but he hadn't even raised an eyebrow.

He pulled up a stool and sat beside her. 'Any pain now?'

'Nothing like it was. Just a dull ache.'

He frowned. 'The morphine may have made the pain in your leg subside, Julia, but your eyes tell me there's another pain. You can tell me about it and it won't go any further than these four walls,' he said quietly.

She bit her lip. It was tempting.

'Okay,' he said. 'I understand. How long since you had anything to eat or drink?'

'A sandwich at lunchtime. Cup of coffee.'

'You lawyers. Anyway, that does mean you can go to theatre straight away.'

He took the notes from his registrar and slotted the X-rays into the illuminated screen on the wall.

'The bullet struck just below the knee joint from a range of about four feet,' he said, reading from the notes. 'Missed the tibia, thank goodness.'

'There's slight loss of feeling and pins and needles,' the registrar explained. 'Entry wound the size of a shirt button, exit wound a 50p piece. Ragged edges. Considerable tissue bruising.'

'There's no bullet inside, Julia,' Martin said, 'but the fibula is broken and there are one or two fragments lying around. The exit wound's a bit of a problem. In case there's any infection we'll only partially sew it up. On Friday morning we'll take you back to theatre, clean it out and sew it up properly.'

'Fine,' she said, attempting to smile. At least the anaesthetic would blank everything out for a few hours and erase these endless floating images.

'Will I be able to walk straight away?' she asked.

Martin raised both hands. 'What's the hurry?'

'I've a busy schedule, Martin.'

'Julia, my dear, when you leave here you'll be using crutches, so you'd better get someone to take over your cases for a while. The bone will knit within five or six weeks.'

She groaned at the thought of the slowness of it all. Martin gave her hand a squeeze. 'See you in theatre,' he said. 'Oh, and by the way, I've told the police you're in no state to answer any questions until at least tomorrow.'

WEDNESDAY

'Ah, Paul,' Bill Brownlow said, looking at Paul with slightly less of a smile than usual. 'Please sit down.'

'If you don't mind, Sir, I'd rather stand.'

'As you wish. I was going to talk to you at our morning meeting, but seeing you're here now, perhaps you'd like to tell me exactly what happened yesterday. And why.'

Paul was amply prepared for this. Both for the abruptness and for the request for detail. Bill Brownlow did not mince his words. Last night, apart from looking after Nicky, going into the guest bedroom every ten minutes to make sure she was all right, he had known it was futile to attempt to sleep and instead had spent most of the night at his dining room table, writing down over and over again the sequence of events on the moorlands and analysing his motives.

The ACC listened without comment. He made a few notes but otherwise kept his eyes fixed on Paul's face. It was a relief that not once did he appear even tempted to say I told you so.

After what seemed like about fifteen minutes of uninterrupted monologue, Paul paused. 'That's about it, Sir. I wanted to be the first to tell you. But since I'm no longer part of an armed response unit and have used a weapon without the necessary authorization of my force, entirely my own decision. I also wanted to pre-empt any decision on your part — ' He stopped and took a deep breath.

The ACC raised his eyebrows. 'Go on, Paul,' he said.

'Sir, I would like you to suspend me from duty.'

Bill Brownlow opened his mouth to speak, but Paul carried on.

'I also need some time to sort out my own affairs. Get away to clear my head. Visit my daughter in Australia whom I haven't seen for years. Let things simmer down here as far as the unauthorised use of the gun is concerned. And . . .' He hesitated, wondering just how far Brownlow's sympathies would stretch, then decided that if he was telling the truth,

329

then better he tell the whole truth. 'And also let things simmer down between myself and Julia Grant. I just want to back out for a while. I need to get away.'

Still holding Paul's gaze, Bill Brownlow rubbed his chin. 'Thank you for being so forthright. I'd been wondering how to get around suspending you. It's something I really didn't want to have to do, but as we all know, in cases of this nature it is normal practice until the investigation is complete. However, now that I'm in possession of all the facts, although in due course I'll have to study the reports from firearms, forensics and various other interested parties, I'm sure we'll be able to sort it all out. Firearms would undoubtedly have been the ones to shoot Smith had it not been for your swift action. But I can't promise you'll be exonerated. However I hope your suspension will only be to . . . maintain appearances, and that's strictly between you and me.'

'Thank you, Sir.'

Paul knew that he should at this moment be feeling a great sense of relief, but just to have Brownlow's understanding was not enough to lift his burden of guilt.

'There's just one more thing, Sir.'

'Yes, Paul. I thought there might be.'

'Jake Burrows. I would like to think that he will be completely absolved for his part in my actions. It was despicable of me to pull rank the way I did. I have the utmost respect for the man, I trained him, dammit, and I know just what a fine policeman he is. He would never have handed over that MP5 if I hadn't deliberately exaggerated my own personal danger because of Smith's well-known hatred of my guts.'

The ACC nodded. 'I know that, Paul. Don't worry. By the time you return from Australia I can only hope that everything will be sorted out.'

- 114 -

Paul tiptoed into Julia's room. He couldn't believe how different she looked. She was propped up on a mound of pillows, with her leg encased in an enormous bandage. Her hair, matted with blood last time he'd seen her, hung shiny and loose around her shoulders. The nursing staff were spot-on in this hospital, he thought.

'Oh, hello Paul.' Her eyes were half-open. She blinked them twice. 'Where's Nicky?'

'She's at school. She's fine. I gave Wendy the night off, so Nicky spent the night with me. I'll bring her in later this afternoon. When all these drips are down.'

Julia's face seemed to brighten up, but only for a moment.

'You look much better,' he said. She'd obviously been smartened up by the nurses after he'd rung to see if he could visit her, but there was something empty and lost about the expression in her eyes.

'Yes,' she said. 'It's an enormous relief that Nicky's safe. Though there's not much else to feel better about.'

He pulled up a bright orange easy-chair and sat down beside the bed. 'The doctor tells me you've been very lucky.'

'Lucky? I expect you mean my leg might have been blown right off.'

'You've also been very brave. But it needn't have happened, Julia.'

She closed her eyes tightly, then opened them and looked up at him like a child about to be chastised. 'You know I could be struck off, don't you? I'll have to stand trial. Probably end up in Styal Prison, not two miles from Hillside House.'

'What the hell are you talking about?'

'Possession of an unlicensed firearm — Exhibit A. And that dagger in your hat, Mrs Grant — Exhibit B.'

'Calm down, Julia. You don't know what you're saying. The morphine has made you delirious.'

'Can't allow people to take the law into their own hands, the judge will say in his summing up.'

'Julia, you're hysterical.'

She pushed herself up on her elbows. 'I killed him, Paul.'

'For God's sake shut up and lie down and listen to me.'

Supporting her head, he eased her down onto the pillows. 'You did not kill Sam Smith. For God's sake, your gun wasn't even loaded.'

She gazed at the window, as though talking to herself. 'If he hadn't seen my gun he wouldn't have shot me. And firearms wouldn't have shot him.' She looked down at her hands, opening them wide as if the answers she was seeking were written on her palms. 'But I'd already killed him. Long before that.'

'I'm not with you,' Paul said.

He held his breath as she told him what she'd done to Smith last Wednesday night, and what Martin Bedlow's prognosis had been.

'Why didn't you tell me?'

'You'd have asked questions. It was too dangerous.'

'So. All along it wasn't the whole police force you didn't trust. It was only me.'

'No, Paul, it wasn't like that. I thought the best way of protecting my child was through my own manipulation of Smith. If I'd told you what was happening he might have harmed Nicky.'

'But he didn't even have Nicky then.'

'No. But I couldn't take any chances, could I? Besides, anyone who could walk into the Magistrates' Court when the entire GM police force was after him, and get away with it, was clearly capable of doing . . . anything.'

Paul's mouth dropped open. 'Oh my God.'

And as the tale of persecution came pouring out, Paul began to understand the full extent of Julia's fear. And of his own transgression. Because of his involvement with Julia . . .

'But, you know,' she said. 'I'm sure that in the beginning he never intended to abduct Nicky. Just as he never intended to kill me. He was certain I'd pay him. He only took Nicky when he was so ill that he knew if he didn't get the cash immediately in order to get out of the country quickly and see a doctor, he would die. It was a last act of self-preservation . . .'

Paul bent down until his eyes were level with Julia's. 'And tell me, Julia, what the hell is it that makes you think he was so sure you'd give him the money?'

She turned her head away and dug her teeth into her bottom lip. 'I don't know, Paul. Don't ask me. I don't know.'

'All right,' he conceded, quite certain that she must have known, and curious about the sudden look of fear that crossed her eyes. 'Who else have you told about that hatpin?' he said.

'No one. Why?'

'I want you to say nothing to the police. He could have got that injury from anyone.'

'But I've told you.'

'Listen carefully. Cause of death was not a puncture wound in the stomach. It was a gunshot wound to the heart delivered in order to stop him shooting you again.' He stood up and marched across the room, then swung round to face her.

'By me.'

'You? Not firearms? But — '

'I told you. He had a gun in his hand. Pointed at you. I had to stop him shooting you again.'

She swung her head from side to side. 'Paul . . . It was me. I killed him. Don't you see? He could easily have shot me in the heart. He was so close it was impossible to miss. But he shot me in the leg. And he died thinking it was me who had shot him . . . me that had killed him.' With her face twisted in pain she screwed her eyes up and turned her head away.

'Christ, if only you'd told me you suspected he was your brother. You could have trusted me. Couldn't you?' He walked back to his chair. 'We could have taken a blood sample from you and done a DNA test and proved months ago whether he was or wasn't. And I'll be quite honest with you. I still don't think he was.'

Julia rolled her eyes at him. 'Can you imagine if it had all come out? Defence lawyer twin sister of serial killer!'

'Julia, Julia. Part of loving is trusting people. You didn't trust me. I wish I could understand you. But I know very little about you really. About your past. You've been bottling so much up. Wouldn't it help if you talked about it now?'

He watched her drag her hand across her brow and purse her lips. He felt a great tide of longing mixed up with a sinking feeling of regret. Perhaps she had never been able to trust anybody. Perhaps this was a new concept for her and it was up to him to help her assimilate it.

'Try,' he said softly. 'It always helps to talk.'

333

She sighed. 'Well, I don't suppose it'll make any difference now.'

And so she told him, sometimes in unstoppable bursts of frenzy, sometimes with slow deliberation, everything she said her adoptive mother had told her on Sunday.

Paul felt anger rise in his chest as he listened to her story. She seemed to be tying herself up in knots, as though there was part of the story she was holding back.

'So why do you still look so guilty, Julia? I get the feeling you've left something out. Have you told me everything?'

For a few moments she said nothing. Then she slid down into the pillows. 'With someone to love him he might have been a different person,' she said. 'But I don't want to discuss it any more. What about you? What's been happening? I've been doing all the talking.'

Paul hesitated. He wished she would tell him now, get it off her chest, but he didn't want to put her under any further strain. 'Well, you'll have to know some time, I suppose. I've been suspended. Pending investigations.'

'What? But they can't do that to you.'

He shrugged. He had no intention of divulging his confidential conversation with Bill Brownlow. It would upset her even more. He would tell her only what she needed to know. 'The media is full of the story today. And I don't know how they've sniffed it out, but there are some suggestions of my link with you. It was even on the news last night. Did I act in the best interests of justice? Why couldn't I just have wounded him?'

He thumped his fist on his knee. 'The bullet had to be either in the head or the heart, Goddamit – in order to stop him pulling the trigger a second time and killing you. That's why.'

'You put your job in jeopardy in order to save my life,' she said softly. 'Your career is everything to you, Paul. It's unthinkable that you might lose your job. Perhaps they're only acting under pressure from the media.'

Just then a nurse carrying a tray covered with a white cloth popped her head around the door. 'I'm afraid you'll have to leave now, Mr Moxon.' She looked at them both, smiled apologetically. 'I'll be back in a moment.'

Paul dutifully stood up. He looked down at Julia. She had told him more than he'd expected to hear, but she was definitely holding something back. Of that he was sure. Each time she seemed to be opening up she would withdraw into herself or completely change the subject.

'I'll drop Nicky in later,' he said. 'Did you know Wendy got married yesterday? That's why she was late.'

'She told me. I didn't take it in at the time. Poor Wendy. What a wedding day! And what a birthday. You were kind to give her the night off.'

He walked to the door. The things that remained unspoken lay like a mountain between them. 'I believe the police will be here in about two hour's time,' he said. 'I hope you'll feel up to answering a few questions. I don't think there'll be a problem. You don't need to give anything more than the bare facts. Nothing about being related. You were clearly a victim. When are you having your second op?'

'On Friday morning, I believe. I hate these anaesthetics. They give me the most dreadful hallucinations.'

He cracked his knuckles, slowly, one by one. 'I hope you make a speedy recovery.'

With his hand on the doorknob he turned and looked at her. A sorry sight. He opened his mouth, then closed it without saying what he wanted to say. That even if Smith were still alive she must know it was a futile relationship. Nothing could ever have come of it. By the time he was released, he could never have been rehabilitated into normal society. But Julia would not have accepted this. She would have thought he was being cruel. But it was true, so for her sake, and for society's, he felt sure it was best that he was dead. He hoped that in time she would agree.

'Nice view of the cricket ground,' he blurted out, then quickly closed the door.

Paul took his beer mug in both hands and swallowed the last drop, then signalled the barman to fill it up. He had a quick look around the room, thinking that of all the downtown Manchester pubs the *Café Rouge* in Deansgate was perhaps the most foolhardy of choices for a clandestine meeting with his colleague.

'How d'you think it went this morning, Kev?' he asked quietly.

'It's early days, boss. But I'm cautiously optimistic.' Resting his elbows on the bar counter he gave Paul the gist of his part in the day's proceedings. He'd been emphatic, when questioned, that in his opinion DS Moxon's insistence on being armed was merely a residue, you might say, from his time leading the firearms team and that he'd had no intention of actually using the weapon. He was quite sure too, that firing the MP5 had been a reflex action in response to Smith's action, rather than one of premeditation. Regretting that lack of space in the small helicopter had made it impossible for him to go with DS Moxon as planned, he felt it was a stroke of genius that DS Moxon had sent the rest of the team ahead in the direction of the *Cat and Fiddle*, from where the phone call to Mrs Grant was made, so that by the time he had the details of Smith's recorded telephone conversation it had been an easy matter to radio the exact pick-up point to the firearms van.

'Thanks, Kev,' Paul said, ensuring that without spelling it out he was more than grateful to Kevin, though still wondering how he was going to present his case when it was his turn to give evidence tomorrow morning.

'We'll just have to wait and see, boss. It's a good thing there are no relatives who might want to do something about Smith's death at the hands of the police.'

'Yes,' Paul said, slowly nodding. 'And in a macabre roundabout way that's the reason I asked you to meet me today.'

Kevin looked at him askance. 'If there's anything I can do to help, just tell me, boss.'

'I appreciate that. But first, there's something you should know. Another coffee?'

'Thanks. Then I must get back to Chester House.'

For the next ten minutes Kevin listened to Paul, not saying a word.

'She's convinced he was her brother,' Paul went on. 'She's being torn apart by guilt. She could easily spend the rest of her life blaming herself for all his ills. For having all the good things in life when he had nothing. For killing him as she is stupidly insisting, when all she was doing was defending herself. That clever bastard had twisted her round his little finger. I still can't believe that ever since his escape she's been carrying a gun. The one solicitor you knew would never do anything underhand or against the law. He warped her thinking, then put the fear of death into her.'

'Steady on, boss. I can understand your feelings. But she may be right. He may have been her twin brother. And of course he'd be entirely different because of the way he was brought up, or dragged up in his case.'

'That's still a matter for debate,' Paul said. 'The latest thinking is that nature has it over nurture.' He took a large swig of beer. 'Actually, as far as I'm concerned, I don't care a damn if he is her twin. Was her twin. Just because an accident of birth may have linked that scum to her doesn't make a blind bit of difference to my opinion of her. We can't choose our siblings any more than we can choose our parents. She is what she is, regardless of who her family were. It's her I'm worried about. And for God's sake she has no positive proof the bastard was related to her.' He took another swill of beer.

'For some unfathomable reason she seems unwilling to talk about it, except when I more or less forced her to give me the barest facts. I'm sure there's something she's holding back. Something she doesn't want to talk about. Something she's scared as hell to talk about.'

'It must have been an awful shock for Mrs Grant when she first realised he was her brother,' Kevin said. 'That was enough to make anyone scared, even though there might be something else.'

Paul scratched his head. 'Or thought he might be,' he said.

'You really don't want to believe it, do you, Chief?'

Paul pushed back his stool. He walked a few paces from the bar then sat down again. 'Twin brother or no twin brother, Kevin, some time before the Smith file goes into records I'd like to know who he really was. Anything you can find out, for no other reason than to put Julia out of her misery. I don't think things will ever be quite the same between us, but at least she deserves not to have to live with that.'

He took a small piece of paper from his pocket.

'She finally agreed to pass on the information she'd got last Sunday from her adoptive parents. Her mother's name was Victoria King. Unmarried at the time. In her teens. Father never identified. Brother's name Nicholas. When they were a day or two old Victoria King left the twins at St Mary's church in Manchester, giving no details except her name. Which could of course have been false, and probably was. The nuns took them to the Touchstone Orphanage. Julia was a bit vague about the next ten years but I gather they were fostered by many different foster-parents, the last one being a teacher, whose wife had become an invalid. Then for some reason she wasn't letting on, the twins were separated and she never saw her brother again. At this point she apparently lost her memory. It was partially regained, but she remembered nothing about the events that led to their separation. And still can't. According to her,' he added, closing his eyes and breathing in through his teeth. 'Well, she landed back in the orphanage for the umpteenth time and was then legally adopted. She was told that her brother had died. But last Sunday, for the first time, her adoptive mother told her this was not true. Something Julia said she had always felt.'

Kevin finished his coffee, nodding as he waited for Paul to carry on.

'Kev, I know you're putting yourself on the line by seeing me while I'm suspended, but I've got one hell of a favour to ask you. Will you help?'

'I will if I can.'

'Right now I don't have access to files or computers or anything, so I'm asking you, as a friend, just nick a copy of his criminal record off the system, will you? I'm damned if I can recall the details — all I ever concentrated on were the facts of the cases we were bringing. Oh, and can you also get a copy of his DNA profile too? Quick as you like.'

'Only 'cause it's for you, boss,' Kevin said. 'And because you'll be back in the job again after all this, and you'll make my life a bloody misery if I refuse.'

FRIDAY

116

Julia opened her eyes. The door was ajar, letting in the sound of voices, footsteps, bells and buzzers. The patch of sky she could see through her window was overcast again, although at six this morning when they'd prepared her for theatre, the sun had been shining. Where had the day gone?

She was sitting up combing her tangled hair when she saw, at the edge of her vision, someone standing motionless in the doorway.

Ben. And he was carrying an enormous bouquet of yellow gladioli.

'Hi, Ben,' she said. 'Come and sit down.'

He walked tentatively towards her. 'I brought you these,' he said, looking around for somewhere to put the flowers. 'Yellow's your favourite colour, isn't it?' Finally he put them on a table near the window, then sat down in the chair next to her bed.

'They're beautiful,' Julia said. 'The nurse will put them in a vase. Thank you, Ben. And thank you for taking over all my cases.'

'It was nothing.' He reached for her hand. 'You'd have done the same for me.'

'I'm glad you've come. I need to make a confession.' And before he could say anything more she told him how she'd been driven to forge his signature. 'I'd have paid back every penny, Ben. Please forgive me.'

'No. It's you who must forgive me. I was such a fool not to guess you were under abnormal stress. But now you can forget all that. We'll get you out of that horrible old house. Start afresh.' He smiled a big smile that lit up his whole face. 'I'd wanted to ask you on Tuesday afternoon, you know. When I picked you up from Crown Square . . .'

Julia felt a wave of pity that started in the depths of her stomach and seemed to engulf her whole body. 'Oh Ben. You've been so good to me. But we'll always be friends.'

He drew his lips together, breathed in deeply then smiled again. But this time it was a different smile. A slow, brave, melting, wistful smile

340

that said more than any words could say. It told Julia that at last he accepted that she could never love him as he loved her.

When he left she collapsed in torrents of tears. *What a shit I've been. I'll never forgive myself for being so awful to him.*

And she was still crying when she heard Nicky's voice.

'Hello, darling,' she said, straightening her face and wiping her eyes.

Her pulse quickened as she watched Nicky walk slowly towards her, a small bunch of yellow flowers in her hand. *Daisies she must have picked from the garden,* Julia thought.

She took the flowers from Nicky's outstretched hand. With her other hand she touched Nicky's cheek and for a few moments remained absolutely still. Then, as though she was drowning, she flung her arms around her daughter and held her close, oblivious of the avalanche of yellow daisies that flew into the air then wafted like sun-kissed snowflakes melting onto the sheets.

'I like that, Mummy. But Mummy, why are you crying?'

'I'm not crying, darling. I'm just so happy to see you,' she said, attempting to gather up the daisies.

'But you saw me yesterday. And the day before.' Nicky squeezed her mother's hand, her eyes shining with unconditional love.

Julia couldn't stop the tears spilling down her cheeks. It had been like this since Tuesday night. Crying for the relief of Nicky being unhurt. For the enormity of the death she had caused. And for the other one she had caused all those years ago. Crying for the slightest reason. Or for no reason at all. And there was nothing she could do to stop it. Ben's act of kindness had exacerbated it, but it had taken even less than that to set her off. Martin suggested some medication to calm her nerves but she was adamant in her rejection.

She felt Nicky stir. She knew at once from her daughter's tense reaction that there was someone else in the room. She opened her eyes and there was Paul, standing at the door, gazing at her and Nicky entwined in each other's arms, a bunch of yellow roses in his hands which he placed next to the gladioli. *Was all this yellow going to make her happy?*

'I've come to say goodbye,' he said

It was as though someone had thumped her in the stomach, like they'd been taught to do in Mike's class. Hard. Number ten. 'I didn't know you were going away,' she said, groping under her pillow for a tissue.

'I gave my evidence this morning. The enquiry may take weeks. It's a good opportunity to visit Tandy. I might not get another chance for years.'

'Australia?'

He nodded.

That would mean he would see Jane as well, she thought.

'The roses are magnificent,' she said.

He nodded. She wished he would sit down on the bed, next to her and Nicky. She didn't mind if he said nothing, just as long as he was close to them. The three of them together, like they were in those few precious minutes on that idyllic morning that seemed so distant now. 'Pull up that chair,' she said. 'I'll ring for some tea. It's good to see you. And thank you for the lovely flowers.'

She'd had so many visitors, including Wendy and Alan, Janey, David and Jessie all the way by train from Southport, Geoff Atherton, Fred Kennedy whom she had frantically phoned on Wednesday morning to cancel the transaction, and all the office staff. And of course Martin several times a day. But she hadn't seen Paul alone since the morning after the shooting. Each time he had brought Nicky to visit he had insisted on waiting outside to give Nicky as much time with her mother as possible. Or so he said.

He moved a few steps closer. 'Don't worry about the tea. I can't stay long, but I have some news for you.'

Julia could think of nothing that could possibly be good news. Unless it was that Paul had been re-instated. And it was far too soon for that.

He stood absolutely still, looking down at her, so close that she could see tiny muscles moving in his neck. He took the chair and placed it so that he was facing her. She glanced at Nicky and was surprised to see that she was fast asleep.

'Yes, Julia,' he said softly. 'He was your brother.'

What was this? More punishment?

'I know. So why are you telling me?'

'I saw what it was doing to you. I wanted to be sure. Tracing antecedents usually takes months, but some years ago when Smith had been charged with robbery and rape, an investigation was apparently carried out to track down any relatives or possible witnesses. I asked Kevin Moorsley to help. He dug deep and in a remarkably short time found some interesting facts.'

A rash of perspiration burst out on Julia's face and trickled down between her breasts. Interesting facts? Which interesting facts, she wondered. 'And?' she asked. The only person who knew about the worst one of all was dead. So what did he mean? Had Forensics managed to decipher the letter in Smith's pocket after all?

'He took the name of Sam Woodgate when he was fostered by a Mr and Mrs Woodgate. Mr Woodgate divorced his wife Ada some months later. The authorities slipped up there. The child should have been moved on to a more stable home. Ada Woodgate died when Sam was thirteen, of a stab wound for which no suspect out of many was ever charged. Things get a bit vague here, but some time after that he called himself Smith. Before that his name had been Nicholas King. He had a twin sister called Julia. No further record of Julia was recorded in this survey.'

Paul's face was straight, the policeman through and through.

'Is that all?' she asked, her knees shivering under the blanket.

'No,' he said. 'When he was only ten years old he was sent briefly to a secure unit, but was almost immediately returned to the orphanage where he was kept under observation. Do you want to know why, Julia?'

'Yes,' she said, for how could she say no.

'The report says he had attacked his then foster father — Mr Robert St John Spencer, headmaster of a well-known public school — with a brass lamp found at the scene. There were multiple wounds, one of which was in his chest, presumably caused by a piece of broken glass from the lamp and which proved to be fatal. The boy and his sister escaped from the house. The forensic report showed there had been a great deal of violence in the bedroom before Mr Spencer died. It appears close neighbours must have called an ambulance, as his invalid wife had been drugged and was still asleep. Mr Spencer was dead on arrival at the hospital. Police apprehended the two children three days later, in a field, both with serious wounds and bruises. Covered in blood. Starving and freezing cold and delirious with fright. Are you sure you want to hear it all, Julia?'

Hardly able to breathe, she nodded.

'In hindsight there was an obvious cover-up, though there are no details of how this was achieved. The deceased was clearly a man who'd had power and connection so that letting it out that he had been a paedophile all those years would have caused huge embarrassment in certain circles. The report states the girl was suffering from post traumatic shock and amnesia, and that admissions the boy made were considered potentially to be unreliable, having been uttered in informal circumstances without the benefit of legal advice, never repeated under caution, or in an admissible form. He was therefore returned to the orphanage, but with advice that he should not be offered for legal adoption. Several foster parents threw him out before he was eventually fostered by the Woodgates.'

Julia felt her chest expanding as if it would burst. Apart from the fact that she had been the one to deal the fatal blows, not Nicholas, there was something in this bizarre report that didn't quite add up, but she was damned if she could identify the anomaly. 'And what does that prove,' she asked, mentally crossing her fingers, 'apart from the fact that my brother's life became hell because he had protected me.'

'That's one way of looking at it,' Paul said, and Julia was relieved that he did not mention the paedophile reference again, although now that it was apparently common knowledge she would at least be spared the indignity of revealing it herself.

'Nothing surprises us about Smith in this report,' he said. 'But you can't argue against a DNA test that proves you're siblings.'

'A DNA test? On me?'

'Your doctor, Martin Bedlow, who tells me he's known you for many years, made a professional decision. He agreed with me that the circumstances warranted it, for your health's sake and nothing else. In case you'd been mistaken.'

Julia stared at Paul's face, trying to follow it as it swam around the room.

'I'll be honest, Julia, I didn't believe it at first. I overheard part of your conversation just before Smith died. But I had to make sure.'

'Sometimes I wasn't sure either,' she whispered. 'Sometimes I wondered whether I'd imagined it all. Whether he was using everything I'd told him about myself at Strangeways when I'd been trying to make it easier for him to talk about himself. Just storing it up, knowing he could use it as a weapon against me. I told him my twin brother had died but that I still dreamt I would one day find him. Right up to the end I wasn't sure. And then . . . '

'Well?' Paul said.

'I saw the swan.'

'The swan?'

'The birthmark on his neck.' She turned her head away. 'He's dead but he isn't dead. He's still here with me. I can't help it, Paul.'

'Sam Smith *is* dead. The person who died out there on the moors was no longer your twin, but a man who became Sam Smith, regardless of who he was when he was born. You've been mourning an illusion.'

'No. I don't think so,' she said. 'You see, you can't erase the past.'

'Past or no past. Don't you think it's time to say goodbye to that dream? Look what it's done to you. Look what it's doing to you now. I've never seen you look like this.'

Paul stood up and walked to the window and back again towards the bed. In the silence that followed Julia looked down at Nicky resting on her arm. The child's eyes were wide open and she realised that far from being asleep her daughter was listening to every word they said.

Slowly Nicky sat up. She looked first at Paul, then at Julia. Then again at Paul, who held out his arms towards her. With a little whoop she jumped off the bed and ran into his arms.

'Well, I must be off,' he said, still holding Nicky. 'Wendy said she wanted to see you. Still blaming herself for everything.' He looked at his watch. 'She'll be here in half an hour and will take Nicky home. You did a fine thing, Julia, sending her and Alan a cheque to cover a deposit on a little house. But a bit over the top, I'd have said.'

Julia ignored his remark. He would never understand. 'Can't you stay a little longer?' she said.

'I have to pack. My flight leaves tomorrow.'

Nicky clung to Paul.

He kissed her on the forehead. 'Come on now, Princess. I must be going.' He unwrapped her arms from his neck and put her down. She rushed back to Julia, glancing at Paul like a frightened deer caught between two hunters.

'Will you be away long?' Julia gripped Nicky's hand. She felt as though every last breath was being sucked from her lungs.

'Three weeks. My first holiday for two years. But who knows? I might stay longer.'

Julia managed a smile. 'Well, have a good time. I hope everything is sorted out by the time you get home. Thank you for the lovely roses. And for the news,' she added, avoiding his gaze.

Paul walked towards her bed. He bent down and kissed Nicky, rested his hand on Julia's head for a moment, and then without looking back he walked quickly to the door.

TUESDAY

Eleven days later

It was two weeks since Julia was shot when Wendy drove her to Martin Bedlow's outpatient clinic. He removed the bandages, sent her for another X-ray, took the stitches out and re-applied the cast.

'The wounds are healing well, Julia,' Martin told her, 'and the bone is mending. But you'll need physio three times a week from now on. Come and see me again in four weeks time.'

'Will I be completely better then?' she asked.

'Don't look so miserable, Julia. You're doing just fine. You'll be walking without crutches when you see me next. Though you might have a slight limp for a further few weeks.'

Martin was always so precise and thorough. It was good to know exactly where she stood, though she was appalled at how long it would take.

'Just one more question. No, two. When can I go back to work? And when can I drive?'

'I wondered when you'd ask me that. Work in about a month. Driving, I'm afraid, must wait another six weeks.'

'That's impossible. I can't sit around all that time.'

'If you had an automatic you could drive sooner.'

'But I have an automatic. And it's my left leg that's injured.'

He smiled. 'Then I'll leave it up to you. Your leg will tell you when it's ready.'

347

FRIDAY

Four and a half weeks later

'Mummy, why are we here? You said Paul was on holiday.'

'I heard he came back last week so I thought we'd surprise him. He told me once how he loved curries. I've made a chicken curry so he won't have to cook when he comes home.'

Julia still thought it was outrageously presumptuous of her, but there didn't seem to be anything she could do to stop herself. She'd tried the curry out on Wendy who, once she'd got over the shock of seeing Julia in an apron with a wooden spoon in her hand, had said it was fabulous.

'Oh, I love surprises, Mummy. Like when you took me to see *Swan Lake* last night.' Nicky ran up three steps, then down two, keeping level with Julia as she lumbered slowly up the stairs. 'Is that why you bought that recipe book?'

Julia bent down and kissed the top of Nicky's head. She picked out the shiny new key on her key-ring, remembering those few silent moments when she and Paul had held it together, his fingers touching hers.

She rang the bell first. When there was no reply she inserted the key and opened the door. Kevin Moorsley had told her Paul was still suspended, but that he'd been advising a film company in Leeds who were making a documentary about the police force, and was due back today. If the traffic was heavy he might be hours getting home.

She propped up her crutches just inside the front door. Even though she'd had the plaster off three days ago, she still needed them for climbing stairs.

There was a slightly damp smell in the flat from having been closed up for so long. She found the central heating switch and turned it on. A ten minute blast on a low temperature would get rid of the mustiness

348

while she chopped up some salads and heated the curry and the rice.

Soon the flat was filled with the delicious aroma of eastern spices. The wine and the beer were in the fridge and she'd arranged a bowl of yellow roses on the table in the hall.

Nicky heard the key in the lock before Julia did.

'Shh, Mummy. Paul's coming. Shall we hide?'

'No, darling. We'll just stand here, and see what happens.' She was perfectly aware that she was using her own daughter as a shield to make sure he could not reject her outright, as he might do if she were on her own.

Seeing one of the roses out of place she quickly repositioned it. What if he'd found someone new while he was on holiday? Or gone back to his ex-wife, she wondered. She should have thought of that before she embarked on this ridiculous harebrained scheme.

The door opened and Paul walked in.

'Julia. What a surprise!'

He switched his gaze to Nicky, his eyes lighting up as she ran into his arms.

Julia leaned against the table. Was this what she wanted?

'Paul, Mummy's cooked a chicken curry and we're going to have strawberries and ice cream and I've set the table.'

He put Nicky down. Still holding her hand he walked slowly towards Julia.

'Why?' he asked softly.

It wasn't often Julia had no immediate answer. She smiled, feeling absurdly awkward. 'We missed you,' she said at last.

She'd had hours and days and weeks to consider the differences in their professional attitudes that had so often led to conflict. But in the end it wasn't a question of who was right and who was wrong. It was what Jessie had said. The respect they had for each other was what counted. It was also impossible to forget that Paul had jeopardised his career to save her life, though she doubted he would admit to that.

He looked down at Nicky. 'I missed you too,' he said.

The meal surprised even Julia. After the first mouthful Paul raised his eyebrows.

'Delicious.'

'Thank you,' she said, and for the first time in her life she realised what a buzz it could give you to cook for someone else's enjoyment.

They ate in almost total silence, Nicky looking from Paul to Julia as though she was at a tennis match. Paul helped himself to more, adding a liberal sprinkling of chopped tomatoes, cucumbers and sliced bananas, and a seriously hot mango chutney. 'I'm impressed. Who said you couldn't cook?'

'Everyone,' she said, and they all laughed.

Nicky asked if she could watch television. Paul put on the stern face he usually reserved for criminals. 'Just this once, young lady,' he said, scooping her up and placing her on his reclining chair in front of the big wide screen.

Julia thought achingly what a normal domestic scene it almost was.

They carried the dishes to the kitchen and Paul stacked the dishwasher. He hadn't mentioned Tandy or Jane, and Julia wondered whether his unusual quietness was because he was thinking of them, or because he resented her presence when he'd made it pretty clear before going away that her apparent lack of trust had been unacceptable to him.

He put the kettle on and took cups and saucers from a cupboard. 'How've you been?' he asked.

'Okay, now that I'm back at work. It was lovely when Nicky was on her half term holiday. But when she was at school the house was so quiet. Wendy always busy or out with Alan looking for a house. The kittens gone and no Duke. Duchess is a poppet, but she's really only Nicky's dog.'

'D'you mind if I ask you something personal? It's been puzzling me for weeks.'

'What is it?'

'Most adopted people want to know fairly early in their lives about their real family. Yet until very recently you didn't find out anything about them or about your early childhood. Why?'

Somehow I'll just have to muddle through this, Julia thought, and took a deep breath. 'When David and Jessie adopted me they told me they were now my parents and all the dreadful things that had happened before no longer existed. But I felt lonely and incomplete and even when the little boy next door came round to play and I thought he was my brother, and I was accused of — '

'Of what?'

'Even then they didn't explain.'

'Accused of what, Julia? Tell me.'

'Of . . . molesting him.'

He switched off the kettle, then slowly turned and looked at her.

'And did you?'

'Of course not. But . . . oh, don't ask me, Paul.'

'No. Wait, Julia. You're getting sidetracked. I understand it was terrible for you, but which dreadful thing in particular?'

'I don't know. I can't remember.'

'Why did you really come here tonight?'

'A whole lot of reasons,' she said, relieved that it looked as though he had decided not to pursue questioning her about her past. She had seen a look on his face that she knew well. One he always had when he thought he was getting close to capturing his prey.

'Tell me one.'

'Nicky can't live without seeing you now and then,' she added, not wanting to sound too melodramatic.

'And what else? Isn't there something special you wanted to tell me? Something about your past. That you've not told me before?'

She picked up a sponge and wiped the sink and the worktop. He wasn't letting it go. He was going to get it out of her if she wasn't careful. She should never under-estimate his powers of detection, and should be prepared for a question that might trip her up.

'Julia?' He waited. 'Okay. But I thought you said there were a lot of reasons.'

'There are,' she said, puzzled at why he was deliberately muddying the line of his questioning, chopping from one thing to another.

'Well? Tell me another one.'

She stood at the empty sink looking through the window at the twilight sky. There were no stars out yet, but above the window a cloud of moths circled the outside light. I'm just like those moths, she thought. Free to fly wherever they like, but trapped by their need to keep on flying round and round that light.

'And neither can I,' she whispered.

There. I've said it, she thought, not really surprised at his apparent lack of response, since his mind was clearly targeted in another direction. Now the ball is in his court. Or is it still in mine? It will be impossible for us to move a single inch forward while this rock of doubt stands between us. He knows there's something big on my mind. Something I'm deliberately withholding. I can't bear his silence.

'Paul . . .'

'What?'

'You're right. I do have something to tell you.'

'I'm glad,' he said. 'But first I have something to tell you.'

He opened a drawer and took out a handful of teaspoons which he rattled together as though he was playing castanets. 'I may be out of turn in mentioning this,' he said at last, 'but I have a feeling you may be totally unaware of something forensics found when they carried out Smith's autopsy.'

She stared at him but was unable to speak.

The letter.

So it was catching up with her after all. She felt the blood drain from her head. She felt like an animal trapped in a snare, unable to escape. The end, she thought. This is the end . . .

'It may help to fine-tune your memory. Fill in a few gaps.'

Julia felt as though something was blocking her windpipe.

He paused, but when she still said nothing he carried on. 'Forensics had a hell of a job deciphering it, but when they did, it made interesting reading. A letter in his pocket, drenched in blood, perforated by a bullet, but stamped and addressed to the Chief Constable Greater Manchester Police. Informing him that — '

'Stop! I don't want to hear it.' She hid her face in her hands.

'Informing him that before he could drag you away into hiding, afraid for your safety he said, you had insisted on dialling 999, in spite of your own horrendous wounds, to say there'd been a serious accident at Mr Robert St John Spencer's house and would they send an ambulance for him straight away. Is that true, Julia?'

Oh, Nicholas . . .

The floodgates of her memory sprang open, but only momentarily. And just wide enough to see herself running barefoot into the hallway trying to dodge the broken glass on the floor but not succeeding, and picking up the phone — before they clashed closed again and she was left with a blank screen and far more sorrow in her heart than relief, and yet more fragments of a picture that refused to slot into place.

Paul sighed, impatient with her hesitance.

'Yes,' she said. 'That bit is true. Strange. I've only just this moment remembered it.'

'And the other bit?'

'Oh, I don't know, Paul. I'm not sure of it myself.'

'Try, Julia. Try.'

She stood behind him and slid her arms around his waist. It was one way of not letting him see her eyes.

'Remember I told you about Smith's phone call the morning after he'd broken into my house, when he demanded a quarter of a million pounds. I told you he said he would not guarantee Nicky's safety if I didn't pay by the deadline he imposed.'

'Go on,' Paul said, his voice like a blank white wall.

'Well . . . that wasn't all he threatened.'

'I knew there was something else.'

'He said . . . he said if I didn't pay he would make some . . . interesting facts public. A very juicy piece of news about me. He said he could tell the authorities a thing or two.'

Paul straightened her arms and swivelled round to face her.

'And what were those facts?'

She wanted more than anything to break this impasse between them, but she'd been stupid to start something she couldn't finish. Not only could she not finish, she couldn't even begin. She would have to tell him that at first she had tolerated the sexual abuse. *It's our special secret, Julia* . . . Before that, no other human being except her brother had loved her. No one apart from her brother had ever cared . . .

353

Paul stood looking down at her. His eyes never left her face as he waited for her answer.

Oh, how clever, Julia thought. He had timed the surprising news of the letter to perfection, knowing it would make it almost impossible for her not to elaborate further.

'Go on, Julia.'

She turned her head away. 'Well . . . I suppose, oh, I don't know . . . I suppose it was . . . well, just that — that I was his sister.'

He looked up at the ceiling and shook his head and breathed in long and slowly through his mouth. 'And you really think that would have injured your reputation? Do you think that would have worried me?'

'You hated Smith. You despised him.'

'You must have known that would cut no ice with me. You weren't Siamese twins for God's sake. He was Smith. And you're right. I despised him. But you were two separate people.' He paused. 'No, Julia. I know you better than you think. There's something else, isn't there. What is it? Surely you can tell me?'

And in that split second she recalled Smith's dying words. They'd been lurking in the back of her mind for weeks, not forming themselves. Now suddenly, like mountains emerging from a thick mist, they stood out, clearly etched against the sky.

It was lucky I came into your room when I did . . . sometimes we do what we have to do . . . he deserved to die . . .

The room waved and heaved as she strove to remember the detail, feeling it touching her then receding, touching and receding, and longing for it to jump into sharp focus.

'You need some rest, Julia. You'd better get home.'

He seemed about to say something else, but instead he gently pushed past her.

'Bed time, Nicky,' he called, leaving Julia in stunned silence to gather up her things.

When they were ready to go, he gave Nicky a hug, then turned to

354

Julia. 'Thank you. That was a superb curry. I'll see you to the car.'

MONDAY

Three days later

- 119 -

Paul was still in bed when the phone rang. Today was Monday, the day when good things used to happen to him but now was like any other empty day. Bill Brownlow had said everything would be sorted out by the time he returned from Australia. At the back of his mind he wanted to believe this but so far nothing had been said and he needed it to be confirmed either verbally or in writing before he could relax.

It was more than forty-eight hours since he'd treated Julia so abominably, selfishly letting his own problems, his preoccupation about his future with the force blind him to her emotional needs – being impatient with her on-off decision to tell him something. He'd rehearsed his speech of apology should she phone, though this he knew was highly unlikely. In any case it should be the other way around.

He should be phoning her.

Time had passed, but the burden of frustration was still inside him. His work on the film had ended. There was nothing really to get up for, and he had a good mind to just let the phone ring.

But finally his innate sense of duty made him pick it up.

'Paul. I think you're off the hook.'

Bill Brownlow's words hit him like a cricket ball at mid stumps. He hadn't been near Chester House since his suspension. Apart from giving evidence at his enquiry, he'd had no contact with any of the staff except his two unofficial meetings with Kevin before he had left for Australia, and then Kevin's unauthorised phone call about Smith's bloodstained letter.

'Are you still there, Paul?'

'Yeah. I'm here, Sir.' And in one movement he sat up and swung his legs over the side of the bed. 'Do you think you could just say that again, Sir?'

'Unofficially, Paul, I've just received a call. Everything's fine.'

* * *

When he set out an hour later in his newly polished Honda CRX, with a rug on the back seat to protect the upholstery, and a song in his heart that he didn't know how to suppress, he had no idea how the rest of the day would turn out.

- 120 -

In courtroom number two in the Manchester Crown Court Julia bowed to the judge, gathered up her files and waited till everyone had left the courtroom before she shuffled carefully up the steps to the swing doors. With a final glance at the dock, where all day she'd seen only one face, she hobbled out into the corridor, where her seven months pregnant client was waiting to have a word. She was tired, but was unable to resist the woman's eager smile.

'I'll never forget you, Mrs Grant. You won't mind, will you, if I call my daughter Julia?'

She put her arms around the woman and hugged her. 'Good luck for the future,' she said, before turning and making her way along the concourse to the lifts.

Then something made her stop dead. Suddenly bombarded with a tumult of never-before-glimpsed scenes that hurtled across her vision as though she was looking at a giant TV screen on fast-forward with the sound on full blast, she turned back towards courtroom number two.

Dodging the outgoing crowds, her painful leg forgotten, she careered along the concourse. Outside the empty courtroom she stood for a moment, took a deep breath, then opened the door and walked in.

There was an eerie, fluttery sound as though a breeze had crept in behind her, brushing the hairs on her neck and moving the hem of her skirt.

She stared at the dock.

He was there, his mouth quivering, his eyes fixed on hers. He must have known she would come back, she thought, feeling the pull of his eyes.

Slowly she mouthed the words that had been hammering in her head all day.

Nicholas. It was me. You were right. I killed him. I see it all at last.

Lying in my bed. Eyes tight closed. Knowing. Waiting. Watching.

The door opens. I smell the stale tobacco and the chocolates. Hear his soft padding footsteps. I lie rigid. A cold sweat makes me shiver. I hear his panting. Hear him switch on the brass lamp. Close my eyes tighter.

He rips the blanket off the bed. His big hairy hand touches me, runs down my body, lifts my nightgown as he slides his grotesque body next to mine. Look at me, Julia, he says and thrusts a chocolate in my mouth. In the dim light I see the leer in his eyes. I see a swirl of jagged red shapes surging towards me. Hear a roaring and a rushing in my ears. Sit up with a jerk and spit the chocolate in his face.

He gasps. Wipes his face with his hand. Shoves me back down. Rips my nightgown off. Heaves his huge hulk on top of me but I wriggle clear and grab the lamp and smash it down on him. He leaps up. Holds me by my hair with one hand. Lashes out with the other, over and over again. I scream and scream, but nothing stops him and as usual Mrs Spencer doesn't wake up. Blood runs down my face, my arms, my legs. He is like a maniac, landing blow after blow until I can't see and can no longer feel anything but the pain.

You come rushing in. You switch on the ceiling light. Go, Nicholas! Go back to bed, I shout, or he will kill you too. But you fly at him with all your might. He lets go of my hair, drops me to the floor. His eyes are ablaze, like molten tar. He lands punch after punch at your head and your wiry little body. Blood pours from your nose.

I have to save you. I grab the shattered lamp. With all my strength I lift it up and once more smash it down on him. He stops beating you. Picks you up by one arm and hurls you across the room. Your head hits the wall. I think you are dead. Now free of you he turns to me. Lifts me off my feet with one hand. Grabs the broken lamp with his other hand. Swings the lamp back and aims it at my head and at that moment like a meteor your flick knife shoots across the room. The lamp crashes to the ground. One last gasp and his gross body crashes down and envelopes mine like a ton of solidifying cement. You drag him off me. Help to put my nightgown on. Pull the knife from his chest. Blood pours everywhere. I run to the phone. You try to stop me. I call 999. You take my hand. Come quickly, Julia, you say. I'll look after you, you say as you drag me out the door and down the driveway. Faster, you say as the next-door lights flood the garden and the neighbours appear. Just keep running, you say. Never mind the lights and the sirens . . . I'll look after you . . .

I know that you are making for the field where we often go to play on the way home from school, the one with the dense clumps of bushes and trees where we sometimes sit in the shade and day-dream. And where we sometimes come at night, creeping out at dead of night to see the stars and watch the full moon rise. Remember?

We have no shoes. We stumble over stones. Long grass cuts our legs and our already bleeding feet. I can't go any faster but you hold my hand tighter and pull me along and at last we reach the field and the bushes and the trees. You take the flick-knife from your pocket and throw it deep into the shadows. We lie down. You take off your pyjama jacket and cover me with it and you hold me tight and keep me warm . . .

She paused, but only long enough to take a deep breath, for his vision was fading from the dock and there were still things she had to say to him.

We did it together, Nicholas. He would have killed us, but you saved my life and your own. It was my fault but you took all the blame. Why didn't you tell them? It was all my fault.

'It was all my fault,' she said again, then lifted her eyes to the ceiling where the criss-cross pattern of lights shone like a canopy of stars on a cloudless night.

She heard his voice:

Watch my eyes, Julia, and I'll watch yours. And together we'll see the stars float on the moon . . .

Quickly she looked back at the dock. She could no longer see him clearly. With both hands she reached out towards him, trying to hang on to the final shreds of his image, fearful that this would be the last time he would ever visit her. For a moment it felt as though part of her body was being sucked out of her, as though someone had pulled out a plug and left her to drain away.

And then the dock was empty.

Julia saw him the moment she came through the smoky glass doors. He was standing outside the Bar San Giorgio directly opposite the Crown Court. She rested her leg for a few seconds, holding her hand to her forehead before she limped out of the covered area into the bright afternoon sunshine.

And only then did she see the dog. It was so like Duke that for a moment she thought she was still hallucinating. But all she could think of was telling Paul now.

She walked towards him, watching his face. He looked as though he wasn't sure why he was there, or what he was going to say to her. But before he said anything he thrust the end of a shiny new leather lead into her hand.

'Well, don't look at me like that,' he said at last. 'I'm not going to take him for a walk.'

When she still didn't answer he put his arm around her shoulder. 'Why are you crying?' he asked. 'Hasn't anyone given you a present before?'

Still speechless she stroked the dog's golden head, all the unspoken words receding like a morning mist at sunrise.

Another time, she thought. Another day.

THE END

Made in the USA
Charleston, SC
14 October 2011